HARRY POTTER

and the Prisoner of Azkaban

DRAGO DORMIENS NUNQUAM TITILLANDUS

*Titles available in the Harry Potter series
(in reading order):*
Harry Potter and the Philosopher's Stone
Harry Potter and the Chamber of Secrets
Harry Potter and the Prisoner of Azkaban
Harry Potter and the Goblet of Fire
Harry Potter and the Order of the Phoenix
Harry Potter and the Half-Blood Prince
Harry Potter and the Deathly Hallows

*Titles available in the Harry Potter series
(in Latin):*
Harry Potter and the Philosopher's Stone
Harry Potter and the Chamber of Secrets
(in Welsh, Ancient Greek and Irish):
Harry Potter and the Philosopher's Stone

HARRY POTTER

and the Prisoner of Azkaban

J. K. ROWLING

BLOOMSBURY

LONDON BERLIN NEW YORK

First published in Great Britain in 1999 by Bloomsbury Publishing Plc
36 Soho Square, London, W1D 3QY

Bloomsbury Publishing, London, Berlin and New York

This edition first published in 2004

ISBN 978 0 7475 7376 0

FSC

Mixed Sources
Product group from well-managed
forests and other controlled sources

Cert no. SGS - COC - 2061
www.fsc.org
© 1996 Forest Stewardship Council

Typeset by Dorchester Typesetting
Printed in Great Britain by Clays Ltd, St Ives plc

11

www.bloomsbury.com/harrypotter

To Jill Prewett and Aine Kiely,
the Godmothers of Swing

— CHAPTER ONE —

Owl Post

Harry Potter was a highly unusual boy in many ways. For one thing, he hated the summer holidays more than any other time of year. For another, he really wanted to do his homework, but was forced to do it in secret, in the dead of night. And he also happened to be a wizard.

It was nearly midnight, and he was lying on his front in bed, the blankets drawn right over his head like a tent, a torch in one hand and a large leather-bound book (*A History of Magic*, by Bathilda Bagshot) propped open against the pillow. Harry moved the tip of his eagle-feather quill down the page, frowning as he looked for something that would help him write his essay, 'Witch-Burning in the Fourteenth Century Was Completely Pointless – discuss'.

The quill paused at the top of a likely-looking paragraph. Harry pushed his round glasses up his nose, moved his torch closer to the book and read:

> *Non-magic people (more commonly known as Muggles) were particularly afraid of magic in medieval times, but not very good at recognising it. On the rare occasion that they did catch a real witch or wizard, burning had no effect whatsoever. The witch or wizard would perform a basic Flame-Freezing Charm and then pretend to shriek with pain while enjoying a gentle, tickling sensation. Indeed, Wendelin the Weird enjoyed being burnt so much that she allowed herself to be caught no fewer than forty-seven times in various disguises.*

Harry put his quill between his teeth and reached underneath his pillow for his ink bottle and a roll of parchment. Slowly and very carefully he unscrewed the ink bottle, dipped his quill into it and began to write, pausing every now and then to listen, because if any of the Dursleys heard the scratching of his quill on their way to the bathroom, he'd probably find himself locked in the cupboard under the stairs for the rest of the summer.

The Dursley family of number four, Privet Drive, was the reason that Harry never enjoyed his summer holidays. Uncle Vernon, Aunt Petunia and their son, Dudley, were Harry's only living relatives. They were Muggles, and they had a very medieval attitude towards magic. Harry's dead parents, who had been a witch and wizard themselves, were never mentioned under the Dursleys' roof. For years, Aunt Petunia and Uncle Vernon had hoped that if they kept Harry as downtrodden as possible, they would be able to squash the magic out of him. To their fury, they had been unsuccessful, and now lived in terror of anyone finding out that Harry had spent most of the last two years at Hogwarts School of Witchcraft and Wizardry. The most the Dursleys could do these days was to lock away Harry's spellbooks, wand, cauldron and broomstick at the start of the summer holidays, and forbid him to talk to the neighbours.

This separation from his spellbooks had been a real problem for Harry, because his teachers at Hogwarts had given him a lot of holiday work. One of the essays, a particularly nasty one about Shrinking Potions, was for Harry's least favourite teacher, Professor Snape, who would be delighted to have an excuse to give Harry detention for a month. Harry had therefore seized his chance in the first week of the holidays. While Uncle Vernon, Aunt Petunia and Dudley had gone out into the front garden to admire Uncle Vernon's new company car (in very loud voices, so that the rest of the street would notice it too), Harry had crept downstairs, picked the lock on the cupboard under the stairs, grabbed some of his books and hidden them in his bedroom. As long as he didn't leave spots of ink on the sheets, the Dursleys need never know that he was studying magic by night.

Harry was keen to avoid trouble with his aunt and uncle at the moment, as they were already in a bad mood with him, all because he'd received a telephone call from a fellow wizard one week into the school holidays.

Ron Weasley, who was one of Harry's best friends at Hogwarts, came from a whole family of wizards. This meant that he knew a lot of things Harry didn't, but had never used a telephone before. Most unluckily, it had been Uncle Vernon who had answered the call.

'Vernon Dursley speaking.'

Harry, who happened to be in the room at the time, froze as he heard Ron's voice answer.

'HELLO? HELLO? CAN YOU HEAR ME? I – WANT – TO – TALK – TO – HARRY – POTTER!'

Ron was yelling so loudly that Uncle Vernon jumped and held the receiver a foot away from his ear, staring at it with an expression of mingled fury and alarm.

'WHO IS THIS?' he roared in the direction of the mouthpiece. 'WHO ARE YOU?'

'RON – WEASLEY!' Ron bellowed back, as though he and Uncle Vernon were speaking from opposite ends of a football pitch. 'I'M – A – FRIEND – OF – HARRY'S – FROM – SCHOOL –'

Uncle Vernon's small eyes swivelled around to Harry, who was rooted to the spot.

'THERE IS NO HARRY POTTER HERE!' he roared, now holding the receiver at arm's length, as though frightened it might explode. 'I DON'T KNOW WHAT SCHOOL YOU'RE TALKING ABOUT! NEVER CONTACT ME AGAIN! DON'T YOU COME NEAR MY FAMILY!'

And he threw the receiver back onto the telephone as if dropping a poisonous spider.

The row that had followed had been one of the worst ever.

'HOW DARE YOU GIVE THIS NUMBER TO PEOPLE LIKE – PEOPLE LIKE YOU!' Uncle Vernon had roared, spraying Harry with spit.

Ron obviously realised that he'd got Harry into trouble, because he hadn't called again. Harry's other best friend from Hogwarts, Hermione Granger, hadn't been in touch either. Harry suspected that Ron had warned Hermione not to call, which was a pity, because Hermione, the cleverest witch in Harry's year, had Muggle parents, knew perfectly well how to use a telephone, and would probably have had enough sense not to say that she went to Hogwarts.

So Harry had had no word from any of his wizarding friends for five long weeks, and this summer was turning out to be almost as bad as the last one. There was just one, very small improvement:

after swearing that he wouldn't use her to send letters to any of his friends, Harry had been allowed to let his owl, Hedwig, out at night. Uncle Vernon had given in because of the racket Hedwig made if she was locked in her cage all the time.

Harry finished writing about Wendelin the Weird and paused to listen again. The silence in the dark house was broken only by the distant, grunting snores of his enormous cousin, Dudley. It must be very late. Harry's eyes were itching with tiredness. Perhaps he'd finish this essay tomorrow night ...

He replaced the top of the ink bottle, pulled an old pillowcase from under his bed, put the torch, *A History of Magic,* his essay, quill and ink inside it, got out of bed and hid the lot under a loose floorboard under his bed. Then he stood up, stretched, and checked the time on the luminous alarm clock on his bedside table.

It was one o'clock in the morning. Harry's stomach gave a funny jolt. He had been thirteen years old, without realising it, for a whole hour.

Yet another unusual thing about Harry was how little he looked forward to his birthdays. He had never received a birthday card in his life. The Dursleys had completely ignored his last two birthdays, and he had no reason to suppose they would remember this one.

Harry walked across the dark room, past Hedwig's large, empty cage, to the open window. He leant on the sill, the cool night air pleasant on his face after a long time under the blankets. Hedwig had been absent for two nights now. Harry wasn't worried about her – she'd been gone this long before – but he hoped she'd be back soon. She was the only living creature in this house who didn't flinch at the sight of him.

Harry, though still rather small and skinny for his age, had grown a few inches over the last year. His jet-black hair, however, was just as it always had been: stubbornly untidy, whatever he did to it. The eyes behind his glasses were bright green, and on his forehead, clearly visible through his hair, was a thin scar, shaped like a bolt of lightning.

Of all the unusual things about Harry, this scar was the most extraordinary of all. It was not, as the Dursleys had pretended for ten years, a souvenir of the car crash that had killed Harry's parents, because Lily and James Potter had not died in a car crash. They had been murdered, murdered by the most feared Dark wizard for a hundred years, Lord Voldemort. Harry had escaped from the same attack with nothing more than a scar on his forehead, when Voldemort's curse, instead of killing him, had rebounded upon its originator. Barely alive, Voldemort had fled ...

But Harry had come face to face with him since at Hogwarts. Remembering their last meeting as he stood at the dark window, Harry had to admit he was lucky even to have reached his thirteenth birthday.

He scanned the starry sky for a sign of Hedwig, perhaps soaring back to him with a dead mouse dangling from her beak, expecting praise. Gazing absently over the rooftops, it was a few seconds before Harry realised what he was seeing.

Silhouetted against the golden moon, and growing larger every moment, was a large, strangely lop-sided creature, and it was flapping in Harry's direction. He stood quite still, watching it sink lower and lower. For a split second, he hesitated, his hand on the window-latch, wondering whether to slam it shut, but then the bizarre creature soared over one of the streetlamps of Privet Drive, and Harry, realising what it was, leapt aside.

Through the window soared three owls, two of them holding up the third, which appeared to be unconscious. They landed with a soft *flump* on Harry's bed, and the middle owl, which was large and grey, keeled right over and lay motionless. There was a large package tied to its legs.

Harry recognised the unconscious owl at once – his name was Errol, and he belonged to the Weasley family. Harry dashed to the bed at once, untied the cords around Errol's legs, took off the parcel and then carried Errol to Hedwig's cage. Errol opened one bleary eye, gave a feeble hoot of thanks, and began to gulp some water.

Harry turned back to the remaining owls. One of them, the large snowy female, was his own Hedwig. She, too, was carrying a parcel, and looked extremely pleased with herself. She gave Harry an affectionate nip with her beak as he removed her burden, then flew across the room to join Errol.

Harry didn't recognise the third owl, a handsome tawny one, but he knew at once where it had come from, because in addition to a third parcel, it was carrying a letter bearing the Hogwarts crest. When Harry relieved this owl of its post it ruffled its feathers importantly, stretched its wings and took off through the window into the night.

Harry sat down on his bed, grabbed Errol's package, ripped off the brown paper and discovered a present wrapped in gold, and his first ever birthday card. Fingers trembling slightly, he opened the envelope. Two pieces of paper fell out – a letter and a newspaper cutting.

The cutting had clearly come out of the wizarding newspaper, the *Daily Prophet*, because the people in the black and white picture were moving. Harry picked up the cutting, smoothed it out and read:

MINISTRY OF MAGIC EMPLOYEE SCOOPS GRAND PRIZE

Arthur Weasley, Head of the Misuse of Muggle Artefacts Office at the Ministry of Magic, has won the annual Daily Prophet *Grand Prize Galleon Draw.*

A delighted Mr Weasley told the Daily Prophet, 'We will be spending the gold on a summer holiday in Egypt, where our eldest son, Bill, works as a curse breaker for Gringotts Wizarding Bank.'

The Weasley family will be spending a month in Egypt, returning for the start of the new school year at Hogwarts, which five of the Weasley children currently attend.

Harry scanned the moving photograph, and a grin spread across his face as he saw all nine of the Weasleys waving furiously at him, standing in front of a large pyramid. Plump little Mrs Weasley, tall, balding Mr Weasley, six sons and one daughter, all (though the black and white picture didn't show it) with flaming red hair. Right in the middle of the picture was Ron, tall and gangling, with his pet rat Scabbers on his shoulder and his arm around his little sister, Ginny.

Harry couldn't think of anyone who deserved to win a large pile of gold more than the Weasleys, who were very nice and extremely poor. He picked up Ron's letter and unfolded it.

Dear Harry,

Happy birthday!

Look, I'm really sorry about that telephone call. I hope the Muggles didn't give you a hard time. I asked Dad, and he reckons I shouldn't have shouted.

It's brilliant here in Egypt. Bill's taken us round all the tombs and you wouldn't believe the curses those old Egyptian wizards put on them. Mum wouldn't let Ginny come in the last one. There were all these mutant skeletons in there, of Muggles who'd broken in and grown extra heads and stuff.

I couldn't believe it when Dad won the Daily Prophet Draw. Seven hundred galleons! Most of it's gone on this holiday, but they're going to buy me a new wand for next year.

Harry remembered only too well the occasion when Ron's old wand had snapped. It had happened when the car the two of them had been flying to Hogwarts had crashed into a tree in the school grounds.

We'll be back about a week before term starts and we'll be going up to London to get my wand and our new books. Any chance of meeting you there?

Don't let the Muggles get you down!

Try and come to London,

Ron

PS: Percy's Head Boy. He got the letter last week.

Harry glanced back at the photograph. Percy, who was in his seventh and final year at Hogwarts, was looking particularly smug. He had pinned his Head Boy badge to the fez perched jauntily on top of his neat hair, his horn-rimmed glasses flashing in the Egyptian sun.

Harry now turned to his present and unwrapped it. Inside was what looked like a miniature glass spinning top. There was another note from Ron beneath it.

Harry – this is a Pocket Sneakoscope. If there's someone untrustworthy around, it's supposed to light up and spin. Bill says it's rubbish sold for wizard tourists and isn't reliable, because it kept lighting up at dinner last night. But he didn't realise Fred and George had put beetles in his soup.

Bye – Ron

Harry put the Pocket Sneakoscope on his bedside table, where it stood quite still, balanced on its point, reflecting the luminous hands of his clock. He looked at it happily for a few seconds, then picked up the parcel Hedwig had brought.

Inside this, too, there was a wrapped present, a card and a letter, this time from Hermione.

Dear Harry,

Ron wrote to me and told me about his phone call to your Uncle Vernon. I do hope you're all right.

I'm on holiday in France at the moment and I didn't know how I was going to send this to you – what if they'd opened it at Customs? – but then Hedwig turned up! I think she wanted to make sure you got something for your birthday for a change. I bought your present by owl-order; there was an advertisement in the Daily Prophet (I've been getting it delivered, it's so good to keep up with what's going on in the wizarding world). Did you see that picture of Ron and his family a week ago? I bet he's learning loads, I'm really jealous – the ancient Egyptian wizards were fascinating.

There's some interesting local history of witchcraft here, too. I've re-written my whole History of Magic essay to include some of the things I've found out. I hope it's not too long, it's two rolls of parchment more than Professor Binns asked for.

Ron says he's going to be in London in the last week of the holidays. Can you make it? Will your aunt and uncle let you come? I really hope you can. If not, I'll see you on the Hogwarts Express on September the first!

Love from
Hermione

P.S. Ron says Percy's Head Boy. I'll bet Percy's really pleased. Ron doesn't seem too happy about it.

Harry laughed again as he put Hermione's letter aside and picked up her present. It was very heavy. Knowing Hermione, he was sure it would be a large book full of very difficult spells – but it wasn't. His heart gave a huge bound as he ripped back the paper and saw a sleek black leather case with silver words stamped across it: *Broomstick Servicing Kit.*

'Wow, Hermione!' Harry whispered, unzipping the case to look inside.

There was a large jar of Fleetwood's High-Finish Handle Polish, a pair of gleaming silver Tail-Twig Clippers, a tiny brass compass to clip onto your broom for long journeys, and a *Handbook of Do-it-Yourself Broomcare*.

Apart from his friends, the thing that Harry missed most about Hogwarts was Quidditch, the most popular sport in the magical world – highly dangerous, very exciting and played on broomsticks. Harry happened to be a very good Quidditch player; he had been the youngest person in a century to be picked for one of the Hogwarts house teams. One of Harry's most prized possessions was his Nimbus Two Thousand racing broom.

Harry put the leather case aside and picked up his last parcel. He recognised the untidy scrawl on the brown paper at once: this was from Hagrid, the Hogwarts gamekeeper. He tore off the top layer of paper and glimpsed something green and leathery, but before he could unwrap it properly, the parcel gave a strange quiver, and whatever was inside it snapped loudly – as though it had jaws.

Harry froze. He knew that Hagrid would never send him anything dangerous on purpose, but then, Hagrid didn't have a normal person's view of what was dangerous. Hagrid had been known to befriend giant spiders, buy vicious, three-headed dogs from men in pubs and sneak illegal dragon eggs into his cabin.

Harry poked the parcel nervously. It snapped loudly again. Harry reached for the lamp on his bedside table, gripped it firmly in one hand and raised it over his head, ready to strike. Then he seized the rest of the wrapping paper in his other hand and pulled.

And out fell – a book. Harry just had time to register its handsome green cover, emblazoned with the golden title, *The Monster Book of Monsters*, before it flipped onto its edge and scuttled sideways along the bed like some weird crab.

'Uh oh,' Harry muttered.

The book toppled off the bed with a loud clunk and shuffled rapidly across the room. Harry followed it stealthily. The book was hiding in the dark space under his desk. Praying that the Dursleys were still fast asleep, Harry got down on his hands and knees and reached towards it.

'Ouch!'

The book snapped shut on his hand and then flapped past him, still scuttling on its covers. Harry scrambled around, threw himself forward and managed to flatten it. Uncle Vernon gave a loud, sleepy grunt in the room next door.

Hedwig and Errol watched interestedly as Harry clamped the struggling book tightly in his arms, hurried to his chest of drawers and pulled out a belt, which he buckled tightly around it. *The Monster Book* shuddered angrily, but could no longer flap and snap, so Harry threw it down on the bed and reached for Hagrid's card.

Dear Harry,
   Happy Birthday!
   Think you might find this useful for next year. Won't say no more here. Tell you when I see you.
   Hope the Muggles are treating you right.
   All the best,
   Hagrid

It struck Harry as ominous that Hagrid thought a biting book would come in useful, but he put up Hagrid's card next to Ron and Hermione's, grinning more broadly than ever. Now there was only the letter from Hogwarts left.

Noticing that it was rather thicker than usual, Harry slit open the envelope, pulled out the first page of parchment within and read:

Dear Mr Potter,
   Please note that the new school year will begin on September the first. The Hogwarts Express will leave from King's Cross Station, platform nine and three-quarters, at eleven o'clock.
   Third-years are permitted to visit the village of Hogsmeade at certain weekends. Please give the enclosed permission form to your parent or guardian to sign.
   A list of books for next year is enclosed.
   Yours sincerely,
   Professor M. McGonagall
   Deputy Headmistress

Harry pulled out the Hogsmeade permission form and looked

at it, no longer grinning. It would be wonderful to visit Hogsmeade at weekends; he knew it was an entirely wizarding village, and he had never set foot there. But how on earth was he going to persuade Uncle Vernon or Aunt Petunia to sign the form?

He looked over at the alarm clock. It was now two o'clock in the morning.

Deciding that he'd worry about the Hogsmeade form when he woke up, Harry got back into bed and reached up to cross off another day on the chart he'd made for himself, counting down the days left until his return to Hogwarts. Then he took off his glasses and lay down, eyes open, facing his three birthday cards.

Extremely unusual though he was, at that moment Harry Potter felt just like everyone else: glad, for the first time in his life, that it was his birthday.

CHAPTER TWO

Aunt Marge's Big Mistake

Harry went down to breakfast next morning to find the three Dursleys already sitting around the kitchen table. They were watching a brand-new television, a welcome-home-for-the-summer present for Dudley, who had been complaining loudly about the long walk between the fridge and the television in the living room. Dudley had spent most of the summer in the kitchen, his piggy little eyes fixed on the screen and his five chins wobbling as he ate continually.

Harry sat down between Dudley and Uncle Vernon, a large, beefy man with very little neck and a lot of moustache. Far from wishing Harry a happy birthday, none of the Dursleys gave any sign that they had noticed Harry enter the room, but Harry was far too used to this to care. He helped himself to a piece of toast and then looked up at the newsreader on the television, who was halfway through a report on an escaped convict.

'... the public is warned that Black is armed and extremely dangerous. A special hotline has been set up, and any sighting of Black should be reported immediately.'

'No need to tell us *he's* no good,' snorted Uncle Vernon, staring over the top of his newspaper at the prisoner. 'Look at the state of him, the filthy layabout! Look at his hair!'

He shot a nasty look sideways at Harry, whose untidy hair had always been a source of great annoyance to Uncle Vernon. Compared to the man on the television, however, whose gaunt face was surrounded by a matted, elbow-length tangle, Harry felt very well groomed indeed.

The newsreader had reappeared.

'The Ministry of Agriculture and Fisheries will announce today –'

'Hang on!' barked Uncle Vernon, staring furiously at the newsreader. 'You didn't tell us where that maniac's escaped from! What use is that? Lunatic could be coming up the street right now!'

Aunt Petunia, who was bony and horse-faced, whipped around and peered intently out of the kitchen window. Harry knew Aunt Petunia would simply love to be the one to call the hotline number. She was the nosiest woman in the world and spent most of her life spying on her boring, law-abiding neighbours.

'When will they *learn*,' said Uncle Vernon, pounding the table with his large purple fist, 'that hanging's the only way to deal with these people?'

'Very true,' said Aunt Petunia, who was still squinting into next door's runner-beans.

Uncle Vernon drained his teacup, glanced at his watch and added, 'I'd better be off in a minute, Petunia, Marge's train gets in at ten.'

Harry, whose thoughts had been upstairs with the Broomstick Servicing Kit, was brought back to earth with an unpleasant bump.

'Aunt Marge?' he blurted out. 'Sh-*she*'s not coming here, is she?'

Aunt Marge was Uncle Vernon's sister. Even though she was not a blood relative of Harry's (whose mother had been Aunt Petunia's sister), he had been forced to call her 'Aunt' all his life. Aunt Marge lived in the country, in a house with a large garden, where she bred bulldogs. She didn't often stay in Privet Drive, because she couldn't bear to leave her precious dogs, but each of her visits stood out horribly vividly in Harry's mind.

At Dudley's fifth birthday party, Aunt Marge had whacked Harry around the shins with her walking stick to stop him beating Dudley at musical statues. A few years later, she had turned up at Christmas with a computerised robot for Dudley and a box of dog biscuits for Harry. On her last visit, the year before Harry had started at Hogwarts, Harry had accidentally trodden on the paw of her favourite dog. Ripper had chased Harry out into the garden and up a tree, and Aunt Marge had refused to call him off until past midnight. The memory of this incident still brought tears of laughter to Dudley's eyes.

'Marge'll be here for a week,' Uncle Vernon snarled, 'and while we're on the subject,' he pointed a fat finger threateningly at Harry, 'we need to get a few things straight before I go and collect her.'

Dudley smirked and withdrew his gaze from the television.

Watching Harry being bullied by Uncle Vernon was Dudley's favourite form of entertainment.

'Firstly,' growled Uncle Vernon, 'you'll keep a civil tongue in your head when you're talking to Marge.'

'All right,' said Harry bitterly, 'if she does when she's talking to me.'

'Secondly,' said Uncle Vernon, acting as though he had not heard Harry's reply, 'as Marge doesn't know anything about your *abnormality*, I don't want any – any *funny* stuff while she's here. You behave yourself, got me?'

'I will if she does,' said Harry through gritted teeth.

'And thirdly,' said Uncle Vernon, his mean little eyes now slits in his great purple face, 'we've told Marge you attend St Brutus's Secure Centre for Incurably Criminal Boys.'

'*What?*' Harry yelled.

'And you'll be sticking to that story, boy, or there'll be trouble,' spat Uncle Vernon.

Harry sat there, white-faced and furious, staring at Uncle Vernon, hardly able to believe it. Aunt Marge coming for a week-long visit – it was the worst birthday present the Dursleys had ever given him, including that pair of Uncle Vernon's old socks.

'Well, Petunia,' said Uncle Vernon, getting heavily to his feet, 'I'll be off to the station, then. Want to come along for the ride, Dudders?'

'No,' said Dudley, whose attention had returned to the television now that Uncle Vernon had finished threatening Harry.

'Duddy's got to make himself smart for his auntie,' said Aunt Petunia, smoothing Dudley's thick blond hair. 'Mummy's bought him a lovely new bow-tie.'

Uncle Vernon clapped Dudley on his porky shoulder.

'See you in a bit, then,' he said, and he left the kitchen.

Harry, who had been sitting in a kind of horrified trance, had a sudden idea. Abandoning his toast, he got quickly to his feet and followed Uncle Vernon to the front door.

Uncle Vernon was pulling on his car coat.

'I'm not taking *you*,' he snarled, as he turned to see Harry watching him.

'Like I wanted to come,' said Harry coldly. 'I want to ask you something.'

Uncle Vernon eyed him suspiciously.

'Third-years at Hog – at my school are allowed to visit the village sometimes,' said Harry.

'So?' snapped Uncle Vernon, taking his car keys from a hook next to the door.

'I need you to sign the permission form,' said Harry in a rush.

'And why should I do that?' sneered Uncle Vernon.

'Well,' said Harry, choosing his words carefully, 'it'll be hard work, pretending to Aunt Marge I go to that St Whatsits ...'

'St Brutus's Secure Centre for Incurably Criminal Boys!' bellowed Uncle Vernon, and Harry was pleased to hear a definite note of panic in Uncle Vernon's voice.

'Exactly,' said Harry, looking calmly up into Uncle Vernon's large, purple face. 'It's a lot to remember. I'll have to make it sound convincing, won't I? What if I accidentally let something slip?'

'You'll get the stuffing knocked out of you, won't you?' roared Uncle Vernon, advancing on Harry with his fist raised. But Harry stood his ground.

'Knocking the stuffing out of me won't make Aunt Marge forget what I could tell her,' he said grimly.

Uncle Vernon stopped, his fist still raised, his face an ugly puce.

'But if you sign my permission form,' Harry went on quickly, 'I swear I'll remember where I'm supposed to go to school, and I'll act like a Mug – like I'm normal and everything.'

Harry could tell that Uncle Vernon was thinking it over, even if his teeth were bared and a vein was throbbing in his temple.

'Right,' he snapped finally. 'I shall monitor your behaviour carefully during Marge's visit. If, at the end of it, you've toed the line and kept to the story, I'll sign your ruddy form.'

He wheeled around, pulled open the front door and slammed it so hard that one of the little panes of glass at the top fell out.

Harry didn't return to the kitchen. He went back upstairs to his bedroom. If he was going to act like a real Muggle, he'd better start now. Slowly and sadly he gathered up all his presents and his birthday cards and hid them under the loose floorboard with his homework. Then he went to Hedwig's cage. Errol seemed to have recovered; he and Hedwig were both asleep, heads under their wings. Harry sighed, then poked them both awake.

'Hedwig,' he said gloomily, 'you're going to have to clear off for a week. Go with Errol, Ron'll look after you. I'll write him a note, explaining. And don't look at me like that' – Hedwig's large amber eyes were reproachful, 'it's not my fault. It's the only way I'll be allowed to visit Hogsmeade with Ron and Hermione.'

Ten minutes later, Errol and Hedwig (who had a note to Ron bound to her leg) soared out of the window and out of sight. Harry, now feeling thoroughly miserable, put the empty cage away inside the wardrobe.

But Harry didn't have long to brood. In next to no time, Aunt Petunia was shrieking up the stairs for Harry to come down and get ready to welcome their guest.

'Do something about your hair!' Aunt Petunia snapped as he reached the hall.

Harry couldn't see the point of trying to make his hair lie flat. Aunt Marge loved criticising him, so the untidier he looked, the happier she would be.

All too soon, there was a crunch of gravel outside as Uncle Vernon's car pulled back into the driveway, then the clunk of the car doors, and footsteps on the garden path.

'Get the door!' Aunt Petunia hissed at Harry.

A feeling of great gloom in his stomach, Harry pulled the door open.

On the threshold stood Aunt Marge. She was very like Uncle Vernon; large, beefy and purple-faced, she even had a moustache, though not as bushy as his. In one hand she held an enormous suitcase, and tucked under the other was an old and evil-tempered bulldog.

'Where's my Dudders?' roared Aunt Marge. 'Where's my neffy poo?'

Dudley came waddling down the hall, his blond hair plastered flat to his fat head, a bow-tie just visible under his many chins. Aunt Marge thrust the suitcase into Harry's stomach, knocking the wind out of him, seized Dudley in a tight one-armed hug and planted a large kiss on his cheek.

Harry knew perfectly well that Dudley only put up with Aunt Marge's hugs because he was well paid for it, and sure enough, when they broke apart, Dudley had a crisp twenty-pound note clutched in his fat fist.

'Petunia!' shouted Aunt Marge, striding past Harry as though he was a hat-stand. Aunt Marge and Aunt Petunia kissed, or rather, Aunt Marge bumped her large jaw against Aunt Petunia's bony cheekbone.

Uncle Vernon now came in, smiling jovially as he shut the door.

'Tea, Marge?' he said. 'And what will Ripper take?'

'Ripper can have some tea out of my saucer,' said Aunt Marge, as they all trooped into the kitchen, leaving Harry alone in the hall with the suitcase. But Harry wasn't complaining; any excuse not to be with Aunt Marge was fine by him, so he began to heave the case upstairs into the spare bedroom, taking as long as he could.

By the time he got back to the kitchen, Aunt Marge had been supplied with tea and fruitcake and Ripper was lapping noisily in the corner. Harry saw Aunt Petunia wince slightly as specks of tea and drool flecked her clean floor. Aunt Petunia hated animals.

'Who's looking after the other dogs, Marge?' Uncle Vernon asked.

'Oh, I've got Colonel Fubster managing them,' boomed Aunt Marge. 'He's retired now, good for him to have something to do. But I couldn't leave poor old Ripper. He pines if he's away from me.'

Ripper began to growl again as Harry sat down. This directed Aunt Marge's attention to Harry for the first time.

'So!' she barked. 'Still here, are you?'

'Yes,' said Harry.

'Don't you say "yes" in that ungrateful tone,' Aunt Marge growled. 'It's damn good of Vernon and Petunia to keep you. Wouldn't have done it myself. You'd have gone straight to an orphanage if you'd been dumped on *my* doorstep.'

Harry was bursting to say that he'd rather live in an orphanage than with the Dursleys, but the thought of the Hogsmeade form stopped him. He forced his face into a painful smile.

'Don't you smirk at me!' boomed Aunt Marge. 'I can see you haven't improved since I last saw you. I hoped school would knock some manners into you.' She took a large gulp of tea, wiped her moustache and said, 'Where is it that you send him, again, Vernon?'

'St Brutus's,' said Uncle Vernon promptly. 'It's a first-rate institution for hopeless cases.'

'I see,' said Aunt Marge. 'Do they use the cane at St Brutus's, boy?' she barked across the table.

'Er –'

Uncle Vernon nodded curtly behind Aunt Marge's back.

'Yes,' said Harry. Then, feeling he might as well do the thing properly, he added, 'All the time.'

'Excellent,' said Aunt Marge. 'I won't have this namby-pamby, wishy-washy nonsense about not hitting people who deserve it. A good thrashing is what's needed in ninety-nine cases out of a hundred. Have *you* been beaten often?'

'Oh, yeah,' said Harry, 'loads of times.'

Aunt Marge narrowed her eyes.

'I still don't like your tone, boy,' she said. 'If you can speak of your beatings in that casual way, they clearly aren't hitting you hard enough. Petunia, I'd write if I were you. Make it clear that you approve the use of extreme force in this boy's case.'

Perhaps Uncle Vernon was worried that Harry might forget their bargain; in any case, he changed the subject abruptly.

'Heard the news this morning, Marge? What about that escaped prisoner, eh?'

*

As Aunt Marge started to make herself at home, Harry caught himself thinking almost longingly of life at number four without her. Uncle Vernon and Aunt Petunia usually encouraged Harry to stay out of their way, which Harry was only too happy to do. Aunt Marge, on the other hand, wanted Harry under her eye at all times, so that she could boom out suggestions for his improvement. She delighted in comparing Harry with Dudley, and took huge pleasure in buying Dudley expensive presents while glaring at Harry, as though daring him to ask why he hadn't got a present too. She also kept throwing out dark hints about what made Harry such an unsatisfactory person.

'You mustn't blame yourself for the way the boy's turned out, Vernon,' she said over lunch on the third day. 'If there's something rotten on the *inside*, there's nothing anyone can do about it.'

Harry tried to concentrate on his food, but his hands shook and his face was starting to burn with anger. *Remember the form,* he told himself. *Think about Hogsmeade. Don't say anything. Don't rise –*

Aunt Marge reached for her glass of wine.

'It's one of the basic rules of breeding,' she said. 'You see it all the time with dogs. If there's something wrong with the bitch, there'll be something wrong with the pup –'

At that moment, the wine glass Aunt Marge was holding exploded in her hand. Shards of glass flew in every direction and Aunt Marge spluttered and blinked, her great ruddy face dripping.

'Marge!' squealed Aunt Petunia. 'Marge, are you all right?'

'Not to worry,' grunted Aunt Marge, mopping her face with her napkin. 'Must have squeezed it too hard. Did the same thing at Colonel Fubster's the other day. No need to fuss, Petunia, I have a very firm grip ...'

But Aunt Petunia and Uncle Vernon were both looking at Harry suspiciously, so he decided he'd better skip pudding and escape from the table as soon as he could.

Outside in the hall, he leant against the wall, breathing deeply. It had been a long time since he'd lost control and made something explode. He couldn't afford to let it happen again. The Hogsmeade form wasn't the only thing at stake – if he carried on like that, he'd be in trouble with the Ministry of Magic.

Harry was still an underage wizard, and he was forbidden by wizard law to do magic outside school. His record wasn't exactly clean, either. Only last summer he'd got an official warning which had stated quite clearly that if the Ministry got wind of any more magic in Privet Drive, Harry would face expulsion from Hogwarts.

He heard the Dursleys leaving the table and hurried upstairs out of the way.

*

Harry got through the next three days by forcing himself to think about his *Handbook of Do-it-Yourself Broomcare* whenever Aunt Marge started on him. This worked quite well, though it seemed to give him a glazed look, because Aunt Marge started voicing the opinion that he was mentally subnormal.

At last, at long last, the final evening of Marge's stay arrived. Aunt Petunia cooked a fancy dinner and Uncle Vernon uncorked several bottles of wine. They got all the way through the soup and the salmon without a single mention of Harry's faults; during the lemon meringue pie, Uncle Vernon bored them all with a long talk about Grunnings, his drill-making company; then Aunt Petunia made coffee and Uncle Vernon brought out a bottle of brandy.

'Can I tempt you, Marge?'

Aunt Marge had already had rather a lot of wine. Her huge face was very red.

'Just a small one, then,' she chuckled. 'A bit more than that ... and a bit more ... that's the boy.'

Dudley was eating his fourth slice of pie. Aunt Petunia was sipping coffee with her little finger sticking out. Harry really wanted to disappear into his bedroom, but he met Uncle Vernon's angry little eyes and knew he would have to sit it out.

'Aah,' said Aunt Marge, smacking her lips and putting the empty brandy glass back down. 'Excellent nosh, Petunia. It's normally just a fry-up for me of an evening, with twelve dogs to look after ...' She burped richly and patted her great tweed stomach. 'Pardon me. But I do like to see a healthy-sized boy,' she went on, winking at Dudley. 'You'll be a proper-sized man, Dudders, like your father. Yes, I'll have a spot more brandy, Vernon ...'

'Now, this one here –'

She jerked her head at Harry, who felt his stomach clench. *The Handbook*, he thought quickly.

'This one's got a mean, runty look about him. You get that with dogs. I had Colonel Fubster drown one last year. Ratty little thing it was. Weak. Underbred.'

Harry was trying to remember page twelve of his book: *A Charm to Cure Reluctant Reversers*.

'It all comes down to blood, as I was saying the other day. Bad blood will out. Now, I'm saying nothing against your family, Petunia' – she patted Aunt Petunia's bony hand with her shovel-like one, 'but your sister was a bad egg. They turn up in the best families. Then she ran off with a wastrel and here's the result right in front of us.'

Harry was staring at his plate, a funny ringing in his ears. *Grasp your broom firmly by the tail,* he thought. But he couldn't remember what came next. Aunt Marge's voice seemed to be boring into him like one of Uncle Vernon's drills.

'This Potter,' said Aunt Marge loudly, seizing the brandy bottle and splashing more into her glass and over the tablecloth, 'you never told me what he did?'

Uncle Vernon and Aunt Petunia were looking extremely tense. Dudley had even looked up from his pie to gape at his parents.

'He – didn't work,' said Uncle Vernon, with half a glance at Harry. 'Unemployed.'

'As I expected!' said Aunt Marge, taking a huge swig of brandy and wiping her chin on her sleeve. 'A no-account, good-for-nothing, lazy scrounger who –'

'He was not,' said Harry suddenly. The table went very quiet. Harry was shaking all over. He had never felt so angry in his life.

'MORE BRANDY!' yelled Uncle Vernon, who had gone very white. He emptied the bottle into Aunt Marge's glass. 'You, boy,' he snarled at Harry. 'Go to bed, go on –'

'No, Vernon,' hiccoughed Aunt Marge, holding up a hand, her tiny bloodshot eyes fixed on Harry's. 'Go on, boy, go on. Proud of your parents, are you? They go and get themselves killed in a car crash (drunk, I expect) –'

'They didn't die in a car crash!' said Harry, who found himself on his feet.

'They died in a car crash, you nasty little liar, and left you to be a burden on their decent, hardworking relatives!' screamed Aunt Marge, swelling with fury. 'You are an insolent, ungrateful little –'

But Aunt Marge suddenly stopped speaking. For a moment, it looked as though words had failed her. She seemed to be swelling with inexpressible anger – but the swelling didn't stop. Her great red face started to expand, her tiny eyes bulged and her mouth stretched too tightly for speech. Next second, several buttons burst from her tweed jacket and pinged off the walls – she was inflating like a monstrous balloon, her stomach bursting free of her tweed waistband, each of her fingers blowing up like a salami ...

'MARGE!' yelled Uncle Vernon and Aunt Petunia together, as Aunt Marge's whole body began to rise off her chair towards the ceiling. She was entirely round, now, like a vast life buoy with piggy eyes, and her hands and feet stuck out weirdly as she drifted up into the air, making apoplectic popping noises. Ripper came skidding into the room, barking madly.

'NOOOOOOO!'

Uncle Vernon seized one of Marge's feet and tried to pull her down again, but was almost lifted from the floor himself. Next second, Ripper had leapt forward and sunk his teeth into Uncle Vernon's leg.

Harry tore from the dining room before anyone could stop him, heading for the cupboard under the stairs. The cupboard door burst magically open as he reached it. In seconds, he had heaved his trunk to the front door. He sprinted upstairs and threw him-self under the bed, wrenched up the loose floorboard and grabbed the pillowcase full of his books and birthday presents. He wriggled out, seized Hedwig's empty cage and dashed back downstairs to his trunk, just as Uncle Vernon burst out of the dining room, his trouser leg in bloody tatters.

'COME BACK IN HERE!' he bellowed. 'COME BACK AND PUT HER RIGHT!'

But a reckless rage had come over Harry. He kicked his trunk open, pulled out his wand and pointed it at Uncle Vernon.

'She deserved it,' Harry said, breathing very fast. 'She deserved what she got. You keep away from me.'

He fumbled behind him for the catch on the door.

'I'm going,' Harry said. 'I've had enough.'

And next moment, he was out in the dark, quiet street, heaving his heavy trunk behind him, Hedwig's cage under his arm.

— CHAPTER THREE —

The Knight Bus

Harry was several streets away before he collapsed onto a low wall in Magnolia Crescent, panting from the effort of dragging his trunk. He sat quite still, anger still surging through him, listening to the frantic thumping of his heart.

But after ten minutes alone in the dark street, a new emotion overtook him: panic. Whichever way he looked at it, he had never been in a worse fix. He was stranded, quite alone, in the dark Muggle world, with absolutely nowhere to go. And the worst of it was, he had just done serious magic, which meant that he was almost certainly expelled from Hogwarts. He had broken the Decree for the Restriction of Underage Wizardry so badly, he was surprised Ministry of Magic representatives weren't swooping down on him where he sat.

Harry shivered and looked up and down Magnolia Crescent. What was going to happen to him? Would he be arrested, or would he simply be outlawed from the wizarding world? He thought of Ron and Hermione, and his heart sank even lower. Harry was sure that, criminal or not, Ron and Hermione would want to help him now, but they were both abroad, and with Hedwig gone, he had no means of contacting them.

He didn't have any Muggle money, either. There was a little wizard gold in the moneybag at the bottom of his trunk, but the rest of the fortune his parents had left him was stored in a vault at Gringotts Wizarding Bank in London. He'd never be able to drag his trunk all the way to London. Unless ...

He looked down at his wand, which he was still clutching in his hand. If he was already expelled (his heart was now thumping painfully fast), a bit more magic couldn't hurt. He had the Invisibility Cloak he had inherited from his father – what if he bewitched the trunk to make it feather-light, tied it to his broomstick, covered himself in the Cloak and flew to London? Then he could get the rest of his money out of his vault and ... begin his life as an outcast. It was a horrible prospect, but he couldn't sit on this wall for ever or he'd find himself trying to explain to Muggle police why he was out in the dead of night with a trunkful of spellbooks and a broomstick.

Harry opened his trunk again and pushed the contents aside, looking for the Invisibility Cloak – but before he had found it, he straightened up suddenly, looking around him once more.

A funny prickling on the back of his neck had made Harry feel he was being watched, but the street appeared to be deserted, and no lights shone from any of the large square houses.

He bent over his trunk again, but almost immediately stood up once more, his hand clenched on his wand. He had sensed rather than heard it: someone or something was standing in the narrow gap between the garage and the fence behind him. Harry squinted at the black alleyway. If only it would move, then he'd know whether it was just a stray cat or – something else.

'Lumos,' Harry muttered, and a light appeared at the end of his wand, almost dazzling him. He held it high over his head, and the pebble-dashed walls of number two suddenly sparkled; the garage door gleamed, and between them, Harry saw, quite distinctly, the hulking outline of something very big, with wide, gleaming eyes.

Harry stepped backwards. His legs hit his trunk and he tripped. His wand flew out of his hand as he flung out an arm to break his fall, and he landed, hard, in the gutter.

There was a deafening BANG and Harry threw up his hands to shield his eyes against a sudden blinding light ...

With a yell, he rolled back onto the pavement, just in time. A second later, a gigantic pair of wheels and headlights had screeched to a halt exactly where Harry had just been lying. They belonged, as Harry saw when he raised his head, to a triple-decker, violently purple bus, which had appeared out of thin air. Gold lettering over the windscreen spelled *The Knight Bus*.

For a split second, Harry wondered if he had been knocked silly by his fall. Then a conductor in a purple uniform leapt out of the bus and began to speak loudly to the night.

'Welcome to the Knight Bus, emergency transport for the stranded witch or wizard. Just stick out your wand hand, step on board and we can take you anywhere you want to go. My name is

Stan Shunpike, and I will be your conductor this eve–'

The conductor stopped abruptly. He had just caught sight of Harry, who was still sitting on the ground. Harry snatched up his wand again and scrambled to his feet. Close to, he saw that Stan Shunpike was only a few years older than he was; eighteen or nineteen at most, with large, protruding ears and a fair few pimples.

'What were you doin' down there?' said Stan, dropping his professional manner.

'Fell over,' said Harry.

''Choo fall over for?' sniggered Stan.

'I didn't do it on purpose,' said Harry, annoyed. One of the knees in his jeans was torn, and the hand he had thrown out to break his fall was bleeding. He suddenly remembered why he had fallen over, and turned around quickly to stare at the alleyway between the garage and fence. The Knight Bus's headlamps were flooding it with light, and it was empty.

''Choo lookin' at?' said Stan.

'There was a big black thing,' said Harry, pointing uncertainly into the gap. 'Like a dog ... but massive ...'

He looked around at Stan, whose mouth was slightly open. With a feeling of unease, Harry saw Stan's eyes move to the scar on Harry's forehead.

'Woss that on your 'ead?' said Stan abruptly.

'Nothing,' said Harry quickly, flattening his hair over his scar. If the Ministry of Magic was looking for him, he didn't want to make it too easy for them.

'Woss your name?' Stan persisted.

'Neville Longbottom,' said Harry, saying the first name that came into his head. 'So – so this bus,' he went on quickly, hoping to distract Stan, 'did you say it goes *anywhere*?'

'Yep,' said Stan proudly, 'anywhere you like, long's it's on land. Can't do nuffink underwater. 'Ere,' he said, looking suspicious again, 'you *did* flag us down, dincha? Stuck out your wand 'and, dincha?'

'Yes,' said Harry quickly. 'Listen, how much would it be to get to London?'

'Eleven Sickles,' said Stan, 'but for firteen you get 'ot chocolate, and for fifteen you get an 'ot-water bottle an' a toofbrush in the colour of your choice.'

Harry rummaged once more in his trunk, extracted his money

bag and shoved some silver into Stan's hand. He and Stan then lifted his trunk, with Hedwig's cage balanced on top, up the steps of the bus.

There were no seats; instead, half-a-dozen brass bedsteads stood beside the curtained windows. Candles were burning in brackets beside each bed, illuminating the wood-panelled walls. A tiny wizard in a nightcap at the rear of the bus muttered, 'Not now, thanks, I'm pickling some slugs,' and rolled over in his sleep.

'You 'ave this one,' Stan whispered, shoving Harry's trunk under the bed right behind the driver, who was sitting in an armchair in front of the steering wheel. 'This is our driver, Ernie Prang. This is Neville Longbottom, Ern.'

Ernie Prang, an elderly wizard wearing very thick glasses, nodded to Harry, who nervously flattened his fringe again and sat down on his bed.

'Take 'er away, Ern,' said Stan, sitting down in the armchair next to Ernie's.

There was another tremendous BANG, and next moment Harry found himself flat on his bed, thrown backwards by the speed of the Knight Bus. Pulling himself up, Harry stared out of the dark window and saw that they were now bowling along a completely different street. Stan was watching Harry's stunned face with great enjoyment.

'This is where we was before you flagged us down,' he said. 'Where are we, Ern? Somewhere in Wales?'

'Ar,' said Ernie.

'How come the Muggles don't hear the bus?' said Harry.

'Them!' said Stan contemptuously. 'Don' listen properly, do they? Don' look properly either. Never notice nuffink, they don'.'

'Best go wake up Madam Marsh, Stan,' said Ern. 'We'll be in Abergavenny in a minute.'

Stan passed Harry's bed and disappeared up a narrow wooden staircase. Harry was still looking out of the window, feeling increasingly nervous. Ernie didn't seem to have mastered the use of a steering wheel. The Knight Bus kept mounting the pavement, but it didn't hit anything; lines of lamp posts, letter-boxes and bins jumped out of its way as it approached and back into position once it had passed.

Stan came back downstairs, followed by a faintly green witch wrapped in a travelling cloak.

''Ere you go, Madam Marsh,' said Stan happily, as Ern stamped on the brake and the beds slid a foot or so towards the front of the bus. Madam Marsh clamped a handkerchief to her mouth and tottered down the steps. Stan threw her bag out after her and rammed the doors shut; there was another loud BANG, and they were thundering down a narrow country lane, trees leaping out of the way.

Harry wouldn't have been able to sleep even if he had been travelling on a bus that didn't keep banging loudly and jumping a hundred miles at a time. His stomach churned as he fell back to wondering what was going to happen to him, and whether the Dursleys had managed to get Aunt Marge off the ceiling yet.

Stan had unfurled a copy of the *Daily Prophet* and was now reading with his tongue between his teeth. A large photograph of a sunken-faced man with long, matted hair blinked slowly at Harry from the front page. He looked strangely familiar.

'That man!' Harry said, forgetting his troubles for a moment. 'He was on the Muggle news!'

Stanley turned to the front page and chuckled.

'Sirius Black,' he said, nodding. ''Course 'e was on the Muggle news, Neville. Where you been?'

He gave a superior sort of chuckle at the blank look on Harry's face, removed the front page and handed it to Harry.

'You oughta read the papers more, Neville.'

Harry held the paper up to the candlelight and read:

BLACK STILL AT LARGE

Sirius Black, possibly the most infamous prisoner ever to be held in Azkaban fortress, is still eluding capture, the Ministry of Magic confirmed today.

'We are doing all we can to recapture Black,' said the Minister for Magic, Cornelius Fudge, this morning, 'and we beg the magical community to remain calm.'

Fudge has been criticised by some members of the International Federation of Warlocks for informing the Muggle Prime Minister of the crisis.

'Well, really, I had to, don't you know,' said an irritable Fudge. 'Black is mad. He's a danger to anyone who crosses him, magic or Muggle. I have the Prime Minister's assurance that he will not breathe a word of Black's true identity to anyone. And let's face it – who'd believe him if he did?'

While Muggles have been told that Black is carrying a gun
(a kind of metal wand which Muggles use to kill each other),
the magical community lives in fear of a massacre like that of
twelve years ago, when Black murdered thirteen people with a
single curse.

Harry looked into the shadowed eyes of Sirius Black, the only part
of the sunken face that seemed alive. Harry had never met a vampire, but he had seen pictures of them in his Defence Against the
Dark Arts classes, and Black, with his waxy white skin, looked
just like one.

'Scary-lookin' fing, inee?' said Stan, who had been watching
Harry read.

'He murdered *thirteen people*?' said Harry, handing the page
back to Stan, 'with *one curse*?'

'Yep,' said Stan. 'In front of witnesses an' all. Broad daylight. Big
trouble it caused, dinnit, Ern?'

'Ar,' said Ern darkly.

Stan swivelled in his armchair, his hands on the back, the better to look at Harry.

'Black woz a big supporter of You-Know-'Oo,' he said.

'What, Voldemort?' said Harry, without thinking.

Even Stan's pimples went white; Ern jerked the steering wheel
so hard that a whole farmhouse had to jump aside to avoid the
bus.

'You outta your tree?' yelped Stan. ''Choo say 'is name for?'

'Sorry,' said Harry hastily. 'Sorry, I – I forgot –'

'Forgot!' said Stan weakly. 'Blimey, my 'eart's goin' that fast ...'

'So – so Black was a supporter of You-Know-Who?' Harry
prompted apologetically.

'Yeah,' said Stan, still rubbing his chest. 'Yeah, that's right. Very
close to You-Know-'Oo, they say ... anyway, when little 'Arry
Potter put paid to You-Know-'Oo' – Harry nervously flattened his
fringe down again – 'all You-Know-'Oo's supporters was tracked
down, wasn't they, Ern? Most of 'em knew it was all over, wiv You-
Know-'Oo gone, and they came quiet. But not Sirius Black. I 'eard
he thought 'e'd be second-in-command once You-Know-'Oo 'ad
taken over.

'Anyway, they cornered Black in the middle of a street full of
Muggles an' Black took out 'is wand and 'e blasted 'alf the street

apart, an' a wizard got it, an' so did a dozen Muggles what got in the way. 'Orrible, eh? An' you know what Black did then?' Stan continued in a dramatic whisper.

'What?' said Harry.

'*Laughed*,' said Stan. 'Jus' stood there an' laughed. An' when reinforcements from the Ministry of Magic got there, 'e went wiv 'em quiet as anyfink, still laughing 'is 'ead off. 'Cos 'e's mad, inee, Ern? Inee mad?'

'If he weren't when he went to Azkaban, he will be now,' said Ern in his slow voice. 'I'd blow meself up before I set foot in that place. Serves him right, mind ... after what he did ...'

'They 'ad a job coverin' it up, din' they, Ern?' Stan said. ''Ole street blown up an' all them Muggles dead. What was it they said 'ad 'appened, Ern?'

'Gas explosion,' grunted Ernie.

'An' now 'e's out,' said Stan, examining the newspaper picture of Black's gaunt face again. 'Never been a breakout from Azkaban before, 'as there, Ern? Beats me 'ow 'e did it. Frightenin', eh? Mind, I don't fancy 'is chances against them Azkaban guards, eh, Ern?'

Ernie suddenly shivered.

'Talk about summat else, Stan, there's a good lad. Them Azkaban guards give me the collywobbles.'

Stan put the paper away reluctantly and Harry leant against the window of the Knight Bus, feeling worse than ever. He couldn't help imagining what Stan might be telling his passengers in a few nights' time.

''Ear about that 'Arry Potter? Blew up 'is Aunt! We 'ad 'im 'ere on the Knight Bus, di'n't we, Ern? 'E was tryin' to run for it ...'

He, Harry, had broken wizard law just like Sirius Black. Was inflating Aunt Marge bad enough to land him in Azkaban? Harry didn't know anything about the wizard prison, though everyone he'd ever heard speak of it did so in the same fearful tone. Hagrid the Hogwarts gamekeeper had spent two months there only last year. Harry wouldn't soon forget the look of terror on Hagrid's face when he had been told where he was going, and Hagrid was one of the bravest people Harry knew.

The Knight Bus rolled through the darkness, scattering bushes and bollards, telephone boxes and trees, and Harry lay, restless and miserable, on his feather bed. After a while, Stan remembered that Harry had paid for hot chocolate, but poured it all over Harry's pillow when the bus moved abruptly from Anglesey to Aberdeen. One by one, wizards and witches in dressing-gowns and slippers descended from the upper floors to leave the bus. They all looked very pleased to go.

Finally, Harry was the only passenger left.

'Right then, Neville,' said Stan, clapping his hands, 'whereabouts in London?'

'Diagon Alley,' said Harry.

'Righto,' said Stan, ''old tight, then ...'

BANG!

They were thundering along Charing Cross Road. Harry sat up and watched buildings and benches squeezing themselves out of the Knight Bus's way. The sky was getting a little lighter. He would lie low for a couple of hours, go to Gringotts the moment it opened, then set off – where, he didn't know.

Ern slammed on the brakes and the Knight Bus skidded to a halt in front of a small and shabby-looking pub, the Leaky Cauldron, behind which lay the magical entrance to Diagon Alley.

'Thanks,' Harry said to Ern.

He jumped down the steps and helped Stan lower his trunk and Hedwig's cage onto the pavement.

'Well,' said Harry, 'bye then!'

But Stan wasn't paying attention. Still standing in the doorway to the bus, he was goggling at the shadowy entrance to the Leaky Cauldron.

'*There* you are, Harry,' said a voice.

Before Harry could turn, he felt a hand on his shoulder. At the same time, Stan shouted, 'Blimey! Ern, come 'ere! Come *'ere*!'

Harry looked up at the owner of the hand on his shoulder and felt a bucketful of ice cascade into his stomach – he had walked right into Cornelius Fudge, the Minister for Magic himself.

Stan leapt onto the pavement beside them.

'What didja call Neville, Minister?' he said excitedly.

Fudge, a portly little man in a long, pinstriped cloak, looked cold and exhausted.

'Neville?' he repeated, frowning. 'This is Harry Potter.'

'I knew it!' Stan shouted gleefully. 'Ern! Ern! Guess 'oo Neville is, Ern! 'E's 'Arry Potter! I can see 'is scar!'

'Yes,' said Fudge testily. 'Well, I'm very glad the Knight Bus picked Harry up, but he and I need to step inside the Leaky Cauldron now ...'

Fudge increased the pressure on Harry's shoulder, and Harry found himself being steered inside the pub. A stooping figure bearing a lantern appeared through the door behind the bar. It was Tom, the wizened, toothless landlord.

'You've got him, Minister!' said Tom. 'Will you be wanting anything? Beer? Brandy?'

'Perhaps a pot of tea,' said Fudge, who still hadn't let go of Harry.

There was a loud scraping and puffing from behind them, and Stan and Ern appeared, carrying Harry's trunk and Hedwig's cage and looking around excitedly.

''Ow come you di'n't tell us 'oo you are, eh, Neville?' said Stan, beaming at Harry, while Ernie's owlish face peered interestedly over Stan's shoulder.

'And a *private* parlour, please, Tom,' said Fudge pointedly.

'Bye,' Harry said miserably to Stan and Ern, as Tom beckoned Fudge towards the passage that led from the bar.

'Bye, Neville!' called Stan.

Fudge marched Harry along the narrow passage after Tom's lantern, and then into a small parlour. Tom clicked his fingers, a fire burst into life in the grate, and he bowed himself out of the room.

'Sit down, Harry,' said Fudge, indicating a chair by the fire.

Harry sat down, feeling goosebumps rising up his arms despite the glow of the fire. Fudge took off his pinstriped cloak and tossed it aside, then hitched up the trousers of his bottle-green suit and sat down opposite Harry.

'I am Cornelius Fudge, Harry. The Minister for Magic.'

Harry already knew this, of course; he had seen Fudge once before, but as he had been wearing his father's Invisibility Cloak at the time, Fudge wasn't to know that.

Tom the innkeeper reappeared, wearing an apron over his nightshirt and bearing a tray of tea and crumpets. He placed the tray on a table between Fudge and Harry, and left the parlour, closing the door behind him.

'Well, Harry,' said Fudge, pouring out tea, 'you've had us all in a right flap, I don't mind telling you. Running away from your aunt and uncle's house like that! I'd started to think ... but you're safe, and that's what matters.'

Fudge buttered himself a crumpet and pushed the plate towards Harry.

'Eat, Harry, you look dead on your feet. Now then ... You will be pleased to hear that we have dealt with the unfortunate blowing-up of Miss Marjorie Dursley. Two members of the Accidental Magic Reversal Squad were dispatched to Privet Drive a few hours ago. Miss Dursley has been punctured and her memory has been modified. She has no recollection of the incident at all. So that's that, and no harm done.'

Fudge smiled at Harry over the rim of his teacup, rather like an uncle surveying a favourite nephew. Harry, who couldn't believe his ears, opened his mouth to speak, couldn't think of anything to say, and closed it again.

'Ah, you're worrying about the reaction of your aunt and uncle?' said Fudge. 'Well, I won't deny that they are extremely angry, Harry, but they are prepared to take you back next summer as long as you stay at Hogwarts for the Christmas and Easter holidays.'

Harry unstuck his throat.

'I *always* stay at Hogwarts for the Christmas and Easter holidays,' he said, 'and I don't ever want to go back to Privet Drive.'

'Now, now, I'm sure you'll feel differently once you've calmed down,' said Fudge in a worried tone. 'They are your family, after all, and I'm sure you are fond of each other – er – *very* deep down.'

It didn't occur to Harry to put Fudge right. He was still waiting to hear what was going to happen to him now.

'So all that remains,' said Fudge, now buttering himself a second crumpet, 'is to decide where you're going to spend the last three weeks of your holidays. I suggest you take a room here at the Leaky Cauldron and –'

'Hang on,' blurted Harry, 'what about my punishment?'

Fudge blinked.

'Punishment?'

'I broke the law!' Harry said. 'The Decree for the Restriction of Underage Wizardry!'

'Oh, my dear boy, we're not going to punish you for a little thing like that!' cried Fudge, waving his crumpet impatiently. 'It was an accident! We don't send people to Azkaban just for blowing up their aunts!'

But this didn't tally at all with Harry's past dealings with the Ministry of Magic.

'Last year, I got an official warning just because a house-elf smashed a pudding in my uncle's house!' said Harry, frowning. 'The Ministry of Magic said I'd be expelled from Hogwarts if there was any more magic there!'

Unless Harry's eyes were deceiving him, Fudge was suddenly looking awkward.

'Circumstances change, Harry ... we have to take into account ... in the present climate ... surely you don't *want* to be expelled?'

'Of course I don't,' said Harry.

'Well then, what's all the fuss about?' laughed Fudge airily. 'Now, have a crumpet, Harry, while I go and see if Tom's got a room for you.'

Fudge strode out of the parlour and Harry stared after him. There was something extremely odd going on. Why had Fudge been waiting for him at the Leaky Cauldron, if not to punish him for what he'd done? And now Harry came to think of it, surely it wasn't usual for the Minister for Magic *himself* to get involved in matters of underage magic?

Fudge came back, accompanied by Tom the innkeeper.

'Room eleven's free, Harry,' said Fudge. 'I think you'll be very comfortable. Just one thing, and I'm sure you'll understand: I don't want you wandering off into Muggle London, all right? Keep to Diagon Alley. And you're to be back here before dark each night. Sure you'll understand. Tom will be keeping an eye on you for me.'

'OK,' said Harry slowly, 'but why –?'

'Don't want to lose you again, do we?' said Fudge with a hearty laugh. 'No, no ... best we know where you are ... I mean ...'

Fudge cleared his throat loudly and picked up his pinstriped cloak.

'Well, I'll be off, plenty to do, you know.'

'Have you had any luck with Black yet?' Harry asked.

Fudge's fingers slipped on the silver fastenings of his cloak.

'What's that? Oh, you've heard – well, no, not yet, but it's only a matter of time. The Azkaban guards have never yet failed ... and they are angrier than I've ever seen them.'

Fudge shuddered slightly.

'So, I'll say goodbye.'

He held out his hand and Harry, shaking it, had a sudden idea.

'Er – Minister? Can I ask you something?'

'Certainly,' smiled Fudge.

'Well, third-years at Hogwarts are allowed to visit Hogsmeade, but my aunt and uncle didn't sign the permission form. D'you think you could?'

Fudge was looking uncomfortable.

'Ah,' he said. 'No. No, I'm very sorry, Harry, but as I'm not your parent or guardian –'

'But you're the Minister for Magic,' said Harry eagerly. 'If you gave me permission –'

'No, I'm sorry, Harry, but rules are rules,' said Fudge flatly. 'Perhaps you'll be able to visit Hogsmeade next year. In fact, I think it best if you don't ... yes ... well, I'll be off. Enjoy your stay, Harry.'

And with a last smile and shake of Harry's hand, Fudge left the room. Tom now moved forward, beaming at Harry.

'If you'll follow me, Mr Potter,' he said. 'I've already taken your things up ...'

Harry followed Tom up a handsome wooden staircase to a door with a brass number eleven on it, which Tom unlocked and opened for him.

Inside was a very comfortable-looking bed, some highly polished oak furniture, a cheerfully crackling fire and, perched on top of the wardrobe –

'Hedwig!' Harry gasped.

The snowy owl clicked her beak and fluttered down onto Harry's arm.

'Very smart owl you've got there,' chuckled Tom. 'Arrived about five minutes after you did. If there's anything you need, Mr Potter, don't hesitate to ask.'

He gave another bow and left.

Harry sat on his bed for a long time, absent-mindedly stroking Hedwig. The sky outside the window was changing rapidly from deep, velvety blue to cold, steely grey and then, slowly, to pink shot with gold. Harry could hardly believe that he'd only left Privet Drive a few hours ago, that he wasn't expelled, and that he was now facing three completely Dursley-free weeks.

'It's been a very weird night, Hedwig,' he yawned.

And without even removing his glasses, he slumped back onto his pillows and fell asleep.

— CHAPTER FOUR —

The Leaky Cauldron

It took Harry several days to get used to his strange new freedom. Never before had he been able to get up whenever he wanted or eat whatever he fancied. He could even go wherever he liked, as long as it was in Diagon Alley, and as this long cobbled street was packed with the most fascinating wizarding shops in the world, Harry felt no desire to break his word to Fudge and stray back into the Muggle world.

Harry ate breakfast each morning in the Leaky Cauldron, where he liked watching the other guests: funny little witches from the country, up for a day's shopping; venerable-looking wizards arguing over the latest article in *Transfiguration Today*; wild-looking warlocks, raucous dwarfs and, once, what looked suspiciously like a hag, who ordered a plate of raw liver from behind a thick woollen balaclava.

After breakfast Harry would go out into the back yard, take out his wand, tap the third brick from the left above the dustbin, and stand back as the archway into Diagon Alley opened in the wall.

Harry spent the long sunny days exploring the shops and eating under the brightly coloured umbrellas outside cafés, where his fellow diners were showing each other their purchases ('it's a lunascope, old boy – no more messing around with moon charts, see?') or else discussing the case of Sirius Black ('personally, I won't let any of the children out alone until he's back in Azkaban'). Harry didn't have to do his homework under the blankets by torchlight any more; now he could sit in the bright sunshine outside Florean Fortescue's Ice-Cream Parlour, finishing all his essays with occasional help from Florean Fortescue himself, who, apart from knowing a great deal about medieval witch-burnings, gave Harry free sundaes every half hour.

Once Harry had refilled his money bag with gold Galleons,

silver Sickles and bronze Knuts from his vault at Gringotts, he needed to exercise a lot of self-control not to spend the whole lot at once. He had to keep reminding himself that he had five years to go at Hogwarts, and how it would feel to ask the Dursleys for money for spellbooks, to stop himself buying a handsome set of solid gold Gobstones (a wizarding game rather like marbles, in which the stones squirted a nasty-smelling liquid into the other player's face when they lost a point). He was sorely tempted, too, by the perfect, moving model of the galaxy in a large glass ball, which would have meant he never had to take another Astronomy lesson. But the thing that tested Harry's resolution most appeared in his favourite shop, Quality Quidditch Supplies, a week after he'd arrived at the Leaky Cauldron.

Curious to know what the crowd in the shop was staring at, Harry edged his way inside and squeezed in amongst the excited witches and wizards until he glimpsed a newly erected podium on which was mounted the most magnificent broom he had ever seen in his life.

'Just come out ... prototype ...' a square-jawed wizard was telling his companion.

'It's the fastest broom in the world, isn't it, Dad?' squeaked a boy younger than Harry, who was swinging off his father's arm.

'Irish International Side's just put in an order for seven of these beauties!' the proprietor of the shop told the crowd. 'And they're favourites for the World Cup!'

A large witch in front of Harry moved, and he was able to read the sign next to the broom:

THE FIREBOLT

This state-of-the-art racing broom sports a streamlined, super-fine handle of ash, treated with a diamond-hard polish and hand-numbered with its own registration number. Each individually selected birch twig in the broomtail has been honed to aerodynamic perfection, giving the Firebolt unsurpassable balance and pinpoint precision. The Firebolt has an acceleration of 0–150 miles an hour in ten seconds and incorporates an unbreakable braking charm. Price on request.

Price on request ... Harry didn't like to think how much gold the

Firebolt would cost. He had never wanted anything so much in his whole life – but he had never lost a Quidditch match on his Nimbus Two Thousand, and what was the point in emptying his Gringotts vault for the Firebolt, when he had a very good broom already? Harry didn't ask for the price, but he returned, almost every day after that, just to look at the Firebolt.

There were, however, things that Harry needed to buy. He went to the apothecary to replenish his store of Potions' ingredients, and as his school robes were now several inches too short in the arm and leg, he visited Madam Malkin's Robes for All Occasions and bought new ones. Most important of all, he had to buy his new school books, which would include those for his two new subjects, Care of Magical Creatures and Divination.

Harry got a surprise as he looked in at the bookshop window. Instead of the usual display of gold-embossed spellbooks the size of paving slabs, there was a large iron cage behind the glass which held about a hundred copies of *The Monster Book of Monsters*. Torn pages were flying everywhere as the books grappled with each other, locked together in furious wrestling matches and snapping aggressively.

Harry pulled his booklist out of his pocket and consulted it for the first time. *The Monster Book of Monsters* was listed as the set book for Care of Magical Creatures. Now Harry understood why Hagrid had said it would come in useful. He felt relieved; he had been wondering whether Hagrid wanted help with some terrifying new pet.

As Harry entered Flourish and Blotts, the manager came hurrying towards him.

'Hogwarts?' he said abruptly. 'Come to get your new books?'

'Yes,' said Harry. 'I need –'

'Get out of the way,' said the manager impatiently, brushing Harry aside. He drew on a pair of very thick gloves, picked up a large, knobbly walking stick and proceeded towards the door of the *Monster Books*' cage.

'Hang on,' said Harry quickly, 'I've already got one of those.'

'Have you?' A look of enormous relief spread over the manager's face. 'Thank heavens for that, I've been bitten five times already this morning –'

A loud ripping noise rent the air; two of the *Monster Books* had seized a third and were pulling it apart.

'Stop it! Stop it!' cried the manager, poking the walking stick through the bars and knocking the books apart. 'I'm never stocking them again, never! It's been bedlam! I thought we'd seen the worst when we bought two hundred copies of *The Invisible Book of Invisibility* – cost a fortune, and we never found them ... Well, is there anything else I can help you with?'

'Yes,' said Harry, looking down his booklist. 'I need *Unfogging the Future,* by Cassandra Vablatsky.'

'Ah, starting Divination, are you?' said the manager, stripping off his gloves and leading Harry into the back of the shop, where there was a corner devoted to fortune-telling. A small table was stacked with volumes such as *Predicting the Unpredictable: Insulate Yourself against Shocks* and *Broken Balls: When Fortunes Turn Foul.*

'Here you are,' said the manager, who had climbed a set of steps to take down a thick, black-bound book. '*Unfogging the Future*. Very good guide to all your basic fortune-telling methods – palmistry, crystal balls, bird entrails ...'

But Harry wasn't listening. His eyes had fallen on another book, which was among a display on a small table: *Death Omens: What to Do When You Know the Worst Is Coming.*

'Oh, I wouldn't read that if I were you,' said the assistant lightly, looking to see what Harry was staring at. 'You'll start seeing death omens everywhere, it's enough to frighten anyone to death.'

But Harry continued to stare at the front cover of the book; it showed a black dog large as a bear, with gleaming eyes. It looked oddly familiar ...

The assistant pressed *Unfogging the Future* into Harry's hands.

'Anything else?' he said.

'Yes,' said Harry, tearing his eyes away from the dog's and dazedly consulting his booklist. 'Er – I need *Intermediate Transfiguration* and *The Standard Book of Spells, Grade Three.*'

Harry emerged from Flourish and Blotts ten minutes later with his new books under his arms, and made his way back to the Leaky Cauldron, hardly noticing where he was going and bumping into several people.

He tramped up the stairs to his room, went inside and tipped his books onto his bed. Somebody had been in to tidy; the windows were open and sun was pouring inside. Harry could hear the buses rolling by in the unseen Muggle street behind him, and the sound of the invisible crowd below in Diagon Alley. He caught sight of himself in the mirror over the basin.

'It can't have been a death omen,' he told his reflection defiantly. 'I was panicking when I saw that thing in Magnolia Crescent. It was probably just a stray dog ...'

He raised his hand automatically and tried to make his hair lie flat.

'You're fighting a losing battle there, dear,' said his mirror in a wheezy voice.

*

As the days slipped by, Harry started looking wherever he went for a sign of Ron or Hermione. Plenty of Hogwarts students were arriving in Diagon Alley now, with the start of term so near. Harry met Seamus Finnigan and Dean Thomas, his fellow Gryffindors, in Quality Quidditch Supplies, where they, too, were ogling the Firebolt; he also ran into the real Neville Longbottom, a round-faced, forgetful boy, outside Flourish and Blotts. Harry didn't stop to chat; Neville appeared to have mislaid his booklist, and was being told off by his very formidable-looking grandmother. Harry hoped she never found out that he'd pretended to be Neville while on the run from the Ministry of Magic.

Harry woke on the last day of the holidays, thinking that he would at least meet Ron and Hermione tomorrow, on the Hogwarts Express. He got up, dressed, went for a last look at the Firebolt, and was just wondering where he'd have lunch, when someone yelled his name and he turned.

'Harry! HARRY!'

They were there, both of them, sitting outside Florean Fortescue's Ice-Cream Parlour, Ron looking incredibly freckly, Hermione very brown, both waving frantically at him.

'Finally!' said Ron, grinning at Harry as he sat down. 'We went to the Leaky Cauldron, but they said you'd left, and we went to Flourish and Blotts, and Madam Malkin's, and –'

'I got all my school stuff last week,' Harry explained. 'And how come you know I'm staying at the Leaky Cauldron?'

'Dad,' said Ron simply.

Mr Weasley, who worked at the Ministry of Magic, would of course have heard the whole story of what had happened to Aunt Marge.

'Did you *really* blow up your aunt, Harry?' said Hermione in a very serious voice.

'I didn't mean to,' said Harry, while Ron roared with laughter. 'I just – lost control.'

'It's not funny, Ron,' said Hermione sharply. 'Honestly, I'm amazed Harry wasn't expelled.'

'So am I,' admitted Harry. 'Forget expelled, I thought I was going to be arrested.' He looked at Ron. 'Your dad doesn't know why Fudge let me off, does he?'

'Probably 'cause it's you, isn't it?' shrugged Ron, still chuckling. 'Famous Harry Potter and all that. I'd hate to see what the Ministry'd do to *me* if I blew up an aunt. Mind you, they'd have to dig me up first, because Mum would've killed me. Anyway, you can ask Dad yourself this evening. We're staying at the Leaky Cauldron tonight, too! So you can come to King's Cross with us tomorrow! Hermione's there as well!'

Hermione nodded, beaming. 'Mum and Dad dropped me off this morning with all my Hogwarts things.'

'Excellent!' said Harry happily. 'So, have you got all your new books and stuff?'

'Look at this,' said Ron, pulling a long thin box out of a bag and opening it. 'Brand-new wand. Fourteen inches, willow, containing one unicorn tail-hair. And we've got all our books' – he pointed at a large bag under his chair. 'What about those *Monster Books*, eh? The assistant nearly cried when we said we wanted two.'

'What's all that, Hermione?' Harry asked, pointing at not one, but three, bulging bags in the chair next to her.

'Well, I'm taking more new subjects than you, aren't I?' said Hermione. 'Those are my books for Arithmancy, Care of Magical Creatures, Divination, Study of Ancient Runes, Muggle Studies –'

'What are you doing Muggle Studies for?' said Ron, rolling his eyes at Harry. 'You're Muggle-born! Your mum and dad are Muggles! You already know all about Muggles!'

'But it'll be fascinating to study them from the wizarding point of view,' said Hermione earnestly.

'Are you planning to eat or sleep at all this year, Hermione?' asked Harry, while Ron sniggered. Hermione ignored them.

'I've still got ten Galleons,' she said, checking her purse. 'It's my birthday in September, and Mum and Dad gave me some money to get myself an early birthday present.'

'How about a nice *book*?' said Ron innocently.

'No, I don't think so,' said Hermione composedly. 'I really want an owl. I mean, Harry's got Hedwig and you've got Errol –'

'I haven't,' said Ron. 'Errol's a family owl. All I've got is Scabbers.' He pulled his pet rat out of his pocket. 'And I want to get him checked over,' he added, placing Scabbers on the table in front of them. 'I don't think Egypt agreed with him.'

Scabbers was looking thinner than usual, and there was a definite droop to his whiskers.

'There's a magical-creature shop just over there,' said Harry, who knew Diagon Alley very well by now. 'You can see if they've got anything for Scabbers, and Hermione can get her owl.'

So they paid for their ice-creams and crossed the street to the Magical Menagerie.

There wasn't much room inside. Every inch of wall was hidden by cages. It was smelly and very noisy because the occupants of these cages were all squeaking, squawking, jabbering or hissing. The witch behind the counter was already advising a wizard on the care of double-ended newts, so Harry, Ron and Hermione waited, examining the cages.

A pair of enormous purple toads sat gulping wetly and feasting on dead blowflies. A gigantic tortoise with a jewel-encrusted shell was glittering near the window. Poisonous orange snails were oozing slowly up the side of their glass tank, and a fat white rabbit kept changing into a silk top hat and back again with a loud popping noise. Then there were cats of every colour, a noisy cage of ravens, a basket of funny custard-coloured furballs that were humming loudly, and, on the counter, a vast cage of sleek black rats which were playing some sort of skipping game using their long bald tails.

The double-ended-newt wizard left and Ron approached the counter.

'It's my rat,' he told the witch. 'He's been a bit off-colour ever since I brought him back from Egypt.'

'Bang him on the counter,' said the witch, pulling a pair of heavy black spectacles out of her pocket.

Ron lifted Scabbers out of his inside pocket and placed him next to the cage of his fellow rats, who stopped their skipping tricks and scuffled to the wire for a better look.

Like nearly everything Ron owned, Scabbers the rat was second-hand (he had once belonged to Ron's brother Percy) and a bit battered. Next to the glossy rats in the cage, he looked especially woebegone.

'Hm,' said the witch, picking Scabbers up. 'How old is this rat?'

'Dunno,' said Ron. 'Quite old. He used to belong to my brother.'

'What powers does he have?' said the witch, examining Scabbers closely.

'Er –' said Ron. The truth was that Scabbers had never shown the faintest trace of interesting powers. The witch's eyes moved from Scabbers's tattered left ear to his front paw, which had a toe missing, and tutted loudly.

'He's been through the mill, this one,' she said.

'He was like that when Percy gave him to me,' said Ron defensively.

'An ordinary, common or garden rat like this can't be expected to live longer than three years or so,' said the witch. 'Now, if you were looking for something a bit more hard-wearing, you might like one of these ...'

She indicated the black rats, who promptly started skipping again. Ron muttered, 'Show-offs.'

'Well, if you don't want a replacement, you can try this Rat Tonic,' said the witch, reaching under the counter and bringing out a small red bottle.

'OK,' said Ron. 'How much – OUCH!'

Ron buckled as something huge and orange came soaring from the top of the highest cage, landed on his head and then propelled itself, spitting madly, at Scabbers.

'NO, CROOKSHANKS, NO!' cried the witch, but Scabbers shot from between her hands like a bar of soap, landed splay-legged on the floor and then scarpered for the door.

'Scabbers!' Ron shouted, haring out of the shop after him; Harry followed.

It took them nearly ten minutes to find Scabbers, who had taken refuge under a wastepaper bin outside Quality Quidditch Supplies. Ron stuffed the trembling rat back into his pocket and straightened up, massaging his head.

'What *was* that?'

'It was either a very big cat or quite a small tiger,' said Harry.

'Where's Hermione?'

'Probably getting her owl.'

They made their way back up the crowded street to the Magical Menagerie. As they reached it, Hermione came out, but she wasn't carrying an owl. Her arms were clamped tightly around the enormous ginger cat.

'You *bought* that monster?' said Ron, his mouth hanging open.

'He's *gorgeous*, isn't he?' said Hermione, glowing.

That was a matter of opinion, thought Harry. The cat's ginger fur was thick and fluffy, but it was definitely a bit bow-legged and its face looked grumpy and oddly squashed, as though it had run headlong into a brick wall. Now that Scabbers was out of sight, however, the cat was purring contentedly in Hermione's arms.

'Hermione, that thing nearly scalped me!' said Ron.

'He didn't mean to, did you, Crookshanks?' said Hermione.

'And what about Scabbers?' said Ron, pointing at the lump in his chest pocket. 'He needs rest and relaxation! How's he going to get it with that thing around?'

'That reminds me, you forgot your Rat Tonic,' said Hermione, slapping the small red bottle into Ron's hand. 'And stop *worrying*, Crookshanks will be sleeping in my dormitory and Scabbers in yours. What's the problem? Poor Crookshanks, that witch said he'd been in there for ages: no one wanted him.'

'I wonder why,' said Ron sarcastically, as they set off towards the Leaky Cauldron.

They found Mr Weasley sitting in the bar, reading the *Daily Prophet*.

'Harry!' he said, smiling as he looked up. 'How are you?'

'Fine, thanks,' said Harry, as he, Ron and Hermione joined Mr Weasley with all their shopping.

Mr Weasley put down his paper, and Harry saw the now familiar picture of Sirius Black staring up at him.

'They still haven't caught him, then?' he asked.

'No,' said Mr Weasley, looking extremely grave. 'They've pulled us all off our regular jobs at the Ministry to try and find him, but no luck so far.'

'Would we get a reward if we caught him?' asked Ron. 'It'd be good to get some more money –'

'Don't be ridiculous, Ron,' said Mr Weasley, who on closer inspection looked very strained. 'Black's not going to be caught by a thirteen-year-old wizard. It's the Azkaban guards who'll get him back, you mark my words.'

At that moment Mrs Weasley entered the bar, laden with shopping and followed by the twins, Fred and George, who were about to start their fifth year at Hogwarts, the newly elected Head Boy, Percy, and the Weasleys' youngest child and only girl, Ginny.

Ginny, who had always been very taken with Harry, seemed even more heartily embarrassed than usual when she saw him, perhaps because he had saved her life during their last term at Hogwarts. She went very red and muttered 'hello' without looking at him. Percy, however, held out his hand solemnly as though he and Harry had never met and said, 'Harry. How nice to see you.'

'Hello, Percy,' said Harry, trying not to laugh.

'I hope you're well?' said Percy pompously, shaking hands. It was rather like being introduced to the mayor.

'Very well, thanks –'

'Harry!' said Fred, elbowing Percy out of the way and bowing deeply. 'Simply *splendid* to see you, old boy –'

'Marvellous,' said George, pushing Fred aside and seizing Harry's hand in turn. 'Absolutely spiffing.'

Percy scowled.

'That's enough, now,' said Mrs Weasley.

'Mum!' said Fred, as though he'd only just spotted her, and seized her hand, too. 'How really corking to see you –'

'I said, that's enough,' said Mrs Weasley, depositing her shopping in an empty chair. 'Hello, Harry, dear. I suppose you've heard our exciting news?' She pointed at the brand-new silver badge on Percy's chest. 'Second Head Boy in the family!' she said, swelling with pride.

'And last,' Fred muttered under his breath.

'I don't doubt that,' said Mrs Weasley, frowning suddenly. 'I notice they haven't made you two Prefects.'

'What do we want to be Prefects for?' said George, looking revolted at the very idea. 'It'd take all the fun out of life.'

Ginny giggled.

'You want to set a better example to your sister!' snapped Mrs Weasley.

'Ginny's got other brothers to set her an example, Mother,' said Percy loftily. 'I'm going up to change for dinner ...'

He disappeared and George heaved a sigh.

'We tried to shut him in a pyramid,' he told Harry. 'But Mum spotted us.'

*

Dinner that night was a very enjoyable affair. Tom the innkeeper put three tables together in the parlour and the seven Weasleys, Harry and Hermione ate their way through five delicious courses.

'How're we getting to King's Cross tomorrow, Dad?' asked Fred, as they tucked into a sumptuous chocolate pudding.

'The Ministry's providing a couple of cars,' said Mr Weasley.

Everyone looked up at him.

'Why?' said Percy curiously.

'It's because of you, Perce,' said George seriously. 'And there'll be little flags on the bonnets, with HB on them –'

'– for Humungous Bighead,' said Fred.

Everyone except Percy and Mrs Weasley snorted into their pudding.

'Why are the Ministry providing cars, Father?' Percy asked again, in a dignified voice.

'Well, as we haven't got one any more,' said Mr Weasley, 'and as I work there, they're doing me a favour ...'

His voice was casual, but Harry couldn't help noticing that Mr Weasley's ears had gone red, just like Ron's did when he was under pressure.

'Good job, too,' said Mrs Weasley briskly. 'Do you realise how much luggage you've all got between you? A nice sight you'd be on the Muggle Underground ... You are all packed, aren't you?'

'Ron hasn't put all his new things in his trunk yet,' said Percy, in a long-suffering voice. 'He's dumped them on my bed.'

'You'd better go and pack properly, Ron, because we won't have much time in the morning,' Mrs Weasley called down the table. Ron scowled at Percy.

After dinner everyone felt very full and sleepy. One by one they made their way upstairs to their rooms to check their things for the next day. Ron and Percy were next door to Harry. He had just closed and locked his own trunk when he heard angry voices through the wall, and went to see what was going on.

The door of number twelve was ajar and Percy was shouting.

'It was *here*, on the bedside table, I took it off for polishing –'

'I haven't touched it, all right?' Ron roared back.

'What's up?' said Harry.

'My Head Boy badge has gone,' said Percy, rounding on Harry.

'So's Scabbers's Rat Tonic,' said Ron, throwing things out of his trunk to look. 'I think I might've left it in the bar –'

'You're not going anywhere till you've found my badge!' yelled Percy.

'I'll get Scabbers's stuff, I'm packed,' Harry said to Ron, and he went downstairs.

Harry was halfway along the passage to the bar, which was now very dark, when he heard another pair of angry voices coming from the parlour. A second later, he recognised them as Mr and Mrs Weasley's. He hesitated, not wanting them to know he'd heard them rowing, when the sound of his own name made him stop, then move closer to the parlour door.

'... makes no sense not to tell him,' Mr Weasley was saying heatedly. 'Harry's got a right to know. I've tried to tell Fudge, but he insists on treating Harry like a child. He's thirteen years old and –'

'Arthur, the truth would terrify him!' said Mrs Weasley shrilly. 'Do you really want to send Harry back to school with that hanging over him? For heaven's sake, he's *happy* not knowing!'

'I don't want to make him miserable, I want to put him on his guard!' retorted Mr Weasley. 'You know what Harry and Ron are like, wandering off by themselves – they've even ended up in the Forbidden Forest! But Harry mustn't do that this year! When I think what could have happened to him that night he ran away from home! If the Knight Bus hadn't picked him up, I'm prepared to bet he would have been dead before the Ministry found him.'

'But he's *not* dead, he's fine, so what's the point –'

'Molly, they say Sirius Black's mad, and maybe he is, but he was clever enough to escape from Azkaban, and that's supposed to be impossible. It's been a month now, and no one's seen hide nor hair of him, and I don't care what Fudge keeps telling the *Daily Prophet*, we're no nearer catching Black than inventing self-spelling wands. The only thing we know for sure is what Black's after –'

'But Harry will be perfectly safe at Hogwarts.'

'We thought Azkaban was perfectly safe. If Black can break out of Azkaban, he can break into Hogwarts.'

'But no one's really sure that Black's after Harry –'

There was a thud on wood, and Harry was sure Mr Weasley had banged his fist on the table.

'Molly, how many times do I have to tell you? They didn't

report it in the press because Fudge wanted it kept quiet, but Fudge went out to Azkaban the night Black escaped. The guards told Fudge that Black's been talking in his sleep for a while now. Always the same words: "He's at Hogwarts ... he's at Hogwarts." Black is deranged, Molly, and he wants Harry dead. If you ask me, he thinks murdering Harry will bring You-Know-Who back to power. Black lost everything the night Harry stopped You-Know-Who, and he's had twelve years alone in Azkaban to brood on that ...'

There was a silence. Harry leant still closer to the door, desperate to hear more.

'Well, Arthur, you must do what you think is right. But you're forgetting Albus Dumbledore. I don't think anything could hurt Harry at Hogwarts while Dumbledore's Headmaster. I suppose he knows about all this?'

'Of course he knows. We had to ask him if he minds the Azkaban guards stationing themselves around the entrances to the school grounds. He wasn't happy about it, but he agreed.'

'Not happy? Why shouldn't he be happy, if they're there to catch Black?'

'Dumbledore isn't fond of the Azkaban guards,' said Mr Weasley heavily. 'Nor am I, if it comes to that ... but when you're dealing with a wizard like Black, you sometimes have to join forces with those you'd rather avoid.'

'If they save Harry –'

'– then I will never say another word against them,' said Mr Weasley wearily. 'It's late, Molly, we'd better go up ...'

Harry heard chairs move. As quietly as he could, he hurried down the passage to the bar and out of sight. The parlour door opened, and a few seconds later footsteps told him that Mr and Mrs Weasley were climbing the stairs.

The bottle of Rat Tonic was lying under the table they had sat at earlier. Harry waited until he heard Mr and Mrs Weasley's bedroom door close, then headed back upstairs with the bottle.

Fred and George were crouching in the shadows on the landing, heaving with laughter as they listened to Percy dismantling his and Ron's room in the search for his badge.

'We've got it,' Fred whispered to Harry. 'We've been improving it.'

The badge now read *Bighead Boy*.

Harry forced a laugh, went to give Ron the rat tonic, then shut himself in his room and lay down on his bed.

So Sirius Black was after him. That explained everything. Fudge had been lenient with him because he was so relieved to find him alive. He'd made Harry promise to stay in Diagon Alley, where there were plenty of wizards to keep an eye on him. And he was sending two Ministry cars to take them all to the station tomorrow, so that the Weasleys could look after Harry until he was on the train.

Harry lay listening to the muffled shouting next door and wondered why he didn't feel more scared. Sirius Black had murdered thirteen people with one curse; Mr and Mrs Weasley obviously thought Harry would be panic-stricken if he knew the truth. But Harry happened to agree whole-heartedly with Mrs Weasley that the safest place on earth was wherever Albus Dumbledore happened to be. Didn't people always say that Dumbledore was the only person Lord Voldemort had ever been afraid of? Surely Black, as Voldemort's right-hand man, would be just as frightened of him?

And then there were these Azkaban guards everyone kept talking about. They seemed to scare most people senseless, and if they were stationed all around the school, Black's chances of getting inside seemed very remote.

No, all in all, the thing that bothered Harry most was the fact that his chances of visiting Hogsmeade now looked like zero. Nobody would want Harry to leave the safety of the castle until Black was caught; in fact, Harry suspected his every move would be carefully watched until the danger had passed.

He scowled at the dark ceiling. Did they think he couldn't look after himself? He'd escaped Lord Voldemort three times, he wasn't completely useless ...

Unbidden, the image of the beast in the shadows of Magnolia Crescent crossed his mind. *What to do when you know the worst is coming ...*

'I'm *not* going to be murdered,' Harry said out loud.

'That's the spirit, dear,' said his mirror sleepily.

CHAPTER FIVE

The Dementor

Tom woke Harry next morning with his usual toothless grin and a cup of tea. Harry got dressed and was just persuading a disgruntled Hedwig to get back into her cage when Ron banged his way into the room, pulling a sweatshirt over his head and looking irritable.

'The sooner we get on the train, the better,' he said. 'At least I can get away from Percy at Hogwarts. Now he's accusing me of dripping tea on his photo of Penelope Clearwater. You know,' Ron grimaced, 'his *girlfriend*. She's hidden her face under the frame because her nose has gone all blotchy ...'

'I've got something to tell you,' Harry began, but they were interrupted by Fred and George, who had looked in to congratulate Ron on infuriating Percy again.

They headed down to breakfast, where Mr Weasley was reading the front page of the *Daily Prophet* with a furrowed brow and Mrs Weasley was telling Hermione and Ginny about a Love Potion she'd made as a young girl. All three of them were rather giggly.

'What were you saying?' Ron asked Harry, as they sat down.

'Later,' Harry muttered, as Percy stormed in.

Harry had no chance to speak to Ron or Hermione in the chaos of leaving; they were too busy heaving all their trunks down the Leaky Cauldron's narrow staircase and piling them up near the door, with Hedwig and Hermes, Percy's screech owl, perched on top in their cages. A small wickerwork basket stood beside the heap of trunks, spitting loudly.

'It's all right, Crookshanks,' Hermione cooed through the wickerwork, 'I'll let you out on the train.'

'You won't,' snapped Ron. 'What about poor Scabbers, eh?'

He pointed at his chest, where a large lump indicated that Scabbers was curled up in his pocket.

Mr Weasley, who had been outside waiting for the Ministry cars, stuck his head inside.

'They're here,' he said. 'Harry, come on.'

Mr Weasley marched Harry across the short stretch of pavement towards the first of two old-fashioned dark green cars, each of which was driven by a furtive-looking wizard, wearing a suit of emerald velvet.

'In you get, Harry,' said Mr Weasley, glancing up and down the crowded street.

Harry got into the back of the car, and was shortly joined by Hermione, Ron and, to Ron's disgust, Percy.

The journey to King's Cross was very uneventful compared to Harry's trip on the Knight Bus. The Ministry of Magic cars seemed almost ordinary, though Harry noticed that they could slide through gaps that Uncle Vernon's new company car certainly couldn't have managed. They reached King's Cross with twenty minutes to spare; the Ministry drivers found them trolleys, unloaded their trunks, touched their hats to Mr Weasley and drove away, somehow managing to jump to the head of an unmoving queue for the traffic lights.

Mr Weasley kept close to Harry's elbow all the way into the station.

'Right then,' he said, glancing around them. 'Let's do this in pairs, as there are so many of us. I'll go through first with Harry.'

Mr Weasley strolled towards the barrier between platforms nine and ten, pushing Harry's trolley and apparently very interested in the InterCity 125 that had just arrived at platform nine. With a meaningful look at Harry, he leant casually against the barrier. Harry imitated him.

Next moment, they had fallen sideways through the solid metal onto platform nine and three-quarters and looked up to see the Hogwarts Express, a scarlet steam engine, puffing smoke over a platform packed with witches and wizards seeing their children onto the train.

Percy and Ginny suddenly appeared behind Harry. They were panting, and had apparently taken the barrier at a run.

'Ah, there's Penelope!' said Percy, smoothing his hair and going pink again. Ginny caught Harry's eye and they both turned away to hide their laughter as Percy strode over to a girl with long, curly hair, walking with his chest thrown out so that she couldn't miss his shiny badge.

Once the remaining Weasleys and Hermione had joined them, Harry and Mr Weasley led the way to the end of the train, past packed compartments, to a carriage that looked quite empty. They loaded the trunks onto it, stowed Hedwig and Crookshanks in the luggage rack, then went back outside to say goodbye to Mr and Mrs Weasley.

Mrs Weasley kissed all her children, then Hermione, and finally, Harry. He was embarrassed, but really quite pleased, when she gave him an extra hug.

'Do take care, won't you, Harry?' she said as she straightened up, her eyes oddly bright. Then she opened her enormous hand-bag and said, 'I've made you all sandwiches. Here you are, Ron ... no, they're not corned beef ... Fred? Where's Fred? Here you are, dear ...'

'Harry,' said Mr Weasley quietly, 'come over here a moment.'

He jerked his head towards a pillar, and Harry followed him behind it, leaving the others crowded around Mrs Weasley.

'There's something I've got to tell you before you leave –' said Mr Weasley, in a tense voice.

'It's all r ght, Mr Weasley,' said Harry, 'I already know.'

'You know? How could you know?'

'I – er – I heard you and Mrs Weasley talking last night. I couldn't help hearing,' Harry added quickly. 'Sorry –'

'That's not the way I'd have chosen for you to find out,' said Mr Weasley, looking anxious.

'No – honestly, it's OK. This way, you haven't broken your word to Fudge and I know what's going on.'

'Harry, you must be very scared –'

'I'm not,' said Harry sincerely. 'Really,' he added, because Mr Weasley was looking disbelieving. 'I'm not trying to be a hero, but seriously, Sirius Black can't be worse than Voldemort, can he?'

Mr Weasley flinched at the sound of the name, but overlooked it.

'Harry, I knew you were, well, made of stronger stuff than Fudge seems to think, and I'm obviously pleased that you're not scared, but –'

'Arthur!' called Mrs Weasley, who was now shepherding the rest onto the train. 'Arthur, what are you doing? It's about to go!'

'He's coming, Molly!' said Mr Weasley, but he turned back to

Harry and kept talking in a lower and more hurried voice. 'Listen,
I want you to give me your word –'

'– that I'll be a good boy and stay in the castle?' said Harry
gloomily.

'Not entirely,' said Mr Weasley, who looked more serious than
Harry had ever seen him. 'Harry, swear to me you won't go *looking*
for Black.'

Harry stared. 'What?'

There was a loud whistle. Guards were walking along the train,
slamming all the doors shut.

'Promise me, Harry,' said Mr Weasley, talking more quickly still,
'that whatever happens –'

'Why would I go looking for someone I know wants to kill me?'
said Harry blankly.

'Swear to me that whatever you might hear –'

'Arthur, quickly!' cried Mrs Weasley.

Steam was billowing from the train; it had started to move.
Harry ran to the compartment door and Ron threw it open and
stood back to let him on. They leant out of the window and
waved at Mr and Mrs Weasley until the train turned a corner and
blocked them from view.

'I need to talk to you in private,' Harry muttered to Ron and
Hermione as the train picked up speed.

'Go away, Ginny,' said Ron.

'Oh, that's nice,' said Ginny huffily, and she stalked off.

Harry, Ron and Hermione set off down the corridor, looking for
an empty compartment, but all were full except for the one at the
very end of the train.

This only had one occupant, a man sitting fast asleep next to
the window. Harry, Ron and Hermione checked on the threshold.
The Hogwarts Express was usually reserved for students and they
had never seen an adult there before, except for the witch who
pushed the food trolley.

The stranger was wearing an extremely shabby set of wizard's
robes which had been darned in several places. He looked ill and
exhausted. Though he seemed quite young, his light-brown hair
was flecked with grey.

'Who d'you reckon he is?' Ron hissed, as they sat down and slid
the door shut, taking the seats furthest away from the window.

'Professor R. J. Lupin,' whispered Hermione at once.

'How d'you know that?'

'It's on his case,' replied Hermione, pointing at the luggage rack over the man's head, where there was a small, battered case held together with a large quantity of neatly knotted string. The name 'Professor R. J. Lupin' was stamped across one corner in peeling letters.

'Wonder what he teaches?' said Ron, frowning at Professor Lupin's pallid profile.

'That's obvious,' whispered Hermione. 'There's only one vacancy, isn't there? Defence Against the Dark Arts.'

Harry, Ron and Hermione had already had two Defence Against the Dark Arts teachers, both of whom had only lasted one year. There were rumours that the job was jinxed.

'Well, I hope he's up to it,' said Ron doubtfully. 'He looks like one good hex would finish him off, doesn't he? Anyway ...' he turned to Harry, 'what were you going to tell us?'

Harry explained all about Mr and Mrs Weasley's argument and the warning Mr Weasley had just given him. When he'd finished, Ron looked thunderstruck, and Hermione had her hands over her mouth. She finally lowered them to say, 'Sirius Black escaped to come after *you*? Oh, Harry ... you'll have to be really, really careful. Don't go looking for trouble, Harry ...'

'I don't go looking for trouble,' said Harry, nettled. 'Trouble usually finds *me*.'

'How thick would Harry have to be, to go looking for a nutter who wants to kill him?' said Ron shakily.

They were taking the news worse than Harry had expected. Both Ron and Hermione seemed to be much more frightened of Black than he was.

'No one knows how he got out of Azkaban,' said Ron uncomfortably. 'No one's ever done it before. And he was a top-security prisoner, too.'

'But they'll catch him, won't they?' said Hermione earnestly. 'I mean, they've got all the Muggles looking out for him, too ...'

'What's that noise?' said Ron suddenly.

A faint, tinny sort of whistle was coming from somewhere. They looked all around the compartment.

'It's coming from your trunk, Harry,' said Ron, standing up and reaching into the luggage rack. A moment later he had pulled the Pocket Sneakoscope out from between Harry's robes. It was spinning very fast in the palm of Ron's hand, and glowing brilliantly.

'Is that a *Sneakoscope*?' said Hermione interestedly, standing up for a better look.

'Yeah ... mind you, it's a very cheap one,' Ron said. 'It went haywire just as I was tying it to Errol's leg to send it to Harry.'

'Were you doing anything untrustworthy at the time?' said Hermione shrewdly.

'No! Well ... I wasn't supposed to be using Errol. You know he's not really up to long journeys ... but how else was I supposed to get Harry's present to him?'

'Stick it back in the trunk,' Harry advised, as the Sneakoscope whistled piercingly, 'or it'll wake him up.'

He nodded towards Professor Lupin. Ron stuffed the Sneakoscope into a particularly horrible pair of Uncle Vernon's old socks, which deadened the sound, then closed the lid of the trunk on it.

'We could get it checked in Hogsmeade,' said Ron, sitting back down. 'They sell that sort of thing in Dervish and Banges, magical instruments and stuff, Fred and George told me.'

'Do you know much about Hogsmeade?' asked Hermione keenly. 'I've read it's the only entirely non-Muggle settlement in Britain –'

'Yeah, I think it is,' said Ron in an offhand sort of way, 'but that's not why I want to go. I just want to get inside Honeydukes!'

'What's that?' said Hermione.

'It's this sweetshop,' said Ron, a dreamy look coming over his face, 'where they've got *everything* ... Pepper Imps – they make you smoke at the mouth – and great fat Chocoballs full of strawberry mousse and clotted cream, and really excellent sugar quills which you can suck in class and just look like you're thinking what to write next –'

'But Hogsmeade's a very interesting place, isn't it?' Hermione pressed on eagerly. 'In *Sites of Historical Sorcery* it says the inn was the headquarters for the 1612 goblin rebellion, and the Shrieking Shack's supposed to be the most severely haunted building in Britain –'

'– and massive sherbet balls that make you levitate a few inches off the ground while you're sucking them,' said Ron, who was plainly not listening to a word Hermione was saying.

Hermione looked around at Harry.

'Won't it be nice to get out of school for a bit and explore Hogsmeade?'

''Spect it will,' said Harry heavily. 'You'll have to tell me when you've found out.'

'What d'you mean?' said Ron.

'I can't go. The Dursleys didn't sign my permission form, and Fudge wouldn't, either.'

Ron looked horrified.

'*You're not allowed to come?* But – no way – McGonagall or someone will give you permission –'

Harry gave a hollow laugh. Professor McGonagall, Head of Gryffindor house, was very strict.

'– or we can ask Fred and George, they know every secret passage out of the castle –'

'Ron!' said Hermione sharply. 'I don't think Harry should be sneaking out of school with Black on the loose –'

'Yeah, I expect that's what McGonagall will say when I ask for permission,' said Harry bitterly.

'But if *we*'re with him,' said Ron spiritedly to Hermione, 'Black wouldn't dare –'

'Oh, Ron, don't talk rubbish,' snapped Hermione. 'Black's already murdered a whole bunch of people in the middle of a crowded street, do you really think he's going to worry about attacking Harry just because *we're* there?'

She was fumbling with the straps of Crookshanks's basket as she spoke.

'Don't let that thing out!' Ron said, but too late; Crookshanks leapt lightly from the basket, stretched, yawned, and sprang onto Ron's knees; the lump in Ron's pocket trembled and he shoved Crookshanks angrily away.

'Get out of it!'

'Ron, don't!' said Hermione angrily.

Ron was about to answer back when Professor Lupin stirred. They watched him apprehensively, but he simply turned his head the other way, mouth slightly open, and slept on.

The Hogwarts Express moved steadily north and the scenery outside the window became wilder and darker while the clouds overhead thickened. People were chasing backwards and forwards past the door of their compartment. Crookshanks had now settled in an empty seat, his squashed face turned towards Ron, his yellow eyes on Ron's top pocket.

At one o'clock the plump witch with the food trolley arrived at the compartment door.

'D'you think we should wake him up?' Ron asked awkwardly, nodding towards Professor Lupin. 'He looks like he could do with some food.'

Hermione approached Professor Lupin cautiously.

'Er – Professor?' she said. 'Excuse me – Professor?'

He didn't move.

'Don't worry, dear,' said the witch, as she handed Harry a large stack of Cauldron Cakes. 'If he's hungry when he wakes, I'll be up front with the driver.'

'I suppose he *is* asleep?' said Ron quietly, as the witch slid the compartment door closed. 'I mean – he hasn't died, has he?'

'No, no, he's breathing,' whispered Hermione, taking the Cauldron Cake Harry passed her.

He might not be very good company, but Professor Lupin's presence in their compartment had its uses. Mid-afternoon, just as it had started to rain, blurring the rolling hills outside the window, they heard footsteps in the corridor again, and their three least favourite people appeared at the door: Draco Malfoy, flanked by his cronies, Vincent Crabbe and Gregory Goyle.

Draco Malfoy and Harry had been enemies ever since they had met on their very first train journey to Hogwarts. Malfoy, who had a pale, pointed, sneering face, was in Slytherin house; he played Seeker on the Slytherin Quidditch team, the same position that Harry played on the Gryffindor team. Crabbe and Goyle seemed to exist to do Malfoy's bidding. They were both wide and muscly; Crabbe was the taller, with a pudding-basin haircut and a very thick neck; Goyle had short, bristly hair and long, gorilla arms.

'Well, look who it is,' said Malfoy in his usual lazy drawl, pulling open the compartment door. 'Potty and the Weasel.'

Crabbe and Goyle chuckled trollishly.

'I heard your father finally got his hands on some gold this summer, Weasley,' said Malfoy. 'Did your mother die of shock?'

Ron stood up so quickly he knocked Crookshanks's basket to the floor. Professor Lupin gave a snort.

'Who's that?' said Malfoy, taking an automatic step backwards as he spotted Lupin.

'New teacher,' said Harry, who had got to his feet, too, in case he needed to hold Ron back. 'What were you saying, Malfoy?'

Malfoy's pale eyes narrowed; he wasn't fool enough to pick a fight right under a teacher's nose.

'C'mon,' he muttered resentfully to Crabbe and Goyle, and they disappeared.

Harry and Ron sat down again, Ron massaging his knuckles.

'I'm not going to take any rubbish from Malfoy this year,' he said angrily. 'I mean it. If he makes one more crack about my family, I'm going to get hold of his head and –'

Ron made a violent gesture in mid-air.

'Ron,' hissed Hermione, pointing at Professor Lupin, 'be *careful* ...'

But Professor Lupin was still fast asleep.

The rain thickened as the train sped yet further north; the windows were now a solid, shimmering grey, which gradually darkened until lanterns flickered into life all along the corridors and over the luggage racks. The train rattled, the rain hammered, the wind roared, but still, Professor Lupin slept.

'We must be nearly there,' said Ron, leaning forward to look past Professor Lupin at the now completely black window.

The words had hardly left him when the train started to slow down.

'Brilliant,' said Ron, getting up and walking carefully past Professor Lupin to try and see outside. 'I'm starving, I want to get to the feast ...'

'We can't be there yet,' said Hermione, checking her watch.

'So why're we stopping?'

The train was getting slower and slower. As the noise of the pistons fell away, the wind and rain sounded louder than ever against the windows.

Harry, who was nearest the door, got up to look into the corridor. All along the carriage, heads were sticking curiously out of their compartments.

The train came to a stop with a jolt and distant thuds and bangs told them that luggage had fallen out of the racks. Then, without warning, all the lamps went out and they were plunged into total darkness.

'What's going on?' said Ron's voice from behind Harry.

'Ouch!' gasped Hermione. 'Ron, that was my foot!'

Harry felt his way back to his seat.

'D'you think we've broken down?'

'Dunno ...'

There was a squeaking sound, and Harry saw the dim black outline of Ron, wiping a patch clean on the window and peering out.

'There's something moving out there,' Ron said. 'I think people are coming aboard ...'

The compartment door suddenly opened and someone fell painfully over Harry's legs.

'Sorry! D'you know what's going on? Ouch! Sorry –'

'Hello, Neville,' said Harry, feeling around in the dark and pulling Neville up by his cloak.

'Harry? Is that you? What's happening?'

'No idea! Sit down –'

There was a loud hissing and a yelp of pain; Neville had tried to sit on Crookshanks.

'I'm going to go and ask the driver what's going on,' came Hermione's voice. Harry felt her pass him, heard the door slide open again and then a thud and two loud squeals of pain.

'Who's that?'

'Who's *that*?'

'Ginny?'

'Hermione?'

'What are you doing?'

'I was looking for Ron –'

'Come in and sit down –'

'Not here!' said Harry hurriedly. 'I'm here!'

'Ouch!' said Neville.

'Quiet!' said a hoarse voice suddenly.

Professor Lupin appeared to have woken up at last. Harry could hear movements in his corner. None of them spoke.

There was a soft, crackling noise and a shivering light filled the compartment. Professor Lupin appeared to be holding a handful of flames. They illuminated his tired grey face, but his eyes looked alert and wary.

'Stay where you are,' he said, in the same hoarse voice, and he got slowly to his feet with his handful of fire held out in front of him.

But the door slid slowly open before Lupin could reach it.

Standing in the doorway, illuminated by the shivering flames in Lupin's hand, was a cloaked figure that towered to the ceiling. Its face was completely hidden beneath its hood. Harry's eyes darted downwards, and what he saw made his stomach contract. There was a hand protruding from the cloak and it was glistening, grey-ish, slimy-looking and scabbed, like something dead that had decayed in water ...

It was visible only for a split second. As though the creature beneath the cloak sensed Harry's gaze, the hand was suddenly withdrawn into the folds of the black material.

And then the thing beneath the hood, whatever it was, drew a long, slow, rattling breath, as though it was trying to suck some-thing more than air from its surroundings.

An intense cold swept over them all. Harry felt his own breath catch in his chest. The cold went deeper than his skin. It was inside his chest, it was inside his very heart ...

Harry's eyes rolled up into his head. He couldn't see. He was drowning in cold. There was a rushing in his ears as though of water. He was being dragged downwards, the roaring growing louder ...

And then, from far away, he heard screaming, terrible, terrified, pleading screams. He wanted to help whoever it was, he tried to move his arms, but couldn't ... a thick white fog was swirling around him, inside him –

'Harry! Harry! Are you all right?'

Someone was slapping his face.

'W-what?'

Harry opened his eyes. There were lanterns above him, and the floor was shaking – the Hogwarts Express was moving again and the lights had come back on. He seemed to have slid out of his seat onto the floor. Ron and Hermione were kneeling next to him, and above them he could see Neville and Professor Lupin watch-ing. Harry felt very sick; when he put up his hand to push his glasses back on, he felt cold sweat on his face.

Ron and Hermione heaved him back onto his seat.

'Are you OK?' Ron asked nervously.

'Yeah,' said Harry, looking quickly towards the door. The hood-ed creature had vanished. 'What happened? Where's that – that thing? Who screamed?'

'No one screamed,' said Ron, more nervously still.

Harry looked around the bright compartment. Ginny and Neville looked back at him, both very pale.

'But I heard screaming –'

A loud snap made them all jump. Professor Lupin was breaking an enormous slab of chocolate into pieces.

'Here,' he said to Harry, handing him a particularly large piece. 'Eat it. It'll help.'

Harry took the chocolate but didn't eat it.

'What was that thing?' he asked Lupin.

'A Dementor,' said Lupin, who was now giving chocolate to everyone else. 'One of the Dementors of Azkaban.'

Everyone stared at him. Professor Lupin crumpled up the empty chocolate wrapper and put it in his pocket.

'Eat,' he repeated. 'It'll help. I need to speak to the driver, excuse me ...'

He strolled past Harry and disappeared into the corridor.

'Are you sure you're OK, Harry?' said Hermione, watching Harry anxiously.

'I don't get it ... what happened?' said Harry, wiping more sweat off his face.

'Well – that thing – the Dementor – stood there and looked around (I mean, I think it did, I couldn't see its face) – and you – you –'

'I thought you were having a fit or something,' said Ron, who still looked scared. 'You went sort of rigid and fell out of your seat and started twitching –'

'And Professor Lupin stepped over you, and walked towards the Dementor, and pulled out his wand,' said Hermione. 'And he said, "None of us is hiding Sirius Black under our cloaks. Go." But the Dementor didn't move, so Lupin muttered something, and a silvery thing shot out of his wand at it, and it turned round and sort of glided away ...'

'It was horrible,' said Neville, in a higher voice than usual. 'Did you feel how cold it went when it came in?'

'I felt weird,' said Ron, shifting his shoulders uncomfortably. 'Like I'd never be cheerful again ...'

Ginny, who was huddled in her corner looking nearly as bad as Harry felt, gave a small sob; Hermione went over and put a comforting arm around her.

'But didn't any of you – fall off your seats?' said Harry awkwardly.

'No,' said Ron, looking anxiously at Harry again. 'Ginny was shaking like mad, though ...'

Harry didn't understand. He felt weak and shivery, as though he was recovering from a bad bout of flu; he also felt the beginnings of shame. Why had he gone to pieces like that, when no one else had?

Professor Lupin had come back. He paused as he entered, looked around and said, with a small smile, 'I haven't poisoned that chocolate, you know ...'

Harry took a bite and to his great surprise felt warmth spread suddenly to the tips of his fingers and toes.

'We'll be at Hogwarts in ten minutes,' said Professor Lupin. 'Are you all right, Harry?'

Harry didn't ask how Professor Lupin knew his name.

'Fine,' he muttered, embarrassed.

They didn't talk much during the remainder of the journey. At long last, the train stopped at Hogsmeade station, and there was a great scramble to get out; owls hooted, cats miaowed, and Neville's pet toad croaked loudly from under his hat. It was freezing on the tiny platform; rain was driving down in icy sheets.

'Firs'-years this way!' called a familiar voice. Harry, Ron and Hermione turned and saw the gigantic outline of Hagrid at the other end of the platform, beckoning the terrified-looking new students forward for their traditional journey across the lake.

'All righ', you three?' Hagrid yelled over the heads of the crowd. They waved at him, but had no chance to speak to him because the mass of people around them was shunting them away along the platform. Harry, Ron and Hermione followed the rest of the school out onto a rough mud track, where at least a hundred stagecoaches awaited the remaining students, each pulled, Harry could only assume, by an invisible horse, because when they climbed inside one and shut the door, the coach set off all by itself, bumping and swaying in procession.

The coach smelled faintly of mould and straw. Harry felt better since the chocolate, but still weak. Ron and Hermione kept looking at him sideways, as though frightened he might collapse again.

As the carriage trundled towards a pair of magnificent wrought-iron gates, flanked with stone columns topped with winged boars, Harry saw two more towering, hooded Dementors, standing guard on either side. A wave of cold sickness threatened to engulf him again; he leant back into the lumpy seat and closed his eyes until they had passed through the gates. The carriage picked up speed on the long, sloping drive up to the castle; Hermione was leaning out of the tiny window, watching the many turrets and towers draw nearer. At last, the carriage swayed to a halt, and Hermione and Ron got out.

As Harry stepped down, a drawling, delighted voice sounded in his ear.

'You *fainted*, Potter? Is Longbottom telling the truth? You actually *fainted*?'

Malfoy elbowed past Hermione to block Harry's way up the stone steps to the castle, his face gleeful and his pale eyes glinting maliciously.

'Shove off, Malfoy,' said Ron, whose jaw was clenched.

'Did you faint as well, Weasley?' said Malfoy loudly. 'Did the scary old Dementor frighten you, too, Weasley?'

'Is there a problem?' said a mild voice. Professor Lupin had just got out of the next carriage.

Malfoy gave Professor Lupin an insolent stare, which took in the patches on his robes and the dilapidated suitcase. With a tiny hint of sarcasm in his voice, he said, 'Oh, no – er – *Professor*,' then he smirked at Crabbe and Goyle, and led them up the steps into the castle.

Hermione prodded Ron in the back to make him hurry, and the three of them joined the crowd swarming up the steps, through the giant oak front doors, and into the cavernous Entrance Hall, which was lit with flaming torches and housed a magnificent marble staircase which led to the upper floors.

The door into the Great Hall stood open at the right; Harry followed the crowd towards it, but had barely glimpsed the enchanted ceiling, which was black and cloudy tonight, when a voice called, 'Potter! Granger! I want to see you both!'

Harry and Hermione turned around, surprised. Professor McGonagall, Transfiguration teacher and Head of Gryffindor house, was calling over the heads of the crowd. She was a stern-looking witch who wore her hair in a tight bun; her sharp eyes were framed with square spectacles. Harry fought his way over to her with a feeling of foreboding; Professor McGonagall had a way of making him feel he must have done something wrong.

'There's no need to look so worried – I just want a word in my office,' she told them. 'Move along there, Weasley.'

Ron stared as Professor McGonagall ushered Harry and Hermione away from the chattering crowd; they accompanied her across the Entrance Hall, up the marble staircase and along a corridor.

Once they were in her office, a small room with a large, welcoming fire, Professor McGonagall motioned Harry and Hermione to sit down. She settled herself behind her desk and said abruptly, 'Professor Lupin sent an owl ahead to say that you were taken ill on the train, Potter.'

Before Harry could reply, there was a soft knock on the door and Madam Pomfrey, the matron, came bustling in.

Harry felt himself going red in the face. It was bad enough that he'd passed out, or whatever he had done, without everyone making all this fuss.

'I'm fine,' he said. 'I don't need anything –'

'Oh, it's you, is it?' said Madam Pomfrey, ignoring this and bending down to stare closely at him. 'I suppose you've been doing something dangerous again?'

'It was a Dementor, Poppy,' said Professor McGonagall.

They exchanged a dark look and Madam Pomfrey clucked disapprovingly.

'Setting Dementors around a school,' she muttered, pushing Harry's hair back and feeling his forehead. 'He won't be the first one who collapses. Yes, he's all clammy. Terrible things, they are, and the effect they have on people who are already delicate –'

'I'm not delicate!' said Harry crossly.

'Of course you're not,' said Madam Pomfrey absent-mindedly, now taking his pulse.

'What does he need?' said Professor McGonagall crisply. 'Bed rest? Should he perhaps spend tonight in the hospital wing?'

'I'm *fine*!' said Harry, jumping up. The idea of what Draco Malfoy would say if he had to go to the hospital wing was torture.

'Well, he should have some chocolate, at the very least,' said Madam Pomfrey, who was now trying to peer into Harry's eyes.

'I've already had some,' said Harry. 'Professor Lupin gave me some. He gave it to all of us.'

'Did he, now?' said Madam Pomfrey approvingly. 'So we've finally got a Defence Against the Dark Arts teacher who knows his remedies.'

'Are you sure you feel all right, Potter?' said Professor McGonagall sharply.

'*Yes,*' said Harry.

'Very well. Kindly wait outside while I have a quick word with Miss Granger about her timetable, then we can go down to the feast together.'

Harry went back into the corridor with Madam Pomfrey, who left for the hospital wing, muttering to herself. He only had to wait a few minutes; then Hermione emerged looking very happy about something, followed by Professor McGonagall, and the three of them made their way back down the marble staircase to the Great Hall.

It was a sea of pointed black hats; each of the long house tables was lined with students, their faces glimmering by the light of thousands of candles, which were floating over the tables in mid-air. Professor Flitwick, who was a tiny little wizard with a shock of white hair, was carrying an ancient hat and a three-legged stool out of the Hall.

'Oh,' said Hermione softly, 'we've missed the Sorting!'

New students at Hogwarts were sorted into houses by trying on the Sorting Hat, which shouted out the house they were best suited to (Gryffindor, Ravenclaw, Hufflepuff or Slytherin). Professor McGonagall strode off towards her empty seat at the staff table, and Harry and Hermione set off in the other direction, as quietly as possible, towards the Gryffindor table. People looked around at them as they passed along the back of the Hall, and a few of them pointed at Harry. Had the story of him collapsing in front of the Dementor travelled that fast?

He and Hermione sat down on either side of Ron, who had saved them seats.

'What was all that about?' he muttered to Harry.

Harry started to explain in a whisper, but at that moment the Headmaster stood up to speak, and he broke off.

Professor Dumbledore, though very old, always gave an impression of great energy. He had several feet of long silver hair and beard, half-moon spectacles and an extremely crooked nose. He was often described as the greatest wizard of the age, but that wasn't why Harry respected him. You couldn't help trusting Albus Dumbledore, and as Harry watched him beaming around at the students, he felt really calm for the first time since the Dementor had entered the train compartment.

'Welcome!' said Dumbledore, the candlelight shimmering on

his beard. 'Welcome to another year at Hogwarts! I have a few things to say to you all, and as one of them is very serious, I think it best to get it out of the way before you become befuddled by our excellent feast ...'

Dumbledore cleared his throat and continued. 'As you will all be aware after their search of the Hogwarts Express, our school is presently playing host to some of the Dementors of Azkaban, who are here on Ministry of Magic business.'

He paused, and Harry remembered what Mr Weasley had said about Dumbledore not being happy with the Dementors guarding the school.

'They are stationed at every entrance to the grounds,' Dumbledore continued, 'and while they are with us, I must make it plain that nobody is to leave school without permission. Dementors are not to be fooled by tricks or disguises – or even Invisibility Cloaks,' he added blandly, and Harry and Ron glanced at each other. 'It is not in the nature of a Dementor to understand pleading or excuses. I therefore warn each and every one of you to give them no reason to harm you. I look to the Prefects, and our new Head Boy and Girl, to make sure that no student runs foul of the Dementors.'

Percy, who was sitting a few seats along from Harry, puffed out his chest again and stared around impressively. Dumbledore paused again; he looked very seriously around the Hall, and nobody moved or made a sound.

'On a happier note,' he continued, 'I am pleased to welcome two new teachers to our ranks this year.

'Firstly, Professor Lupin, who has kindly consented to fill the post of Defence Against the Dark Arts teacher.'

There was some scattered, rather unenthusiastic, applause. Only those who had been in the compartment on the train with Professor Lupin clapped hard, Harry among them. Professor Lupin looked particularly shabby next to all the other teachers in their best robes.

'Look at Snape!' Ron hissed in Harry's ear.

Professor Snape, the Potions master, was staring along the staff table at Professor Lupin. It was common knowledge that Snape wanted the Defence Against the Dark Arts job, but even Harry, who hated Snape, was startled at the expression twisting his thin, sallow face. It was beyond anger: it was loathing. Harry knew that expression only too well; it was the look Snape wore every time he set eyes on Harry.

'As to our second new appointment,' Dumbledore continued, as the lukewarm applause for Professor Lupin died away, 'well, I am sorry to tell you that Professor Kettleburn, our Care of Magical Creatures teacher, retired at the end of last year in order to enjoy more time with his remaining limbs. However, I am delighted to say that his place will be filled by none other than Rubeus Hagrid, who has agreed to take on this teaching job in addition to his gamekeeping duties.'

Harry, Ron and Hermione stared at each other, stunned. Then they joined in with the applause, which was tumultuous at the Gryffindor table in particular. Harry leant forward to see Hagrid, who was ruby red in the face and staring down at his enormous hands, his wide grin hidden in the tangle of his black beard.

'We should've known!' Ron roared, pounding the table. 'Who else would have set us a biting book?'

Harry, Ron and Hermione were the last to stop clapping, and as Professor Dumbledore started speaking again, they saw that Hagrid was wiping his eyes on the tablecloth.

'Well, I think that's everything of importance,' said Dumbledore. 'Let the feast begin!'

The golden plates and goblets before them filled suddenly with food and drink. Harry, suddenly ravenous, helped himself to everything he could reach and began to eat.

It was a delicious feast; the Hall echoed with talk, laughter and the clatter of knives and forks. Harry, Ron and Hermione, however, were eager for it to finish so that they could talk to Hagrid. They knew how much being made a teacher would mean to him. Hagrid wasn't a fully qualified wizard; he had been expelled from Hogwarts in his third year, for a crime he had not committed. It had been Harry, Ron and Hermione who had cleared Hagrid's name last year.

At long last, when the last morsels of pumpkin tart had melted from the golden platters, Dumbledore gave the word that it was time for them all to go to bed, and they got their chance.

'Congratulations, Hagrid!' Hermione squealed, as they reached the teachers' table.

'All down ter you three,' said Hagrid, wiping his shining face on his napkin as he looked up at them. 'Can' believe it ... great man,

Dumbledore ... came straight down to me hut after Professor Kettleburn said he'd had enough ... it's what I always wanted ...'

Overcome with emotion, he buried his face in his napkin, and Professor McGonagall shooed them away.

Harry, Ron and Hermione joined the Gryffindors streaming up the marble staircase and, very tired now, along more corridors, up more and more stairs, to the hidden entrance to Gryffindor Tower. A large portrait of a fat lady in a pink dress asked them, 'Password?'

'Coming through, coming through!' Percy called from behind the crowd. 'The new password's *Fortuna Major*!'

'Oh no,' said Neville Longbottom sadly. He always had trouble remembering the passwords.

Through the portrait hole and across the common room, the girls and boys divided towards their separate staircases. Harry climbed the spiral stairs with no thought in his head except how glad he was to be back. They reached their familiar, circular dormitory with its five four-poster beds and Harry, looking around, felt he was home at last.

— CHAPTER SIX —

Talons and Tea Leaves

When Harry, Ron and Hermione entered the Great Hall for breakfast next day, the first thing they saw was Draco Malfoy, who seemed to be entertaining a large group of Slytherins with a very funny story. As they passed, Malfoy did a ridiculous impression of a swooning fit and there was a roar of laughter.

'Ignore him,' said Hermione, who was right behind Harry. 'Just ignore him, it's not worth it ...'

'Hey, Potter!' shrieked Pansy Parkinson, a Slytherin girl with a face like a pug. 'Potter! The Dementors are coming, Potter! *Wooooooooo!*'

Harry dropped into a seat at the Gryffindor table, next to George Weasley.

'New third-year timetables,' said George, passing them over. 'What's up with you, Harry?'

'Malfoy,' said Ron, sitting down on George's other side and glaring over at the Slytherin table.

George looked up in time to see Malfoy pretending to faint with terror again.

'That little git,' he said calmly. 'He wasn't so cocky last night when the Dementors were down our end of the train. Came running into our compartment, didn't he, Fred?'

'Nearly wet himself,' said Fred, with a contemptuous glance at Malfoy.

'I wasn't too happy myself,' said George. 'They're horrible things, those Dementors ...'

'Sort of freeze your insides, don't they?' said Fred.

'You didn't pass out, though, did you?' said Harry in a low voice.

'Forget it, Harry,' said George bracingly. 'Dad had to go out to Azkaban one time, remember, Fred? And he said it was the worst place he'd ever been. He came back all weak and shaking ... They suck the happiness out of a place, Dementors. Most of the prisoners go mad in there.'

'Anyway, we'll see how happy Malfoy looks after our first Quidditch match,' said Fred. 'Gryffindor versus Slytherin, first game of the season, remember?'

The only time Harry and Malfoy had faced each other in a Quidditch match, Malfoy had definitely come off worse. Feeling slightly more cheerful, Harry helped himself to sausages and fried tomatoes.

Hermione was examining her new timetable.

'Ooh, good, we're starting some new subjects today,' she said happily.

'Hermione,' said Ron, frowning as he looked over her shoulder, 'they've messed up your timetable. Look – they've got you down for about ten subjects a day. There isn't enough *time*.'

'I'll manage. I've fixed it all with Professor McGonagall.'

'But look,' said Ron, laughing, 'see this morning? Nine o'clock, Divination. And underneath, nine o'clock, Muggle Studies. And –' Ron leant closer to the timetable, disbelieving, '*look* – underneath that, Arithmancy, *nine o'clock*. I mean, I know you're good, Hermione, but no one's *that* good. How're you supposed to be in three classes at once?'

'Don't be silly,' said Hermione shortly. 'Of course I won't be in three classes at once.'

'Well, then –'

'Pass the marmalade,' said Hermione.

'But –'

'Oh, Ron, what's it to you if my timetable's a bit full?' Hermione snapped. 'I told you, I've fixed it all with Professor McGonagall.'

Just then, Hagrid entered the Great Hall. He was wearing his long moleskin overcoat and was absent-mindedly swinging a dead polecat from one enormous hand.

'All righ'?' he said eagerly, pausing on the way to the staff table. 'Yer in my firs' ever lesson! Right after lunch! Bin up since five gettin' everythin' ready ... hope it's OK ... me, a teacher ... hones'ly ...'

He grinned broadly at them and headed off to the staff table, still swinging the polecat.

'Wonder what he's been getting ready?' said Ron, a note of anxiety in his voice.

The Hall was starting to empty as people headed off towards their first lesson. Ron checked his timetable.

'We'd better go, look, Divination's at the top of North Tower. It'll take us ten minutes to get there ...'

They finished their breakfast hastily, said goodbye to Fred and George and walked back through the Hall. As they passed the Slytherin table, Malfoy did yet another impression of a fainting fit. The shouts of laughter followed Harry into the Entrance Hall.

The journey through the castle to North Tower was a long one. Two years at Hogwarts hadn't taught them everything about the castle, and they had never been inside North Tower before.

'There's – got – to – be – a – short – cut,' Ron panted, as they climbed their seventh long staircase and emerged on an unfamiliar landing, where there was nothing but a large painting of a bare stretch of grass hanging on the stone wall.

'I think it's this way,' said Hermione, peering down the empty passage to the right.

'Can't be,' said Ron. 'That's south. Look, you can see a bit of the lake out of the window ...'

Harry was watching the painting. A fat, dapple-grey pony had just ambled onto the grass and was grazing nonchalantly. Harry was used to the subjects of Hogwarts paintings moving around and leaving their frames to visit each other, but he always enjoyed watching them. A moment later, a short, squat knight in a suit of armour had clanked into the picture after his pony. By the look of the grass stains on his metal knees, he had just fallen off.

'Aha!' he yelled, seeing Harry, Ron and Hermione. 'What villains are these that trespass upon my private lands? Come to scorn at my fall, perchance? Draw, you knaves, you dogs!'

They watched in astonishment as the little knight tugged his sword out of its scabbard and began brandishing it violently, hopping up and down in rage. But the sword was too long for him; a particularly wild swing made him overbalance, and he landed face down in the grass.

'Are you all right?' said Harry, moving closer to the picture.

'Get back, you scurvy braggart! Back, you rogue!'

The knight seized his sword again and used it to push himself back up, but the blade sank deeply into the grass and, though he pulled with all his might, he couldn't get it out again. Finally he had to flop back down onto the grass and push up his visor to mop his sweating face.

'Listen,' said Harry, taking advantage of the knight's exhaustion, 'we're looking for the North Tower. You don't know the way, do you?'

'A quest!' The knight's rage seemed to vanish instantly. He clanked to his feet and shouted, 'Come follow me, dear friends, and we shall find our goal, or else shall perish bravely in the charge!'

He gave the sword another fruitless tug, tried and failed to mount the fat pony, and cried, 'On foot then, good sirs and gentle lady! On! On!'

And he ran, clanking loudly, into the left-hand side of the frame and out of sight.

They hurried after him along the corridor, following the sound of his armour. Every now and then they spotted him running through a picture ahead.

'Be of stout heart, the worst is yet to come!' yelled the knight, and they saw him reappear in front of an alarmed group of women in crinolines, whose picture hung on the wall of a narrow spiral staircase.

Puffing loudly, Harry, Ron and Hermione climbed the tightly spiralling steps, getting dizzier and dizzier, until at last they heard the murmur of voices above them, and knew they had reached the classroom.

'Farewell!' cried the knight, popping his head into a painting of some sinister-looking monks. 'Farewell, my comrades-in-arms! If ever you have need of noble heart and steely sinew, call upon Sir Cadogan!'

'Yeah, we'll call you,' muttered Ron, as the knight disappeared, 'if we ever need someone mental.'

They climbed the last few steps and emerged onto a tiny landing, where most of the class was already assembled. There were no doors off this landing; Ron nudged Harry and pointed at the ceiling, where there was a circular trap door with a brass plaque on it.

'Sybill Trelawney, Divination teacher,' Harry read. 'How're we supposed to get up there?'

As though in answer to his question, the trap door suddenly opened, and a silvery ladder descended right at Harry's feet. Everyone went quiet.

'After you,' said Ron, grinning, so Harry climbed the ladder first.

He emerged into the strangest-looking classroom he had ever seen. In fact, it didn't look like a classroom at all; more like a cross between someone's attic and an old-fashioned teashop. At least twenty small, circular tables were crammed inside it, all surround-ed by chintz armchairs and fat little pouffes. Everything was lit with a dim, crimson light; the curtains at the windows were all closed, and the many lamps were draped with dark red scarves. It was stiflingly warm, and the fire which was burning under the crowded mantelpiece was giving off a heavy, sickly sort of per-fume as it heated a large copper kettle. The shelves running around the circular walls were crammed with dusty-looking feath-ers, stubs of candles, many packs of tattered playing cards, count-less silvery crystal balls and a huge array of teacups.

Ron appeared at Harry's shoulder as the class assembled around them, all talking in whispers.

'Where is she?' Ron said.

A voice came suddenly out of the shadows, a soft, misty sort of voice.

'Welcome,' it said. 'How nice to see you in the physical world at last.'

Harry's immediate impression was of a large, glittering insect. Professor Trelawney moved into the firelight, and they saw that she was very thin; her large glasses magnified her eyes to several times their natural size, and she was draped in a gauzy spangled shawl. Innumerable chains and beads hung around her spindly neck, and her arms and hands were encrusted with bangles and rings.

'Sit, my children, sit,' she said, and they all climbed awkwardly into armchairs or sank onto pouffes. Harry, Ron and Hermione sat themselves around the same round table.

'Welcome to Divination,' said Professor Trelawney, who had seated herself in a winged armchair in front of the fire. 'My name is Professor Trelawney. You may not have seen me before. I find that descending too often into the hustle and bustle of the main school clouds my Inner Eye.'

Nobody said anything in answer to this extraordinary pro-nouncement. Professor Trelawney delicately rearranged her shawl and continued, 'So you have chosen to study Divination, the most difficult of all magical arts. I must warn you at the outset that if you do not have the Sight, there is very little I will be able to teach you. Books can take you only so far in this field ...'

At these words, both Harry and Ron glanced, grinning, at Hermione, who looked startled at the news that books wouldn't be much help in this subject.

'Many witches and wizards, talented though they are in the area of loud bangs and smells and sudden disappearings, are yet unable to penetrate the veiled mysteries of the future,' Professor Trelawney went on, her enormous, gleaming eyes moving from face to nervous face. 'It is a Gift granted to few. You, boy,' she said suddenly to Neville, who almost toppled off his pouffe, 'is your grandmother well?'

'I think so,' said Neville tremulously.

'I wouldn't be so sure if I were you, dear,' said Professor Trelawney, the firelight glinting on her long emerald earrings. Neville gulped. Professor Trelawney continued placidly, 'We will be covering the basic methods of Divination this year. The first term will be devoted to reading the tea leaves. Next term we shall progress to palmistry. By the way, my dear,' she shot suddenly at Parvati Patil, 'beware a red-haired man.'

Parvati gave a startled look at Ron, who was right behind her, and edged her chair away from him.

'In the summer term,' Professor Trelawney went on, 'we shall progress to the crystal ball – if we have finished with fire-omens, that is. Unfortunately, classes will be disrupted in February by a nasty bout of flu. I myself will lose my voice. And around Easter, one of our number will leave us for ever.'

A very tense silence followed this pronouncement, but Professor Trelawney seemed unaware of it.

'I wonder, dear,' she said to Lavender Brown, who was nearest and shrank back in her chair, 'if you could pass me the largest silver teapot?'

Lavender, looking relieved, stood up, took an enormous teapot from the shelf and put it down on the table in front of Professor Trelawney.

'Thank you, my dear. Incidentally, that thing you are dreading – it will happen on Friday the sixteenth of October.'

Lavender trembled.

'Now, I want you all to divide into pairs. Collect a teacup from the shelf, come to me and I will fill it. Then sit down and drink;

drink until only the dregs remain. Swill these around the cup three times with the left hand, then turn the cup upside-down on its saucer; wait for the last of the tea to drain away, then give your cup to your partner to read. You will interpret the patterns using pages five and six of *Unfogging the Future*. I shall move among you, helping and instructing. Oh, and dear –' she caught Neville by the arm as he made to stand up, 'after you've broken your first cup, would you be so kind as to select one of the blue patterned ones? I'm rather attached to the pink.'

Sure enough, Neville had no sooner reached the shelf of teacups than there was a tinkle of breaking china. Professor Trelawney swept over to him holding a dustpan and brush and said, 'One of the blue ones, then, dear, if you wouldn't mind ... thank you ...'

When Harry and Ron had had their teacups filled, they went back to their table and tried to drink the scalding tea quickly. They swilled the dregs around as Professor Trelawney had instructed, then drained the cups and swapped them.

'Right,' said Ron, as they both opened their books at pages five and six. 'What can you see in mine?'

'A load of soggy brown stuff,' said Harry. The heavily perfumed smoke in the room was making him feel sleepy and stupid.

'Broaden your minds, my dears, and allow your eyes to see past the mundane!' Professor Trelawney cried through the gloom.

Harry tried to pull himself together.

'Right, you've got a wonky sort of cross ...' he said, consulting *Unfogging the Future*. 'That means you're going to have "trials and suffering" – sorry about that – but there's a thing that could be the sun. Hang on ... that means "great happiness" ... so you're going to suffer but be very happy ...'

'You need your Inner Eye testing, if you ask me,' said Ron, and they both had to stifle their laughs as Professor Trelawney gazed in their direction.

'My turn ...' Ron peered into Harry's teacup, his forehead wrinkled with effort. 'There's a blob a bit like a bowler hat,' he said. 'Maybe you're going to work for the Ministry of Magic ...'

He turned the teacup the other way up.

'But this way it looks more like an acorn ... what's that?' He scanned his copy of *Unfogging the Future*. '"A windfall, unexpected gold." Excellent, you can lend me some. And there's a thing here,' he turned the cup again, 'that looks like an animal. Yeah, if that was its head ... it looks like a hippo ... no, a sheep ...'

Professor Trelawney whirled around as Harry let out a snort of laughter.

'Let me see that, my dear,' she said reprovingly to Ron, sweeping over and snatching Harry's cup from him. Everyone went quiet to watch.

Professor Trelawney was staring into the teacup, rotating it anti-clockwise.

'The falcon ... my dear, you have a deadly enemy.'

'But everyone knows *that*,' said Hermione in a loud whisper. Professor Trelawney stared at her.

'Well, they do,' said Hermione. 'Everybody knows about Harry and You-Know-Who.'

Harry and Ron stared at her with a mixture of amazement and admiration. They had never heard Hermione speak to a teacher like that before. Professor Trelawney chose not to reply. She lowered her huge eyes to Harry's cup again and continued to turn it.

'The club ... an attack. Dear, dear, this is not a happy cup ...'

'I thought that was a bowler hat,' said Ron sheepishly.

'The skull ... danger in your path, my dear ...'

Everyone was staring, transfixed, at Professor Trelawney, who gave the cup a final turn, gasped, and then screamed.

There was another tinkle of breaking china; Neville had smashed his second cup. Professor Trelawney sank into a vacant armchair, her glittering hand at her heart and her eyes closed.

'My dear boy – my poor dear boy – no – it is kinder not to say – no – don't ask me ...'

'What is it, Professor?' said Dean Thomas at once. Everyone had got to their feet, and slowly, they crowded around Harry and Ron's table, pressing close to Professor Trelawney's chair to get a good look at Harry's cup.

'My dear,' Professor Trelawney's huge eyes opened dramatically, 'you have the Grim.'

'The what?' said Harry.

He could tell that he wasn't the only one who didn't understand; Dean Thomas shrugged at him and Lavender Brown looked puzzled, but nearly everybody else clapped their hands to their mouths in horror.

'The Grim, my dear, the Grim!' cried Professor Trelawney, who looked shocked that Harry hadn't understood. 'The giant, spectral dog that haunts churchyards! My dear boy, it is an omen – the worst omen – of *death*!'

Harry's stomach lurched. That dog on the cover of *Death Omens* in Flourish and Blotts – the dog in the shadows of Magnolia Crescent ... Lavender Brown clapped her hands to her mouth, too. Everyone was looking at Harry; everyone except Hermione, who had got up and moved around to the back of Professor Trelawney's chair.

'*I* don't think it looks like a Grim,' she said flatly.

Professor Trelawney surveyed Hermione with mounting dislike.

'You'll forgive me for saying so, my dear, but I perceive very little aura around you. Very little receptivity to the resonances of the future.'

Seamus Finnigan was tilting his head from side to side.

'It looks like a Grim if you do this,' he said, with his eyes almost shut, 'but it looks more like a donkey from here,' he said, leaning to the left.

'When you've all finished deciding whether I'm going to die or not!' said Harry, taking even himself by surprise. Now nobody seemed to want to look at him.

'I think we will leave the lesson here for today,' said Professor Trelawney, in her mistiest voice. 'Yes ... please pack away your things ...'

Silently the class took their teacups back to Professor Trelawney, packed away their books and closed their bags. Even Ron was avoiding Harry's eyes.

'Until we meet again,' said Professor Trelawney faintly, 'fair fortune be yours. Oh, and dear –' she pointed at Neville, 'you'll be late next time, so mind you work extra hard to catch up.'

Harry, Ron and Hermione descended Professor Trelawney's ladder and the winding staircase in silence, then set off for Professor McGonagall's Transfiguration lesson. It took them so long to find her classroom that, early as they had left Divination, they were only just in time.

Harry chose a seat right at the back of the room, feeling as though he was sitting in a very bright spotlight; the rest of the class kept shooting furtive glances at him, as though he was about to drop dead at any moment. He hardly heard what Professor McGonagall was telling them about Animagi (wizards who could transform at will into animals), and wasn't even watching when she transformed herself in front of their eyes into a tabby cat with spectacle markings around her eyes.

'Really, what has got into you all today?' said Professor McGonagall, turning back into herself with a faint *pop,* and staring around at them all. 'Not that it matters, but that's the first time my transformation's not got applause from a class.'

Everybody's heads turned towards Harry again, but nobody spoke. Then Hermione raised her hand.

'Please, Professor, we've just had our first Divination class, and we were reading the tea leaves, and –'

'Ah, of course,' said Professor McGonagall, suddenly frowning. 'There is no need to say any more, Miss Granger. Tell me, which of you will be dying this year?'

Everyone stared at her.

'Me,' said Harry, finally.

'I see,' said Professor McGonagall, fixing Harry with her beady eyes. 'Then you should know, Potter, that Sybill Trelawney has predicted the death of one student a year since she arrived at this school. None of them has died yet. Seeing death omens is her favourite way of greeting a new class. If it were not for the fact that I never speak ill of my colleagues –' Professor McGonagall broke off, and they saw that her nostrils had gone white. She went on, more calmly, 'Divination is one of the most imprecise branches of magic. I shall not conceal from you that I have very little patience with it. True Seers are very rare, and Professor Trelawney ...'

She stopped again, and then said, in a very matter-of-fact tone, 'You look in excellent health to me, Potter, so you will excuse me if I don't let you off homework today. I assure you that if you die, you need not hand it in.'

Hermione laughed. Harry felt a bit better. It was harder to feel scared of a lump of tea leaves away from the dim red light and befuddling perfume of Professor Trelawney's classroom. Not everyone was convinced, however. Ron still looked worried, and Lavender whispered, 'But what about Neville's cup?'

When the Transfiguration class had finished, they joined the crowd thundering towards the Great Hall for lunch.

'Ron, cheer up,' said Hermione, pushing a dish of stew towards him. 'You heard what Professor McGonagall said.'

Ron spooned stew onto his plate and picked up his fork but didn't start.

'Harry,' he said, in a low, serious voice, 'you *haven't* seen a great black dog anywhere, have you?'

'Yeah, I have,' said Harry. 'I saw one the night I left the Dursleys.'

Ron let his fork fall with a clatter.

'Probably a stray,' said Hermione calmly.

Ron looked at Hermione as though she had gone mad.

'Hermione, if Harry's seen a Grim, that's – that's bad,' he said. 'My – my Uncle Bilius saw one and – and he died twenty-four hours later!'

'Coincidence,' said Hermione airily, pouring herself some pumpkin juice.

'You don't know what you're talking about!' said Ron, starting to get angry. 'Grims scare the living daylights out of most wizards!'

'There you are, then,' said Hermione in a superior tone. 'They see the Grim and die of fright. The Grim's not an omen, it's the cause of death! And Harry's still with us because he's not stupid enough to see one and think, right, well, I'd better pop my clogs then!'

Ron mouthed wordlessly at Hermione, who opened her bag, took out her new Arithmancy book and propped it open against the juice jug.

'I think Divination seems very woolly,' she said, searching for her page. 'A lot of guesswork, if you ask me.'

'There was nothing woolly about the Grim in that cup!' said Ron hotly.

'You didn't seem quite so confident when you were telling Harry it was a sheep,' said Hermione coolly.

'Professor Trelawney said you didn't have the right aura! You just don't like being rubbish at something for a change!'

He had touched a nerve. Hermione slammed her Arithmancy book down on the table so hard that bits of meat and carrot flew everywhere.

'If being good at Divination means I have to pretend to see death omens in a lump of tea leaves, I'm not sure I'll be studying it much longer! That lesson was absolute rubbish compared to my Arithmancy class!'

She snatched up her bag and stalked away.

Ron frowned after her.

'What's she talking about?' he said to Harry. 'She hasn't been to an Arithmancy class yet.'

*

Harry was pleased to get out of the castle after lunch. Yesterday's rain had cleared; the sky was a clear, pale grey and the grass was springy and damp underfoot as they set off for their first ever Care of Magical Creatures class.

Ron and Hermione weren't speaking to each other. Harry walked beside them in silence as they went down the sloping lawns to Hagrid's hut on the edge of the Forbidden Forest. It was only when he spotted three only-too-familiar backs ahead of them that he realised they must be having these lessons with the Slytherins. Malfoy was talking animatedly to Crabbe and Goyle, who were chortling. Harry was quite sure he knew what they were talking about.

Hagrid was waiting for his class at the door of his hut. He stood in his moleskin overcoat, with Fang the boarhound at his heels, looking impatient to start.

'C'mon, now, get a move on!' he called, as the class approached. 'Got a real treat for yeh today! Great lesson comin' up! Everyone here? Right, follow me!'

For one nasty moment, Harry thought that Hagrid was going to lead them into the Forest; Harry had had enough unpleasant experiences in there to last him a lifetime. However, Hagrid strolled off around the edge of the trees, and five minutes later, they found themselves outside a kind of paddock. There was nothing in there.

'Everyone gather round the fence here!' he called. 'That's it – make sure yeh can see. Now, firs' thing yeh'll want ter do is open yer books –'

'How?' said the cold, drawling voice of Draco Malfoy.

'Eh?' said Hagrid.

'How do we open our books?' Malfoy repeated. He took out his copy of *The Monster Book of Monsters*, which he had bound shut with a length of rope. Other people took theirs out, too; some, like Harry, had belted their book shut; others had crammed them inside tight bags or clamped them together with bullclips.

'Hasn' – hasn' anyone bin able ter open their books?' said

Hagrid, looking crestfallen.

The class all shook their heads.

'Yeh've got ter *stroke* 'em,' said Hagrid, as though this was the most obvious thing in the world. 'Look ...'

He took Hermione's copy and ripped off the Spellotape that bound it. The book tried to bite, but Hagrid ran a giant forefinger down its spine, and the book shivered, and then fell open and lay quiet in his hand.

'Oh, how silly we've all been!' Malfoy sneered. 'We should have *stroked* them! Why didn't we guess!'

'I ... I thought they were funny,' Hagrid said uncertainly to Hermione.

'Oh, tremendously funny!' said Malfoy. 'Really witty, giving us books that try and rip our hands off!'

'Shut up, Malfoy,' said Harry quietly. Hagrid was looking downcast and Harry wanted Hagrid's first lesson to be a success.

'Righ' then,' said Hagrid, who seemed to have lost his thread, 'so ... so yeh've got yer books an' ... an' ... now yeh need the Magical Creatures. Yeah. So I'll go an' get 'em. Hang on ...'

He strode away from them into the Forest and out of sight.

'God, this place is going to the dogs,' said Malfoy loudly. 'That oaf teaching classes, my father'll have a fit when I tell him –'

'Shut up, Malfoy,' Harry repeated.

'Careful, Potter, there's a Dementor behind you –'

'Oooooooh!' squealed Lavender Brown, pointing towards the opposite side of the paddock.

Trotting towards them were a dozen of the most bizarre creatures Harry had ever seen. They had the bodies, hind legs and tails of horses, but the front legs, wings and heads of what seemed to be giant eagles, with cruel, steel-coloured beaks and large, brilliantly orange eyes. The talons on their front legs were half a foot long and deadly-looking. Each of the beasts had a thick leather collar around its neck, which was attached to a long chain, and the ends of all of these were held in the vast hands of Hagrid, who came jogging into the paddock behind the creatures.

'Gee up, there!' he roared, shaking the chains and urging the creatures towards the fence where the class stood. Everyone drew back slightly as Hagrid reached them and tethered the creatures to the fence.

'Hippogriffs!' Hagrid roared happily, waving a hand at them.

'Beau'iful, aren' they?'

Harry could sort of see what Hagrid meant. Once you had got over the first shock of seeing something that was half-horse, half-bird, you started to appreciate the Hippogriffs' gleaming coats, changing smoothly from feather to hair, each of them a different colour: stormy grey, bronze, a pinkish roan, gleaming chestnut and inky black.

'So,' said Hagrid, rubbing his hands together and beaming around, 'if yeh wan' ter come a bit nearer ...'

No one seemed to want to. Harry, Ron and Hermione, however, approached the fence cautiously.

'Now, firs' thing yeh gotta know abou' Hippogriffs is they're proud,' said Hagrid. 'Easily offended, Hippogriffs are. Don't never insult one, 'cause it might be the last thing yeh do.'

Malfoy, Crabbe and Goyle weren't listening; they were talking in an undertone and Harry had a nasty feeling they were plotting how best to disrupt the lesson.

'Yeh always wait fer the Hippogriff ter make the firs' move,' Hagrid continued. 'It's polite, see? Yeh walk towards him, and yeh bow, an' yeh wait. If he bows back, yeh're allowed ter touch him. If he doesn' bow, then get away from him sharpish, 'cause those talons hurt.'

'Right – who wants ter go first?'

Most of the class backed further away in answer. Even Harry, Ron and Hermione had misgivings. The Hippogriffs were tossing their fierce heads and flexing their powerful wings; they didn't seem to like being tethered like this.

'No one?' said Hagrid, with a pleading look.

'I'll do it,' said Harry.

There was an intake of breath from behind him and both Lavender and Parvati whispered, 'Oooh, no, Harry, remember your tea leaves!'

Harry ignored them. He climbed over the paddock fence.

'Good man, Harry!' roared Hagrid. 'Right then – let's see how yeh get on with Buckbeak.'

He untied one of the chains, pulled the grey Hippogriff away from his fellows and slipped off his leather collar. The class on the other side of the paddock seemed to be holding its breath. Malfoy's eyes were narrowed maliciously.

'Easy, now, Harry,' said Hagrid quietly. 'Yeh've got eye contact, now try not ter blink – Hippogriffs don' trust yeh if yeh blink too much ...'

Harry's eyes immediately began to water, but he didn't shut them. Buckbeak had turned his great, sharp head, and was staring at Harry with one fierce orange eye.

'Tha's it,' said Hagrid. 'Tha's it, Harry ... now, bow ...'

Harry didn't feel much like exposing the back of his neck to Buckbeak, but he did as he was told. He gave a short bow and then looked up.

The Hippogriff was still staring haughtily at him. It didn't move.

'Ah,' said Hagrid, sounding worried. 'Right – back away, now, Harry, easy does it –'

But then, to Harry's enormous surprise, the Hippogriff suddenly bent his scaly front knees, and sank into what was an unmistake-able bow.

'Well done, Harry!' said Hagrid, ecstatic. 'Right – yeh can touch him! Pat his beak, go on!'

Feeling that a better reward would have been to back away, Harry moved slowly towards the Hippogriff and reached out towards him. He patted the beak several times and the Hippogriff closed his eyes lazily, as though enjoying it.

The class broke into applause, all except for Malfoy, Crabbe and Goyle, who were looking deeply disappointed.

'Righ' then, Harry,' said Hagrid, 'I reckon he migh' let yeh ride him!'

This was more than Harry had bargained for. He was used to a broomstick; but he wasn't sure a Hippogriff would be quite the same.

'Yeh climb up there, jus' behind the wing joint,' said Hagrid, 'an' mind yeh don' pull any of his feathers out, he won' like that ...'

Harry put his foot on the top of Buckbeak's wing and hoisted himself onto his back. Buckbeak stood up. Harry wasn't sure where to hold on; everything in front of him was covered in feathers.

'Go on, then!' roared Hagrid, slapping the Hippogriff's hindquarters.

Without warning, twelve-foot wings flapped open on either side of Harry; he just had time to seize the Hippogriff around the neck before he was soaring upwards. It was nothing like a broom-stick, and Harry knew which one he preferred; the Hippogriff's wings were beating uncomfortably on either side of him, catching him under his legs and making him feel he was about to be thrown off; the glossy feathers slipped under his fingers and he didn't dare get a stronger grip; instead of the smooth action of his Nimbus Two Thousand, he now felt himself rocking backwards and forwards as the hindquarters of the Hippogriff rose and fell with his wings.

Buckbeak flew him once around the paddock and then headed back to the ground; this was the bit Harry had been dreading; he leant back as the smooth neck lowered, feeling he was going to slip off over the beak; then he felt a heavy thud as the four ill-assorted feet hit the ground, and just managed to hold on and push himself straight again.

'Good work, Harry!' roared Hagrid, as everyone except Malfoy, Crabbe and Goyle cheered. 'OK, who else wants a go?'

Emboldened by Harry's success, the rest of the class climbed cautiously into the paddock. Hagrid untied the Hippogriffs one by one, and soon people were bowing nervously, all over the paddock. Neville ran repeatedly backwards from his, which didn't seem to want to bend its knees. Ron and Hermione practised on the chestnut, while Harry watched.

Malfoy, Crabbe and Goyle had taken over Buckbeak. He had bowed to Malfoy, who was now patting his beak, looking disdainful.

'This is very easy,' Malfoy drawled, loud enough for Harry to hear him. 'I knew it must have been, if Potter could do it ... I bet you're not dangerous at all, are you?' he said to the Hippogriff. 'Are you, you ugly great brute?'

It happened in a flash of steely talons; Malfoy let out a high-pitched scream and next moment, Hagrid was wrestling Buckbeak back into his collar as he strained to get at Malfoy, who lay curled in the grass, blood blossoming over his robes.

'I'm dying!' Malfoy yelled, as the class panicked. 'I'm dying, look at me! It's killed me!'

'Yer not dyin'!' said Hagrid, who had gone very white. 'Someone help me – gotta get him outta here –'

Hermione ran to open the gate while Hagrid lifted Malfoy easily. As they passed, Harry saw that there was a long, deep gash in Malfoy's arm; blood splattered the grass and Hagrid ran with him, up the slope towards the castle.

Very shaken, the Care of Magical Creatures class followed at a walk. The Slytherins were all shouting about Hagrid.

'They should sack him straight away!' said Pansy Parkinson, who was in tears.

'It was Malfoy's fault!' snapped Dean Thomas. Crabbe and Goyle flexed their muscles threateningly.

They all climbed the stone steps into the deserted Entrance Hall.

'I'm going to see if he's OK!' said Pansy, and they all watched her run up the marble staircase. The Slytherins, still muttering about Hagrid, headed away in the direction of their dungeon common room; Harry, Ron and Hermione proceeded upstairs to Gryffindor Tower.

'D'you think he'll be all right?' said Hermione nervously.

''Course he will, Madam Pomfrey can mend cuts in about a second,' said Harry, who had had far worse injuries mended magically by the matron.

'That was a really bad thing to happen in Hagrid's first class, though, wasn't it?' said Ron, looking worried. 'Trust Malfoy to mess things up for him ...'

They were among the first to reach the Great Hall at dinnertime, hoping to see Hagrid, but he wasn't there.

'They *wouldn't* sack him, would they?' said Hermione anxiously, not touching her steak-and-kidney pudding.

'They'd better not,' said Ron, who wasn't eating either.

Harry was watching the Slytherin table. A large group including Crabbe and Goyle were huddled together, deep in conversation. Harry was sure they were cooking up their own version of how Malfoy had got injured.

'Well, you can't say it wasn't an interesting first day back,' said Ron gloomily.

They went up to the crowded Gryffindor common room after dinner and tried to do the homework Professor McGonagall had set them, but all three of them kept breaking off and glancing out of the tower window.

'There's a light on in Hagrid's window,' Harry said suddenly.

Ron looked at his watch.

'If we hurried, we could go down and see him, it's still quite early ...'

'I don't know,' Hermione said slowly, and Harry saw her glance at him.

'I'm allowed to walk across the *grounds*,' he said pointedly. 'Sirius Black hasn't got past the Dementors here, has he?'

So they put their things away and headed out of the portrait hole, glad not to meet anybody on their way to the front doors, as they weren't entirely sure they were supposed to be out.

The grass was still wet and looked almost black in the twilight. When they reached Hagrid's hut, they knocked, and a voice growled, 'C'min.'

Hagrid was sitting in his shirt-sleeves at his scrubbed wooden table; his boarhound, Fang, had his head in Hagrid's lap. One look told them that Hagrid had been drinking a lot; there was a pewter tankard almost as big as a bucket in front of him, and he seemed to be having difficulty in getting them into focus.

''Spect it's a record,' he said thickly, when he recognised them. 'Don' reckon they've ever had a teacher who on'y lasted a day before.'

'You haven't been sacked, Hagrid!' gasped Hermione.

'Not yet,' said Hagrid miserably, taking a huge gulp of whatever was in the tankard. 'But 's only a matter o' time, i'n't it, after Malfoy ...'

'How is he?' said Ron, as they all sat down. 'It wasn't serious, was it?'

'Madam Pomfrey fixed him best she could,' said Hagrid dully, 'but he's sayin' it's still agony ... covered in bandages ... moanin' ...'

'He's faking it,' said Harry at once. 'Madam Pomfrey can mend anything. She regrew half my bones last year. Trust Malfoy to milk it for all it's worth.'

'School gov'nors have bin told, o' course,' said Hagrid miserably. 'They reckon I started too big. Shoulda left Hippogriffs fer later ... done Flobberworms or summat ... jus' thought it'd make a good firs' lesson ... 's all my fault ...'

'It's all *Malfoy's* fault, Hagrid!' said Hermione earnestly.

'We're witnesses,' said Harry. 'You said Hippogriffs attack if you insult them. It's Malfoy's problem he wasn't listening. We'll tell Dumbledore what really happened.'

'Yeah, don't worry, Hagrid, we'll back you up,' said Ron.

Tears leaked out of the crinkled corners of Hagrid's beetle-black eyes. He grabbed both Harry and Ron and pulled them into a bone-breaking hug.

'I think you've had enough to drink, Hagrid,' said Hermione

firmly. She took the tankard from the table and went outside to empty it.

'Ar, maybe she's right,' said Hagrid, letting go of Harry and Ron, who both staggered away, rubbing their ribs. Hagrid heaved himself out of his chair and followed Hermione unsteadily outside. They heard a loud splash.

'What's he done?' said Harry nervously, as Hermione came back in with the empty tankard.

'Stuck his head in the water barrel,' said Hermione, putting the tankard away.

Hagrid came back, his long hair and beard sopping wet, wiping the water out of his eyes.

'Tha's better,' he said, shaking his head like a dog and drenching them all. 'Listen, it was good of yeh ter come an' see me, I really –'

Hagrid stopped dead, staring at Harry as though he'd only just realised he was there.

'WHAT D'YEH THINK YOU'RE DOIN', EH?' he roared, so suddenly that they jumped a foot in the air. 'YEH'RE NOT TO GO WANDERIN' AROUND AFTER DARK, HARRY! AN' YOU TWO! LETTIN' HIM!'

Hagrid strode over to Harry, grabbed his arm and pulled him to the door.

'C'mon!' Hagrid said angrily. 'I'm takin' yer all back up ter school, an' don' let me catch yeh walkin' down ter see me after dark again. I'm not worth that!'

CHAPTER SEVEN

The Boggart in the Wardrobe

Malfoy didn't reappear in classes until late on Thursday morning, when the Slytherins and Gryffindors were halfway through double Potions. He swaggered into the dungeon, his right arm covered in bandages and bound up in a sling, acting, in Harry's opinion, as though he was the heroic survivor of some dreadful battle.

'How is it, Draco?' simpered Pansy Parkinson. 'Does it hurt much?'

'Yeah,' said Malfoy, putting on a brave sort of grimace. But Harry saw him wink at Crabbe and Goyle when Pansy had looked away.

'Settle down, settle down,' said Professor Snape idly.

Harry and Ron scowled at each other; Snape wouldn't have said 'settle down' if *they*'d walked in late, he'd have given them detention. But Malfoy had always been able to get away with anything in Snape's classes; Snape was Head of Slytherin house, and generally favoured his own students before all others.

They were making a new potion today, a Shrinking Solution. Malfoy set up his cauldron right next to Harry and Ron, so that they were preparing their ingredients on the same table.

'Sir,' Malfoy called, 'sir, I'll need help cutting up these daisy roots, because of my arm –'

'Weasley, cut up Malfoy's roots for him,' said Snape, without looking up.

Ron went brick red.

'There's nothing wrong with your arm,' he hissed at Malfoy.

Malfoy smirked across the table.

'Weasley, you heard Professor Snape, cut up these roots.'

Ron seized his knife, pulled Malfoy's roots towards him and began to chop them roughly, so that they were all different sizes.

'Professor,' drawled Malfoy, 'Weasley's mutilating my roots, sir.'

Snape approached their table, stared down his hooked nose at the roots, then gave Ron an unpleasant smile from beneath his long, greasy black hair.

'Change roots with Malfoy, Weasley.'

'But sir –!'

Ron had spent the last quarter of an hour carefully shredding his own roots into exactly equal pieces.

'*Now,*' said Snape in his most dangerous voice.

Ron shoved his own beautifully cut roots across the table at Malfoy, then took up the knife again.

'And, sir, I'll need this Shrivelfig skinned,' said Malfoy, his voice full of malicious laughter.

'Potter, you can skin Malfoy's Shrivelfig,' said Snape, giving Harry the look of loathing he always reserved just for him.

Harry took Malfoy's Shrivelfig as Ron set about trying to repair the damage to the roots he now had to use. Harry skinned the Shrivelfig as fast as he could and flung it back across the table at Malfoy without speaking. Malfoy was smirking more broadly than ever.

'Seen your pal Hagrid lately?' he asked them quietly.

'None of your business,' said Ron jerkily, without looking up.

'I'm afraid he won't be a teacher much longer,' said Malfoy, in a tone of mock sorrow. 'Father's not very happy about my injury –'

'Keep talking, Malfoy, and I'll give you a real injury,' snarled Ron.

'– he's complained to the school governors. *And* to the Ministry of Magic. Father's got a lot of influence, you know. And a lasting injury like this –' he gave a huge, fake sigh, 'who knows if my arm'll ever be the same again?'

'So that's why you're putting it on,' said Harry, accidentally beheading a dead caterpillar because his hand was shaking in anger. 'To try and get Hagrid sacked.'

'Well,' said Malfoy, lowering his voice to a whisper, '*partly,* Potter. But there are other benefits, too. Weasley, slice my caterpillars for me.'

A few cauldrons away, Neville was in trouble. Neville regularly went to pieces in Potions lessons; it was his worst subject, and his great fear of Professor Snape made things ten times worse. His potion, which was supposed to be a bright, acid green, had turned –

'Orange, Longbottom,' said Snape, ladling some up and allowing it to splash back into the cauldron, so that everyone could see. 'Orange. Tell me, boy, does anything penetrate that thick skull of yours? Didn't you hear me say, quite clearly, that only one rat spleen was needed? Didn't I state plainly that a dash of leech juice would suffice? What do I have to do to make you understand, Longbottom?'

Neville was pink and trembling. He looked as though he was on the verge of tears.

'Please, sir,' said Hermione, 'please, I could help Neville put it right –'

'I don't remember asking you to show off, Miss Granger,' said Snape coldly, and Hermione went as pink as Neville. 'Longbottom, at the end of this lesson we will feed a few drops of this potion to your toad and see what happens. Perhaps that will encourage you to do it properly.'

Snape moved away, leaving Neville breathless with fear.

'Help me!' he moaned to Hermione.

'Hey, Harry,' said Seamus Finnigan, leaning over to borrow Harry's brass scales, 'have you heard? *Daily Prophet* this morning – they reckon Sirius Black's been sighted.'

'Where?' said Harry and Ron quickly. On the other side of the table, Malfoy looked up, listening closely.

'Not too far from here,' said Seamus, who looked excited. 'It was a Muggle who saw him. 'Course, she didn't really understand. The Muggles think he's just an ordinary criminal, don't they? So she 'phoned the telephone hotline. By the time the Ministry of Magic got there, he was gone.'

'Not too far from here ...' Ron repeated, looking significantly at Harry. He turned around and saw Malfoy watching closely. 'What, Malfoy? Need something else skinning?'

But Malfoy's eyes were shining malevolently, and they were fixed on Harry. He leant across the table.

'Thinking of trying to catch Black single-handed, Potter?'

'Yeah, that's right,' said Harry offhandedly.

Malfoy's thin mouth was curving in a mean smile.

'Of course, if it was me,' he said quietly, 'I'd have done something before now. I wouldn't be staying in school like a good boy, I'd be out there looking for him.'

'What are you talking about, Malfoy?' said Ron roughly.

'Don't you *know*, Potter?' breathed Malfoy, his pale eyes narrowed.

'Know what?'

Malfoy let out a low, sneering laugh.

'Maybe you'd rather not risk your neck,' he said. 'Want to leave it to the Dementors, do you? But if it was me, I'd want revenge. I'd hunt him down myself.'

'*What are you talking about?*' said Harry angrily, but at that moment Snape called, 'You should have finished adding your ingredients by now. This potion needs to stew before it can be drunk; clear away while it simmers and then we'll test Longbottom's ...'

Crabbe and Goyle laughed openly, watching Neville sweat as he stirred his potion feverishly. Hermione was muttering instructions to him out of the corner of her mouth, so that Snape wouldn't see. Harry and Ron packed away their unused ingredients and went to wash their hands and ladles in the stone basin in the corner.

'What did Malfoy mean?' Harry muttered to Ron, as he stuck his hands under the icy jet that poured from a gargoyle's mouth. 'Why would I want revenge on Black? He hasn't done anything to me – yet.'

'He's making it up,' said Ron, savagely, 'he's trying to make you do something stupid ...'

The end of the lesson in sight, Snape strode over to Neville, who was cowering by his cauldron.

'Everyone gather round,' said Snape, his black eyes glittering, 'and watch what happens to Longbottom's toad. If he has managed to produce a Shrinking Solution, it will shrink to a tadpole. If, as I don't doubt, he has done it wrong, his toad is likely to be poisoned.'

The Gryffindors watched fearfully. The Slytherins looked excited. Snape picked up Trevor the toad in his left hand, and dipped a small spoon into Neville's potion, which was now green. He trickled a few drops down Trevor's throat.

There was a moment of hushed silence, in which Trevor gulped; then there was a small *pop*, and Trevor the tadpole was wriggling in Snape's palm.

The Gryffindors burst into applause. Snape, looking sour, pulled a small bottle from the pocket of his robe, poured a few drops on top of Trevor and he reappeared suddenly, fully grown.

'Five points from Gryffindor,' said Snape, which wiped the smiles from every face. 'I told you not to help him, Miss Granger. Class dismissed.'

Harry, Ron and Hermione climbed the steps to the Entrance Hall. Harry was still thinking about what Malfoy had said, while Ron was seething about Snape.

'Five points from Gryffindor because the potion was all right! Why didn't you lie, Hermione? You should've said Neville did it all by himself!'

Hermione didn't answer. Ron looked around.

'Where is she?'

Harry turned, too. They were at the top of the steps now, watching the rest of the class pass them, heading for the Great Hall and lunch.

'She was right behind us,' said Ron, frowning.

Malfoy passed them, walking between Crabbe and Goyle. He smirked at Harry and disappeared.

'There she is,' said Harry.

Hermione was panting slightly, hurrying up the stairs; one hand was clutching her bag, the other seemed to be tucking something down the front of her robes.

'How did you do that?' said Ron.

'What?' said Hermione, joining them.

'One minute you were right behind us, and next moment, you were back at the bottom of the stairs again.'

'What?' Hermione looked slightly confused. 'Oh – I had to go back for something. Oh, no ...'

A seam had split on Hermione's bag. Harry wasn't surprised; he could see that it was crammed with at least a dozen large and heavy books.

'Why are you carrying all these around with you?' Ron asked her.

'You know how many subjects I'm taking,' said Hermione breathlessly. 'Couldn't hold these for me, could you?'

'But –' Ron was turning over the books she had handed him, looking at the covers – 'you haven't got any of these subjects today. It's only Defence Against the Dark Arts this afternoon.'

'Oh, yes,' said Hermione vaguely, but she packed all the books back into her bag just the same. 'I hope there's something good for lunch, I'm starving,' she added, and she marched off towards the Great Hall.

'D'you get the feeling Hermione's not telling us something?' Ron asked Harry.

*

Professor Lupin wasn't there when they arrived at his first Defence Against the Dark Arts lesson. They all sat down, took out their books, quills and parchment, and were talking when he finally entered the room. Lupin smiled vaguely and placed his tatty old briefcase on the teacher's desk. He was as shabby as ever but looked healthier than he had on the train, as though he had had a few square meals.

'Good afternoon,' he said. 'Would you please put all your books back in your bags. Today's will be a practical lesson. You will only need your wands.'

A few curious looks were exchanged as the class put away their books. They had never had a practical Defence Against the Dark Arts before, unless you counted the memorable class last year when their old teacher had brought a cageful of pixies to class and set them loose.

'Right then,' said Professor Lupin, when everyone was ready, 'if you'd follow me.'

Puzzled but interested, the class got to its feet and followed Professor Lupin out of the classroom. He led them along the deserted corridor and around a corner, where the first thing they saw was Peeves the poltergeist, who was floating upside-down in mid-air and stuffing the nearest keyhole with chewing gum.

Peeves didn't look up until Professor Lupin was two feet away, then he wiggled his curly-toed feet and broke into song.

'Loony, loopy Lupin,' Peeves sang. 'Loony, loopy Lupin, loony, loopy Lupin –'

Rude and unmanageable as he almost always was, Peeves usually showed some respect towards the teachers. Everyone looked quickly at Professor Lupin to see how he would take this; to their surprise, he was still smiling.

'I'd take that gum out of the keyhole, if I were you, Peeves,' he said pleasantly. 'Mr Filch won't be able to get in to his brooms.'

Filch was the Hogwarts caretaker, a bad-tempered, failed wizard who waged a constant war against the students and, indeed, Peeves. However, Peeves paid no attention to Professor Lupin's words, except to blow a loud wet raspberry.

Professor Lupin gave a small sigh and took out his wand.

'This is a useful little spell,' he told the class over his shoulder. 'Please watch closely.'

He raised the wand to shoulder height, said '*Waddiwasi!*' and pointed it at Peeves.

With the force of a bullet, the wad of chewing gum shot out of the keyhole and straight down Peeves's left nostril; he whirled right way up and zoomed away, cursing.

'Cool, sir!' said Dean Thomas in amazement.

'Thank you, Dean,' said Professor Lupin, putting his wand away again. 'Shall we proceed?'

They set off again, the class looking at shabby Professor Lupin with increased respect. He led them down a second corridor and stopped, right outside the staff-room door.

'Inside, please,' said Professor Lupin, opening it and standing back.

The staff room, a long, panelled room full of old, mismatched chairs, was empty except for one teacher. Professor Snape was sitting in a low armchair, and he looked around as the class filed in. His eyes were glittering and there was a nasty sneer playing around his mouth. As Professor Lupin came in and made to close the door behind him, Snape said, 'Leave it open, Lupin. I'd rather not witness this.' He got to his feet and strode past the class, his black robes billowing behind him. At the doorway he turned on his heel and said, 'Possibly no one's warned you, Lupin, but this class contains Neville Longbottom. I would advise you not to entrust him with anything difficult. Not unless Miss Granger is hissing instructions in his ear.'

Neville went scarlet. Harry glared at Snape; it was bad enough that he bullied Neville in his own classes, let alone doing it in front of other teachers.

Professor Lupin had raised his eyebrows.

'I was hoping that Neville would assist me with the first stage of the operation,' he said, 'and I am sure he will perform it admirably.'

Neville's face went, if possible, even redder. Snape's lip curled, but he left, shutting the door with a snap.

'Now, then,' said Professor Lupin, beckoning the class towards the end of the room, where there was nothing except an old wardrobe in which the teachers kept their spare robes. As Professor Lupin went to stand next to it, the wardrobe gave a sudden wobble, banging off the wall.

'Nothing to worry about,' said Professor Lupin calmly, as a few people jumped backwards in alarm. 'There's a Boggart in there.'

Most people seemed to feel that this *was* something to worry about. Neville gave Professor Lupin a look of pure terror, and Seamus Finnigan eyed the now rattling doorknob apprehensively.

'Boggarts like dark, enclosed spaces,' said Professor Lupin. 'Wardrobes, the gap beneath beds, the cupboards under sinks – I once met one that had lodged itself in a grandfather clock. *This* one moved in yesterday afternoon, and I asked the Headmaster if the staff would leave it to give my third-years some practice.

'So, the first question we must ask ourselves is, what *is* a Boggart?'

Hermione put up her hand.

'It's a shape-shifter,' she said. 'It can take the shape of whatever it thinks will frighten us most.'

'Couldn't have put it better myself,' said Professor Lupin, and Hermione glowed. 'So the Boggart sitting in the darkness within has not yet assumed a form. He does not yet know what will frighten the person on the other side of the door. Nobody knows what a Boggart looks like when he is alone, but when I let him out, he will immediately become whatever each of us most fears.

'This means,' said Professor Lupin, choosing to ignore Neville's small splutter of terror, 'that we have a huge advantage over the Boggart before we begin. Have you spotted it, Harry?'

Trying to answer a question with Hermione next to him, bobbing up and down on the balls of her feet with her hand in the air, was very off-putting, but Harry had a go.

'Er – because there are so many of us, it won't know what shape it should be?'

'Precisely,' said Professor Lupin, and Hermione put her hand down looking a little disappointed. 'It's always best to have company when you're dealing with a Boggart. He becomes confused. Which should he become, a headless corpse or a flesh-eating slug? I once saw a Boggart make that very mistake – tried to frighten two people at once and turned himself into half a slug. Not remotely frightening.

'The charm that repels a Boggart is simple, yet it requires force of mind. You see, the thing that really finishes a Boggart is *laughter*. What you need to do is force it to assume a shape that you find amusing.

'We will practise the charm without wands first. After me, please ... *riddikulus!*'

'Riddikulus!' said the class together.

'Good,' said Professor Lupin. 'Very good. But that was the easy part, I'm afraid. You see, the word alone is not enough. And this is where you come in, Neville.'

The wardrobe shook again, though not as much as Neville, who walked forward as though he was heading for the gallows.

'Right, Neville,' said Professor Lupin. 'First things first: what would you say is the thing that frightens you most in the world?'

Neville's lips moved, but no noise came out.

'Didn't catch that, Neville, sorry,' said Professor Lupin cheerfully.

Neville looked around rather wildly, as though begging someone to help him, then said, in barely more than a whisper, 'Professor Snape.'

Nearly everyone laughed. Even Neville grinned apologetically. Professor Lupin, however, looked thoughtful.

'Professor Snape ... hmmm ... Neville, I believe you live with your grandmother?'

'Er – yes,' said Neville nervously. 'But – I don't want the Boggart to turn into her, either.'

'No, no, you misunderstand me,' said Professor Lupin, now smiling. 'I wonder, could you tell us what sort of clothes your grandmother usually wears?'

Neville looked startled, but said, 'Well ... always the same hat. A tall one with a stuffed vulture on top. And a long dress ... green, normally ... and sometimes a fox-fur scarf.'

'And a handbag?' prompted Professor Lupin.

'A big red one,' said Neville.

'Right then,' said Professor Lupin. 'Can you picture those clothes very clearly, Neville? Can you see them in your mind's eye?'

'Yes,' said Neville uncertainly, plainly wondering what was coming next.

'When the Boggart bursts out of this wardrobe, Neville, and sees you, it will assume the form of Professor Snape,' said Lupin. 'And you will raise your wand – thus – and cry "Riddikulus" – and concentrate hard on your grandmother's clothes. If all goes well, Professor Boggart Snape will be forced into that vulture-topped hat, that green dress, that big red handbag.'

There was a great shout of laughter. The wardrobe wobbled more violently.

'If Neville is successful, the Boggart is likely to turn his attention to each of us in turn,' said Professor Lupin. 'I would like all of you to take a moment now to think of the thing that scares you most, and imagine how you might force it to look comical ...'

The room went quiet. Harry thought ... What scared him most in the world?

His first thought was Lord Voldemort – a Voldemort returned to full strength. But before he had even started to plan a possible counter-attack on a Boggart-Voldemort, a horrible image came floating to the surface of his mind ...

A rotting, glistening hand, slithering back beneath a black cloak ... a long, rattling breath from an unseen mouth ... then a cold so penetrating it felt like drowning ...

Harry shivered, then looked around, hoping no one had noticed. Many people had their eyes shut tight. Ron was muttering to himself, 'Take its legs off.' Harry was sure he knew what that was about. Ron's greatest fear was spiders.

'Everyone ready?' said Professor Lupin.

Harry felt a lurch of fear. He wasn't ready. How could you make a Dementor less frightening? But he didn't want to ask for more time; everyone else was nodding and rolling up their sleeves.

'Neville, we're going to back away,' said Professor Lupin. 'Let you have a clear field, all right? I'll call the next person forward ... everyone back, now, so Neville can get a clear shot –'

They all retreated, backing against the walls, leaving Neville alone beside the wardrobe. He looked pale and frightened, but he had pushed up the sleeves of his robes and was holding his wand ready.

'On the count of three, Neville,' said Professor Lupin, who was pointing his own wand at the handle of the wardrobe. 'One – two – three – now!'

A jet of sparks shot from the end of Professor Lupin's wand and hit the doorknob. The wardrobe burst open. Hook-nosed and menacing, Professor Snape stepped out, his eyes flashing at Neville.

Neville backed away, his wand up, mouthing wordlessly. Snape was bearing down upon him, reaching inside his robes.

'R-r-riddikulus!' squeaked Neville.

There was a noise like a whip-crack. Snape stumbled; he was wearing a long, lace-trimmed dress and a towering hat topped with a moth-eaten vulture, and swinging a huge crimson handbag from his hand.

There was a roar of laughter; the Boggart paused, confused, and Professor Lupin shouted, 'Parvati! Forward!'

Parvati walked forward, her face set. Snape rounded on her. There was another crack, and where he had stood was a blood-stained, bandaged mummy; its sightless face was turned to Parvati and it began to walk towards her, very slowly, dragging its feet, its stiff arms rising –

'Riddikulus!' cried Parvati.

A bandage unravelled at the mummy's feet; it became entangled, fell face forwards and its head rolled off.

'Seamus!' roared Professor Lupin.

Seamus darted past Parvati.

Crack! Where the mummy had been was a woman with floor-length black hair and a skeletal, green-tinged face – a banshee. She opened her mouth wide, and an unearthly sound filled the room, a long, wailing shriek which made the hair on Harry's head stand on end –

'Riddikulus!' shouted Seamus.

The banshee made a rasping noise and clutched her throat; her voice was gone.

Crack! The banshee turned into a rat, which chased its tail in a circle, then – *crack!* – became a rattlesnake, which slithered and writhed before – *crack!* – becoming a single, bloody eyeball.

'It's confused!' shouted Lupin. 'We're getting there! Dean!'

Dean hurried forward.

Crack! The eyeball became a severed hand, which flipped over, and began to creep along the floor like a crab.

'Riddikulus!' yelled Dean.

There was a snap, and the hand was trapped in a mousetrap.

'Excellent! Ron, you next!'

Ron leapt forward.

'Crack!'

Quite a few people screamed. A giant spider, six feet tall and covered in hair, was advancing on Ron, clicking its pincers menacingly. For a moment, Harry thought Ron had frozen. Then –

'Riddikulus!' bellowed Ron, and the spider's legs vanished. It rolled over and over; Lavender Brown squealed and ran out of its way and it came to a halt at Harry's feet. He raised his wand, ready, but –

'Here!' shouted Professor Lupin suddenly, hurrying forward.

Crack!

The legless spider had vanished. For a second, everyone looked wildly around to see where it was. Then they saw a silvery white orb hanging in the air in front of Lupin, who said 'Riddikulus!' almost lazily.

Crack!

'Forward, Neville, and finish him off!' said Lupin, as the Boggart landed on the floor as a cockroach. *Crack!* Snape was back. This time Neville charged forward looking determined.

'Riddikulus!' he shouted, and they had a split second's view of Snape in his lacy dress before Neville let out a great 'Ha!' of laughter, and the Boggart exploded, burst into a thousand tiny wisps of smoke, and was gone.

'Excellent!' cried Professor Lupin, as the class broke into applause. 'Excellent, Neville. Well done, everyone. Let me see ... five points to Gryffindor for every person to tackle the Boggart – ten for Neville because he did it twice – and five each to Hermione and Harry.'

'But I didn't do anything,' said Harry.

'You and Hermione answered my questions correctly at the start of the class, Harry,' Lupin said lightly. 'Very well, everyone, an excellent lesson. Homework, kindly read the chapter on Boggarts and summarise it for me ... to be handed in on Monday. That will be all.'

Talking excitedly, the class left the staff room. Harry, however, wasn't feeling cheerful. Professor Lupin had deliberately stopped him tackling the Boggart. Why? Was it because he'd seen Harry collapse on the train, and thought he wasn't up to much? Had he thought Harry would pass out again?

But no one else seemed to have noticed anything.

'Did you see me take that banshee?' shouted Seamus.

'And the hand!' said Dean, waving his own around.

'And Snape in that hat!'

'And my mummy!'

'I wonder why Professor Lupin's frightened of crystal balls?' said Lavender thoughtfully.

'That was the best Defence Against the Dark Arts lesson we've ever had, wasn't it?' said Ron excitedly, as they made their way back to the classroom to get their bags.

'He seems a very good teacher,' said Hermione approvingly. 'But I wish I could have had a turn with the Boggart –'

'What would it have been for you?' said Ron, sniggering. 'A piece of homework that only got nine out of ten?'

— CHAPTER EIGHT —

Flight of the Fat Lady

In no time at all, Defence Against the Dark Arts had become most people's favourite class. Only Draco Malfoy and his gang of Slytherins had anything bad to say about Professor Lupin.

'Look at the state of his robes,' Malfoy would say in a loud whisper as Professor Lupin passed. 'He dresses like our old house-elf.'

But no one else cared that Professor Lupin's robes were patched and frayed. His next few lessons were just as interesting as the first. After Boggarts, they studied Red Caps, nasty little goblin-like creatures that lurked wherever there had been bloodshed, in the dungeons of castles and the potholes of deserted battlefields, waiting to bludgeon those who had got lost. From Red Caps they moved on to Kappas, creepy water-dwellers that looked like scaly monkeys, with webbed hands itching to strangle unwitting waders in their ponds.

Harry only wished he was as happy with some of his other classes. Worst of all was Potions. Snape was in a particularly vindictive mood these days, and no one was in any doubt why. The story of the Boggart assuming Snape's shape, and the way that Neville had dressed it in his grandmother's clothes, had travelled through the school like wildfire. Snape didn't seem to find it funny. His eyes flashed menacingly at the very mention of Professor Lupin's name, and he was bullying Neville worse than ever.

Harry was also growing to dread the hours he spent in Professor Trelawney's stifling tower room, deciphering lop-sided shapes and symbols, trying to ignore the way Professor Trelawney's enormous eyes filled with tears every time she looked at him. He couldn't like Professor Trelawney, even though she was treated with respect bordering on reverence by many of the class. Parvati Patil and Lavender Brown had taken to haunting Professor Trelawney's tower room at lunchtimes, and always returned with annoyingly superior looks on their faces, as though they knew things the others didn't. They had also started using hushed voices whenever they spoke to Harry, as though he was on his deathbed.

Nobody really liked Care of Magical Creatures, which, after the action-packed first class, had become extremely dull. Hagrid seemed to have lost his confidence. They were now spending lesson after lesson learning how to look after Flobberworms, which had to be some of the most boring creatures in existence.

'Why would anyone *bother* looking after them?' said Ron, after yet another hour of poking shredded lettuce down the Flobberworms' slimy throats.

At the start of October, however, Harry had something else to occupy him, something so enjoyable it made up for his unsatisfactory classes. The Quidditch season was approaching, and Oliver Wood, captain of the Gryffindor team, called a meeting one Thursday evening to discuss tactics for the new season.

There were seven people on a Quidditch team: three Chasers, whose job it was to score goals by putting the Quaffle (a red, football-sized ball) through one of the fifty-foot-high hoops at each end of the pitch; two Beaters, who were equipped with heavy bats to repel the Bludgers (two heavy black balls which zoomed around trying to attack the players); a Keeper, who defended the goalposts, and the Seeker, who had the hardest job of all, that of catching the Golden Snitch, a tiny, winged, walnut-sized ball, whose capture ended the game and earned the Seeker's team an extra one hundred and fifty points.

Oliver Wood was a burly seventeen-year-old, now in his seventh and final year at Hogwarts. There was a quiet sort of desperation in his voice as he addressed his six fellow team members in the chilly changing rooms on the edge of the darkening Quidditch pitch.

'This is our last chance – *my* last chance – to win the Quidditch Cup,' he told them, striding up and down in front of them. 'I'll be leaving at the end of this year. I'll never get another shot at it.

'Gryffindor haven't won for seven years now. OK, so we've had the worst luck in the world – injuries – then the tournament getting called off last year ...' Wood swallowed, as though the memory still brought a lump to his throat. 'But we also know we've got the *best – ruddy – team – in – the – school*,' he said, punching a fist into his other hand, the old manic glint back in his eye.

'We've got three *superb* Chasers.'

Wood pointed at Alicia Spinnet, Angelina Johnson and Katie Bell.

'We've got two *unbeatable* Beaters.'

'Stop it, Oliver, you're embarrassing us,' said Fred and George Weasley together, pretending to blush.

'And we've got a Seeker who has *never failed to win us a match*!' Wood rumbled, glaring at Harry with a kind of furious pride. 'And me,' he added, as an afterthought.

'We think you're very good, too, Oliver,' said George.

'Cracking Keeper,' said Fred.

'The point is,' Wood went on, resuming his pacing, 'the Quidditch Cup should have had our name on it these last two years. Ever since Harry joined the team, I've thought the thing was in the bag. But we haven't got it, and this year's the last chance we'll get to finally see our name on the thing ...'

Wood spoke so dejectedly that even Fred and George looked sympathetic.

'Oliver, this year's our year,' said Fred.

'We'll do it, Oliver!' said Angelina.

'Definitely,' said Harry.

Full of determination, the team started training sessions, three evenings a week. The weather was getting colder and wetter, the nights darker, but no amount of mud, wind or rain could tarnish Harry's wonderful vision of finally winning the huge silver Quidditch Cup.

Harry returned to the Gryffindor common room one evening after training, cold and stiff but pleased with the way practice had gone, to find the room buzzing excitedly.

'What's happened?' he asked Ron and Hermione, who were sitting in two of the best chairs by the fireside and completing some star charts for Astronomy.

'First Hogsmeade weekend,' said Ron, pointing at a notice that had appeared on the battered old noticeboard. 'End of October. Hallowe'en.'

'Excellent,' said Fred, who had followed Harry through the portrait hole. 'I need to visit Zonko's, I'm nearly out of Stink Pellets.'

Harry threw himself into a chair beside Ron, his high spirits ebbing away. Hermione seemed to read his mind.

'Harry, I'm sure you'll be able to go next time,' she said. 'They're bound to catch Black soon, he's been sighted once already.'

'Black's not fool enough to try anything in Hogsmeade,' said Ron. 'Ask McGonagall if you can go this time, Harry, the next one might not be for ages –'

'*Ron!*' said Hermione. 'Harry's supposed to stay *in school* –'

'He can't be the only third-year left behind,' said Ron. 'Ask McGonagall, go on, Harry –'

'Yeah, I think I will,' said Harry, making up his mind.

Hermione opened her mouth to argue, but at that moment Crookshanks leapt lightly onto her lap. A large, dead spider was dangling from his mouth.

'Does he have to eat that in front of us?' said Ron, scowling.

'Clever Crookshanks, did you catch that all by yourself?' said Hermione.

Crookshanks slowly chewed up the spider, his yellow eyes fixed insolently on Ron.

'Just keep him over there, that's all,' said Ron irritably, turning back to his star chart. 'I've got Scabbers asleep in my bag.'

Harry yawned. He really wanted to go to bed, but he still had his own star chart to complete. He pulled his bag towards him, took out parchment, ink and quill, and started work.

'You can copy mine, if you like,' said Ron, labelling his last star with a flourish and shoving the chart towards Harry.

Hermione, who disapproved of copying, pursed her lips, but didn't say anything. Crookshanks was still staring unblinkingly at Ron, flicking the end of his bushy tail. Then, without warning, he pounced.

'OY!' Ron roared, seizing his bag, as Crookshanks sank four sets of claws deeply into it, and began tearing ferociously. 'GET OFF, YOU STUPID ANIMAL!'

Ron tried to pull the bag away from Crookshanks, but Crookshanks clung on, spitting and slashing.

'Ron, don't hurt him!' squealed Hermione. The whole common room was watching; Ron whirled the bag around, Crookshanks still clinging to it, and Scabbers came flying out of the top –

'CATCH THAT CAT!' Ron yelled, as Crookshanks freed himself from the remnants of the bag, sprang over the table and chased after the terrified Scabbers.

George Weasley made a lunge for Crookshanks but missed;

Scabbers streaked through twenty pairs of legs and shot beneath an old chest of drawers. Crookshanks skidded to a halt, crouched low on his bandy legs and started making furious swipes beneath the chest of drawers with his front paw.

Ron and Hermione hurried over; Hermione grabbed Crookshanks around the middle and heaved him away; Ron threw himself onto his stomach and, with great difficulty, pulled Scabbers out by the tail.

'Look at him!' he said furiously to Hermione, dangling Scabbers in front of her. 'He's skin and bone! You keep that cat away from him!'

'Crookshanks doesn't understand it's wrong!' said Hermione, her voice shaking. 'All cats chase rats, Ron!'

'There's something funny about that animal!' said Ron, who was trying to persuade a frantically wiggling Scabbers back into his pocket. 'It heard me say that Scabbers was in my bag!'

'Oh, what rubbish,' said Hermione impatiently. 'Crookshanks could *smell* him, Ron, how else d'you think –'

'That cat's got it in for Scabbers!' said Ron, ignoring the people around him, who were starting to giggle. 'And Scabbers was here first, *and* he's ill!'

Ron marched through the common room and out of sight up the stairs to the boys' dormitories.

*

Ron was still in a bad mood with Hermione next day. He barely talked to her all through Herbology, even though he, Harry and Hermione were working together on the same Puffapod.

'How's Scabbers?' Hermione asked timidly, as they stripped fat pink pods from the plants and emptied the shining beans into a wooden pail.

'He's hiding at the bottom of my bed, shaking,' said Ron angrily, missing the pail and scattering beans over the greenhouse floor.

'Careful, Weasley, careful!' cried Professor Sprout, as the beans burst into bloom before their very eyes.

They had Transfiguration next. Harry, who had resolved to ask Professor McGonagall after the lesson whether he could go into Hogsmeade with the rest, joined the queue outside the classroom, trying to decide how he was going to argue his case. He was distracted, however, by a disturbance at the front of the line.

Lavender Brown seemed to be crying. Parvati had her arm

around her, and was explaining something to Seamus Finnigan and Dean Thomas, who were looking very serious.

'What's the matter, Lavender?' said Hermione anxiously, as she, Harry and Ron went to join the group.

'She got a letter from home this morning,' Parvati whispered. 'It's her rabbit, Binky. He's been killed by a fox.'

'Oh,' said Hermione. 'I'm sorry, Lavender.'

'I should have known!' said Lavender tragically. 'You know what day it is?'

'Er –'

'The sixteenth of October! "That thing you're dreading, it will happen on the sixteenth of October!" Remember? She was right, she was right!'

The whole class was gathered around Lavender now. Seamus shook his head seriously. Hermione hesitated; then she said, 'You – you were dreading Binky being killed by a fox?'

'Well, not necessarily by a *fox*,' said Lavender, looking up at Hermione with streaming eyes, 'but I was *obviously* dreading him dying, wasn't I?'

'Oh,' said Hermione. She paused again. Then –

'Was Binky an *old* rabbit?'

'N-no!' sobbed Lavender. 'H-he was only a baby!'

Parvati tightened her arm around Lavender's shoulders.

'But then, why would you dread him dying?' said Hermione.

Parvati glared at her.

'Well, look at it logically,' said Hermione, turning to the rest of the group. 'I mean, Binky didn't even die today, did he, Lavender just got the news today –' Lavender wailed loudly '– and she *can't* have been dreading it, because it's come as a real shock –'

'Don't mind Hermione, Lavender,' said Ron loudly, 'she doesn't think other people's pets matter very much.'

Professor McGonagall opened the classroom door at that moment, which was perhaps lucky; Hermione and Ron were looking daggers at each other, and when they got into class, they seated themselves either side of Harry, and didn't talk to each other all lesson.

Harry still hadn't decided what he was going to say to Professor McGonagall when the bell rang at the end of the lesson, but it was she who brought up the subject of Hogsmeade first.

'One moment, please!' she called, as the class made to leave. 'As you're all in my house, you should hand Hogsmeade permission forms to me before Hallowe'en. No form, no visiting the village, so don't forget!'

Neville put up his hand.

'Please, Professor, I – I think I've lost –'

'Your grandmother sent yours to me directly, Longbottom,' said Professor McGonagall. 'She seemed to think it was safer. Well, that's all, you may leave.'

'Ask her now,' Ron hissed at Harry.

'Oh, but –' Hermione began.

'Go for it, Harry,' said Ron stubbornly.

Harry waited for the rest of the class to disappear, then headed nervously for Professor McGonagall's desk.

'Yes, Potter?'

Harry took a deep breath.

'Professor, my aunt and uncle – er – forgot to sign my form,' he said.

Professor McGonagall looked over her square spectacles at him, but didn't say anything.

'So – er – d'you think it would be all right – I mean, will it be OK if I – if I go to Hogsmeade?'

Professor McGonagall looked down and began shuffling papers on her desk.

'I'm afraid not, Potter,' she said. 'You heard what I said. No form, no visiting the village. That's the rule.'

'But – Professor, my aunt and uncle – you know, they're Muggles, they don't really understand about – about Hogwarts forms and stuff,' Harry said, while Ron egged him on with vigorous nods. 'If you said I could go –'

'But I don't say so,' said Professor McGonagall, standing up and piling her papers neatly into a drawer. 'The form clearly states that the parent or guardian must give permission.' She turned to look at him, with an odd expression on her face. Was it pity? 'I'm sorry, Potter, but that's my final word. You had better hurry, or you'll be late for your next lesson.'

*

There was nothing to be done. Ron called Professor McGonagall a lot of names that greatly annoyed Hermione; Hermione assumed an 'all for the best' expression that made Ron even angrier, and Harry had to endure everyone in the class talking loudly and happily about what they were going to do first, once they got into Hogsmeade.

'There's always the feast,' said Ron, in an effort to cheer Harry up. 'You know, the Hallowe'en feast, in the evening.'

'Yeah,' said Harry, gloomily, 'great.'

The Hallowe'en feast was always good, but it would taste a lot better if he was coming to it after a day in Hogsmeade with everyone else. Nothing anyone said made him feel any better about being left behind. Dean Thomas, who was good with a quill, had offered to forge Uncle Vernon's signature on the form, but as Harry had already told Professor McGonagall he hadn't had it signed, that was no good. Ron half-heartedly suggested the Invisibility Cloak, but Hermione stamped on that one, reminding Ron what Dumbledore had told them about the Dementors being able to see through them. Percy had what were possibly the least helpful words of comfort.

'They make a fuss about Hogsmeade, but I assure you, Harry, it's not all it's cracked up to be,' he said seriously. 'All right, the sweetshop's rather good, but Zonko's Joke Shop's frankly dangerous, and yes, the Shrieking Shack's always worth a visit, but really, Harry, apart from that, you're not missing anything.'

*

On Hallowe'en morning, Harry awoke with the rest and went down to breakfast feeling thoroughly depressed, though doing his best to act normally.

'We'll bring you lots of sweets back from Honeydukes,' said Hermione, looking desperately sorry for him.

'Yeah, loads,' said Ron. He and Hermione had finally forgotten their squabble about Crookshanks in the face of Harry's disappointment.

'Don't worry about me,' said Harry, in what he hoped was an offhand voice. 'I'll see you at the feast. Have a good time.'

He accompanied them to the Entrance Hall, where Filch, the caretaker, was standing inside the front doors, checking off names against a long list, peering suspiciously into every face, and making sure that no one was sneaking out who shouldn't be going.

'Staying here, Potter?' shouted Malfoy, who was standing in line with Crabbe and Goyle. 'Scared of passing the Dementors?'

Harry ignored him and made his solitary way up the marble staircase, through the deserted corridors, and back to Gryffindor Tower.

'Password?' said the Fat Lady, jerking out of a doze.

'Fortuna Major,' said Harry listlessly.

The portrait swung open and he climbed through the hole into the common room. It was full of chattering first- and second-years, and a few older students who had obviously visited Hogsmeade so often the novelty had worn off.

'Harry! Harry! Hi, Harry!'

It was Colin Creevey, a second-year who was deeply in awe of Harry and never missed an opportunity to speak to him.

'Aren't you going to Hogsmeade, Harry? Why not? Hey –' Colin looked eagerly around at his friends, 'you can come and sit with us, if you like, Harry!'

'Er – no, thanks, Colin,' said Harry, who wasn't in the mood to have a lot of people staring avidly at the scar on his forehead. 'I – I've got to go to the library, got to get some work done.'

After that, he had no choice but to turn right around and head back out of the portrait hole again.

'What was the point of waking me up?' the Fat Lady called grumpily after him as he walked away.

Harry wandered dispiritedly towards the library, but halfway there he changed his mind; he didn't feel like working. He turned around and came face to face with Filch, who had obviously just seen off the last of the Hogsmeade visitors.

'What are you doing?' Filch snarled suspiciously.

'Nothing,' said Harry truthfully.

'Nothing!' spat Filch, his jowls quivering unpleasantly. 'A likely story! Sneaking around on your own, why aren't you in Hogsmeade buying Stink Pellets and Belch Powder and Whizzing Worms like the rest of your nasty little friends?'

Harry shrugged.

'Well, get back to your common room where you belong!' snapped Filch, and he stood glaring until Harry had passed out of sight.

But Harry didn't go back to the common room; he climbed a staircase, thinking vaguely of visiting the Owlery to see Hedwig, and was walking along another corridor when a voice from inside one of the rooms said, 'Harry?'

Harry doubled back to see who had spoken and met Professor Lupin, looking around his office door.

'What are you doing?' said Lupin, in a very different voice from Filch. 'Where are Ron and Hermione?'

'Hogsmeade,' said Harry, in a would-be casual voice.

'Ah,' said Lupin. He considered Harry for a moment. 'Why don't you come in? I've just taken delivery of a Grindylow for our next lesson.'

'A what?' said Harry.

He followed Lupin into his office. In the corner stood a very large tank of water. A sickly-green creature with sharp little horns had its face pressed against the glass, pulling faces and flexing its long, spindly fingers.

'Water demon,' said Lupin, surveying the Grindylow thoughtfully. 'We shouldn't have much difficulty with him, not after the Kappas. The trick is to break his grip. You notice the abnormally long fingers? Strong, but very brittle.'

The Grindylow bared its green teeth and then buried itself in a tangle of weed in a corner.

'Cup of tea?' Lupin said, looking around for his kettle. 'I was just thinking of making one.'

'All right,' said Harry awkwardly.

Lupin tapped the kettle with his wand and a blast of steam issued suddenly from the spout.

'Sit down,' said Lupin, taking the lid off a dusty tin. 'I've only got teabags, I'm afraid – but I daresay you've had enough of tea leaves?'

Harry looked at him. Lupin's eyes were twinkling.

'How did you know about that?' Harry asked.

'Professor McGonagall told me,' said Lupin, passing Harry a chipped mug of tea. 'You're not worried, are you?'

'No,' said Harry.

He thought for a moment of telling Lupin about the dog he'd seen in Magnolia Crescent, but decided not to. He didn't want Lupin to think he was a coward, especially since Lupin already seemed to think he couldn't cope with a Boggart.

Something of Harry's thoughts seemed to have shown on his face, because Lupin said, 'Anything worrying you, Harry?'

'No,' Harry lied. He drank a bit of tea and watched the Grindylow brandishing a fist at him. 'Yes,' he said suddenly, putting his tea down on Lupin's desk. 'You know that day we fought the Boggart?'

'Yes,' said Lupin slowly.

'Why didn't you let me fight it?' said Harry abruptly.

Lupin raised his eyebrows.

'I would have thought that was obvious, Harry,' he said, sounding surprised.

Harry, who had expected Lupin to deny that he'd done any such thing, was taken aback.

'Why?' he said again.

'Well,' said Lupin, frowning slightly, 'I assumed that if the Boggart faced you, it would assume the shape of Lord Voldemort.'

Harry stared. Not only was this the last answer he'd expected, but Lupin had said Voldemort's name. The only person Harry had ever heard say the name aloud (apart from himself) was Professor Dumbledore.

'Clearly, I was wrong,' said Lupin, still frowning at Harry. 'But I didn't think it a good idea for Lord Voldemort to materialise in the staff room. I imagined that people would panic.'

'I did think of Voldemort first,' said Harry honestly. 'But then I – I remembered those Dementors.'

'I see,' said Lupin thoughtfully. 'Well, well ... I'm impressed.' He smiled slightly at the look of surprise on Harry's face. 'That suggests that what you fear most of all is – fear. Very wise, Harry.'

Harry didn't know what to say to that, so he drank some more tea.

'So you've been thinking that I didn't believe you capable of fighting the Boggart?' said Lupin shrewdly.

'Well ... yeah,' said Harry. He was suddenly feeling a lot happier. 'Professor Lupin, you know the Dementors –'

He was interrupted by a knock on the door.

'Come in,' called Lupin.

The door opened, and in came Snape. He was carrying a goblet, which was smoking faintly, and stopped at the sight of Harry, his black eyes narrowing.

'Ah, Severus,' said Lupin, smiling. 'Thanks very much. Could you leave it here on the desk for me?'

Snape set the smoking goblet down, his eyes wandering between Harry and Lupin.

'I was just showing Harry my Grindylow,' said Lupin pleasantly, pointing at the tank.

'Fascinating,' said Snape, without looking at it. 'You should drink that directly, Lupin.'

'Yes, yes, I will,' said Lupin.

'I made an entire cauldronful,' Snape continued. 'If you need more.'

'I should probably take some again tomorrow. Thanks very much, Severus.'

'Not at all,' said Snape, but there was a look in his eye Harry didn't like. He backed out of the room, unsmiling and watchful.

Harry looked curiously at the goblet. Lupin smiled.

'Professor Snape has very kindly concocted a potion for me,' he said. 'I have never been much of a potion-brewer and this one is particularly complex.' He picked up the goblet and sniffed it. 'Pity sugar makes it useless,' he added, taking a sip and shuddering.

'Why –?' Harry began. Lupin looked at him and answered the unfinished question.

'I've been feeling a bit off-colour,' he said. 'This potion is the only thing that helps. I am very lucky to be working alongside Professor Snape; there aren't many wizards who are up to making it.'

Professor Lupin took another sip and Harry had a mad urge to knock the goblet out of his hands.

'Professor Snape's very interested in the Dark Arts,' he blurted out.

'Really?' said Lupin, looking only mildly interested as he took another gulp of potion.

'Some people reckon –' Harry hesitated, then plunged recklessly on, 'some people reckon he'd do anything to get the Defence Against the Dark Arts job.'

Lupin drained the goblet and pulled a face.

'Disgusting,' he said. 'Well, Harry, I'd better get back to work. I'll see you at the feast later.'

'Right,' said Harry, putting his empty teacup down.

The empty goblet was still smoking.

*

'There you go,' said Ron. 'We got as much as we could carry.'

A shower of brilliantly coloured sweets fell into Harry's lap. It was dusk, and Ron and Hermione had just turned up in the common room, pink-faced from the cold wind and looking as though they'd had the time of their lives.

'Thanks,' said Harry, picking up a packet of tiny black Pepper

Imps. 'What's Hogsmeade like? Where did you go?'

By the sound of it – everywhere. Dervish and Banges, the wiz-arding equipment shop, Zonko's Joke Shop, into the Three Broomsticks for foaming mugs of hot Butterbeer and many places besides.

'The post office, Harry! About two hundred owls, all sitting on shelves, all colour-coded depending on how fast you want your letter to get there!'

'Honeydukes have got a new kind of fudge, they were giving out free samples, there's a bit, look –'

'We *think* we saw an ogre, honestly, they get all sorts at the Three Broomsticks –'

'Wish we could have brought you some Butterbeer, really warms you up –'

'What did you do?' said Hermione, looking anxious. 'Did you get any work done?'

'No,' said Harry. 'Lupin made me a cup of tea in his office. And then Snape came in ...'

He told them all about the goblet. Ron's mouth fell open.

'*Lupin drank it?*' he gasped. 'Is he mad?'

Hermione checked her watch.

'We'd better go down, you know, the feast'll be starting in five minutes ...' They hurried through the portrait hole and into the crowd, still discussing Snape.

'But if he – you know –' Hermione dropped her voice, glancing nervously around, 'if he *was* trying to – to poison Lupin – he wouldn't have done it in front of Harry.'

'Yeah, maybe,' said Harry, as they reached the Entrance Hall and crossed into the Great Hall. It had been decorated with hundreds and hundreds of candle-filled pumpkins, a cloud of fluttering live bats and many flaming orange streamers, which were swimming lazily across the stormy ceiling like brilliant watersnakes.

The food was delicious; even Hermione and Ron, who were full to bursting with Honeydukes sweets, managed second helpings of everything. Harry kept glancing at the staff table. Professor Lupin looked cheerful and as well as he ever did; he was talking animat-edly to tiny little Professor Flitwick, the Charms teacher. Harry moved his eyes along the table, to the place where Snape sat. Was he imagining it, or were Snape's eyes flickering towards Lupin more often than was natural?

The feast finished with an entertainment provided by the Hogwarts ghosts. They popped out of the walls and tables to do a spot of formation gliding; Nearly Headless Nick, the Gryffindor ghost, had a great success with a re-enactment of his own botched beheading.

It had been such a good evening that Harry's good mood couldn't even be spoiled by Malfoy, who shouted through the crowd as they all left the Hall, 'The Dementors send their love, Potter!'

Harry, Ron and Hermione followed the rest of the Gryffindors along the usual path to Gryffindor Tower, but when they reached the corridor which ended with the portrait of the Fat Lady, they found it jammed with students.

'Why isn't anyone going in?' said Ron curiously.

Harry peered over the heads in front of him. The portrait seemed to be closed.

'Let me through, please,' came Percy's voice, and he came bustling importantly through the crowd. 'What's the hold-up here? You can't all have forgotten the password – excuse me, I'm Head Boy –'

And then a silence fell over the crowd, from the front first, so that a chill seemed to spread down the corridor. They heard Percy say, in a suddenly sharp voice, 'Somebody get Professor Dumbledore. Quick.'

People's heads turned; those at the back were standing on tiptoe.

'What's going on?' said Ginny, who had just arrived.

Next moment, Professor Dumbledore was there, sweeping towards the portrait; the Gryffindors squeezed together to let him through, and Harry, Ron and Hermione moved closer to see what the trouble was.

'Oh, my –' Hermione exclaimed and grabbed Harry's arm.

The Fat Lady had vanished from her portrait, which had been slashed so viciously that strips of canvas littered the floor; great chunks of it had been torn away completely.

Dumbledore took one quick look at the ruined painting and turned, his eyes sombre, to see Professors McGonagall, Lupin and Snape hurrying towards him.

'We need to find her,' said Dumbledore. 'Professor McGonagall, please go to Mr Filch at once and tell him to search every painting in the castle for the Fat Lady.'

'You'll be lucky!' said a cackling voice.

It was Peeves the poltergeist, bobbing over the crowd and look-ing delighted, as he always did, at the sight of wreckage or worry.

'What do you mean, Peeves?' said Dumbledore calmly, and Peeves's grin faded a little. He didn't dare taunt Dumbledore. Instead he adopted an oily voice that was no better than his cackle.

'Ashamed, Your Headship, sir. Doesn't want to be seen. She's a horrible mess. Saw her running through the landscape up on the fourth floor, sir, dodging between the trees. Crying something dreadful,' he said happily. 'Poor thing,' he added, unconvincingly.

'Did she say who did it?' said Dumbledore quietly.

'Oh, yes, Professorhead,' said Peeves, with the air of one cradling a large bombshell in his arms. 'He got very angry when she wouldn't let him in, you see.' Peeves flipped over, and grinned at Dumbledore from between his own legs. 'Nasty temper he's got, that Sirius Black.'

CHAPTER NINE

Grim Defeat

Professor Dumbledore sent all the Gryffindors back to the Great Hall, where they were joined ten minutes later by the students from Hufflepuff, Ravenclaw and Slytherin, who all looked extremely confused.

'The teachers and I need to conduct a thorough search of the castle,' Professor Dumbledore told them as Professors McGonagall and Flitwick closed all doors into the Hall. 'I'm afraid that, for your own safety, you will have to spend the night here. I want the Prefects to stand guard over the entrances to the Hall and I am leaving the Head Boy and Girl in charge. Any disturbance should be reported to me immediately,' he added to Percy, who was looking immensely proud and important. 'Send word with one of the ghosts.'

Professor Dumbledore paused, about to the leave the Hall, and said, 'Oh, yes, you'll be needing ...'

One casual wave of his wand and the long tables flew to the edges of the Hall and stood themselves against the walls; another wave, and the floor was covered with hundreds of squashy purple sleeping bags.

'Sleep well,' said Professor Dumbledore, closing the door behind him.

The Hall immediately began to buzz excitedly; the Gryffindors were telling the rest of the school what had just happened.

'Everyone into their sleeping bags!' shouted Percy. 'Come on now, no more talking! Lights out in ten minutes!'

'C'mon,' Ron said to Harry and Hermione; they seized three sleeping bags and dragged them into a corner.

'Do you think Black's still in the castle?' Hermione whispered anxiously.

'Dumbledore obviously thinks he might be,' said Ron.

'It's very lucky he picked tonight, you know,' said Hermione, as they climbed fully dressed into their sleeping bags and propped themselves on their elbows to talk. 'The one night we weren't in the Tower ...'

'I reckon he's lost track of time, being on the run,' said Ron. 'Didn't realise it was Hallowe'en. Otherwise he'd have come bursting in here.'

Hermione shuddered.

All around them, people were asking each other the same question: *'How did he get in?'*

'Maybe he knows how to Apparate,' said a Ravenclaw a few feet away. 'Just appear out of thin air, you know.'

'Disguised himself, probably,' said a Hufflepuff fifth-year.

'He could've flown in,' suggested Dean Thomas.

'Honestly, am I the *only* person who's ever bothered to read *Hogwarts, A History*?' said Hermione crossly to Harry and Ron.

'Probably,' said Ron. 'Why?'

'Because the castle's protected by more than *walls,* you know,' said Hermione. 'There are all sorts of enchantments on it, to stop people entering by stealth. You can't just Apparate in here. And I'd like to see the disguise that could fool those Dementors. They're guarding every single entrance to the grounds. They'd have seen him fly in, too. And Filch knows all the secret passages, they'll have them covered ...'

'The lights are going out now!' Percy shouted. 'I want everyone in their sleeping bags and no more talking!'

The candles all went out at once. The only light now came from the silvery ghosts, who were drifting about talking seriously to the Prefects, and the enchanted ceiling, which, like the sky outside, was scattered with stars. What with that, and the whispering that still filled the Hall, Harry felt as though he was sleeping out of doors in a light wind.

Once every hour, a teacher would reappear in the Hall to check that everything was quiet. Around three in the morning, when many students had finally fallen asleep, Professor Dumbledore came in. Harry watched him looking around for Percy, who had been prowling between the sleeping bags, telling people off for talking. Percy was only a short way away from Harry, Ron and Hermione, who quickly pretended to be asleep as Dumbledore's footsteps drew nearer.

'Any sign of him, Professor?' asked Percy in a whisper.

'No. All well here?'

'Everything under control, sir.'

'Good. There's no point moving them all now. I've found a temporary guardian for the Gryffindor portrait hole. You'll be able to move them back in tomorrow.'

'And the Fat Lady, sir?'

'Hiding in a map of Argyllshire on the second floor. Apparently she refused to let Black in without the password, so he attacked. She's still very distressed, but once she's calmed down, I'll have Mr Filch restore her.'

Harry heard the door of the Hall creak open again, and more footsteps.

'Headmaster?' It was Snape. Harry kept quite still, listening hard. 'The whole of the third floor has been searched. He's not there. And Filch has done the dungeons; nothing there, either.'

'What about the Astronomy Tower? Professor Trelawney's room? The Owlery?'

'All searched ...'

'Very well, Severus. I didn't really expect Black to linger.'

'Have you any theory as to how he got in, Professor?' asked Snape.

Harry raised his head very slightly off his arms to free his other ear.

'Many, Severus, each of them as unlikely as the next.'

Harry opened his eyes a fraction and squinted up to where they stood; Dumbledore's back was to him, but he could see Percy's face, rapt with attention, and Snape's profile, which looked angry.

'You remember the conversation we had, Headmaster, just before – ah – the start of term?' said Snape, who was barely opening his lips, as though trying to block Percy out of the conversation.

'I do, Severus,' said Dumbledore, and there was something like warning in his voice.

'It seems – almost impossible – that Black could have entered the school without inside help. I did express my concerns when you appointed –'

'I do not believe a single person inside this castle would have helped Black enter it,' said Dumbledore, and his tone made it so clear that the subject was closed that Snape didn't reply. 'I must go down to the Dementors,' said Dumbledore. 'I said I would inform them when our search was complete.'

'Didn't they want to help, sir?' said Percy.

'Oh yes,' said Dumbledore coldly. 'But I'm afraid no Dementor will cross the threshold of this castle while I am Headmaster.'

Percy looked slightly abashed. Dumbledore left the Hall, walking quickly and quietly. Snape stood for a moment, watching the Headmaster with an expression of deep resentment on his face, then he, too, left.

Harry glanced sideways at Ron and Hermione. Both of them had their eyes open, too, reflecting the starry ceiling.

'What was all that about?' Ron mouthed.

*

The school talked of nothing but Sirius Black for the next few days. The theories about how he had entered the castle became wilder and wilder; Hannah Abbott, from Hufflepuff, spent much of their next Herbology class telling anyone who'd listen that Black could turn into a flowering shrub.

The Fat Lady's ripped canvas had been taken off the wall and replaced with the portrait of Sir Cadogan and his fat grey pony. Nobody was very happy about this. Sir Cadogan spent half his time challenging people to duels, and the rest thinking up ridiculously complicated passwords, which he changed at least twice a day.

'He's barking mad,' said Seamus Finnigan angrily to Percy. 'Can't we get anyone else?'

'None of the other pictures wanted the job,' said Percy. 'Frightened of what happened to the Fat Lady. Sir Cadogan was the only one brave enough to volunteer.'

Sir Cadogan, however, was the least of Harry's worries. He was now being closely watched. Teachers found excuses to walk along corridors with him and Percy Weasley (acting, Harry suspected, on his mother's orders) was tailing him everywhere like an extremely pompous guard dog. To cap it all, Professor McGonagall summoned Harry into her office, with such a sombre expression on her face Harry thought someone must have died.

'There's no point hiding it from you any longer, Potter,' she said, in a very serious voice. 'I know this will come as a shock to you, but Sirius Black –'

'I know he's after me,' said Harry wearily. 'I heard Ron's dad telling his mum. Mr Weasley works for the Ministry of Magic.'

Professor McGonagall seemed very taken aback. She stared at Harry for a moment or two, then said, 'I see! Well, in that case, Potter, you'll understand why I don't think it's a good idea for you to be practising Quidditch in the evenings. Out on the pitch with only your team members, it's very exposed, Potter –'

'We've got our first match on Saturday!' said Harry, outraged. 'I've got to train, Professor!'

Professor McGonagall considered him intently. Harry knew she was deeply interested in the Gryffindor team's prospects; it had been she, after all, who'd suggested him as Seeker in the first place. He waited, holding his breath.

'Hmm ...' Professor McGonagall stood up and stared out of the window at the Quidditch pitch, just visible through the rain. 'Well ... goodness knows, I'd like to see us win the Cup at last ... but all the same, Potter ... I'd be happier if a teacher were present. I'll ask Madam Hooch to oversee your training sessions.'

*

The weather worsened steadily as the first Quidditch match drew nearer. Undaunted, the Gryffindor team were training harder than ever under the eye of Madam Hooch. Then, at their final training session before Saturday's match, Oliver Wood gave his team some unwelcome news.

'We're not playing Slytherin!' he told them, looking very angry. 'Flint's just been to see me. We're playing Hufflepuff instead.'

'Why?' chorused the rest of the team.

'Flint's excuse is that their Seeker's arm's still injured,' said Wood, grinding his teeth furiously. 'But it's obvious why they're doing it. Don't want to play in this weather. Think it'll damage their chances ...'

There had been strong winds and heavy rain all day, and as Wood spoke, they heard a distant rumble of thunder.

'There's *nothing wrong* with Malfoy's arm!' said Harry furiously. 'He's faking it!'

'I know that, but we can't prove it,' said Wood bitterly. 'And we've been practising all those moves assuming we're playing Slytherin, and instead it's Hufflepuff, and their style's quite different. They've got a new captain and Seeker, Cedric Diggory –'

Angelina, Alicia and Katie suddenly giggled.

'What?' said Wood, frowning at this light-hearted behaviour.

'He's that tall, good-looking one, isn't he?' said Angelina.

'Strong and silent,' said Katie, and they started to giggle again.

'He's only silent because he's too thick to string two words together,' said Fred impatiently. 'I don't know why you're worried, Oliver, Hufflepuff are a pushover. Last time we played them, Harry caught the Snitch in about five minutes, remember?'

'We were playing in completely different conditions!' Wood shouted, his eyes bulging slightly. 'Diggory's put a very strong side together! He's an excellent Seeker! I was afraid you'd take it like this! We mustn't relax! We must keep our focus! Slytherin are trying to wrong-foot us! We *must* win!'

'Oliver, calm down!' said Fred, looking slightly alarmed. 'We're taking Hufflepuff very seriously. *Seriously.*'

*

The day before the match, the winds reached howling point and the rain fell harder than ever. It was so dark inside the corridors and classrooms that extra torches and lanterns were lit. The Slytherin team were looking very smug indeed, and none more so than Malfoy.

'Ah, if only my arm was feeling a bit better!' he sighed, as the gale outside pounded the windows.

Harry had no room in his head to worry about anything except the match next day. Oliver Wood kept hurrying up to him between classes and giving him tips. The third time this happened, Wood talked for so long that Harry suddenly realised he was ten minutes late for Defence Against the Dark Arts, and set off at a run with Wood shouting after him, 'Diggory's got a very fast swerve, Harry, so you might want to try looping him –'

Harry skidded to a halt outside the Defence Against the Dark Arts classroom, pulled the door open and dashed inside.

'Sorry I'm late, Professor Lupin, I –'

But it wasn't Professor Lupin who looked up at him from the teacher's desk; it was Snape.

'This lesson began ten minutes ago, Potter, so I think we'll make it ten points from Gryffindor. Sit down.'

But Harry didn't move.

'Where's Professor Lupin?' he said.

'He says he is feeling too ill to teach today,' said Snape with a twisted smile. 'I believe I told you to sit down?'

But Harry stayed where he was.

'What's wrong with him?'

Snape's black eyes glittered.

'Nothing life-threatening,' he said, looking as though he wished it was. 'Five more points from Gryffindor, and if I have to ask you to sit down again, it will be fifty.'

Harry walked slowly to his seat and sat down. Snape looked around at the class.

'As I was saying before Potter interrupted, Professor Lupin has not left any record of the topics you have covered so far –'

'Please, sir, we've done Boggarts, Red Caps, Kappas and Grindylows,' said Hermione quickly, 'and we're just about to start –'

'Be quiet,' said Snape coldly. 'I did not ask for information. I was merely commenting on Professor Lupin's lack of organisation.'

'He's the best Defence Against the Dark Arts teacher we've ever had,' said Dean Thomas boldly, and there was a murmur of agreement from the rest of the class. Snape looked more menacing than ever.

'You are easily satisfied. Lupin is hardly over-taxing you – I would expect first-years to be able to deal with Red Caps and Grindylows. Today we shall discuss –'

Harry watched him flick through the textbook, to the very back chapter, which he must know they hadn't covered.

'– werewolves,' said Snape.

'But, sir,' said Hermione, seemingly unable to restrain herself, 'we're not supposed to do werewolves yet, we're due to start Hinkypunks –'

'Miss Granger,' said Snape, in a voice of deadly calm, 'I was under the impression that I was taking this lesson, not you. And I am telling you all to turn to page three hundred and ninety-four.' He glanced around again. '*All* of you! *Now!*'

With many bitter sidelong looks and some sullen muttering, the class opened their books.

'Which of you can tell me how we distinguish between the werewolf and the true wolf?' said Snape.

Everyone sat in motionless silence; everyone except Hermione, whose hand, as it so often did, had shot straight into the air.

'Anyone?' Snape said, ignoring Hermione. His twisted smile was back. 'Are you telling me that Professor Lupin hasn't even taught you the basic distinction between –'

'We told you,' said Parvati suddenly, 'we haven't got as far as werewolves yet, we're still on –'

'*Silence!*' snarled Snape. 'Well, well, well, I never thought I'd meet a third-year class who wouldn't even recognise a werewolf when they saw one. I shall make a point of informing Professor Dumbledore how very behind you all are ...'

'Please, sir,' said Hermione, whose hand was still in the air, 'the werewolf differs from the true wolf in several small ways. The snout of the werewolf –'

'That is the second time you have spoken out of turn, Miss Granger,' said Snape coolly. 'Five more points from Gryffindor for being an insufferable know-it-all.'

Hermione went very red, put down her hand and stared at the floor with her eyes full of tears. It was a mark of how much the class loathed Snape that they were all glaring at him, because every one of them had called Hermione a know-it-all at least once, and Ron, who told Hermione she was a know-it-all at least twice a week, said loudly, 'You asked us a question and she knows the answer! Why ask if you don't want to be told?'

The class knew instantly he'd gone too far. Snape advanced on Ron slowly, and the room held its breath.

'Detention, Weasley,' Snape said silkily, his face very close to Ron's. 'And if I ever hear you criticise the way I teach a class again, you will be very sorry indeed.'

No one made a sound throughout the rest of the lesson. They sat and made notes on werewolves from the textbook, while Snape prowled up and down the rows of desks, examining the work they had been doing with Professor Lupin.

'Very poorly explained ... that is incorrect, the Kappa is more commonly found in Mongolia ... Professor Lupin gave this eight out of ten? I wouldn't have given it three ...'

When the bell rang at last, Snape held them back.

'You will each write an essay, to be handed in to me, on the ways you recognise and kill werewolves. I want two rolls of parchment on the subject, and I want them by Monday morning. It is time somebody took this class in hand. Weasley, stay behind, we need to arrange your detention.'

Harry and Hermione left the room with the rest of the class, who waited until they were well out of earshot, then burst into a furious tirade about Snape.

'Snape's never been like this with any of our other Defence Against the Dark Arts teachers, even if he did want the job,' Harry said to Hermione. 'Why's he got it in for Lupin? D'you think this is all because of the Boggart?'

'I don't know,' said Hermione pensively. 'But I really hope Professor Lupin gets better soon ...'

Ron caught up with them five minutes later, in a towering rage.

'D'you know what that –' (he called Snape something that made Hermione say 'Ron!') '– is making me do? I've got to scrub out the bedpans in the hospital wing. *Without magic!*' He was breathing deeply, his fists clenched. 'Why couldn't Black have hidden in Snape's office, eh? He could have finished him off for us!'

*

Harry woke extremely early next morning; so early that it was still dark. For a moment he thought the roaring of the wind had woken him, then he felt a cold breeze on the back of his neck and sat bolt upright – Peeves the poltergeist had been floating next to him, blowing hard in his ear.

'What did you do that for?' said Harry furiously.

Peeves puffed out his cheeks, blew hard and zoomed backwards out of the room, cackling.

Harry fumbled for his alarm clock and looked at it. It was half past four. Cursing Peeves, he rolled over and tried to get back to sleep, but it was very difficult, now he was awake, to ignore the sounds of the thunder rumbling overhead, the pounding of the wind against the castle walls and the distant creaking of the trees in the Forbidden Forest. In a few hours he would be out on the Quidditch pitch, battling through that gale. Finally he gave up any thought of more sleep, got up, dressed, picked up his Nimbus Two Thousand and walked quietly out of the dormitory.

As Harry opened the door, something brushed against his leg. He bent down just in time to grab Crookshanks by the end of his bushy tail, and drag him outside.

'You know, I reckon Ron was right about you,' Harry told Crookshanks suspiciously. 'There are plenty of mice around this place, go and chase them. Go on,' he added, nudging Crookshanks down the spiral staircase with his foot, 'leave Scabbers alone.'

The noise of the storm was even louder in the common room.

Harry knew better than to think the match would be cancelled; Quidditch matches weren't called off for trifles such as thunderstorms. Nevertheless, he was starting to feel very apprehensive. Wood had pointed out Cedric Diggory to him in the corridor; Diggory was a fifth-year and a lot bigger than Harry. Seekers were usually light and speedy, but Diggory's weight would be an advantage in this weather because he was less likely to be blown off course.

Harry whiled away the hours until dawn in front of the fire, getting up every now and then to stop Crookshanks sneaking up the boys' staircase again. At long last Harry thought it must be time for breakfast, so he headed through the portrait hole alone.

'Stand and fight, you mangy cur!' yelled Sir Cadogan.

'Oh, shut up,' Harry yawned.

He revived a bit over a large bowl of porridge, and by the time he'd started on toast, the rest of the team had turned up.

'It's going to be a tough one,' said Wood, who wasn't eating anything.

'Stop worrying, Oliver,' said Alicia soothingly, 'we don't mind a bit of rain.'

But it was considerably more than a bit of rain. Such was the popularity of Quidditch that the whole school turned out to watch the match as usual, but they ran down the lawns towards the Quidditch pitch, heads bowed against the ferocious wind, umbrellas being whipped out of their hands as they went. Just before he entered the changing room, Harry saw Malfoy, Crabbe and Goyle laughing and pointing at him from under an enormous umbrella on their way to the stadium.

The team changed into their scarlet robes and waited for Wood's usual pre-match pep talk, but it didn't come. He tried to speak several times, made an odd gulping noise, then shook his head hopelessly and beckoned them to follow him.

The wind was so strong that they staggered sideways as they walked out onto the pitch. If the crowd was cheering they couldn't hear it over the fresh rolls of thunder. Rain was splattering over Harry's glasses. How on earth was he going to see the Snitch in this?

The Hufflepuffs were approaching from the opposite side of the pitch, wearing canary-yellow robes. The captains walked up to each other and shook hands; Diggory smiled at Wood but Wood now looked as though he had lockjaw and merely nodded. Harry saw Madam Hooch's mouth form the words, 'Mount your brooms.' He pulled his right foot out of the mud with a squelch and swung it over his Nimbus Two Thousand. Madam Hooch put her whistle to her lips and gave it a blast that sounded shrill and distant – they were off.

Harry rose fast, but his Nimbus was swerving slightly with the wind. He held it as steady as he could and turned, squinting into the rain.

Within five minutes Harry was soaked to his skin and frozen, hardly able to see his team-mates, let alone the tiny Snitch. He flew backwards and forwards across the pitch, past blurred red and yellow shapes, with no idea of what was happening in the rest of the game. He couldn't hear the commentary over the wind. The crowd was hidden beneath a sea of cloaks and battered umbrellas. Twice Harry came very close to being unseated by a Bludger; his vision was so clouded by the rain on his glasses he hadn't seen them coming.

He lost track of time. It was getting harder and harder to hold his broom straight. The sky was getting darker, as though night had decided to come early. Twice Harry nearly hit another player, without knowing whether it was a team-mate or opponent; everyone was now so wet, and the rain so thick, he could hardly tell them apart ...

With the first flash of lightning came the sound of Madam Hooch's whistle; Harry could just see the outline of Wood through the thick rain, gesturing him to the ground. The whole team splashed down into the mud.

'I called for time out!' Wood roared at his team. 'Come on, under here –'

They huddled at the edge of the pitch under a large umbrella; Harry took off his glasses and wiped them hurriedly on his robes.

'What's the score?'

'We're fifty points up,' said Wood, 'but unless we get the Snitch soon, we'll be playing into the night.'

'I've got no chance with these on,' Harry said exasperatedly, waving his glasses.

At that very moment, Hermione appeared at his shoulder; she was holding her cloak over her head and was, inexplicably, beaming.

'I've had an idea, Harry! Give me your glasses, quick!'

He handed them to her and, as the team watched in amazement, Hermione tapped them with her wand and said, '*Impervius!*'

'There!' she said, handing them back to Harry. 'They'll repel water!'

Wood looked as though he could have kissed her.

'Brilliant!' he called hoarsely after her, as she disappeared into the crowd. 'OK, team, let's go for it!'

Hermione's spell had done the trick. Harry was still numb with cold, still wetter than he'd ever been in his life, but he could see. Full of fresh determination, he urged his broom through the turbulent air, staring in every direction for the Snitch, avoiding a Bludger, ducking beneath Diggory, who was streaking in the opposite direction ...

There was another clap of thunder, followed immediately by forked lightning. This was getting more and more dangerous. Harry needed to get the Snitch quickly –

He turned, intending to head back towards the middle of the pitch, but at that moment, another flash of lightning illuminated the stands, and Harry saw something that distracted him completely: the silhouette of an enormous shaggy black dog, clearly imprinted against the sky, motionless in the topmost, empty row of seats.

Harry's numb hands slipped on the broom handle and his Nimbus dropped a few feet. Shaking his sodden fringe out of his eyes, he squinted back into the stands. The dog had vanished.

'Harry!' came Wood's anguished yell from the Gryffindor goal-posts. 'Harry, behind you!'

Harry looked wildly around. Cedric Diggory was pelting up the pitch, and a tiny speck of gold was shimmering in the rain-filled air between them ...

With a jolt of panic, Harry threw himself flat to the broom handle and zoomed towards the Snitch.

'Come on!' he growled at his Nimbus, as the rain whipped his face. '*Faster!*'

But something odd was happening. An eerie silence was falling across the stadium. The wind, though as strong as ever, was forgetting to roar. It was as though someone had turned off the sound, as though Harry had gone suddenly deaf – what was going on?

And then a horribly familiar wave of cold swept over him, inside him, just as he became aware of something moving on the pitch below ...

Before he'd had time to think, Harry had taken his eyes off the Snitch and looked down.

At least a hundred Dementors, their hidden faces pointing up at him, were standing below. It was as though freezing water was rising in his chest, cutting at his insides. And then he heard it again ... someone was screaming, screaming inside his head ... a woman ...

'Not Harry, not Harry, please not Harry!'

'Stand aside, you silly girl ... stand aside, now ...'

'Not Harry, please no, take me, kill me instead –'

Numbing, swirling white mist was filling Harry's brain ... What was he doing? Why was he flying? He needed to help her ... she was going to die ... she was going to be murdered ...

He was falling, falling through the icy mist.

'Not Harry! Please ... have mercy ... have mercy ...'

A shrill voice was laughing, the woman was screaming, and Harry knew no more.

*

'Lucky the ground was so soft.'

'I thought he was dead for sure.'

'But he didn't even break his glasses.'

Harry could hear the voices whispering, but they made no sense whatsoever. He didn't have a clue where he was, or how he'd got there, or what he'd been doing before he got there. All he knew was that every inch of him was aching as though it had been beaten.

'That was the scariest thing I've ever seen in my life.'

Scariest ... the scariest thing ... hooded black figures ... cold ... screaming ...

Harry's eyes snapped open. He was lying in the hospital wing. The Gryffindor Quidditch team, spattered with mud from head to foot, was gathered around his bed. Ron and Hermione were also there, looking as though they'd just climbed out of a swimming pool.

'Harry!' said Fred, who looked extremely white underneath the mud. 'How're you feeling?'

It was as though Harry's memory was on fast forward. The

lightning ... the Grim ... the Snitch ... and the Dementors ...

'What happened?' he said, sitting up so suddenly they all gasped.

'You fell off,' said Fred. 'Must've been – what – fifty feet?'

'We thought you'd died,' said Alicia, who was shaking.

Hermione made a small, squeaky noise. Her eyes were extremely bloodshot.

'But the match,' said Harry. 'What happened? Are we having a replay?'

No one said anything. The horrible truth sank into Harry like a stone.

'We didn't – *lose?*'

'Diggory got the Snitch,' said George. 'Just after you fell. He didn't realise what had happened. When he looked back and saw you on the ground, he tried to call it off. Wanted a re-match. But they won fair and square ... even Wood admits it.'

'Where is Wood?' said Harry, suddenly realising he wasn't there.

'Still in the showers,' said Fred. 'We think he's trying to drown himself.'

Harry put his face to his knees, his hands gripping his hair. Fred grabbed his shoulder and shook it roughly.

'C'mon, Harry, you've never missed the Snitch before.'

'There had to be one time you didn't get it,' said George.

'It's not over yet,' said Fred. 'We lost by a hundred points, right? So if Hufflepuff lose to Ravenclaw and we beat Ravenclaw and Slytherin ...'

'Hufflepuff'll have to lose by at least two hundred points,' said George.

'But if they beat Ravenclaw ...'

'No way, Ravenclaw are too good. But if Slytherin lose against Hufflepuff ...'

'It all depends on the points – a margin of a hundred either way –'

Harry lay there, not saying a word. They had lost ... for the first time ever, he had lost a Quidditch match.

After ten minutes or so, Madam Pomfrey came over to tell the team to leave him in peace.

'We'll come and see you later,' Fred told him. 'Don't beat yourself up, Harry, you're still the best Seeker we've ever had.'

The team trooped out, trailing mud behind them. Madam Pomfrey shut the door behind them, looking disapproving. Ron and Hermione moved nearer to Harry's bed.

'Dumbledore was really angry,' Hermione said in a quaking voice. 'I've never seen him like that before. He ran onto the pitch as you fell, waved his wand, and you sort of slowed down before you hit the ground. Then he whirled his wand at the Dementors. Shot silver stuff at them. They left the stadium straight away ... he was furious they'd come into the grounds, we heard him –'

'Then he magicked you onto a stretcher,' said Ron. 'And walked up to school with you floating on it. Everyone thought you were ...'

His voice faded away, but Harry hardly noticed. He was thinking about what the Dementors had done to him ... about the screaming voice. He looked up and saw Ron and Hermione looking at him so anxiously that he quickly cast around for something matter-of-fact to say.

'Did someone get my Nimbus?'

Ron and Hermione looked quickly at each other.

'Er –'

'What?' said Harry, looking from one to the other.

'Well ... when you fell off, it got blown away,' said Hermione hesitantly.

'And?'

'And it hit – it hit – oh, Harry – it hit the Whomping Willow.'

Harry's insides lurched. The Whomping Willow was a very violent tree which stood alone in the middle of the grounds.

'And?' he said, dreading the answer.

'Well, you know the Whomping Willow,' said Ron. 'It – it doesn't like being hit.'

'Professor Flitwick brought it back just before you came round,' said Hermione in a very small voice.

Slowly, she reached down for a bag at her feet, turned it upside-down and tipped a dozen bits of splintered wood and twig onto the bed, the only remains of Harry's faithful, finally beaten broomstick.

CHAPTER TEN

The Marauder's Map

Madam Pomfrey insisted on keeping Harry in the hospital wing for the rest of the weekend. He didn't argue or complain, but he wouldn't let her throw away the shattered remnants of his Nimbus Two Thousand. He knew he was being stupid, knew that the Nimbus was beyond repair, but Harry couldn't help it; he felt as though he'd lost one of his best friends.

He had a stream of visitors, all intent on cheering him up. Hagrid sent him a bunch of earwiggy flowers that looked like yellow cabbages and Ginny Weasley, blushing furiously, turned up with a 'get well' card she had made herself, which sang shrilly unless Harry kept it shut under his bowl of fruit. The Gryffindor team visited again on Sunday morning, this time accompanied by Wood, who told Harry, in a hollow, dead sort of voice, that he didn't blame him in the slightest. Ron and Hermione only left Harry's bedside at night. But nothing anyone said or did could make Harry feel any better, because they only knew half of what was troubling him.

He hadn't told anyone about the Grim, not even Ron and Hermione, because he knew Ron would panic and Hermione would scoff. The fact remained, however, that it had now appeared twice, and both appearances had been followed by near-fatal accidents; the first time, he had nearly been run over by the Knight Bus; the second, fallen fifty feet from his broomstick. Was the Grim going to haunt him until he actually died? Was he going to spend the rest of his life looking over his shoulder for the beast?

And then there were the Dementors. Harry felt sick and humiliated every time he thought of them. Everyone said the Dementors were horrible, but no one else collapsed every time they went near one ... no one else heard echoes in their head of their dying parents.

For Harry knew who that screaming voice belonged to now. He
had heard her words, heard them over and over again during the
night hours in the hospital wing while he lay awake, staring at
the strips of moonlight on the ceiling. When the Dementors
approached him, he heard the last moments of his mother's life,
her attempts to protect him, Harry, from Lord Voldemort, and
Voldemort's laughter before he murdered her ... Harry dozed fit-
fully, sinking into dreams full of clammy, rotted hands and petrified pleading, jerking awake only to dwell again on the sound of
his mother's voice.

*

It was a relief to return on Monday to the noise and bustle of the
main school, where he was forced to think about other things,
even if he had to endure Draco Malfoy's taunting. Malfoy was
almost beside himself with glee at Gryffindor's defeat. He had
finally taken off his bandages, and celebrated having the full use
of both arms again by doing spirited imitations of Harry falling off
his broom. Malfoy spent much of their next Potions class doing
Dementor imitations across the dungeon; Ron finally cracked,
flinging a large, slippery crocodile heart at Malfoy, which hit him
in the face and caused Snape to take fifty points from Gryffindor.

'If Snape's taking Defence Against the Dark Arts again, I'm
going off sick,' said Ron, as they headed towards Lupin's classroom after lunch. 'Check who's in there, Hermione.'

Hermione peered around the classroom door.

'It's OK!'

Professor Lupin was back at work. It certainly looked as
though he had been ill. His old robes were hanging more loosely
on him and there were dark shadows beneath his eyes; nevertheless, he smiled at the class as they took their seats, and they burst
at once into an explosion of complaints about Snape's behaviour
while Lupin had been ill.

'It's not fair, he was only filling in, why should he set us homework?'

'We don't know anything about werewolves –'

'– two rolls of parchment!'

'Did you tell Professor Snape we haven't covered them yet?'
Lupin asked, frowning slightly.

The babble broke out again.

'Yes, but he said we were really behind –'

'– he wouldn't listen –'

'– *two rolls of parchment!*'

Professor Lupin smiled at the look of indignation on every face.

'Don't worry. I'll speak to Professor Snape. You don't have to do the essay.'

'Oh *no*,' said Hermione, looking very disappointed. 'I've already finished it!'

They had a very enjoyable lesson. Professor Lupin had brought along a glass box containing a Hinkypunk, a little one-legged creature who seemed as though he was made of wisps of smoke, rather frail and harmless-looking.

'Lures travellers into bogs,' said Professor Lupin, as they took notes. 'You notice the lantern dangling from his hand? Hops ahead – people follow the light – then –'

The Hinkypunk made a horrible squelching noise against the glass.

When the bell rang, everyone gathered up their things and headed for the door, Harry amongst them, but –

'Wait a moment, Harry,' Lupin called, 'I'd like a word.'

Harry doubled back and watched Professor Lupin covering the Hinkypunk's box with a cloth.

'I heard about the match,' said Lupin, turning back to his desk and starting to pile books into his briefcase, 'and I'm sorry about your broomstick. Is there any chance of fixing it?'

'No,' said Harry. 'The tree smashed it to bits.'

Lupin sighed.

'They planted the Whomping Willow the same year that I arrived at Hogwarts. People used to play a game, trying to get near enough to touch the trunk. In the end, a boy called Davey Gudgeon nearly lost an eye, and we were forbidden to go near it. No broomstick would have a chance.'

'Did you hear about the Dementors, too?' said Harry with difficulty.

Lupin looked at him quickly.

'Yes, I did. I don't think any of us have seen Professor Dumbledore that angry. They have been growing restless for some time ... furious at his refusal to let them inside the grounds ... I suppose they were the reason you fell?'

'Yes,' said Harry. He hesitated, and then the question he had to ask burst from him before he could stop himself. '*Why*? Why do they affect me like that? Am I just –?'

'It has nothing to do with weakness,' said Professor Lupin sharply, as though he had read Harry's mind. 'The Dementors affect you worse than the others because there are horrors in your past that the others don't have.'

A ray of wintry sunlight fell across the classroom, illuminating Lupin's grey hairs and the lines on his young face.

'Dementors are among the foulest creatures that walk this earth. They infest the darkest, filthiest places, they glory in decay and despair, they drain peace, hope and happiness out of the air around them. Even Muggles feel their presence, though they can't see them. Get too near a Dementor and every good feeling, every happy memory, will be sucked out of you. If it can, the Dementor will feed on you long enough to reduce you to something like itself – soulless and evil. You'll be left with nothing but the worst experiences of your life. And the worst that has happened to *you*, Harry, is enough to make anyone fall off their broom. You have nothing to feel ashamed of.'

'When they get near me –' Harry stared at Lupin's desk, his throat tight, 'I can hear Voldemort murdering my mum.'

Lupin made a sudden motion with his arm as though he had made to grip Harry's shoulder, but thought better of it. There was a moment's silence; then –

'Why did they have to come to the match?' said Harry bitterly.

'They're getting hungry,' said Lupin coolly, shutting his briefcase with a snap. 'Dumbledore won't let them into the school, so their supply of human prey has dried up ... I don't think they could resist the large crowd around the Quidditch pitch. All that excitement ... emotions running high ... it was their idea of a feast.'

'Azkaban must be terrible,' Harry muttered. Lupin nodded grimly.

'The fortress is set on a tiny island, way out to sea, but they don't need walls and water to keep the prisoners in, not when they're all trapped inside their own heads, incapable of a single cheerful thought. Most of them go mad within weeks.'

'But Sirius Black escaped from them,' Harry said slowly. 'He got away ...'

Lupin's briefcase slipped from the desk; he had to stoop quickly to catch it.

'Yes,' he said, straightening up. 'Black must have found a way to fight them. I wouldn't have believed it possible ... Dementors are supposed to drain a wizard of his powers if he is left with them too long ...'

'*You* made that Dementor on the train back off,' said Harry suddenly.

'There are – certain defences one can use,' said Lupin. 'But there was only one Dementor on the train. The more there are, the more difficult it becomes to resist.'

'What defences?' said Harry at once. 'Can you teach me?'

'I don't pretend to be an expert at fighting Dementors, Harry – quite the contrary ...'

'But if the Dementors come to another Quidditch match, I need to be able to fight them –'

Lupin looked into Harry's determined face, hesitated, then said, 'Well ... all right. I'll try and help. But it'll have to wait until next term, I'm afraid. I have a lot to do before the holidays. I chose a very inconvenient time to fall ill.'

*

What with the promise of Anti-Dementor lessons from Lupin, the thought that he might never have to hear his mother's death again, and the fact that Ravenclaw flattened Hufflepuff in their Quidditch match at the end of November, Harry's mood took a definite upturn. Gryffindor were not out of the running after all, although they could not afford to lose another match. Wood became repossessed of his manic energy, and worked his team as hard as ever in the chilly haze of rain that persisted into December. Harry saw no hint of a Dementor within the grounds. Dumbledore's anger seemed to be keeping them at their stations at the entrances.

Two weeks before the end of term, the sky lightened suddenly to a dazzling, opaline white and the muddy grounds were revealed one morning covered in glittering frost. Inside the castle, there was a buzz of Christmas in the air. Professor Flitwick, the Charms teacher, had already decorated his classroom with shimmering lights that turned out to be real, fluttering fairies. The students were all happily discussing their plans for the holidays. Both Ron and Hermione had decided to remain at Hogwarts, and though Ron said it was because he couldn't stand two weeks with Percy, and Hermione insisted she needed to use the library, Harry wasn't fooled; they were doing it to keep him company, and he was very grateful.

To everyone's delight except Harry's, there was to be another Hogsmeade trip on the very last weekend of term.

'We can do all our Christmas shopping there!' said Hermione. 'Mum and Dad would really love those Toothflossing Stringmints from Honeydukes!'

Resigned to the fact that he would be the only third-year staying behind again, Harry borrowed a copy of *Which Broomstick* from Wood, and decided to spend the day reading up on the different makes. He had been riding one of the school brooms at team practice, an ancient Shooting Star, which was very slow and jerky; he definitely needed a new broom of his own.

On the Saturday morning of the Hogsmeade trip, Harry bid goodbye to Ron and Hermione, who were wrapped in cloaks and scarves, then turned up the marble staircase alone, and headed back towards Gryffindor Tower. Snow had started to fall outside the windows, and the castle was very still and quiet.

'Psst – Harry!'

He turned, halfway along the third-floor corridor, to see Fred and George peering out at him from behind a statue of a humpbacked, one-eyed witch.

'What are you doing?' said Harry curiously. 'How come you're not going to Hogsmeade?'

'We've come to give you a bit of festive cheer before we go,' said Fred, with a mysterious wink. 'Come in here ...'

He nodded towards an empty classroom to the left of the one-eyed statue. Harry followed Fred and George inside. George closed the door quietly and then turned, beaming, to look at Harry.

'Early Christmas present for you, Harry,' he said.

Fred pulled something from inside his cloak with a flourish and laid it on one of the desks. It was a large, square, very worn piece of parchment with nothing written on it. Harry, suspecting one of Fred and George's jokes, stared at it.

'What's that supposed to be?'

'This, Harry, is the secret of our success,' said George, patting the parchment fondly.

'It's a wrench, giving it to you,' said Fred, 'but we decided last night, your need's greater than ours.'

'Anyway, we know it off by heart,' said George. 'We bequeath it to you. We don't really need it any more.'

'And what do I need with a bit of old parchment?' said Harry.

'A bit of old parchment!' said Fred, closing his eyes with a grimace as though Harry had mortally offended him. 'Explain, George.'

'Well ... when we were in our first year, Harry – young, carefree and innocent –'

Harry snorted. He doubted whether Fred and George had ever been innocent.

'– well, more innocent than we are now – we got into a spot of bother with Filch.'

'We let off a Dungbomb in the corridor and it upset him for some reason –'

'So he hauled us off to his office and started threatening us with the usual –'

'– detention –'

'– disembowelment –'

'– and we couldn't help noticing a drawer in one of his filing cabinets marked *Confiscated and Highly Dangerous*.'

'Don't tell me –' said Harry, starting to grin.

'Well, what would you've done?' said Fred. 'George caused a diversion by dropping another Dungbomb, I whipped the drawer open and grabbed – *this*.'

'It's not as bad as it sounds, you know,' said George. 'We don't reckon Filch ever found out how to work it. He probably suspected what it was, though, or he wouldn't have confiscated it.'

'And you know how to work it?'

'Oh yes,' said Fred, smirking. 'This little beauty's taught us more than all the teachers in this school.'

'You're winding me up,' said Harry, looking at the ragged old bit of parchment.

'Oh, are we?' said George.

He took out his wand, touched the parchment lightly and said, *'I solemnly swear that I am up to no good.'*

And at once, thin ink lines began to spread like a spider's web from the point that George's wand had touched. They joined each other, they criss-crossed, they fanned into every corner of the parchment; then words began to blossom across the top, great, curly green words, that proclaimed:

Messrs Moony, Wormtail, Padfoot and Prongs
Purveyors of Aids to Magical Mischief-Makers
are proud to present
THE MARAUDER'S MAP

It was a map showing every detail of the Hogwarts castle and grounds. But the truly remarkable thing was the tiny ink dots moving around it, each labelled with a name in minuscule writing. Astounded, Harry bent over it. A labelled dot in the top left corner showed that Professor Dumbledore was pacing his study; the caretaker's cat, Mrs Norris, was prowling the second floor, and Peeves the poltergeist was currently bouncing around the trophy room. And as Harry's eyes travelled up and down the familiar corridors, he noticed something else.

This map showed a set of passages he had never entered. And many of them seemed to lead –

'Right into Hogsmeade,' said Fred, tracing one of them with his finger. 'There are seven in all. Now, Filch knows about these four –' he pointed them out, '– but we're sure we're the only ones who know about *these*. Don't bother with the one behind the mirror on the fourth floor. We used it until last winter, but it's caved in – completely blocked. And we don't reckon anyone's ever used this one, because the Whomping Willow's planted right over the entrance. But this one here, this one leads right into the cellar of Honeydukes. We've used it loads of times. And as you might've noticed, the entrance is right outside this room, through that one-eyed old crone's hump.'

'Moony, Wormtail, Padfoot and Prongs,' sighed George, patting the heading of the map. 'We owe them so much.'

'Noble men, working tirelessly to help a new generation of law-breakers,' said Fred solemnly.

'Right,' said George briskly, 'don't forget to wipe it after you've used it –'

'– or anyone can read it,' Fred said warningly.

'Just tap it again and say, "Mischief managed!" And it'll go blank.'

'So, young Harry,' said Fred, in an uncanny impersonation of Percy, 'mind you behave yourself.'

'See you in Honeydukes,' said George, winking.

They left the room, both smirking in a satisfied sort of way.

Harry stood there, gazing at the miraculous map. He watched the tiny ink Mrs Norris turn left and pause to sniff at something on the floor. If Filch really didn't know ... he wouldn't have to pass the Dementors at all ...

But even as he stood there, flooded with excitement, something Harry had once heard Mr Weasley say came floating out of his memory.

Never trust anything that can think for itself, if you can't see where it keeps its brain.

This map was one of those dangerous magical objects Mr Weasley had been warning against ... *Aids to Magical Mischief-Makers* ... but then, Harry reasoned, he only wanted to use it to get into Hogsmeade, it wasn't as though he wanted to steal anything or attack anyone ... and Fred and George had been using it for years without anything horrible happening ...

Harry traced the secret passage to Honeydukes with his finger.

Then, quite suddenly, as though following orders, he rolled up the map, stuffed it inside his robes, and hurried to the door of the classroom. He opened it a couple of inches. There was no one outside. Very carefully, he edged out of the room and slipped behind the statue of the one-eyed witch.

What did he have to do? He pulled out the map again and saw, to his astonishment, that a new ink figure had appeared upon it, labelled 'Harry Potter'. This figure was standing exactly where the real Harry was standing, about halfway down the third-floor corridor. Harry watched carefully. His little ink self appeared to be tapping the witch with his minute wand. Harry quickly took out his real wand and tapped the statue. Nothing happened. He looked back at the map. The tiniest speech bubble had appeared next to his figure. The word inside said '*Dissendium*'.

'*Dissendium!*' Harry whispered, tapping the stone witch again.

At once, the statue's hump opened wide enough to admit a fairly thin person. Harry glanced quickly up and down the corridor, then tucked the map away again, hoisted himself into the hole headfirst, and pushed himself forwards.

He slid a considerable way down what felt like a stone slide, then landed on cold, damp earth. He stood up, looking around. It was pitch dark. He held up his wand, muttered, '*Lumos!*' and saw that he was in a very narrow, low, earthy passageway. He raised the map, tapped it with the tip of his wand and muttered, 'Mischief managed!' The map went blank at once. He folded it carefully, tucked it inside his robes, then, heart beating fast, both excited and apprehensive, he set off.

The passage twisted and turned, more like the burrow of a giant rabbit than anything else. Harry hurried along it, stumbling now and then on the uneven floor, holding his wand out in front of him.

It took ages, but Harry had the thought of Honeydukes to sustain him. After what felt like an hour, the passage began to rise. Panting, Harry sped up, his face hot, his feet very cold.

Ten minutes later, he came to the foot of some worn stone steps which rose out of sight above him. Careful not to make any noise, Harry began to climb. A hundred steps, two hundred steps, he lost count as he climbed, watching his feet ... then, without warning, his head hit something hard.

It seemed to be a trapdoor. Harry stood there, massaging the top of his head, listening. He couldn't hear any sounds above him. Very slowly, he pushed the trapdoor open and peered over the edge.

He was in a cellar which was full of wooden crates and boxes. Harry climbed out of the trapdoor and replaced it – it blended so perfectly with the dusty floor that it was impossible to tell it was there. Harry crept slowly towards the wooden staircase that led upstairs. Now he could definitely hear voices, not to mention the tinkle of a bell and the opening and shutting of a door.

Wondering what he ought to do, he suddenly heard a door open much closer at hand; somebody was about to come downstairs.

'And get another box of Jelly Slugs, dear, they've nearly cleaned us out –' said a woman's voice.

A pair of feet was coming down the staircase. Harry leapt behind an enormous crate and waited for the footsteps to pass. He heard the man shifting boxes against the wall opposite. He might not get another chance –

Quickly and silently, Harry dodged out from his hiding place and climbed the stairs; looking back, he saw an enormous backside and a shiny bald head buried in a box. Harry reached the door at the top of the stairs, slipped through it, and found himself behind the counter of Honeydukes – he ducked, crept sideways and then straightened up.

Honeydukes was so crowded with Hogwarts students that no one looked twice at Harry. He edged amongst them, looking around, and suppressed a laugh as he imagined the look that would spread over Dudley's piggy face if he could see where Harry was now.

There were shelves upon shelves of the most succulent-looking sweets imaginable. Creamy chunks of nougat, shimmering pink squares of coconut ice, fat, honey-coloured toffees; hundreds of different kinds of chocolate in neat rows; there was a large barrel of Every Flavour Beans, and another of Fizzing Whizzbees, the levitating sherbet balls that Ron had mentioned; along yet another wall were 'Special Effects' sweets: Drooble's Best Blowing Gum (which filled a room with bluebell-coloured bubbles that refused to pop for days), the strange, splintery Toothflossing Stringmints, tiny black Pepper Imps ('breathe fire for your friends!'), Ice Mice ('hear your teeth chatter and squeak!'), peppermint creams shaped like toads ('hop realistically in the stomach!'), fragile sugar-spun quills and exploding bonbons.

Harry squeezed himself through a crowd of sixth-years and saw a sign hanging in the furthest corner of the shop ('Unusual Tastes'). Ron and Hermione were standing underneath it, examining a tray of blood-flavoured lollipops. Harry sneaked up behind them.

'Urgh, no, Harry won't want one of those, they're for vampires, I expect,' Hermione was saying.

'How about these?' said Ron, shoving a jar of Cockroach Cluster under Hermione's nose.

'Definitely not,' said Harry.

Ron nearly dropped the jar.

'*Harry!*' squealed Hermione. 'What are you doing here? How – how did you –?'

'Wow!' said Ron, looking very impressed. 'You've learnt to Apparate!'

'"Course I haven't,' said Harry. He dropped his voice so that none of the sixth-years could hear him and told them all about the Marauder's Map.

'How come Fred and George never gave it to *me*!' said Ron, out-raged. 'I'm their brother!'

'But Harry isn't going to keep it!' said Hermione, as though the idea was ludicrous. 'He's going to hand it in to Professor McGonagall, aren't you, Harry?'

'No, I'm not!' said Harry.

'Are you mad?' said Ron, goggling at Hermione. 'Hand in something that good?'

'If I hand it in, I'll have to say where I got it! Filch would know Fred and George nicked it!'

'But what about Sirius Black?' Hermione hissed. 'He could be using one of the passages on that map to get into the castle! The teachers have got to know!'

'He can't be getting in through a passage,' said Harry quickly. 'There are seven secret tunnels on the map, right? Fred and George reckon Filch already knows about four of them. And the other three – one of them's caved in, so no one can get through it. One of them's got the Whomping Willow planted over the entrance, so you can't get out of it. And the one I just came through – well – it's really hard to see the entrance to it down in the cellar – so unless he knew it was there –'

Harry hesitated. What if Black did know the passage was there? Ron, however, cleared his throat significantly, and pointed to a notice pasted on the inside of the sweetshop door.

BY ORDER OF THE MINISTRY OF MAGIC

Customers are reminded that until further notice, Dementors will be patrolling the streets of Hogsmeade every night after sundown. This measure has been put in place for the safety of Hogsmeade residents and will be lifted upon the recapture of Sirius Black. It is therefore advisable that you complete your shopping well before nightfall.

Merry Christmas!

'See?' said Ron quietly. 'I'd like to see Black try and break into Honeydukes with Dementors swarming all over the village. Anyway, Hermione, the Honeydukes owners would hear a break-in, wouldn't they? They live over the shop!'

'Yes, but – but –' Hermione seemed to be struggling to find another problem. 'Look, Harry still shouldn't be coming into Hogsmeade, he hasn't got a signed form! If anyone finds out, he'll be in so much trouble! And it's not nightfall yet – what if Sirius Black turns up today? Now?'

'He'd have a job spotting Harry in this,' said Ron, nodding through the mullioned windows at the thick, swirling snow.

'Come on, Hermione, it's Christmas, Harry deserves a break.'

Hermione bit her lip, looking extremely worried.

'Are you going to report me?' Harry asked her, grinning.

'Oh – of course not – but honestly, Harry –'

'Seen the Fizzing Whizzbees, Harry?' said Ron, grabbing him and leading him over to their barrel. 'And the Jelly Slugs? And the Acid Pops? Fred gave me one of those when I was seven – it burnt a hole right through my tongue. I remember Mum walloping him with her broomstick.' Ron stared broodingly into the Acid Pop box. 'Reckon Fred'd take a bit of Cockroach Cluster if I told him they were peanuts?'

When Ron and Hermione had paid for all their sweets, the three of them left Honeydukes for the blizzard outside.

Hogsmeade looked like a Christmas card; the little thatched cottages and shops were all covered in a layer of crisp snow; there were holly wreaths on the doors and strings of enchanted candles hanging in the trees.

Harry shivered; unlike the other two, he didn't have his cloak. They headed up the street, heads bowed against the wind, Ron and Hermione shouting through their scarves.

'That's the Post Office –'

'Zonko's is up there –'

'We could go up to the Shrieking Shack –'

'Tell you what,' said Ron, his teeth chattering, 'shall we go for a Butterbeer in the Three Broomsticks?'

Harry was more than willing; the wind was fierce and his hands were freezing, so they crossed the road, and in a few minutes were entering the tiny inn.

It was extremely crowded, noisy, warm and smoky. A curvy sort of woman with a pretty face was serving a bunch of rowdy war-locks up at the bar.

'That's Madam Rosmerta,' said Ron. 'I'll get the drinks, shall I?' he added, going slightly red.

Harry and Hermione made their way to the back of the room, where there was a small, vacant table between the window and a handsome Christmas tree which stood next to the fireplace. Ron came back five minutes later, carrying three foaming tankards of hot Butterbeer.

'Happy Christmas!' he said happily, raising his tankard.

Harry drank deeply. It was the most delicious thing he'd ever tasted and seemed to heat every bit of him from the inside.

A sudden breeze ruffled his hair. The door of the Three Broomsticks had opened again. Harry looked over the rim of his tankard and choked.

Professors McGonagall and Flitwick had just entered the pub in a flurry of snowflakes, shortly followed by Hagrid, who was deep in conversation with a portly man in a lime-green bowler hat and a pinstriped cloak: Cornelius Fudge, Minister for Magic.

In an instant, Ron and Hermione had both placed hands on the top of Harry's head and forced him off his stool and under the table. Dripping with Butterbeer and crouching out of sight, Harry clutched his empty tankard and watched the teachers' and Fudge's feet move towards the bar, pause, then turn and walk right towards him.

Somewhere above him, Hermione whispered, '*Mobiliarbus!*'

The Christmas tree beside their table rose a few inches off the ground, drifted sideways and landed with a soft thump right in front of their table, hiding them from view. Staring through the dense lower branches, Harry saw four sets of chair legs move back from the table right beside theirs, then heard the grunts and sighs of the teachers and Minister as they sat down.

Next he saw another pair of feet, wearing sparkly turquoise high heels, and heard a woman's voice.

'A small Gillywater –'

'Mine,' said Professor McGonagall's voice.

'Four pints of mulled mead –'

'Ta, Rosmerta,' said Hagrid.

'A cherry syrup and soda with ice and umbrella –'

'Mmm!' said Professor Flitwick, smacking his lips.

'So you'll be the redcurrant rum, Minister.'

'Thank you, Rosmerta, m'dear,' said Fudge's voice. 'Lovely to see you again, I must say. Have one yourself, won't you? Come and join us ...'

'Well, thank you very much, Minister.'

Harry watched the glittering heels march away and back again. His heart was pounding uncomfortably in his throat. Why hadn't it occurred to him that this was the last weekend of term for the teachers, too? And how long were they going to sit there? He needed time to sneak back into Honeydukes if he wanted to return to school tonight ... Hermione's leg gave a nervous twitch next to him.

'So, what brings you to this neck of the woods, Minister?' came Madam Rosmerta's voice.

Harry saw the lower part of Fudge's thick body twist in his chair as though he was checking for eavesdroppers. Then he said in a quiet voice, 'What else, m'dear, but Sirius Black? I daresay you heard what happened up at the school at Hallowe'en?'

'I did hear a rumour,' admitted Madam Rosmerta.

'Did you tell the whole pub, Hagrid?' said Professor McGonagall exasperatedly.

'Do you think Black's still in the area, Minister?' whispered Madam Rosmerta.

'I'm sure of it,' said Fudge shortly.

'You know that the Dementors have searched my pub twice?' said Madam Rosmerta, a slight edge to her voice. 'Scared all my customers away ... it's very bad for business, Minister.'

'Rosmerta, m'dear, I don't like them any more than you do,' said Fudge uncomfortably. 'Necessary precaution ... unfortunate, but there you are ... I've just met some of them. They're in a fury against Dumbledore – he won't let them inside the castle grounds.'

'I should think not,' said Professor McGonagall sharply. 'How are we supposed to teach with those horrors floating around?'

'Hear, hear!' squeaked tiny Professor Flitwick, whose feet were dangling a foot from the ground.

'All the same,' demurred Fudge, 'they are here to protect you all from something much worse ... we all know what Black's capable of ...'

'Do you know, I still have trouble believing it,' said Madam Rosmerta thoughtfully. 'Of all the people to go over to the Dark side, Sirius Black was the last I'd have thought ... I mean, I remember him when he was a boy at Hogwarts. If you'd told me then what he was going to become, I'd have said you'd had too much mead.'

'You don't know the half of it, Rosmerta,' said Fudge gruffly. 'The worst he did isn't widely known.'

'The worst?' said Madam Rosmerta, her voice alive with curiosity. 'Worse than murdering all those poor people, you mean?'

'I certainly do,' said Fudge.

'I can't believe that. What could possibly be worse?'

'You say you remember him at Hogwarts, Rosmerta,' murmured

Professor McGonagall. 'Do you remember who his best friend was?'

'Naturally,' said Madam Rosmerta, with a small laugh. 'Never saw one without the other, did you? The number of times I had them in here – ooh, they used to make me laugh. Quite the double act, Sirius Black and James Potter!'

Harry dropped his tankard with a loud clunk. Ron kicked him.

'Precisely,' said Professor McGonagall. 'Black and Potter. Ringleaders of their little gang. Both very bright, of course – exceptionally bright, in fact – but I don't think we've ever had such a pair of troublemakers –'

'I dunno,' chuckled Hagrid. 'Fred and George Weasley could give 'em a run fer their money.'

'You'd have thought Black and Potter were brothers!' chimed in Professor Flitwick. 'Inseparable!'

'Of course they were,' said Fudge. 'Potter trusted Black beyond all his other friends. Nothing changed when they left school. Black was best man when James married Lily. Then they named him godfather to Harry. Harry has no idea, of course. You can imagine how the idea would torment him.'

'Because Black turned out to be in league with You-Know-Who?' whispered Madam Rosmerta.

'Worse even than that, m'dear ...' Fudge dropped his voice and proceeded in a sort of low rumble. 'Not many people are aware that the Potters knew You-Know-Who was after them. Dumbledore, who was of course working tirelessly against You-Know-Who, had a number of useful spies. One of them tipped him off, and he alerted James and Lily at once. He advised them to go into hiding. Well, of course, You-Know-Who wasn't an easy person to hide from. Dumbledore told them that their best chance was the Fidelius Charm.'

'How does that work?' said Madam Rosmerta, breathless with interest. Professor Flitwick cleared his throat.

'An immensely complex spell,' he said squeakily, 'involving the magical concealment of a secret inside a single, living soul. The information is hidden inside the chosen person, or Secret Keeper, and is henceforth impossible to find – unless, of course, the Secret Keeper chooses to divulge it. As long as the Secret Keeper refused to speak, You-Know-Who could search the village where Lily and James were staying for years and never find them, not even if he had his nose pressed against their sitting-room window!'

'So Black was the Potters' Secret Keeper?' whispered Madam Rosmerta.

'Naturally,' said Professor McGonagall. 'James Potter told Dumbledore that Black would die rather than tell where they were, that Black was planning to go into hiding himself ... and yet, Dumbledore remained worried. I remember him offering to be the Potters' Secret Keeper himself.'

'He suspected Black?' gasped Madam Rosmerta.

'He was sure that somebody close to the Potters had been keeping You-Know-Who informed of their movements,' said Professor McGonagall darkly. 'Indeed, he had suspected for some time that someone on our side had turned traitor and was passing a lot of information to You-Know-Who.'

'But James Potter insisted on using Black?'

'He did,' said Fudge heavily. 'And then, barely a week after the Fidelius Charm had been performed –'

'Black betrayed them?' breathed Madam Rosmerta.

'He did indeed. Black was tired of his double-agent role, he was ready to declare his support openly for You-Know-Who, and he seems to have planned this for the moment of the Potters' death. But, as we all know, You-Know-Who met his downfall in little Harry Potter. Powers gone, horribly weakened, he fled. And this left Black in a very nasty position indeed. His Master had fallen at the very moment when he, Black, had shown his true colours as a traitor. He had no choice but to run for it –'

'Filthy, stinkin' turncoat!' Hagrid said, so loudly that half the bar went quiet.

'Shh!' said Professor McGonagall.

'I met him!' growled Hagrid. 'I musta bin the last ter see him before he killed all them people! It was me what rescued Harry from Lily an' James's house after they was killed! Jus' got him outta the ruins, poor little thing, with a great slash across his forehead, an' his parents dead ... an' Sirius Black turns up, on that flyin' motorbike he used ter ride. Never occurred ter me what he was doin' there. I didn' know he'd bin Lily an' James's Secret Keeper. Thought he'd jus' heard the news o' You-Know-Who's attack an' come ter see what he could do. White an' shakin', he was. An' yeh know what I did? I COMFORTED THE MURDERIN' TRAITOR!' Hagrid roared.

'Hagrid, please!' said Professor McGonagall. 'Keep your voice down!'

'How was I ter know he wasn' upset abou' Lily an' James? It was You-Know-Who he cared abou'! An' then he says, "Give Harry ter me, Hagrid, I'm his godfather, I'll look after him –" Ha! But I'd had me orders from Dumbledore, an' I told Black no, Dumbledore said Harry was ter go ter his aunt an' uncle's. Black argued, but in the end he gave in. Told me ter take his motorbike ter get Harry there. "I won' need it any more," he says.

'I shoulda known there was somethin' fishy goin' on then. He loved that motorbike, what was he givin' it ter me for? Why wouldn' he need it any more? Fact was, it was too easy ter trace. Dumbledore knew he'd bin the Potters' Secret Keeper. Black knew he was goin' ter have ter run fer it that night, knew it was a matter o' hours before the Ministry was after him.

'*But what if I'd given Harry to him, eh?* I bet he'd've pitched him off the bike halfway out ter sea. His bes' friend's son! But when a wizard goes over ter the dark side, there's nothin' and no one that matters to 'em any more ...'

A long silence followed Hagrid's story. Then Madam Rosmerta said with some satisfaction, 'But he didn't manage to disappear, did he? The Ministry of Magic caught up with him next day!'

'Alas, if only we had,' said Fudge bitterly. 'It was not we who found him. It was little Peter Pettigrew – another of the Potters' friends. Maddened by grief, no doubt, and knowing that Black had been the Potters' Secret Keeper, he went after Black himself.'

'Pettigrew ... that fat little boy who was always tagging around after them at Hogwarts?' said Madam Rosmerta.

'Hero-worshipped Black and Potter,' said Professor McGonagall. 'Never quite in their league, talent-wise. I was often rather sharp with him. You can imagine how I – how I regret that now ...' She sounded as though she had a sudden head cold.

'There, now, Minerva,' said Fudge kindly, 'Pettigrew died a hero's death. Eye-witnesses – Muggles, of course, we wiped their memories later – told us how Pettigrew cornered Black. They say he was sobbing. "Lily and James, Sirius! How could you!" And then he went for his wand. Well, of course, Black was quicker. Blew Pettigrew to smithereens ...'

Professor McGonagall blew her nose and said thickly, 'Stupid boy ... foolish boy ... he was always hopeless at duelling ... should have left it to the Ministry ...'

'I tell yeh, if I'd got ter Black before little Pettigrew did, I wouldn't've messed around with wands – I'd've ripped him limb – from – limb,' Hagrid growled.

'You don't know what you're talking about, Hagrid,' said Fudge sharply. 'Nobody but trained Hit Wizards from the Magical Law Enforcement Squad would have stood a chance against Black once he was cornered. I was Junior Minister in the Department of Magical Catastrophes at the time, and I was one of the first on the scene after Black murdered all those people. I – I will never forget it. I still dream about it sometimes. A crater in the middle of the street, so deep it had cracked the sewer below. Bodies everywhere. Muggles screaming. And Black standing there laughing, with what was left of Pettigrew in front of him ... a heap of blood-stained robes and a few – a few fragments –'

Fudge's voice stopped abruptly. There was the sound of five noses being blown.

'Well, there you have it, Rosmerta,' said Fudge thickly. 'Black was taken away by twenty members of the Magical Law Enforcement Patrol and Pettigrew received the Order of Merlin, First Class, which I think was some comfort to his poor mother. Black's been in Azkaban ever since.'

Madam Rosmerta let out a long sigh.

'Is it true he's mad, Minister?'

'I wish I could say that he was,' said Fudge slowly. 'I certainly believe his master's defeat unhinged him for a while. The murder of Pettigrew and all those Muggles was the action of a cornered and desperate man – cruel ... pointless. Yet I met Black on my last inspection of Azkaban. You know, most of the prisoners in there sit muttering to themselves in the dark, there's no sense in them ... but I was shocked at how *normal* Black seemed. He spoke quite rationally to me. It was unnerving. You'd have thought he was merely bored – asked if I'd finished with my newspaper, cool as you please, said he missed doing the crossword. Yes, I was astounded at how little effect the Dementors seemed to be having on him – and he was one of the most heavily guarded in the place, you know. Dementors outside his door, day and night.'

'But what do you think he's broken out to do?' said Madam Rosmerta. 'Good gracious, Minister, he isn't trying to rejoin You-Know-Who, is he?'

'I daresay that is his – er – eventual plan,' said Fudge evasively. 'But we hope to catch Black long before that. I must say, You-Know-Who alone and friendless is one thing ... but give him back his most devoted servant, and I shudder to think how quickly he'll rise again ...'

There was a small chink of glass on wood. Someone had set down their glass.

'You know, Cornelius, if you're dining with the Headmaster, we'd better head back up to the castle,' said Professor McGonagall.

One by one, the pairs of feet in front of Harry took the weight of their owners once more; hems of cloaks swung into sight and Madam Rosmerta's glittering heels disappeared behind the bar. The door of the Three Broomsticks opened again, there was another flurry of snow, and the teachers disappeared.

'Harry?'

Ron and Hermione's faces appeared under the table. They were both staring at him, lost for words.

CHAPTER ELEVEN

The Firebolt

Harry didn't have a very clear idea of how he had managed to get back into the Honeydukes cellar, through the tunnel and into the castle once more. All he knew was that the return trip seemed to take no time at all, and that he hardly noticed what he was doing, because his head was still pounding with the conversation he had just heard.

Why had nobody ever told him? Dumbledore, Hagrid, Mr Weasley, Cornelius Fudge ... why hadn't anyone ever mentioned the fact that Harry's parents had died because their best friend had betrayed them?

Ron and Hermione watched Harry nervously all through dinner, not daring to talk about what they'd overheard, because Percy was sitting close by them. When they went upstairs to the crowded common room, it was to find Fred and George had set off half-a-dozen Dungbombs in a fit of end-of-term high spirits. Harry, who didn't want Fred and George asking him whether he'd reached Hogsmeade or not, sneaked quietly up to the empty dormitory, and headed straight for his bedside cabinet. He pushed his books aside and quickly found what he was looking for – the leather-bound photo album Hagrid had given him two years ago, which was full of wizard pictures of his mother and father. He sat down on his bed, drew the hangings around him, and started turning the pages, searching, until ...

He stopped on a picture of his parents' wedding day. There was his father waving up at him, beaming, the untidy black hair Harry had inherited standing up in all directions. There was his mother, alight with happiness, arm in arm with his Dad. And there ... that must be him. Their best man ... Harry had never given him a thought before.

If he hadn't known it was the same person, he would never

have guessed it was Black in this old photograph. His face wasn't sunken and waxy, but handsome, full of laughter. Had he already been working for Voldemort when this picture had been taken? Was he already planning the deaths of the two people next to him? Did he realise he was facing twelve years in Azkaban, twelve years which would make him unrecognisable?

But the Dementors don't affect him, Harry thought, staring into the handsome, laughing face. *He doesn't have to hear my Mum screaming if they get too close –*

Harry slammed the album shut, reached over and stuffed it back into his cabinet, took off his robes and glasses and got into bed, making sure the hangings were hiding him from view.

The dormitory door opened.

'Harry?' said Ron's voice uncertainly.

But Harry lay still, pretending to be asleep. He heard Ron leave again, and rolled over on his back, his eyes wide open.

A hatred such as he had never known before was coursing through Harry like poison. He could see Black laughing at him through the darkness, as though somebody had pasted the picture from the album over his eyes. He watched, as though somebody was playing him a piece of film, Sirius Black blasting Peter Pettigrew (who resembled Neville Longbottom) into a thousand pieces. He could hear (though he had no idea what Black's voice might sound like) a low, excited mutter. 'It has happened, my Lord ... the Potters have made me their Secret Keeper ...' And then came another voice, laughing shrilly, the same laugh that Harry heard inside his head whenever the Dementors drew near ...

*

'Harry, you – you look terrible.'

Harry hadn't got to sleep until daybreak. He had awoken to find the dormitory deserted, dressed and gone down the spiral stair-case to a common room that was completely empty except for Ron, who was eating a Peppermint Toad and massaging his stom-ach, and Hermione, who had spread her homework over three tables.

'Where is everyone?' said Harry.

'Gone! It's the first day of the holidays, remember?' said Ron, watching Harry closely. 'It's nearly lunchtime, I was going to come and wake you up in a minute.'

Harry slumped into a chair next to the fire. Snow was still

falling outside the windows. Crookshanks was spread out in front of the fire like a large, ginger rug.

'You really don't look well, you know,' Hermione said, peering anxiously into his face.

'I'm fine,' said Harry.

'Harry, listen,' said Hermione, exchanging a look with Ron, 'you must be really upset about what we heard yesterday. But the thing is, you mustn't go doing anything stupid.'

'Like what?' said Harry.

'Like trying to go after Black,' said Ron sharply.

Harry could tell they had rehearsed this conversation while he had been asleep. He didn't say anything.

'You won't, will you, Harry?' said Hermione.

'Because Black's not worth dying for,' said Ron.

Harry looked at them. They didn't seem to understand at all.

'D'you know what I see and hear every time a Dementor gets too near me?' Ron and Hermione shook their heads, looking apprehensive. 'I can hear my mum screaming and pleading with Voldemort. And if you'd heard your mum screaming like that, just about to be killed, you wouldn't forget it in a hurry. And if you found out someone who was supposed to be a friend of hers betrayed her and sent Voldemort after her –'

'There's nothing you can do!' said Hermione, looking stricken. 'The Dementors will catch Black and he'll go back to Azkaban and – and serve him right!'

'You heard what Fudge said. Black isn't affected by Azkaban like normal people are. It's not a punishment for him like it is for the others.'

'So what are you saying?' said Ron, looking very tense. 'You want to – to kill Black or something?'

'Don't be silly,' said Hermione in a panicky voice. 'Harry doesn't want to kill anyone, do you, Harry?'

Again, Harry didn't answer. He didn't know what he wanted to do. All he knew was that the idea of doing nothing, while Black was at liberty, was almost more than he could stand.

'Malfoy knows,' he said abruptly. 'Remember what he said to me in Potions? "If it was me, I'd hunt him down myself ... I'd want revenge."'

'You're going to take Malfoy's advice instead of ours?' said Ron furiously. 'Listen ... you know what Pettigrew's mother got back after Black had finished with him? Dad told me – the Order of Merlin, First Class, and Pettigrew's finger in a box. That was the biggest bit of him they could find. Black's a madman, Harry, and he's dangerous –'

'Malfoy's dad must have told him,' said Harry, ignoring Ron. 'He was right in Voldemort's inner circle –'

'Say *You-Know-Who*, will you?' interjected Ron angrily.

'– so obviously, the Malfoys knew Black was working for Voldemort –'

'– and Malfoy'd love to see you blown into about a million pieces, like Pettigrew! Get a grip, Malfoy's just hoping you'll get yourself killed before he has to play you at Quidditch.'

'Harry, *please*,' said Hermione, her eyes now shining with tears, '*please* be sensible. Black did a terrible, terrible thing, but d-don't put yourself in danger, it's what Black wants ... oh, Harry, you'd be playing right into Black's hands if you went looking for him. Your mum and dad wouldn't want you to get hurt, would they? They'd never want you to go looking for Black!'

'I'll never know what they'd have wanted because, thanks to Black, I've never spoken to them,' said Harry shortly.

There was a silence, in which Crookshanks stretched luxuriously, flexing his claws. Ron's pocket quivered.

'Look,' said Ron, obviously casting around for a change of subject, 'it's the holidays! It's nearly Christmas! Let's – let's go down and see Hagrid. We haven't visited him for ages!'

'No!' said Hermione quickly. 'Harry isn't supposed to leave the castle, Ron –'

'Yeah, let's go,' said Harry, sitting up, 'and I can ask him how come he never mentioned Black when he told me all about my parents!'

Further discussion of Sirius Black plainly wasn't what Ron had had in mind.

'Or we could have a game of chess,' he said hastily, 'or Gobstones. Percy left a set –'

'No, let's visit Hagrid,' said Harry firmly.

So they got their cloaks from their dormitories and set off through the portrait hole ('Stand and fight, you yellow-bellied mongrels!'), down through the empty castle and out through the oak front doors.

They made their way slowly down the lawn, making a shallow

trench in the glittering, powdery snow, their socks and the hems of their cloaks soaked and freezing. The Forbidden Forest looked as though it had been enchanted, each tree smattered with silver, and Hagrid's cabin looked like an iced cake.

Ron knocked, but there was no answer.

'He's not out, is he?' said Hermione, who was shivering under her cloak.

Ron had his ear to the door.

'There's a weird noise,' he said. 'Listen – is that Fang?'

Harry and Hermione put their ears to the door, too. From inside the cabin came a series of low, throbbing moans.

'Think we'd better go and get someone?' said Ron nervously.

'Hagrid!' called Harry, thumping the door. 'Hagrid, are you in there?'

There was a sound of heavy footsteps, then the door creaked open. Hagrid stood there with his eyes red and swollen; tears splashing down the front of his leather waistcoat.

'Yeh've heard!' he bellowed, and he flung himself onto Harry's neck.

Hagrid being at least twice the size of a normal man, this was no laughing matter. Harry, about to collapse under Hagrid's weight, was rescued by Ron and Hermione, who each seized Hagrid under an arm and heaved him, Harry helping, back into the cabin. Hagrid allowed himself to be steered into a chair and slumped over the table, sobbing uncontrollably, his face glazed with tears which dripped down into his tangled beard.

'Hagrid, what is it?' said Hermione, aghast.

Harry spotted an official-looking letter lying open on the table.

'What's this, Hagrid?'

Hagrid's sobs redoubled, but he shoved the letter towards Harry, who picked it up and read aloud:

Dear Mr Hagrid,

Further to our inquiry into the attack by a Hippogriff on a student in your class, we have accepted the assurances of Professor Dumbledore that you bear no responsibility for the regrettable incident.

'Well, that's OK, then, Hagrid!' said Ron, clapping Hagrid on the shoulder. But Hagrid continued to sob, and waved one of his gigantic hands, inviting Harry to read on.

> *However, we must register our concern about the Hippogriff in question. We have decided to uphold the official complaint of Mr Lucius Malfoy, and this matter will therefore be taken to the Committee for the Disposal of Dangerous Creatures. The hearing will take place on April 20th, and we ask you to present yourself and your Hippogriff at the Committee's offices in London on that date. In the meantime, the Hippogriff should be kept tethered and isolated.*
>
> *Yours in fellowship ...*

There followed a list of the school governors.

'Oh,' said Ron. 'But you said Buckbeak isn't a bad Hippogriff, Hagrid. I bet he'll get off –'

'Yeh don' know them gargoyles at the Committee fer the Disposal o' Dangerous Creatures!' choked Hagrid, wiping his eyes on his sleeve. 'They've got it in fer interestin' creatures!'

A sudden sound from the corner of Hagrid's cabin made Harry, Ron and Hermione whip around. Buckbeak the Hippogriff was lying in the corner, chomping on something that was oozing blood all over the floor.

'I couldn' leave him tied up out there in the snow!' choked Hagrid. 'All on his own! At Christmas!'

Harry, Ron and Hermione looked at each other. They had never seen eye to eye with Hagrid about what he called 'interesting creatures' and other people called 'terrifying monsters'. On the other hand, there didn't seem to be any particular harm in Buckbeak. In fact, by Hagrid's usual standards, he was positively cute.

'You'll have to put up a good strong defence, Hagrid,' said Hermione, sitting down and laying a hand on Hagrid's massive forearm. 'I'm sure you can prove Buckbeak is safe.'

'Won' make no diff'rence!' sobbed Hagrid. 'Them Disposal devils, they're all in Lucius Malfoy's pocket! Scared o' him! An' if I lose the case, Buckbeak –'

Hagrid drew his finger swiftly across his throat, then gave a great wail and lurched forwards, his face in his arms.

'What about Dumbledore, Hagrid?' said Harry.

'He's done more'n enough fer me already,' groaned Hagrid. 'Got enough on his plate what with keepin' them Dementors outta the castle, an' Sirius Black lurkin' around –'

Ron and Hermione looked quickly at Harry, as though expecting him to start berating Hagrid for not telling him the truth about Black. But Harry couldn't bring himself to do it, not now he saw Hagrid so miserable and scared.

'Listen, Hagrid,' he said, 'you can't give up. Hermione's right, you just need a good defence. You can call us as witnesses –'

'I'm sure I've read about a case of Hippogriff-baiting,' said Hermione thoughtfully, 'where the Hippogriff got off. I'll look it up for you, Hagrid, and see exactly what happened.'

Hagrid howled still more loudly. Harry and Hermione looked at Ron to help them.

'Er – shall I make a cup of tea?' said Ron.

Harry stared at him.

'It's what my mum does whenever someone's upset,' Ron muttered, shrugging.

At last, after many more assurances of help, with a steaming mug of tea in front of him, Hagrid blew his nose on a handkerchief the size of a tablecloth and said, 'Yer right. I can' afford to go ter pieces. Gotta pull meself together ...'

Fang the boarhound came timidly out from under the table and laid his head on Hagrid's knee.

'I've not bin meself lately,' said Hagrid, stroking Fang with one hand and mopping his face with the other. 'Worried abou' Buckbeak, an' no one likin' me classes –'

'We do like them!' lied Hermione at once.

'Yeah, they're great!' said Ron, crossing his fingers under the table. 'Er – how are the Flobberworms?'

'Dead,' said Hagrid gloomily. 'Too much lettuce.'

'Oh, no!' said Ron, his lip twitching.

'An' them Dementors make me feel ruddy terrible an' all,' said Hagrid, with a sudden shudder. 'Gotta walk past 'em ev'ry time I want a drink in the Three Broomsticks. 'S like bein' back in Azkaban –'

He fell silent, gulping his tea. Harry, Ron and Hermione watched him breathlessly. They had never heard Hagrid talk about his brief spell in Azkaban before. After a brief pause, Hermione said timidly, 'Is it awful in there, Hagrid?'

'Yeh've no idea,' said Hagrid quietly. 'Never bin anywhere like it. Thought I was goin' mad. Kep' goin' over horrible stuff in me mind ... the day I got expelled from Hogwarts ... day me Dad died ... day I had ter let Norbert go ...'

His eyes filled with tears. Norbert was the baby dragon Hagrid had once won in a game of cards.

'Yeh can' really remember who yeh are after a while. An' yeh can' see the point o' livin' at all. I used ter hope I'd jus' die in me sleep ... when they let me out, it was like bein' born again, ev'rythin' came floodin' back, it was the bes' feelin' in the world. Mind, the Dementors weren't keen on lettin' me go.'

'But you were innocent!' said Hermione.

Hagrid snorted.

'Think that matters to them? They don' care. Long as they've got a couple o' hundred humans stuck there with 'em, so they can leech all the happiness out of 'em, they don' give a damn who's guilty an' who's not.'

Hagrid went quiet for a moment, staring into his tea. Then he said quietly, 'Thought o' jus' letting Buckbeak go ... tryin' ter make him fly away ... but how d'yeh explain ter a Hippogriff it's gotta go inter hidin'? An' – an' I'm scared o' breakin' the law ...' He looked up at them, tears leaking down his face again. 'I don' ever want ter go back ter Azkaban.'

*

The trip to Hagrid's, though far from fun, had nevertheless had the effect Ron and Hermione had hoped. Though Harry had by no means forgotten about Black, he couldn't brood constantly on revenge if he wanted to help Hagrid win his case against the Committee for the Disposal of Dangerous Creatures. He, Ron and Hermione went to the library next day, and returned to the empty common room laden with books which might help prepare a defence for Buckbeak. The three of them sat in front of the roaring fire, slowly turning the pages of dusty volumes about famous cases of marauding beasts, speaking occasionally when they ran across something relevant.

'Here's something ... there was a case in 1722 ... but the Hippogriff was convicted – urgh, look what they did to it, that's disgusting –'

'This might help, look – a Manticore savaged someone in 1296, and they let the Manticore off – oh – no, that was only because everyone was too scared to go near it ...'

Meanwhile, in the rest of the castle, the usual magnificent

Christmas decorations had been put up, despite the fact that hardly any of the students remained to enjoy them. Thick streamers of holly and mistletoe were strung along the corridors, mysterious lights shone from inside every suit of armour and the Great Hall was filled with its usual twelve Christmas trees, glittering with golden stars. A powerful and delicious smell of cooking pervaded the corridors, and by Christmas Eve, it had grown so strong that even Scabbers poked his nose out of the shelter of Ron's pocket to sniff hopefully at the air.

On Christmas morning, Harry was woken by Ron throwing his pillow at him.

'Oy! Presents!'

Harry reached for his glasses and put them on, squinting through the semi-darkness to the foot of his bed, where a small heap of parcels had appeared. Ron was already ripping the paper off his own presents.

'Another jumper from Mum ... maroon *again* ... see if you've got one.'

Harry had. Mrs Weasley had sent him a scarlet jumper with the Gryffindor lion knitted on the front, also a dozen home-baked mince pies, some Christmas cake and a box of nut brittle. As he moved all these things aside, he saw a long, thin package lying underneath.

'What's that?' said Ron, looking over, a freshly unwrapped pair of maroon socks in his hand.

'Dunno ...'

Harry ripped the parcel open and gasped as a magnificent, gleaming broomstick rolled out onto his bedspread. Ron dropped his socks and jumped off his bed for a closer look.

'I don't believe it,' he said hoarsely.

It was a Firebolt, identical to the dream broom Harry had gone to see every day in Diagon Alley. Its handle glittered as he picked it up. He could feel it vibrating, and let go; it hung in mid-air, unsupported, at exactly the right height for him to mount it. His eyes moved from the golden registration number at the top of the handle right down to the perfectly smooth, streamlined birch twigs that made up the tail.

'Who sent it to you?' said Ron in a hushed voice.

'Look and see if there's a card,' said Harry.

Ron ripped apart the Firebolt's wrappings.

'Nothing! Blimey, who'd spend that much on you?'

'Well,' said Harry, feeling stunned, 'I'm betting it wasn't the Dursleys.'

'I bet it was Dumbledore,' said Ron, now walking round and round the Firebolt, taking in every glorious inch. 'He sent you the Invisibility Cloak anonymously ...'

'That was my dad's, though,' said Harry. 'Dumbledore was just passing it on to me. He wouldn't spend hundreds of Galleons on me. He can't go giving students stuff like this –'

'That's why he wouldn't say it was from him!' said Ron. 'In case some git like Malfoy said it was favouritism. Hey, Harry –' Ron gave a great whoop of laughter, 'Malfoy! Wait 'til he sees you on this! He'll be sick as a pig! This is an international-standard broom, this is!'

'I can't believe this,' Harry muttered, running a hand along the Firebolt, while Ron sank onto Harry's bed, laughing his head off at the thought of Malfoy. 'Who –?'

'I know,' said Ron, controlling himself. 'I know who it could've been – Lupin!'

'What?' said Harry, now starting to laugh himself. 'Lupin? Listen, if he had this much gold, he'd be able to buy himself some new robes.'

'Yeah, but he likes you,' said Ron. 'And he was away when your Nimbus got smashed, and he might've heard about it and decided to visit Diagon Alley and get this for you –'

'What d'you mean, he was away?' said Harry. 'He was ill when I was playing in that match.'

'Well, he wasn't in the hospital wing,' said Ron. 'I was there, cleaning out the bedpans on that detention from Snape, remember?'

Harry frowned at Ron.

'I can't see Lupin affording something like this.'

'What're you two laughing about?'

Hermione had just come in, wearing her dressing-gown and carrying Crookshanks, who was looking very grumpy, with a string of tinsel tied around his neck.

'Don't bring him in here!' said Ron, hurriedly snatching Scabbers from the depths of his bed and stowing him in his pyjama pocket. But Hermione wasn't listening. She dropped Crookshanks onto Seamus's empty bed and stared, open-mouthed, at the Firebolt.

'Oh, *Harry*! Who sent you *that*?'

'No idea,' said Harry. 'There wasn't a card or anything with it.'

To his great surprise, Hermione did not appear either excited or intrigued by this news. On the contrary, her face fell, and she bit her lip.

'What's the matter with you?' said Ron.

'I don't know,' said Hermione slowly, 'but it's a bit odd, isn't it? I mean, this is supposed to be quite a good broom, isn't it?'

Ron sighed exasperatedly.

'It's the best broom there is, Hermione,' he said.

'So it must've been really expensive ...'

'Probably cost more than all the Slytherins' brooms put together,' said Ron happily.

'Well ... who'd send Harry something as expensive as that, and not even tell him they'd sent it?' said Hermione.

'Who cares?' said Ron, impatiently. 'Listen, Harry, can I have a go on it? Can I?'

'I don't think anyone should ride that broom just yet!' said Hermione shrilly.

Harry and Ron looked at her.

'What d'you think Harry's going to do with it – sweep the floor?' said Ron.

But before Hermione could answer, Crookshanks sprang from Seamus's bed, right at Ron's chest.

'GET – HIM – OUT – OF – HERE!' Ron bellowed, as Crookshanks's claws ripped his pyjamas and Scabbers attempted a wild escape over his shoulder. Ron seized Scabbers by the tail and aimed a misjudged kick at Crookshanks which hit the trunk at the end of Harry's bed, knocking it over and causing Ron to hop on the spot, howling with pain.

Crookshanks's fur suddenly stood on end. A shrill, tinny whistling was filling the room. The Pocket Sneakoscope had become dislodged from Uncle Vernon's old socks and was whirling and gleaming on the floor.

'I forgot about that!' Harry said, bending down and picking up the Sneakoscope. 'I never wear those socks if I can help it ...'

The Sneakoscope whirled and whistled in his palm. Crookshanks was hissing and spitting at it.

'You'd better take that cat out of here, Hermione,' said Ron furiously; he was sitting on Harry's bed nursing his toe. 'Can't you shut that thing up?' he added to Harry, as Hermione strode out of the room, Crookshanks's yellow eyes still fixed maliciously on Ron.

Harry stuffed the Sneakoscope back inside the socks and threw it back into his trunk. All that could be heard now was Ron's stifled moans of pain and rage. Scabbers was huddled in Ron's hands. It had been a while since Harry had seen him out of Ron's pocket, and he was unpleasantly surprised to see that Scabbers, once so fat, was now very skinny; patches of fur seemed to have fallen out, too.

'He's not looking too good, is he?' Harry said.

'It's stress!' said Ron. 'He'd be fine if that stupid great furball left him alone!'

But Harry, remembering what the woman at the Magical Menagerie had said about rats only living three years, couldn't help feeling that unless Scabbers had powers he had never revealed, he was reaching the end of his life. And despite Ron's frequent complaints that Scabbers was both boring and useless, he was sure Ron would be very miserable if Scabbers died.

Christmas spirit was definitely thin on the ground in the Gryffindor common room that morning. Hermione had shut Crookshanks in her dormitory, but was furious with Ron for trying to kick him; Ron was still fuming about Crookshanks's fresh attempt to eat Scabbers. Harry gave up trying to make them talk to each other, and devoted himself to examining the Firebolt, which he had brought down to the common room with him. For some reason this seemed to annoy Hermione as well; she didn't say anything, but she kept looking darkly at the broom as though it, too, had been criticising her cat.

At lunchtime they went down to the Great Hall, to find that the house tables had been moved against the walls again, and that a single table, set for twelve, stood in the middle of the room. Professors Dumbledore, McGonagall, Snape, Sprout and Flitwick were there, along with Filch, the caretaker, who had taken off his usual brown coat and was wearing a very old and rather mouldy-looking tail coat. There were only three other students: two extremely nervous-looking first-years and a sullen-faced Slytherin fifth-year.

'Merry Christmas!' said Dumbledore, as Harry, Ron and Hermione approached the table. 'As there are so few of us, it seemed foolish to use the house tables ... sit down, sit down!'

Harry, Ron and Hermione sat down side by side at the end of the table.

'Crackers!' said Dumbledore enthusiastically, offering the end of a large silver one to Snape, who took it reluctantly and tugged. With a bang like a gunshot, the cracker flew apart to reveal a large, pointed witch's hat topped with a stuffed vulture.

Harry, remembering the Boggart, caught Ron's eye and they both grinned; Snape's mouth thinned and he pushed the hat towards Dumbledore, who swapped it for his wizard's hat at once.

'Tuck in!' he advised the table, beaming around.

As Harry was helping himself to roast potatoes, the doors of the Great Hall opened again. It was Professor Trelawney, gliding towards them as though on wheels. She had put on a green sequined dress in honour of the occasion, making her look more than ever like a glittering, oversize dragonfly.

'Sybill, this is a pleasant surprise!' said Dumbledore, standing up.

'I have been crystal-gazing, Headmaster,' said Professor Trelawney, in her mistiest, most faraway voice, 'and to my astonishment, I saw myself abandoning my solitary luncheon and coming to join you. Who am I to refuse the promptings of fate? I at once hastened from my tower, and I do beg you to forgive my lateness ...'

'Certainly, certainly,' said Dumbledore, his eyes twinkling. 'Let me draw you up a chair –'

And he did indeed draw a chair in mid-air with his wand, which revolved for a few seconds before falling with a thud between Professors Snape and McGonagall. Professor Trelawney, however, did not sit down; her enormous eyes had been roving around the table, and she suddenly uttered a kind of soft scream.

'I dare not, Headmaster! If I join the table, we shall be thirteen! Nothing could be more unlucky! Never forget that when thirteen dine together, the first to rise will be the first to die!'

'We'll risk it, Sybill,' said Professor McGonagall impatiently. 'Do sit down, the turkey's getting stone cold.'

Professor Trelawney hesitated, then lowered herself into the empty chair, eyes shut and mouth clenched tight, as though expecting a thunderbolt to hit the table. Professor McGonagall poked a large spoon into the nearest tureen.

'Tripe, Sybill?'

Professor Trelawney ignored her. Eyes open again, she looked around once more and said, 'But where is dear Professor Lupin?'

'I'm afraid the poor fellow is ill again,' said Dumbledore, indicating that everybody should start serving themselves. 'Most unfortunate that it should happen on Christmas Day.'

'But surely you already knew that, Sybill?' said Professor McGonagall, her eyebrows raised.

Professor Trelawney gave Professor McGonagall a very cold look.

'Certainly I knew, Minerva,' she said quietly. 'But one does not parade the fact that one is All-Knowing. I frequently act as though I am not possessed of the Inner Eye, so as not to make others nervous.'

'That explains a great deal,' said Professor McGonagall tartly.

Professor Trelawney's voice suddenly became a good deal less misty.

'If you must know, Minerva, I have seen that poor Professor Lupin will not be with us for very long. He seems aware, himself, that his time is short. He positively fled when I offered to crystal-gaze for him –'

'Imagine that,' said Professor McGonagall drily.

'I doubt,' said Dumbledore, in a cheerful but slightly raised voice, which put an end to Professor McGonagall and Professor Trelawney's conversation, 'that Professor Lupin is in any immediate danger. Severus, you've made the Potion for him again?'

'Yes, Headmaster,' said Snape.

'Good,' said Dumbledore. 'Then he should be up and about in no time ... Derek, have you had any of these chipolatas? They're excellent.'

The first-year boy went furiously red on being addressed directly by Dumbledore, and took the platter of sausages with trembling hands.

Professor Trelawney behaved almost normally until the very end of Christmas dinner, two hours later. Full to bursting with Christmas dinner and still wearing their cracker hats, Harry and Ron got up first from the table and she shrieked loudly.

'My dears! Which of you left his seat first? Which?'

'Dunno,' said Ron, looking uneasily at Harry.

'I doubt it will make much difference,' said Professor

McGonagall coldly, 'unless a mad axe-man is waiting outside the doors to slaughter the first into the Entrance Hall.'

Even Ron laughed. Professor Trelawney looked highly affronted.

'Coming?' Harry said to Hermione.

'No,' Hermione muttered. 'I want a quick word with Professor McGonagall.'

'Probably trying to see if she can take any more classes,' yawned Ron as they made their way into the Entrance Hall, which was completely devoid of mad axe-men.

When they reached the portrait hole they found Sir Cadogan enjoying a Christmas party with a couple of monks, several previous Headmasters of Hogwarts and his fat pony. He pushed up his visor and toasted them with a flagon of mead.

'Merry – hic – Christmas! Password?'

'Scurvy cur,' said Ron.

'And the same to you, sir!' roared Sir Cadogan, as the painting swung forward to admit them.

Harry went straight up to the dormitory, collected his Firebolt and the Broomstick Servicing Kit Hermione had given him for his birthday, brought them downstairs and tried to find something to do to the Firebolt; however, there were no bent twigs to clip, and the handle was so shiny already it seemed pointless to polish it. He and Ron simply sat admiring it from every angle, until the portrait hole opened, and Hermione came in, accompanied by Professor McGonagall.

Though Professor McGonagall was Head of Gryffindor house, Harry had only seen her in the common room once before, and that had been to make a very grave announcement. He and Ron stared at her, both holding the Firebolt. Hermione walked around them, sat down, picked up the nearest book and hid her face behind it.

'So that's it, is it?' said Professor McGonagall beadily, walking over to the fireside and staring at the Firebolt. 'Miss Granger has just informed me that you have been sent a broomstick, Potter.'

Harry and Ron looked around at Hermione. They could see her forehead reddening over the top of her book, which was upside-down.

'May I?' said Professor McGonagall, but she didn't wait for an answer before pulling the Firebolt out of their hands. She examined it carefully from handle to twig-ends. 'Hmm. And there was no note at all, Potter? No card? No message of any kind?'

'No,' said Harry blankly.

'I see ...' said Professor McGonagall. 'Well, I'm afraid I will have to take this, Potter.'

'W-what?' said Harry, scrambling to his feet. 'Why?'

'It will need to be checked for jinxes,' said Professor McGonagall. 'Of course, I'm no expert, but I daresay Madam Hooch and Professor Flitwick will strip it down –'

'Strip it down?' repeated Ron, as though Professor McGonagall was mad.

'It shouldn't take more than a few weeks,' said Professor McGonagall. 'You will have it back if we are sure it is jinx-free.'

'There's nothing wrong with it!' said Harry, his voice shaking slightly. 'Honestly, Professor –'

'You can't know that, Potter,' said Professor McGonagall, quite kindly, 'not until you've flown it, at any rate, and I'm afraid that is out of the question until we are certain that it has not been tampered with. I shall keep you informed.'

Professor McGonagall turned on her heel and carried the Firebolt out of the portrait hole, which closed behind her. Harry stood staring after her, the tin of High-Finish Polish still clutched in his hands. Ron, however, rounded on Hermione.

'*What did you go running to McGonagall for?*'

Hermione threw her book aside. She was still pink in the face, but stood up and faced Ron defiantly.

'Because I thought – and Professor McGonagall agrees with me – that that broom was probably sent to Harry by Sirius Black!'

— CHAPTER TWELVE —

The Patronus

Harry knew that Hermione had meant well, but that didn't stop him being angry with her. He had been the owner of the best broom in the world for a few short hours, and now, because of her interference, he didn't know whether he would ever see it again. He was positive that there was nothing wrong with the Firebolt now, but what sort of state would it be in once it had been subjected to all sorts of anti-jinx tests?

Ron was furious with Hermione, too. As far as he was concerned, the stripping-down of a brand-new Firebolt was nothing less than criminal damage. Hermione, who remained convinced that she had acted for the best, started avoiding the common room. Harry and Ron supposed she had taken refuge in the library, and didn't try and persuade her to come back. All in all, they were glad when the rest of the school returned shortly after New Year, and Gryffindor Tower became crowded and noisy again.

Wood sought Harry out on the night before term started.

'Had a good Christmas?' he said, and then, without waiting for an answer, he sat down, lowered his voice and said, 'I've been doing some thinking over Christmas, Harry. After the last match, you know. If the Dementors come to the next one ... I mean ... we can't afford you to – well –'

Wood broke off, looking awkward.

'I'm working on it,' said Harry quickly. 'Professor Lupin said he'd train me to ward the Dementors off. We should be starting this week; he said he'd have time after Christmas.'

'Ah,' said Wood, his expression clearing. 'Well, in that case – I really didn't want to lose you as Seeker, Harry. And have you ordered a new broom yet?'

'No,' said Harry.

'What! You'd better get a move on, you know – you can't ride that Shooting Star against Ravenclaw!'

'He got a Firebolt for Christmas,' said Ron.

'A *Firebolt*? No! Seriously? A – a real *Firebolt*?'

'Don't get excited, Oliver,' said Harry gloomily. 'I haven't got it any more. It was confiscated.' And he explained all about how the Firebolt was now being checked for jinxes.

'Jinxed? How could it be jinxed?'

'Sirius Black,' Harry said wearily. 'He's supposed to be after me. So McGonagall reckons he might have sent it.'

Waving aside the information that a famous murderer was after his Seeker, Wood said, 'But Black couldn't have bought a Firebolt! He's on the run! The whole country's on the lookout for him! How could he just walk into Quality Quidditch Supplies and buy a broomstick?'

'I know,' said Harry, 'but McGonagall still wants to strip it down –'

Wood went pale.

'I'll go and talk to her, Harry,' he promised. 'I'll make her see reason ... a Firebolt ... a real Firebolt, on our team ... she wants Gryffindor to win as much as we do ... I'll make her see sense ... a *Firebolt* ...'

*

Lessons started again next day. The last thing anyone felt like doing was spending two hours in the grounds on a raw January morning, but Hagrid had provided a bonfire full of salamanders for their enjoyment, and they spent an unusually good lesson collecting dry wood and leaves to keep the fire blazing, while the flame-loving lizards scampered up and down the crumbling, white-hot logs. The first Divination lesson of the new term was much less fun; Professor Trelawney was now teaching them palmistry, and she lost no time in informing Harry that he had the shortest life-lines she had ever seen.

It was Defence Against the Dark Arts that Harry was keen to get to; after his conversation with Wood, he wanted to get started on his Anti-Dementor lessons as soon as possible.

'Ah yes,' said Lupin, when Harry reminded him of his promise at the end of class. 'Let me see ... how about eight o'clock on Thursday evening? The History of Magic classroom should be large enough ... I'll have to think carefully about how we're going

to do this ... we can't bring a real Dementor into the castle to practise on ...'

'Still looks ill, doesn't he?' said Ron, as they walked down the
corridor, heading to dinner. 'What d'you reckon's the matter with
him?'

There was a loud and impatient 'tuh' from behind them. It was
Hermione, who had been sitting at the feet of a suit of armour, re-
packing her bag, which was so full of books it wouldn't close.

'And what are you tutting at us for?' said Ron irritably.

'Nothing,' said Hermione in a lofty voice, heaving her bag back
over her shoulder.

'Yes, you were,' said Ron. 'I said I wonder what's wrong with
Lupin, and you –'

'Well, isn't it *obvious*?' said Hermione, with a look of madden-
ing superiority.

'If you don't want to tell us, don't,' snapped Ron.

'Fine,' said Hermione haughtily, and she marched off.

'She doesn't know,' said Ron, staring resentfully after Hermione.
'She's just trying to get us to talk to her again.'

*

At eight o'clock on Thursday evening, Harry left Gryffindor Tower
for the History of Magic classroom. It was dark and empty when
he arrived, but he lit the lamps with his wand and had waited
only five minutes when Professor Lupin turned up, carrying a
large packing case, which he heaved onto Professor Binns' desk.

'What's that?' said Harry.

'Another Boggart,' said Lupin, stripping off his cloak. 'I've been
combing the castle ever since Tuesday, and very luckily, I found
this one lurking inside Mr Filch's filing cabinet. It's the nearest
we'll get to a real Dementor. The Boggart will turn into a
Dementor when he sees you, so we'll be able to practise on him. I
can store him in my office when we're not using him; there's a
cupboard under my desk he'll like.'

'OK,' said Harry, trying to sound as though he wasn't apprehensive at all and merely glad that Lupin had found such a good sub-
stitute for a real Dementor.

'So ...' Professor Lupin had taken out his own wand, and indicated that Harry should do the same. 'The spell I am going to try
and teach you is highly advanced magic, Harry – well beyond
Ordinary Wizarding Level. It is called the Patronus Charm.'

'How does it work?' said Harry nervously.

'Well, when it works correctly, it conjures up a Patronus,' said Lupin, 'which is a kind of Anti-Dementor – a guardian which acts as a shield between you and the Dementor.'

Harry had a sudden vision of himself crouching behind a Hagrid-sized figure holding a large club. Professor Lupin continued, 'The Patronus is a kind of positive force, a projection of the very things that the Dementor feeds upon – hope, happiness, the desire to survive – but it cannot feel despair, as real humans can, so the Dementors can't hurt it. But I must warn you, Harry, that the Charm might be too advanced for you. Many qualified wizards have difficulty with it.'

'What does a Patronus look like?' said Harry curiously.

'Each one is unique to the wizard who conjures it.'

'And how do you conjure it?'

'With an incantation, which will work only if you are concentrating, with all your might, on a single, very happy memory.'

Harry cast about for a happy memory. Certainly, nothing that had happened to him at the Dursleys' was going to do. Finally, he settled on the moment when he had first ridden a broomstick.

'Right,' he said, trying to recall as exactly as possible the wonderful, soaring sensation in his stomach.

'The incantation is this –' Lupin cleared his throat, '*expecto patronum!*'

'*Expecto patronum*,' Harry repeated under his breath, '*expecto patronum.*'

'Concentrating hard on your happy memory?'

'Oh – yeah –' said Harry, quickly forcing his thoughts back to that first broom-ride. '*Expecto patrono* – no, *patronum* – sorry – *expecto patronum*, *expecto patronum* –'

Something whooshed suddenly out of the end of his wand; it looked like a wisp of silvery gas.

'Did you see that?' said Harry excitedly. 'Something happened!'

'Very good,' said Lupin, smiling. 'Right then – ready to try it on a Dementor?'

'Yes,' Harry said, gripping his wand very tightly, and moving into the middle of the deserted classroom. He tried to keep his mind on flying, but something else kept intruding ... any second now, he might hear his mother again ... but he shouldn't think that, or he *would* hear her again, and he didn't want to ... or did he?

Lupin grasped the lid of the packing case and pulled.

A Dementor rose slowly from the box, its hooded face turned towards Harry, one glistening, scabbed hand gripping its cloak. The lamps around the classroom flickered and went out. The Dementor stepped from the box and started to sweep silently towards Harry, drawing a deep, rattling breath. A wave of piercing cold broke over him –

'*Expecto patronum!*' Harry yelled. '*Expecto patronum! Expecto –*'

But the classroom and the Dementor were dissolving ... Harry was falling again through thick white fog, and his mother's voice was louder than ever, echoing inside his head – '*Not Harry! Not Harry! Please – I'll do anything –*'

'*Stand aside – stand aside, girl –*'

'Harry!'

Harry jerked back to life. He was lying flat on his back on the floor. The classroom lamps were alight again. He didn't have to ask what had happened.

'Sorry,' he muttered, sitting up and feeling cold sweat trickling down behind his glasses.

'Are you all right?' said Lupin.

'Yes ...' Harry pulled himself up on one of the desks and leant against it.

'Here –' Lupin handed him a Chocolate Frog. 'Eat this before we try again. I didn't expect you to do it first time. In fact, I would have been astounded if you had.'

'It's getting worse,' Harry muttered, biting the Frog's head off. 'I could hear her louder that time – and him – Voldemort –'

Lupin looked paler than usual.

'Harry, if you don't want to continue, I will more than understand –'

'I do!' said Harry fiercely, stuffing the rest of the Chocolate Frog into his mouth. 'I've got to! What if the Dementors turn up at our match against Ravenclaw? I can't afford to fall off again. If we lose this game we've lost the Quidditch Cup!'

'All right then ...' said Lupin. 'You might want to select another memory, a happy memory, I mean, to concentrate on ... that one doesn't seem to have been strong enough ...'

Harry thought hard, and decided his feelings when Gryffindor

had won the House Championship last year had definitely qualified as very happy. He gripped his wand tightly again, and took up
his position in the middle of the classroom.

'Ready?' said Lupin, gripping the box lid.

'Ready,' said Harry, trying hard to fill his head with happy
thoughts about Gryffindor winning, and not dark thoughts about
what was going to happen when the box opened.

'Go!' said Lupin, pulling off the lid. The room went icily cold
and dark once more. The Dementor glided forwards, drawing its
rattly breath; one rotting hand was extending towards Harry –

'Expecto patronum!' Harry yelled. 'Expecto patronum! Expecto
pat–'

White fog obscured his senses ... big, blurred shapes were moving around him ... then came a new voice, a man's voice, shouting,
panicking –

'Lily, take Harry and go! It's him! Go! Run! I'll hold him off –'

*The sounds of someone stumbling from a room – a door bursting
open – a cackle of high-pitched laughter –*

'Harry! Harry ... wake up ...'

Lupin was tapping Harry hard on the face. This time it was a
minute before Harry understood why he was lying on a dusty
classroom floor.

'I heard my dad,' Harry mumbled. 'That's the first time I've ever
heard him – he tried to take on Voldemort himself, to give my
mum time to run for it ...'

Harry suddenly realised that there were tears on his face min-
gling with the sweat. He bent his face low as possible, wiping
them off on his robes, pretending to do up his shoelace, so that
Lupin wouldn't see.

'You heard James?' said Lupin, in a strange voice.

'Yeah ...' Face dry, Harry looked up. 'Why – you didn't know my
dad, did you?'

'I – I did, as a matter of fact,' said Lupin. 'We were friends at
Hogwarts. Listen, Harry – perhaps we should leave it here for
tonight. This charm is ridiculously advanced ... I shouldn't have
suggested putting you through this ...'

'No!' said Harry. He got up again. 'I'll have one more go! I'm not
thinking of happy enough things, that's what it is ... hang on ...'

He racked his brains. A really, really happy memory ... one that
he could turn into a good, strong Patronus ...

The moment when he'd first found out he was a wizard, and would be leaving the Dursleys for Hogwarts! If that wasn't a happy memory, he didn't know what was ... concentrating very hard on how he had felt when he'd realised he'd be leaving Privet Drive, Harry got to his feet and faced the packing case once more.

'Ready?' said Lupin, who looked as though he was doing this against his better judgement. 'Concentrating hard? All right – go!'

He pulled off the lid of the case for the third time, and the Dementor rose out of it; the room fell cold and dark –

'EXPECTO PATRONUM!' Harry bellowed. 'EXPECTO PATRONUM! EXPECTO PATRONUM!'

The screaming inside Harry's head had started again – except this time, it sounded as though it was coming from a badly tuned radio. Softer and louder and softer again ... and he could still see the Dementor ... it had halted ... and then a huge, silver shadow came bursting out of the end of Harry's wand, to hover between him and the Dementor, and though Harry's legs felt like water, he was still on his feet ... though for how much longer, he wasn't sure ...

'Riddikulus!' roared Lupin, springing forwards.

There was a loud crack, and Harry's cloudy Patronus vanished along with the Dementor; he sank into a chair, feeling as exhausted as if he'd just run a mile, his legs shaking. Out of the corner of his eye, he saw Professor Lupin forcing the Boggart back into the packing case with his wand; it had turned into a silvery orb again.

'Excellent!' Lupin said, striding over to where Harry sat. 'Excellent, Harry! That was definitely a start!'

'Can we have another go? Just one more go?'

'Not now,' said Lupin firmly. 'You've had enough for one night. Here –'

He handed Harry a large bar of Honeydukes' best chocolate.

'Eat the lot, or Madam Pomfrey will be after my blood. Same time next week?'

'OK,' said Harry. He took a bite of the chocolate and watched Lupin extinguishing the lamps that had rekindled with the disappearance of the Dementor. A thought had just occurred to him.

'Professor Lupin?' he said. 'If you knew my dad, you must've known Sirius Black as well.'

Lupin turned very quickly.

'What gives you that idea?' he said sharply.

'Nothing – I mean, I just knew they were friends at Hogwarts, too ...'

Lupin's face relaxed.

'Yes, I knew him,' he said shortly. 'Or I thought I did. You'd better get off, Harry, it's getting late.'

Harry left the classroom, walked along the corridor and around a corner, then took a detour behind a suit of armour and sank down on its plinth to finish his chocolate, wishing he hadn't mentioned Black, as Lupin was obviously not keen on the subject. Then Harry's thoughts wandered back to his mother and father ...

He felt drained and strangely empty, even though he was so full of chocolate. Terrible though it was to hear his parents' last moments replayed inside his head, these were the only times Harry had heard their voices since he was a very small child. But he'd never be able to produce a proper Patronus if he half wanted to hear his parents again ...

'They're dead,' he told himself sternly. 'They're dead, and listening to echoes of them won't bring them back. You'd better get a grip on yourself if you want that Quidditch Cup.'

He stood up, crammed the last bit of chocolate into his mouth and headed back to Gryffindor Tower.

*

Ravenclaw played Slytherin a week after the start of term. Slytherin won, though narrowly. According to Wood, this was good news for Gryffindor, who would take second place if they beat Ravenclaw too. He therefore increased the number of team practices to five a week. This meant that with Lupin's Anti-Dementor classes, which in themselves were more draining than six Quidditch practices, Harry had just one night a week to do all his homework. Even so, he wasn't showing the strain nearly as much as Hermione, whose immense workload finally seemed to be getting to her. Every night, without fail, Hermione was to be seen in a corner of the common room, several tables spread with books, Arithmancy charts, Rune dictionaries, diagrams of Muggles lifting heavy objects, and file upon file of extensive notes; she barely spoke to anybody, and snapped when she was interrupted.

'How's she doing it?' Ron muttered to Harry one evening, as Harry sat finishing a nasty essay on Undetectable Poisons for Snape. Harry looked up. Hermione was barely visible behind a tottering pile of books.

'Doing what?'

'Getting to all her classes!' Ron said. 'I heard her talking to Professor Vector, that Arithmancy witch, this morning. They were going on about yesterday's lesson, but Hermione can't've been there, because she was with us in Care of Magical Creatures! And Ernie McMillan told me she's never missed a Muggle Studies class, but half of them are at the same time as Divination, and she's never missed one of them, either!'

Harry didn't have time to fathom the mystery of Hermione's impossible timetable at the moment; he really needed to get on with Snape's essay. Two seconds later, however, he was interrupted again, this time by Wood.

'Bad news, Harry. I've just been to see Professor McGonagall about the Firebolt. She – er – got a bit shirty with me. Told me I'd got my priorities wrong. Seemed to think I cared more about winning the Cup than I do about you staying alive. Just because I told her I didn't care if it threw you off, as long as you caught the Snitch on it first.' Wood shook his head in disbelief. 'Honestly, the way she was yelling at me ... you'd think I'd said something terrible. Then I asked her how much longer she was going to keep it ...' He screwed up his face and imitated Professor McGonagall's severe voice, '"As long as necessary, Wood" ... I reckon it's time you ordered a new broom, Harry. There's an order form at the back of *Which Broomstick* ... you could get a Nimbus Two Thousand and One, like Malfoy's got.'

'I'm not buying anything Malfoy thinks is good,' said Harry flatly.

*

January faded imperceptibly into February, with no change in the bitterly cold weather. The match against Ravenclaw was drawing nearer and nearer, but Harry still hadn't ordered a new broom. He was now asking Professor McGonagall for news of the Firebolt after every Transfiguration lesson, Ron standing hopefully at his shoulder, Hermione rushing past with her face averted.

'No, Potter, you can't have it back yet,' Professor McGonagall told him the twelfth time this happened, before he'd even opened his mouth. 'We've checked for most of the usual curses, but Professor Flitwick believes the broom might be carrying a Hurling Hex. I shall *tell* you once we've finished checking it. Now, please stop badgering me.'

To make matters even worse, Harry's Anti-Dementor lessons were not going nearly as well as he had hoped. Several sessions on, he was able to produce an indistinct, silvery shadow every time the Boggart-Dementor approached him, but his Patronus was too feeble to drive the Dementor away. All it did was hover, like a semi-transparent cloud, draining Harry of energy as he fought to keep it there. Harry felt angry with himself, guilty about his secret desire to hear his parents' voices again.

'You're expecting too much of yourself,' said Professor Lupin sternly, in their fourth week of practice. 'For a thirteen-year-old wizard, even an indistinct Patronus is a huge achievement. You aren't passing out any more, are you?'

'I thought a Patronus would – charge the Dementors down or something,' said Harry dispiritedly. 'Make them disappear –'

'The true Patronus does do that,' said Lupin. 'But you've achieved a great deal in a very short space of time. If the Dementors put in an appearance at your next Quidditch match, you will be able to keep them at bay long enough to get back to the ground.'

'You said it's harder if there are loads of them,' said Harry.

'I have complete confidence in you,' said Lupin, smiling. 'Here – you've earned a drink. Something from the Three Broomsticks, you won't have tried it before –'

He pulled two bottles out of his briefcase.

'Butterbeer!' said Harry, without thinking. 'Yeah, I like that stuff!'

Lupin raised an eyebrow.

'Oh – Ron and Hermione brought me some back from Hogsmeade,' Harry lied quickly.

'I see,' said Lupin, though he still looked slightly suspicious. 'Well – let's drink to a Gryffindor victory against Ravenclaw! Not that I'm supposed to take sides, as a teacher ...' he added hastily.

They drank the Butterbeer in silence, until Harry voiced something he'd been wondering for a while.

'What's under a Dementor's hood?'

Professor Lupin lowered his bottle thoughtfully.

'Hmmm ... well, the only people who really know are in no condition to tell us. You see, the Dementor only lowers its hood to use its last and worst weapon.'

'What's that?'

'They call it the Dementors' Kiss,' said Lupin, with a slightly twisted smile. 'It's what Dementors do to those they wish to destroy utterly. I suppose there must be some kind of mouth under there, because they clamp their jaws upon the mouth of the victim and – and suck out his soul.'

Harry accidentally spat out a bit of Butterbeer.

'What – they kill –?'

'Oh, no,' said Lupin. 'Much worse than that. You can exist without your soul, you know, as long as your brain and heart are still working. But you'll have no sense of self any more, no memory, no ... anything. There's no chance at all of recovery. You'll just – exist. As an empty shell. And your soul is gone for ever ... lost.'

Lupin drank a little more Butterbeer, then said, 'It's the fate that awaits Sirius Black. It was in the *Daily Prophet* this morning. The Ministry have given the Dementors permission to perform it if they find him.'

Harry sat stunned for a moment at the idea of someone having their soul sucked out through their mouth. But then he thought of Black.

'He deserves it,' he said suddenly.

'You think so?' said Lupin lightly. 'Do you really think anyone deserves that?'

'Yes,' said Harry defiantly. 'For ... for some things ...'

He would have liked to have told Lupin about the conversation he'd overheard about Black in the Three Broomsticks, about Black betraying his mother and father, but it would have involved revealing that he'd gone to Hogsmeade without permission, and he knew Lupin wouldn't be very impressed by that. So he finished his Butterbeer, thanked Lupin, and left the History of Magic classroom.

Harry half wished that he hadn't asked what was under a Dementor's hood, the answer had been so horrible, and he was so lost in unpleasant thoughts of what it would feel like to have your soul sucked out of you that he walked headlong into Professor McGonagall halfway up the stairs.

'Do watch where you're going, Potter!'

'Sorry, Professor –'

'I've just been looking for you in the Gryffindor common room. Well, here it is, we've done everything we could think of, and there doesn't seem to be anything wrong with it at all – you've got a very good friend somewhere, Potter ...'

Harry's jaw dropped. She was holding out his Firebolt, and it looked as magnificent as ever.

'I can have it back?' Harry said weakly. 'Seriously?'

'Seriously,' said Professor McGonagall, and she was actually smiling. 'I daresay you'll need to get the feel of it before Saturday's match, won't you? And Potter – *do* try and win, won't you? Or we'll be out of the running for the eighth year in a row, as Professor Snape was kind enough to remind me only last night ...'

Speechless, Harry carried the Firebolt back upstairs towards Gryffindor Tower. As he turned a corner, he saw Ron dashing towards him, grinning from ear to ear.

'She gave it to you? Excellent! Listen, can I still have a go on it? Tomorrow?'

'Yeah ... anything ...' said Harry, his heart lighter than it had been in a month. 'You know what – we should make it up with Hermione. She was only trying to help ...'

'Yeah, all right,' said Ron. 'She's in the common room now – working, for a change.'

They turned into the corridor to Gryffindor Tower and saw Neville Longbottom, pleading with Sir Cadogan, who seemed to be refusing him entrance.

'I wrote them down,' Neville was saying tearfully, 'but I must've dropped them somewhere!'

'A likely tale!' roared Sir Cadogan. Then, spotting Harry and Ron, 'Good even, my fine young yeomen! Come clap this loon in irons, he is trying to force entry to the chambers within!'

'Oh, shut up,' said Ron, as he and Harry drew level with Neville.

'I've lost the passwords!' Neville told them miserably. 'I made him tell me what passwords he was going to use this week, because he keeps changing them, and now I don't know what I've done with them!'

'Oddsbodikins,' said Harry to Sir Cadogan, who looked extremely disappointed and reluctantly swung forwards to let them into the common room. There was a sudden, excited murmur as every head turned and the next moment, Harry was surrounded by people exclaiming over his Firebolt.

'Where'd you get it, Harry?'

'Will you let me have a go?'

'Have you ridden it yet, Harry?'

'Ravenclaw'll have no chance, they're all on Cleansweep Sevens!'

'Can I just *hold* it, Harry?'

After ten minutes or so, during which the Firebolt was passed around and admired from every angle, the crowd dispersed and Harry and Ron had a clear view of Hermione, the only person who hadn't rushed over to them, bent over her work, and carefully avoiding their eyes. Harry and Ron approached her table and at last, she looked up.

'I got it back,' said Harry, grinning at her and holding up the Firebolt.

'See, Hermione? There wasn't anything wrong with it!' said Ron.

'Well – there *might* have been!' said Hermione. 'I mean, at least you know now that it's safe!'

'Yeah, I suppose so,' said Harry. 'I'd better put it upstairs –'

'I'll take it!' said Ron eagerly. 'I've got to give Scabbers his Rat Tonic.'

He took the Firebolt, and, holding it as if it were made of glass, carried it away up the boys' staircase.

'Can I sit down, then?' Harry asked Hermione.

'I suppose so,' said Hermione, moving a great stack of parchment off a chair.

Harry looked around at the cluttered table, at the long Arithmancy essay on which the ink was still glistening, at the even longer Muggle Studies essay ('Explain why Muggles Need Electricity') and at the Rune translation Hermione was now poring over.

'How are you getting through all this stuff?' Harry asked her.

'Oh, well – you know – working hard,' said Hermione. Close to, Harry saw that she looked almost as tired as Lupin.

'Why don't you just drop a couple of subjects?' Harry asked, watching her lifting books as she searched for her Rune dictionary.

'I couldn't do that!' said Hermione, looking scandalised.

'Arithmancy looks terrible,' said Harry, picking up a very complicated-looking number chart.

'Oh, no, it's wonderful!' said Hermione earnestly. 'It's my favourite subject! It's –'

But exactly what was wonderful about Arithmancy, Harry never found out. At that precise moment, a strangled yell echoed down the boys' staircase. The whole common room fell silent, staring, petrified, at the entrance. There came hurried footsteps, growing louder and louder – and then, Ron came leaping into view, dragging with him a bedsheet.

'LOOK!' he bellowed, striding over to Hermione's table. 'LOOK!' he yelled, shaking the sheets in her face.

'Ron, what –?'

'SCABBERS! LOOK! SCABBERS!'

Hermione was leaning away from Ron, looking utterly bewildered. Harry looked down at the sheet Ron was holding. There was something red on it. Something that looked horribly like –

'BLOOD!' Ron yelled into the stunned silence. 'HE'S GONE! AND YOU KNOW WHAT WAS ON THE FLOOR?'

'N-no,' said Hermione, in a trembling voice.

Ron threw something down onto Hermione's Rune translation. Hermione and Harry leant forward. Lying on top of the weird, spiky shapes were several long, ginger cat hairs.

CHAPTER THIRTEEN

Gryffindor versus Ravenclaw

It looked like the end of Ron and Hermione's friendship. Each was so angry with the other that Harry couldn't see how they'd ever make it up.

Ron was enraged that Hermione had never taken Crookshanks's attempts to eat Scabbers seriously, hadn't bothered to keep a close enough watch on him and was still trying to pretend that Crookshanks was innocent by suggesting Ron look for Scabbers under all the boys' beds. Hermione, meanwhile, maintained fiercely that Ron had no proof that Crookshanks had eaten Scabbers, that the ginger hairs might have been there since Christmas, and that Ron had been prejudiced against her cat ever since Crookshanks had landed on Ron's head in the Magical Menagerie.

Personally, Harry was sure that Crookshanks had eaten Scabbers, and when he tried to point out to Hermione that the evidence all pointed that way, she lost her temper with Harry, too.

'OK, side with Ron, I knew you would!' she said shrilly. 'First the Firebolt, now Scabbers, everything's my fault, isn't it! Just leave me alone, Harry, I've got a lot of work to do!'

Ron had taken the loss of his rat very hard indeed.

'Come on, Ron, you were always saying how boring Scabbers was,' said Fred bracingly. 'And he's been off-colour for ages, he was wasting away. It was probably better for him to snuff it quickly. One swallow – he probably didn't feel a thing.'

'*Fred!*' said Ginny indignantly.

'All he did was eat and sleep, Ron, you said it yourself,' said George.

'He bit Goyle for us once!' Ron said miserably. 'Remember, Harry?'

'Yeah, that's true,' said Harry.

'His finest hour,' said Fred, unable to keep a straight face. 'Let

the scar on Goyle's finger stand as a lasting tribute to his memory.
Oh, come on, Ron, get yourself down to Hogsmeade and buy a
new rat. What's the point of moaning?'

In a last-ditch attempt to cheer Ron up, Harry persuaded him
to come along to the Gryffindor team's final practice before the
Ravenclaw match, so that he could have a go on the Firebolt after
they'd finished. This did seem to take Ron's mind off Scabbers for
a moment ('Brilliant! Can I try and shoot a few goals on it?') so
they set off for the Quidditch pitch together.

Madam Hooch, who was still overseeing Gryffindor practices to
keep an eye on Harry, was just as impressed with the Firebolt as
everyone else had been. She took it in her hands before take-off
and gave them the benefit of her professional opinion.

'Look at the balance on it! If the Nimbus series has a fault, it's a
slight list to the tail-end – you often find they develop a drag after
a few years. They've updated the handle, too, a bit slimmer than
the Cleansweeps, reminds me of the old Silver Arrows – a pity
they've stopped making them, I learnt to fly on one, and a very
fine old broom it was too ... '

She continued in this vein for some time, until Wood said, 'Er –
Madam Hooch? Is it OK if Harry has the Firebolt back? Only we
need to practise ...'

'Oh – right – here you are, then, Potter,' said Madam Hooch.
'I'll sit over here with Weasley ...'

She and Ron left the pitch to sit in the stadium, and the
Gryffindor team gathered around Wood for his final instructions
for tomorrow's match.

'Harry, I've just found out who Ravenclaw are playing as Seeker.
It's Cho Chang. She's a fourth-year, and she's pretty good ... I really
hoped she wouldn't be fit, she's had some problems with injuries ...'
Wood scowled his displeasure that Cho Chang had made a full
recovery, then said, 'On the other hand, she rides a Comet Two
Sixty, which is going to look like a joke next to the Firebolt.' He
gave Harry's broom a look of fervent admiration, then said, 'OK,
everyone, let's go –'

And at long last, Harry mounted his Firebolt, and kicked off
from the ground.

It was better than he'd ever dreamed. The Firebolt turned with
the lightest touch; it seemed to obey his thoughts rather than his
grip. It sped across the pitch at such speed that the stadium

turned into a green and grey blur; Harry turned it so sharply that Alicia Spinnet screamed, then he went into a perfectly controlled dive, brushing the grassy pitch with his toes before rising thirty, forty, fifty feet into the air again –

'Harry, I'm letting the Snitch out!' Wood called.

Harry turned and raced a Bludger towards the goalposts; he outstripped it easily, saw the Snitch dart out from behind Wood and within ten seconds had caught it tightly in his hand.

The team cheered madly. Harry let the Snitch go again, gave it a minute's head start, then tore after it, weaving in and out of the others; he spotted it lurking near Katie Bell's knee, looped her easily, and caught it again.

It was the best practice ever; the team, inspired by the presence of the Firebolt in their midst, performed their best moves faultlessly, and by the time they hit the ground again, Wood didn't have a single criticism to make, which, as George Weasley pointed out, was a first.

'I can't see what's going to stop us tomorrow!' said Wood. 'Not unless – Harry, you've sorted your Dementor problem, haven't you?'

'Yeah,' said Harry, thinking of his feeble Patronus and wishing it was stronger.

'The Dementors won't turn up again, Oliver, Dumbledore'd do his nut,' said Fred confidently.

'Well, let's hope not,' said Wood. 'Anyway – good work, everyone. Let's get back to the Tower – turn in early ...'

'I'm staying out for a bit, Ron wants a go on the Firebolt,' Harry told Wood, and while the rest of the team headed off to the changing rooms, Harry strode over to Ron, who vaulted the barrier to the stands and came to meet him. Madam Hooch had fallen asleep in her seat.

'Here you go,' said Harry, handing Ron the Firebolt.

Ron, an expression of ecstasy on his face, mounted the broom and zoomed off into the gathering darkness while Harry walked around the edge of the pitch, watching him. Night had fallen before Madam Hooch awoke with a start, told Harry and Ron off for not waking her, and insisted that they go back to the castle.

Harry shouldered the Firebolt and he and Ron walked out of the shadowy stadium, discussing the Firebolt's superbly smooth action, its phenomenal acceleration and its pinpoint turning.

They were halfway towards the castle when Harry, glancing to his left, saw something that made his heart turn over – a pair of eyes, gleaming out of the darkness.

Harry stopped dead, his heart banging against his ribs.

'What's the matter?' said Ron.

Harry pointed. Ron pulled out his wand and muttered, *'Lumos!'*

A beam of light fell across the grass, hit the bottom of a tree and illuminated its branches; there, crouching amongst the budding leaves, was Crookshanks.

'Get out of it!' Ron roared, and he stooped down and seized a stone lying on the grass, but before he could do anything else, Crookshanks had vanished with one swish of his long ginger tail.

'See?' Ron said furiously, chucking the stone down again. 'She's still letting him wander about wherever he wants – probably washing down Scabbers with a couple of birds now ...'

Harry didn't say anything. He took a deep breath as relief seeped through him; he had been sure for a moment that those eyes had belonged to the Grim. They set off for the castle once more. Slightly ashamed of his moment of panic, Harry didn't say anything to Ron – nor did he look left or right until they had reached the well lit Entrance Hall.

*

Harry went down to breakfast next morning with the rest of the boys in his dormitory, all of whom seemed to think the Firebolt deserved a sort of guard of honour. As Harry entered the Great Hall, heads turned in the direction of the Firebolt, and there was a good deal of excited muttering. Harry saw, with enormous satisfaction, that the Slytherin team were all looking thunderstruck.

'Did you see his face?' said Ron gleefully, looking back at Malfoy. 'He can't believe it! This is brilliant!'

Wood, too, was basking in the reflected glory of the Firebolt.

'Put it here, Harry,' he said, laying the broom in the middle of the table and carefully turning it so that its name faced upwards. People from the Ravenclaw and Hufflepuff tables were soon coming over to look. Cedric Diggory came over to congratulate Harry on having acquired such a superb replacement for his Nimbus, and Percy's Ravenclaw girlfriend, Penelope Clearwater, asked if she could actually hold the Firebolt.

'Now, now, Penny, no sabotage!' said Percy heartily, as she examined the Firebolt closely. 'Penelope and I have got a bet on,' he told the team. 'Ten Galleons on the outcome of the match!'

Penelope put the Firebolt down again, thanked Harry and went back to her table.

'Harry – make sure you win,' said Percy, in an urgent whisper. 'I haven't got ten Galleons. Yes, I'm coming, Penny!' And he bustled off to join her in a piece of toast.

'Sure you can manage that broom, Potter?' said a cold, drawling voice.

Draco Malfoy had arrived for a closer look, Crabbe and Goyle right behind him.

'Yeah, reckon so,' said Harry casually.

'Got plenty of special features, hasn't it?' said Malfoy, eyes glittering maliciously. 'Shame it doesn't come with a parachute – in case you get too near a Dementor.'

Crabbe and Goyle sniggered.

'Pity you can't attach an extra arm to yours, Malfoy,' said Harry. 'Then it could catch the Snitch for you.'

The Gryffindor team laughed loudly. Malfoy's pale eyes narrowed, and he stalked away. They watched him rejoin the rest of the Slytherin team, who put their heads together, no doubt asking Malfoy whether Harry's broom really was a Firebolt.

At a quarter to eleven, the Gryffindor team set off for the changing rooms. The weather couldn't have been more different from their match against Hufflepuff. It was a clear, cool day, with a very light breeze; there would be no visibility problems this time, and Harry, though nervous, was starting to feel the excitement only a Quidditch match could bring. They could hear the rest of the school moving into the stadium beyond. Harry took off his black school robes, removed his wand from his pocket, and stuck it inside the T-shirt he was going to wear under his Quidditch robes. He only hoped he wouldn't need it. He wondered suddenly whether Professor Lupin was in the crowd, watching.

'You know what we've got to do,' said Wood, as they prepared to leave the changing rooms. 'If we lose this match, we're out of the running. Just – just fly like you did in practice yesterday, and we'll be OK!'

They walked out onto the pitch to tumultuous applause. The Ravenclaw team, dressed in blue, were already standing in the middle of the pitch. Their Seeker, Cho Chang, was the only girl in their team. She was shorter than Harry by about a head, and

Harry couldn't help noticing, nervous as he was, that she was extremely pretty. She smiled at Harry as the teams faced each other behind their captains, and he felt a slight jolt in the region of his stomach that he didn't think had anything to do with nerves.

'Wood, Davies, shake hands,' Madam Hooch said briskly, and Wood shook hands with the Ravenclaw captain.

'Mount your brooms ... on my whistle ... three – two – one –'

Harry kicked off into the air and the Firebolt zoomed higher and faster than any other broom; he soared around the stadium and began squinting around for the Snitch, listening all the while to the commentary, which was being provided by the Weasley twins' friend, Lee Jordan.

'They're off, and the big excitement this match is the Firebolt which Harry Potter is flying for Gryffindor. According to *Which Broomstick*, the Firebolt's going to be the broom of choice for the national teams at this year's World Championship –'

'Jordan, would you mind telling us what's going on in the match?' interrupted Professor McGonagall's voice.

'Right you are, Professor – just giving a bit of background information. The Firebolt, incidentally, has a built-in auto-brake and –'

'Jordan!'

'OK, OK, Gryffindor in possession, Katie Bell of Gryffindor heading for goal ...'

Harry streaked past Katie in the opposite direction, gazing around for a glint of gold and noticing that Cho Chang was tailing him closely. She was undoubtedly a very good flier – she kept cutting across him, forcing him to change direction.

'Show her your acceleration, Harry!' Fred yelled, as he whooshed past in pursuit of a Bludger that was aiming for Alicia.

Harry urged the Firebolt forward as they rounded the Ravenclaw goalposts and Cho fell behind. Just as Katie succeeded in scoring the first goal of the match, and the Gryffindor end of the pitch went wild, he saw it – the Snitch was close to the ground, flitting near one of the barriers.

Harry dived; Cho saw what he was doing and tore after him. Harry was speeding up, excitement flooding him; dives were his speciality. He was ten feet away –

Then a Bludger, hit by one of the Ravenclaw Beaters, came pelting out of nowhere; Harry veered off course, avoiding it by an inch, and in those few, crucial seconds, the Snitch had vanished.

There was a great 'Ooooooh' of disappointment from the Gryffindor supporters, but much applause for their Beater from the Ravenclaw end. George Weasley vented his feelings by hitting the second Bludger directly at the offending Beater, who was forced to roll right over in mid-air to avoid it.

'Gryffindor lead by eighty points to zero, and look at that Firebolt go! Potter's really putting it through its paces now. See it turn – Chang's Comet is just no match for it. The Firebolt's precision-balance is really noticeable in these long –'

'JORDAN! ARE YOU BEING PAID TO ADVERTISE FIRE-BOLTS? GET ON WITH THE COMMENTARY!'

Ravenclaw were pulling back; they had now scored three goals, which put Gryffindor only fifty points ahead – if Cho got the Snitch before him, Ravenclaw would win. Harry dropped lower, narrowly avoiding a Ravenclaw Chaser, scanning the pitch franti-cally. A glint of gold, a flutter of tiny wings – the Snitch was cir-cling the Gryffindor goalpost ...

Harry accelerated, eyes fixed on the speck of gold ahead – but next second, Cho had appeared out of thin air, blocking him –

'HARRY, THIS IS NO TIME TO BE A GENTLEMAN!' Wood roared, as Harry swerved to avoid a collision. 'KNOCK HER OFF HER BROOM IF YOU HAVE TO!'

Harry turned and caught sight of Cho; she was grinning. The Snitch had vanished again. Harry turned his Firebolt upwards and was soon twenty feet above the game. Out of the corner of his eye, he saw Cho following him ... she'd decided to mark him rather than search for the Snitch herself. Right then ... if she wanted to tail him, she'd have to take the consequences ...

He dived again, and Cho, thinking he'd seen the Snitch, tried to follow. Harry pulled out of the dive very sharply, she hurtled downwards; he rose fast as a bullet once more, and then saw it, for the third time: the Snitch was glittering way above the pitch at the Ravenclaw end.

He accelerated; so, many feet below, did Cho. He was winning, gaining on the Snitch with every second – then –

'Oh!' screamed Cho, pointing.

Distracted, Harry looked down.

Three Dementors, three tall, black, hooded Dementors, were looking up at him.

He didn't stop to think. Plunging a hand down the neck of his robes, he whipped out his wand and roared, *'Expecto patronum!'*

Something silver white, something enormous, erupted from the end of his wand. He knew it had shot directly at the Dementors but didn't pause to watch; his mind still miraculously clear, he looked ahead – he was nearly there. He stretched out the hand still grasping his wand and just managed to close his fingers over the small, struggling Snitch.

Madam Hooch's whistle sounded, Harry turned around in mid-air and saw six scarlet blurs bearing down on him. Next moment, the whole team were hugging him so hard he was nearly pulled off his broom. Down below he could hear the roars of the Gryffindors in the crowd.

'That's my boy!' Wood kept yelling. Alicia, Angelina and Katie had all kissed Harry, and Fred had him in a grip so tight Harry felt as though his head would come off. In complete disarray, the team managed to make its way back to the ground. Harry got off his broom and looked up to see a gaggle of Gryffindor supporters sprinting onto the pitch, Ron in the lead. Before he knew it, he had been engulfed by the cheering crowd.

'Yes!' Ron yelled, yanking Harry's arm into the air. 'Yes! Yes!'

'Well *done*, Harry!' said Percy, looking delighted. 'Ten Galleons to me! Must find Penelope, excuse me –'

'Good on you, Harry!' roared Seamus Finnigan.

'Ruddy brilliant!' boomed Hagrid over the heads of the milling Gryffindors.

'That was quite some Patronus,' said a voice in Harry's ear.

Harry turned around to see Professor Lupin, who looked both shaken and pleased.

'The Dementors didn't affect me at all!' Harry said excitedly. 'I didn't feel a thing!'

'That would be because they – er – weren't Dementors,' said Professor Lupin. 'Come and see –'

He led Harry out of the crowd until they were able to see the edge of the pitch.

'You gave Mr Malfoy quite a fright,' said Lupin.

Harry stared. Lying in a crumpled heap on the ground were Malfoy, Crabbe, Goyle and Marcus Flint, the Slytherin team captain, all struggling to remove themselves from long, black, hooded robes. It looked as though Malfoy had been standing on Goyle's shoulders. Standing over them, with an expression of the utmost fury on her face, was Professor McGonagall.

'An unworthy trick!' she was shouting. 'A low and cowardly attempt to sabotage the Gryffindor Seeker! Detention for all of you, and fifty points from Slytherin! I shall be speaking to Professor Dumbledore about this, make no mistake! Ah, here he comes now!'

If anything could have set the seal on Gryffindor's victory, it was this. Ron, who had fought his way through to Harry's side, doubled up with laughter as they watched Malfoy fighting to extricate himself from the robe, Goyle's head still stuck inside it.

'Come on, Harry!' said George, fighting his way over. 'Party! Gryffindor common room, now!'

'Right,' said Harry, and feeling happier than he had done in ages, he and the rest of the team led the way, still in their scarlet robes, out of the stadium and back up to the castle.

*

It felt as though they had already won the Quidditch Cup; the party went on all day and well into the night. Fred and George Weasley disappeared for a couple of hours and returned with armfuls of bottles of Butterbeer, pumpkin fizz and several bags full of Honeydukes sweets.

'How did you do that?' squealed Angelina Johnson, as George started throwing Peppermint Toads into the crowd.

'With a little help from Moony, Wormtail, Padfoot and Prongs,' Fred muttered in Harry's ear.

Only one person wasn't joining in the festivities. Hermione, incredibly, was sitting in a corner, attempting to read an enormous book entitled *Home Life and Social Habits of British Muggles*. Harry broke away from the table where Fred and George had started juggling Butterbeer bottles, and went over to her.

'Did you even come to the match?' he asked her.

'Of course I did,' said Hermione, in a strangely high-pitched voice, not looking up. 'And I'm very glad we won, and I think you did really well, but I need to read this by Monday.'

'Come on, Hermione, come and have some food,' Harry said, looking over at Ron and wondering whether he was in a good enough mood to bury the hatchet.

'I can't, Harry, I've still got four hundred and twenty-two pages to read!' said Hermione, now sounding slightly hysterical.

'Anyway ...' she glanced over at Ron, too, 'he doesn't want me to join in.'

There was no arguing with this, as Ron chose that moment to say loudly, 'If Scabbers hadn't just been *eaten*, he could have had some of these Fudge Flies, he used to really like them –'

Hermione burst into tears. Before Harry could say or do anything, she had tucked the enormous book under her arm, and, still sobbing, run towards the staircase to the girls' dormitories and out of sight.

'Can't you give her a break?' Harry asked Ron quietly.

'No,' said Ron flatly. 'If she just acted like she was sorry – but she'll never admit she's wrong, Hermione. She's still acting like Scabbers has gone on holiday or something.'

The Gryffindor party only ended when Professor McGonagall turned up in her tartan dressing-gown and hair-net at one in the morning, to insist that they all went to bed. Harry and Ron climbed the stairs to their dormitory, still discussing the match. At last, exhausted, Harry climbed into bed, twitched the hangings of his four-poster shut to block out a ray of moonlight, lay back and felt himself almost instantly drifting off to sleep ...

He had a very strange dream. He was walking through a forest, his Firebolt over his shoulder, following something silvery white. It was winding its way through the trees ahead, and he could only catch glimpses of it between the leaves. Anxious to catch up with it, he sped up, but as he moved faster, so did his quarry. Harry broke into a run and ahead, he heard hooves gathering speed. Now he was running flat out, and ahead he could hear galloping. Then he turned a corner into a clearing and –

'AAAAAAAAAAAAAAARRRRRRRRRRRRGGGHHHHH! NOOOOOOOOOOOOOOOOOO!'

Harry woke as suddenly as though he'd been hit in the face. Disorientated in the total darkness, he fumbled with his hangings – he could hear movements around him, and Seamus Finnigan's voice from the other side of the room.

'What's going on?'

Harry thought he heard the dormitory door slam. At last finding the divide in his curtains, he ripped them back, and at the same moment, Dean Thomas lit his lamp.

Ron was sitting up in bed, the hangings torn from one side, a look of the utmost terror on his face.

'Black! Sirius Black! With a knife!'

'*What?*'

'Here! Just now! Slashed the curtains! Woke me up!'

'You sure you weren't dreaming, Ron?' said Dean.

'Look at the curtains! I tell you, he was here!'

They all scrambled out of bed; Harry reached the dormitory door first, and they sprinted back down the staircase. Doors opened behind them, and sleepy voices called after them.

'Who shouted?'

'What're you doing?'

The common room was lit by the glow of the dying fire, still littered with debris from the party. It was deserted.

'Are you *sure* you weren't dreaming, Ron?'

'I'm telling you, I saw him!'

'What's all the noise?'

'Professor McGonagall told us to go to bed!'

A few of the girls had come down their staircase, pulling on dressing-gowns and yawning. Boys, too, were reappearing.

'Excellent, are we carrying on?' said Fred Weasley brightly.

'Everyone back upstairs!' said Percy, hurrying into the common room and pinning his Head Boy badge to his pyjamas as he spoke.

'Perce – Sirius Black!' said Ron faintly. 'In our dormitory! With a knife! Woke me up!'

The common room went very still.

'Nonsense!' said Percy, looking startled. 'You had too much to eat, Ron – had a nightmare –'

'I'm telling you –'

'Now, really, enough's enough!'

Professor McGonagall was back. She slammed the portrait behind her as she entered the common room and stared furiously around.

'I am delighted that Gryffindor won the match, but this is getting ridiculous! Percy, I expected better of you!'

'I certainly didn't authorise this, Professor!' said Percy, puffing himself up indignantly. 'I was just telling them all to get back to bed! My brother Ron here had a nightmare –'

'IT WASN'T A NIGHTMARE!' Ron yelled. 'PROFESSOR, I WOKE UP, AND SIRIUS BLACK WAS STANDING OVER ME, HOLDING A KNIFE!'

Professor McGonagall stared at him.

'Don't be ridiculous, Weasley, how could he possibly have got through the portrait hole?'

'Ask him!' said Ron, pointing a shaking finger at the back of Sir Cadogan's picture. 'Ask him if he saw –'

Glaring suspiciously at Ron, Professor McGonagall pushed the portrait back open and went outside. The whole common room listened with bated breath.

'Sir Cadogan, did you just let a man enter Gryffindor Tower?'

'Certainly, good lady!' cried Sir Cadogan.

There was a stunned silence, both inside and outside the common room.

'You – you *did*?' said Professor McGonagall. 'But – but the password!'

'He had 'em!' said Sir Cadogan proudly. 'Had the whole week's, my lady! Read 'em off a little piece of paper!'

Professor McGonagall pulled herself back through the portrait hole to face the stunned crowd. She was white as chalk.

'Which person,' she said, her voice shaking, 'which abysmally foolish person wrote down this week's passwords and left them lying around?'

There was utter silence, broken by the smallest of terrified squeaks. Neville Longbottom, trembling from head to fluffy-slippered toes, raised his hand slowly into the air.

— CHAPTER FOURTEEN —

Snape's Grudge

No one in Gryffindor Tower slept that night. They knew that the castle was being searched again, and the whole house stayed awake in the common room, waiting to hear whether Black had been caught. Professor McGonagall came back at dawn, to tell them that he had again escaped.

Everywhere they went next day they saw signs of tighter security; Professor Flitwick could be seen teaching the front doors to recognise a large picture of Sirius Black; Filch was suddenly bustling up and down the corridors, boarding up everything from tiny cracks in the walls to mouse holes. Sir Cadogan had been sacked. His portrait had been taken back to its lonely landing on the seventh floor, and the Fat Lady was back. She had been expertly restored, but was still extremely nervous, and had only agreed to return to her job on condition that she was given extra protection. A bunch of surly security trolls had been hired to guard her. They paced the corridor in a menacing group, talking in grunts and comparing the size of their clubs.

Harry couldn't help noticing that the statue of the one-eyed witch on the third floor remained unguarded and unblocked. It seemed that Fred and George had been right in thinking that they – and now Harry, Ron and Hermione – were the only ones who knew about the hidden passageway within it.

'D'you reckon we should tell someone?' Harry asked Ron.

'We know he's not coming in through Honeydukes,' said Ron dismissively. 'We'd've heard if the shop had been broken into.'

Harry was glad Ron took this view. If the one-eyed witch was boarded up too, he would never be able to go into Hogsmeade again.

Ron had become an instant celebrity. For the first time in his life, people were paying more attention to him than to Harry, and it was clear that Ron was rather enjoying the experience. Though still severely shaken by the night's events, he was happy to tell anyone who asked, what had happened, with a wealth of detail.

'... I was asleep, and I heard this ripping noise, and I thought it was in my dream, you know? But then there was this draught ... I woke up and one side of the hangings on my bed had been pulled down ... I rolled over ... and I saw him standing over me ... like a skeleton, with loads of filthy hair ... holding this great long knife, must've been twelve inches ... and he looked at me, and I looked at him, and then I yelled, and he scarpered.

'Why, though?' Ron added to Harry, as the group of second-year girls who had been listening to his chilling tale departed. 'Why did he scarper?'

Harry had been wondering the same thing. Why had Black, having got the wrong bed, not silenced Ron and proceeded to Harry? Black had proved twelve years ago that he didn't mind murdering innocent people, and this time he had been facing five unarmed boys, four of whom were asleep.

'He must've known he'd have a job getting back out of the castle once you'd yelled and woken people up,' said Harry thoughtfully. 'He'd've had to kill the whole house to get back through the portrait hole ... then he would've met the teachers ...'

Neville was in total disgrace. Professor McGonagall was so furious with him she had banned him from all future Hogsmeade visits, given him a detention and forbidden anyone to give him the password into the Tower. Poor Neville was forced to wait outside the common room every night for somebody to let him in, while the security trolls leered unpleasantly at him. None of these punishments, however, came close to matching the one his grandmother had in store for him. Two days after Black's break-in, she sent Neville the very worst thing a Hogwarts student could receive over breakfast – a Howler.

The school owls swooped into the Great Hall, carrying the post as usual, and Neville choked as a huge barn owl landed in front of him, a scarlet envelope clutched in its beak. Harry and Ron, who were sitting opposite him, recognised the letter as a Howler at once – Ron had got one from his mother the year before.

'Run for it, Neville,' Ron advised.

Neville didn't need telling twice. He seized the envelope and, holding it before him like a bomb, sprinted out of the Hall, while the Slytherin table exploded with laughter at the sight of him. They heard the Howler go off in the Entrance Hall – Neville's grandmother's voice, magically magnified to a hundred times its usual volume, shrieking about how he had brought shame on the whole family.

Harry was too busy feeling sorry for Neville to notice immediately that he had a letter, too. Hedwig got his attention by nipping him sharply on the wrist.

'Ouch! Oh – thanks, Hedwig ...'

Harry tore open the envelope while Hedwig helped herself to some of Neville's cornflakes. The note inside said:

> Dear Harry and Ron,
>   How about having tea with me this evening round six? I'll come and collect you from the castle. WAIT FOR ME IN THE ENTRANCE HALL, YOU'RE NOT ALLOWED OUT ON YOUR OWN.
>   Cheers,
>   Hagrid

'He probably wants to hear all about Black!' said Ron.

So at six o'clock that evening, Harry and Ron left Gryffindor Tower, passed the security trolls at a run, and headed down to the Entrance Hall.

Hagrid was already waiting for them.

'All right, Hagrid!' said Ron. ''S'pose you want to hear about Saturday night, do you?'

'I've already heard all abou' it,' said Hagrid, opening the front doors and leading them outside.

'Oh,' said Ron, looking slightly put out.

The first thing they saw on entering Hagrid's cabin was Buckbeak, who was stretched out on top of Hagrid's patchwork quilt, his enormous wings folded tight to his body, enjoying a large plate of dead ferrets. Averting his eyes from this unpleasant sight, Harry saw a gigantic, hairy brown suit and a very horrible yellow and orange tie hanging from the top of Hagrid's wardrobe door.

'What are they for, Hagrid?' said Harry.

'Buckbeak's case against the Committee fer the Disposal o' Dangerous Creatures,' said Hagrid. 'This Friday. Him an' me'll be goin' down ter London together. I've booked two beds on the Knight Bus ...'

Harry felt a nasty pang of guilt. He had completely forgotten that Buckbeak's trial was so near, and judging by the uneasy look on Ron's face, he had, too. They had also forgotten their promise about helping him prepare Buckbeak's defence; the arrival of the Firebolt had driven it clean out of their minds.

Hagrid poured them tea and offered them a plate of Bath buns, but they knew better than to accept; they had had too much experience of Hagrid's cooking.

'I got somethin' ter discuss with you two,' said Hagrid, sitting himself between them and looking uncharacteristically serious.

'What?' said Harry.

'Hermione,' said Hagrid.

'What about her?' said Ron.

'She's in a righ' state, that's what. She's bin comin' down ter visit me a lot since Chris'mas. Bin feelin' lonely. Firs' yeh weren' talking to her because o' the Firebolt, now yer not talkin' to her because her cat –'

'– ate Scabbers!' Ron interjected angrily.

'Because her cat acted like all cats do,' Hagrid continued doggedly. 'She's cried a fair few times, yeh know. Goin' through a rough time at the moment. Bitten off more'n she can chew, if yeh ask me, all the work she's tryin' ter do. Still found time ter help me with Buckbeak's case, mind ... she's found some really good stuff fer me ... reckon he'll stand a good chance now ...'

'Hagrid, we should've helped as well – sorry –' Harry began awkwardly.

'I'm not blamin' yeh!' said Hagrid, waving Harry's apology aside. 'Gawd knows yeh've had enough ter be gettin' on with, I've seen yeh practisin' Quidditch ev'ry hour o' the day an' night – but I gotta tell yeh, I thought you two'd value yer friend more'n broomsticks or rats. Tha's all.'

Harry and Ron exchanged uncomfortable looks.

'Really upset, she was, when Black nearly stabbed yeh, Ron. She's got her heart in the right place, Hermione has, an' you two not talkin' to her –'

'If she'd just get rid of that cat, I'd speak to her again!' Ron said angrily. 'But she's still sticking up for it! It's a maniac, and she won't hear a word against it!'

'Ah, well, people can be a bit stupid abou' their pets,' said Hagrid wisely. Behind him, Buckbeak spat a few ferret bones onto Hagrid's pillow.

They spent the rest of their visit discussing Gryffindor's improved chances for the Quidditch Cup. At nine o'clock, Hagrid walked them back up to the castle.

A large group of people was bunched around the noticeboard when they returned to the common room.

'Hogsmeade, next weekend!' said Ron, craning over the heads to read the new notice. 'What d'you reckon?' he added quietly to Harry, as they went to sit down.

'Well, Filch hasn't done anything about the passage into Honeydukes ...' Harry said, even more quietly.

'Harry!' said a voice in his right ear. Harry started and looked around at Hermione, who was sitting at the table right behind them and clearing a space in the wall of books that had been hiding her.

'Harry, if you go into Hogsmeade again ... I'll tell Professor McGonagall about that map!' said Hermione.

'Can you hear someone talking, Harry?' growled Ron, not looking at Hermione.

'Ron, how can you let him go with you? After what Sirius Black nearly did to *you*! I mean it, I'll tell –'

'So now you're trying to get Harry expelled!' said Ron furiously. 'Haven't you done enough damage this year?'

Hermione opened her mouth to respond, but with a soft hiss, Crookshanks leapt onto her lap. Hermione took one frightened look at the expression on Ron's face, gathered Crookshanks up and hurried away towards the girls' dormitories.

'So how about it?' Ron said to Harry, as though there had been no interruption. 'Come on, last time we went you didn't see anything. You haven't even been inside Zonko's yet!'

Harry looked around to check that Hermione was well out of earshot.

'OK,' he said. 'But I'm taking the Invisibility Cloak this time.'

*

On Saturday morning, Harry packed his Invisibility Cloak in his bag, slipped the Marauder's Map into his pocket and went down to breakfast with everyone else. Hermione kept shooting suspicious looks down the table at him, but he avoided her eye, and

was careful to let her see him walking back up the marble staircase in the Entrance Hall as everybody else proceeded to the front
doors.

'Bye!' Harry called to Ron. 'See you when you get back!'

Ron grinned and winked.

Harry hurried up to the third floor, slipping the Marauder's
Map out of his pocket as he went. Crouching behind the one-eyed
witch, he smoothed it out. A tiny dot was moving in his direction.
Harry squinted at it. The minuscule writing next to it read 'Neville
Longbottom'.

Harry quickly pulled out his wand, muttered *'Dissendium!'* and
shoved his bag into the statue, but before he could climb in himself, Neville came around the corner.

'Harry! I forgot you weren't going to Hogsmeade either!'

'Hi, Neville,' said Harry, moving swiftly away from the statue
and pushing the map back into his pocket. 'What are you up to?'

'Nothing,' shrugged Neville. 'Want a game of Exploding Snap?'

'Er – not now – I was going to go to the library and do that
vampire essay for Lupin –'

'I'll come with you!' said Neville brightly. 'I haven't done it
either!'

'Er – hang on – yeah, I forgot, I finished it last night!'

'Brilliant, you can help me!' said Neville, his round face anxious. 'I don't understand that thing about the garlic at all – do they
have to eat it, or –'

Neville broke off with a small gasp, looking over Harry's shoulder.

It was Snape. Neville took a quick step behind Harry.

'And what are you two doing here?' said Snape, coming to a
halt and looking from one to the other. 'An odd place to meet –'

To Harry's immense disquiet, Snape's black eyes flicked to the
doorways on either side of them, and then to the one-eyed witch.

'We're not – meeting here,' said Harry. 'We just – met here.'

'Indeed?' said Snape. 'You have a habit of turning up in unexpected places, Potter, and you are rarely there for no reason ... I
suggest the pair of you return to Gryffindor Tower, where you
belong.'

Harry and Neville set off without another word. As they turned
the corner, Harry looked back. Snape was running one of his
hands over the one-eyed witch's head, examining it closely.

Harry managed to shake Neville off at the Fat Lady by telling him the password, then pretending he'd left his vampire essay in the library and doubling back. Once out of sight of the security trolls, he pulled out the map again and held it close to his nose.

The third-floor corridor seemed to be deserted. Harry scanned the map carefully and saw, with a leap of relief, that the tiny dot labelled 'Severus Snape' was now back in its office.

He sprinted back to the one-eyed witch, opened her hump, heaved himself inside and slid down to meet his bag at the bottom of the stone chute. He wiped the Marauder's Map blank again, then set off at a run.

*

Harry, completely hidden beneath the Invisibility Cloak, emerged into the sunlight outside Honeydukes and prodded Ron in the back.

'It's me,' he muttered.

'What kept you?' Ron hissed.

'Snape was hanging around ...'

They set off up the High Street.

'Where are you?' Ron kept muttering out of the corner of his mouth. 'Are you still there? This feels weird ...'

They went to the Post Office; Ron pretended to be checking the price of an owl to Bill in Egypt so that Harry could have a good look around. The owls sat hooting softly down at him, at least three hundred of them; from Great Greys right down to tiny little Scops owls ('Local Deliveries Only') which were so small they could have sat in the palm of Harry's hand.

Then they visited Zonko's, which was so packed with students Harry had to exercise great care not to tread on anyone and cause a panic. There were jokes and tricks to fulfil even Fred and George's wildest dreams; Harry gave Ron whispered orders and passed him some gold from under the Cloak. They left Zonko's with their money bags considerably lighter than they had been on entering, but their pockets bulging with Dungbombs, Hiccough Sweets, Frog Spawn Soap and a Nose-Biting Teacup apiece.

The day was fine and breezy, and neither of them felt like staying indoors, so they walked past the Three Broomsticks and climbed a slope to visit the Shrieking Shack, the most haunted dwelling in Britain. It stood a little way above the rest of the village, and even in daylight was slightly creepy, with its boarded windows and dank overgrown garden.

'Even the Hogwarts ghosts avoid it,' said Ron, as they leaned on the fence, looking up at it. 'I asked Nearly Headless Nick ... he says he's heard a very rough crowd live here. No one can get in. Fred and George tried, obviously, but all the entrances are sealed shut ...'

Harry, feeling hot from their climb, was just considering taking off the Cloak for a few minutes, when they heard voices nearby. Someone was climbing towards the house from the other side of the hill; moments later, Malfoy had appeared, followed closely by Crabbe and Goyle. Malfoy was speaking.

'... should have an owl from Father any time now. He had to go to the hearing to tell them about my arm ... about how I couldn't use it for three months ...'

Crabbe and Goyle sniggered.

'I really wish I could hear that great hairy moron trying to defend himself ... "There's no 'arm in 'im, 'onest –" ... that Hippogriff's as good as dead –'

Malfoy suddenly caught sight of Ron. His pale face split in a malevolent grin.

'What are you doing, Weasley?'

Malfoy looked up at the crumbling house behind Ron.

'Suppose you'd love to live here, wouldn't you, Weasley? Dreaming about having your own bedroom? I heard your family all sleep in one room – is that true?'

Harry seized the back of Ron's robes to stop him leaping on Malfoy.

'Leave him to me,' he hissed in Ron's ear.

The opportunity was too perfect to miss. Harry crept silently around behind Malfoy, Crabbe and Goyle, bent down and scooped a large handful of mud out of the path.

'We were just discussing your friend Hagrid,' Malfoy said to Ron. 'Just trying to imagine what he's saying to the Committee for the Disposal of Dangerous Creatures. D'you think he'll cry when they cut off his Hippogriff's –'

SPLAT!

Malfoy's head jerked forwards as the mud hit him; his silver-blond hair was suddenly dripping in muck.

'What the –?'

Ron had to hold onto the fence to keep himself standing, he was laughing so hard. Malfoy, Crabbe and Goyle spun stupidly on the spot, staring wildly around, Malfoy trying to wipe his hair clean.

'What was that? Who did that?'

'Very haunted up here, isn't it?' said Ron, with the air of one commenting on the weather.

Crabbe and Goyle were looking scared. Their bulging muscles were no use against ghosts. Malfoy was staring madly around at the deserted landscape.

Harry sneaked along the path, where a particularly sloppy puddle yielded some foul-smelling, green sludge.

SPLATTER!

Crabbe and Goyle caught some this time. Goyle hopped furiously on the spot, trying to rub it out of his small, dull eyes.

'It came from over there!' said Malfoy, wiping his face, and staring at a spot some six feet to the left of Harry.

Crabbe blundered forwards, his long arms outstretched like a zombie. Harry dodged around him, picked up a stick, and lobbed it at Crabbe's back. Harry doubled up with silent laughter as Crabbe did a kind of pirouette in mid-air, trying to see who had thrown it. As Ron was the only person Crabbe could see, it was Ron he started towards, but Harry stuck out his leg. Crabbe stumbled – and his huge, flat foot caught the hem of Harry's Cloak. Harry felt a great tug, then the Cloak slid off his face.

For a split second, Malfoy stared at him.

'AAARGH!' he yelled, pointing at Harry's head. Then he turned tail and ran, at breakneck speed, back down the hill, Crabbe and Goyle behind him.

Harry tugged the Cloak up again, but the damage was done.

'Harry!' Ron said, stumbling forward and staring hopelessly at the point where Harry had disappeared, 'you'd better run for it! If Malfoy tells anyone – you'd better get back to the castle, quick –'

'See you later,' said Harry, and without another word, he tore back down the path towards Hogsmeade.

Would Malfoy believe what he had seen? Would anyone believe Malfoy? Nobody knew about the Invisibility Cloak – nobody except Dumbledore. Harry's stomach turned over – Dumbledore would know exactly what had happened, if Malfoy said anything –

Back into Honeydukes, back down the cellar steps, across the stone floor, through the trapdoor – Harry pulled off the Cloak, tucked it under his arm, and ran, flat out, along the passage ...

Malfoy would get back first ... how long would it take him to find a teacher? Panting, a sharp pain in his side, Harry didn't slow down until he reached the stone slide. He would have to leave the Cloak where it was, it was too much of a giveaway if Malfoy had tipped off a teacher. He hid it in a shadowy corner, then started to climb, fast as he could, his sweaty hands slipping on the sides of the chute. He reached the inside of the witch's hump, tapped it with his wand, stuck his head through and hoisted himself out; the hump closed, and just as Harry jumped out from behind the statue, he heard quick footsteps approaching.

It was Snape. He approached Harry at a swift walk, his black robes swishing, then stopped in front of him.

'So,' he said.

There was a look of suppressed triumph about him. Harry tried to look innocent, all too aware of his sweaty face and his muddy hands, which he quickly hid in his pockets.

'Come with me, Potter,' said Snape.

Harry followed him downstairs, trying to wipe his hands clean on the inside of his robes without Snape noticing. They walked down the stairs to the dungeons and then into Snape's office.

Harry had only been in here once before, and he had been in very serious trouble then, too. Snape had acquired a few more horrible slimy things in jars since last time, all standing on shelves behind his desk, glinting in the firelight and adding to the threatening atmosphere.

'Sit,' said Snape.

Harry sat. Snape, however, remained standing.

'Mr Malfoy has just been to see me with a strange story, Potter,' said Snape.

Harry didn't say anything.

'He tells me that he was up by the Shrieking Shack when he ran into Weasley – apparently alone.'

Still, Harry didn't speak.

'Mr Malfoy states that he was standing talking to Weasley, when a large amount of mud hit him on the back of the head. How do you think that could have happened?'

Harry tried to look mildly surprised.

'I don't know, Professor.'

Snape's eyes were boring into Harry's. It was exactly like trying to stare out a Hippogriff. Harry tried hard not to blink.

'Mr Malfoy then saw an extraordinary apparition. Can you imagine what it might have been, Potter?'

'No,' said Harry, now trying to sound innocently curious.

'It was your head, Potter. Floating in mid-air.'

There was a long silence.

'Maybe he'd better go to Madam Pomfrey,' said Harry. 'If he's seeing things like –'

'What would your head have been doing in Hogsmeade, Potter?' said Snape softly. 'Your head is not allowed in Hogsmeade. No part of your body has permission to be in Hogsmeade.'

'I know that,' said Harry, striving to keep his face free of guilt or fear. 'It sounds like Malfoy's having hallucin–'

'Malfoy is not having hallucinations,' snarled Snape, and he bent down, a hand on each arm of Harry's chair, so that their faces were a foot apart. 'If your head was in Hogsmeade, so was the rest of you.'

'I've been up in Gryffindor Tower,' said Harry. 'Like you told –'

'Can anyone confirm that?'

Harry didn't say anything. Snape's thin mouth curled into a horrible smile.

'So,' he said, straightening up again. 'Everyone from the Minister for Magic downwards has been trying to keep famous Harry Potter safe from Sirius Black. But famous Harry Potter is a law unto himself. Let the ordinary people worry about his safety! Famous Harry Potter goes where he wants to, with no thought for the consequences.'

Harry stayed silent. Snape was trying to provoke him into telling the truth. He wasn't going to do it. Snape had no proof – yet.

'How extraordinarily like your father you are, Potter,' Snape said suddenly, his eyes glinting. 'He, too, was exceedingly arrogant. A small amount of talent on the Quidditch pitch made him think he was a cut above the rest of us, too. Strutting around the place with his friends and admirers ... the resemblance between you is uncanny.'

'My dad didn't *strut*,' said Harry, before he could stop himself. 'And nor do I.'

'Your father didn't set much store by rules, either,' Snape went on, pressing his advantage, his thin face full of malice. 'Rules were for lesser mortals, not Quidditch Cup-winners. His head was so swollen –'

'SHUT UP!'

Harry was suddenly on his feet. Rage such as he had not felt since his last night in Privet Drive was thundering through him. He didn't care that Snape's face had gone rigid, the black eyes flashing dangerously.

'What did you say to me, Potter?'

'I told you to shut up about my dad!' Harry yelled. 'I know the truth, all right? He saved your life! Dumbledore told me! You wouldn't even be here if it weren't for my dad!'

Snape's sallow skin had gone the colour of sour milk.

'And did the Headmaster tell you the circumstances in which your father saved my life?' he whispered. 'Or did he consider the details too unpleasant for precious Potter's delicate ears?'

Harry bit his lip. He didn't know what had happened and didn't want to admit it – but Snape seemed to have guessed the truth.

'I would hate you to run away with a false idea of your father, Potter,' he said, a terrible grin twisting his face. 'Have you been imagining some act of glorious heroism? Then let me correct you – your saintly father and his friends played a highly amusing joke on me that would have resulted in my death if your father hadn't got cold feet at the last moment. There was nothing brave about what he did. He was saving his own skin as much as mine. Had their joke succeeded, he would have been expelled from Hogwarts.'

Snape's uneven, yellowish teeth were bared.

'Turn out your pockets, Potter!' he spat suddenly.

Harry didn't move. There was a pounding in his ears.

'Turn out your pockets, or we go straight to the Headmaster! Pull them out, Potter!'

Cold with dread, Harry slowly pulled out the bag of Zonko's tricks and the Marauder's Map.

Snape picked up the Zonko's bag.

'Ron gave them to me,' said Harry, praying he'd get a chance to tip Ron off before Snape saw him. 'He – brought them back from Hogsmeade last time –'

'Indeed? And you've been carrying them round ever since? How very touching ... and what is this?'

Snape had picked up the map. Harry tried with all his might to keep his face impassive.

'Spare bit of parchment,' he shrugged.

Snape turned it over, his eyes on Harry.

'Surely you don't need such a very *old* piece of parchment?' he said. 'Why don't I just – throw this away?'

His hand moved towards the fire.

'No!' Harry said quickly.

'So!' said Snape, his long nostrils quivering. 'Is this another treasured gift from Mr Weasley? Or is it – something else? A letter, perhaps, written in invisible ink? Or – instructions to get into Hogsmeade without passing the Dementors?'

Harry blinked. Snape's eyes gleamed.

'Let me see, let me see ...' he muttered, taking out his wand and smoothing the map out on his desk. 'Reveal your secret!' he said, touching the wand to the parchment.

Nothing happened. Harry clenched his hands to stop them shaking.

'Show yourself!' Snape said, tapping the map sharply.

It stayed blank. Harry was taking deep, calming breaths.

'Professor Severus Snape, master of this school, commands you to yield the information you conceal!' Snape said, hitting the map with his wand.

As though an invisible hand was writing upon it, words appeared on the smooth surface of the map.

'Mr Moony presents his compliments to Professor Snape, and begs him to keep his abnormally large nose out of other people's business.'

Snape froze. Harry stared, dumbstruck, at the message. But the map didn't stop there. More writing was appearing beneath the first.

'Mr Prongs agrees with Mr Moony, and would like to add that Professor Snape is an ugly git.'

It would have been very funny if the situation hadn't been so serious. And there was more ...

'Mr Padfoot would like to register his astonishment that an idiot like that ever became a Professor.'

Harry closed his eyes in horror. When he'd opened them, the map had had its last word.

'Mr Wormtail bids Professor Snape good day, and advises him to wash his hair, the slimeball.'

Harry waited for the blow to fall.

'So ...' said Snape softly. 'We'll see about this ...'

He strode across to his fire, seized a fistful of glittering powder from a jar on the fireplace, and threw it into the flames.

'Lupin!' Snape called into the fire. 'I want a word!'

Utterly bewildered, Harry stared at the fire. A large shape had appeared in it, revolving very fast. Seconds later, Professor Lupin was clambering out of the fireplace, brushing ash off his shabby robes.

'You called, Severus?' said Lupin mildly.

'I certainly did,' said Snape, his face contorted with fury as he strode back to his desk. 'I have just asked Potter to empty his pockets. He was carrying this.'

Snape pointed at the parchment, on which the words of Messrs Moony, Wormtail, Padfoot and Prongs were still shining. An odd, closed expression appeared on Lupin's face.

'Well?' said Snape.

Lupin continued to stare at the map. Harry had the impression that Lupin was doing some very quick thinking.

'Well?' said Snape again. 'This parchment is plainly full of Dark Magic. This is supposed to be your area of expertise, Lupin. Where do you imagine Potter got such a thing?'

Lupin looked up and, by the merest half glance in Harry's direction, warned him not to interrupt.

'Full of Dark Magic?' he repeated mildly. 'Do you really think so, Severus? It looks to me as though it is merely a piece of parchment that insults anybody who tries to read it. Childish, but surely not dangerous? I imagine Harry got it from a joke-shop –'

'Indeed?' said Snape. His jaw had gone rigid with anger. 'You think a joke-shop could supply him with such a thing? You don't think it more likely that he got it *directly from the manufacturers*?'

Harry didn't understand what Snape was talking about. Nor, apparently, did Lupin.

'You mean, from Mr Wormtail or one of these people?' he said. 'Harry, do you know any of these men?'

'No,' said Harry quickly.

'You see, Severus?' said Lupin, turning back to Snape. 'It looks like a Zonko product to me –'

Right on cue, Ron came bursting into the office. He was completely out of breath, and stopped just short of Snape's desk, clutching the stitch in his chest and trying to speak.

'I – gave – Harry – that – stuff,' he choked. 'Bought – it – in

Zonko's – ages – ago ...'

'Well!' said Lupin, clapping his hands together and looking around cheerfully. 'That seems to clear that up! Severus, I'll take this back, shall I?' He folded the map and tucked it inside his robes. 'Harry, Ron, come with me, I need a word about my vampire essay. Excuse us, Severus.'

Harry didn't dare look at Snape as they left his office. He, Ron and Lupin walked all the way back into the Entrance Hall before speaking. Then Harry turned to Lupin.

'Professor, I –'

'I don't want to hear explanations,' said Lupin shortly. He glanced around the empty Entrance Hall and lowered his voice. 'I happen to know that this map was confiscated by Mr Filch many years ago. Yes, I know it's a map,' he said, as Harry and Ron looked amazed. 'I don't want to know how it fell into your possession. I am, however, *astounded* that you didn't hand it in. Particularly after what happened the last time a student left information about the castle lying around. And I can't let you have it back, Harry.'

Harry had expected that, and was too keen for explanations to protest.

'Why did Snape think I'd got it from the manufacturers?'

'Because ...' Lupin hesitated, 'because these mapmakers would have wanted to lure you out of school. They'd think it extremely entertaining.'

'Do you *know* them?' said Harry, impressed.

'We've met,' he said shortly. He was looking at Harry more seriously than ever before.

'Don't expect me to cover up for you again, Harry. I cannot make you take Sirius Black seriously. But I would have thought that what you have heard when the Dementors draw near you would have had more of an effect on you. Your parents gave their lives to keep you alive, Harry. A poor way to repay them – gambling their sacrifice for a bag of magic tricks.'

He walked away, leaving Harry feeling worse by far than he had at any point in Snape's office. Slowly, he and Ron mounted the marble staircase. As Harry passed the one-eyed witch, he remembered the Invisibility Cloak – it was still down there, but he didn't dare go and get it.

'It's my fault,' said Ron abruptly. 'I persuaded you to go. Lupin's right, it was stupid, we shouldn't've done it –'

He broke off; they had reached the corridor where the security trolls were pacing, and Hermione was walking towards them. One look at her face convinced Harry that she had heard what had happened. His heart plummeted – had she told Professor McGonagall?

'Come to have a good gloat?' said Ron savagely, as she stopped in front of them. 'Or have you just been to tell on us?'

'No,' said Hermione. She was holding a letter in her hands and her lip was trembling. 'I just thought you ought to know ... Hagrid lost his case. Buckbeak is going to be executed.'

— CHAPTER FIFTEEN —

The Quidditch Final

'He – he sent me this,' Hermione said, holding out the letter.

Harry took it. The parchment was damp, and enormous teardrops had smudged the ink so badly in places that it was very difficult to read.

> *Dear Hermione,*
> *We lost. I'm allowed to bring him back to Hogwarts.*
> *Execution date to be fixed.*
> *Beaky has enjoyed London.*
> *I won't forget all the help you gave us.*
> *Hagrid*

'They can't do this,' said Harry. 'They can't. Buckbeak isn't dangerous.'

'Malfoy's dad's frightened the Committee into it,' said Hermione, wiping her eyes. 'You know what he's like. They're a bunch of doddery old fools, and they were scared. There'll be an appeal, though, there always is. Only I can't see any hope ... nothing will have changed.'

'Yeah, it will,' said Ron fiercely. 'You won't have to do all the work alone this time, Hermione. I'll help.'

'Oh, Ron!'

Hermione flung her arms around Ron's neck and broke down completely. Ron, looking quite terrified, patted her very awkwardly on the top of the head. Finally, Hermione drew away.

'Ron, I'm really, really sorry about Scabbers ...' she sobbed.

'Oh – well – he was old,' said Ron, looking thoroughly relieved that she had let go of him. 'And he was a bit useless. You never know, Mum and Dad might get me an owl now.'

*

The safety measures imposed on the students since Black's second break-in made it impossible for Harry, Ron and Hermione to go and visit Hagrid in the evenings. Their only chance of talking to him was during Care of Magical Creatures lessons.

He seemed numb with shock at the verdict.

''S all my fault. Got all tongue-tied. They was all sittin' there in black robes an' I kep' droppin' me notes and forgettin' all them dates yeh looked up fer me, Hermione. An' then Lucius Malfoy stood up an' said his bit, and the Committee jus' did exac'ly what he told 'em ...'

'There's still the appeal!' said Ron fiercely. 'Don't give up yet, we're working on it!'

They were walking back up to the castle with the rest of the class. Ahead they could see Malfoy, who was walking with Crabbe and Goyle, and kept looking back, laughing derisively.

''S no good, Ron,' said Hagrid sadly as they reached the castle steps. 'That Committee's in Lucius Malfoy's pocket. I'm jus' gonna make sure the rest o' Beaky's time is the happiest he's ever had. I owe him that ...'

Hagrid turned round and hurried back towards his cabin, his face buried in his handkerchief.

'Look at him blubber!'

Malfoy, Crabbe and Goyle had been standing just inside the castle doors, listening.

'Have you ever seen anything quite as pathetic?' said Malfoy. 'And he's supposed to be our teacher!'

Harry and Ron both made furious moves towards Malfoy, but Hermione got there first – SMACK!

She had slapped Malfoy around the face with all the strength she could muster. Malfoy staggered. Harry, Ron, Crabbe and Goyle stood flabbergasted as Hermione raised her hand again.

'Don't you *dare* call Hagrid pathetic, you foul – you evil –'

'Hermione!' said Ron weakly, and he tried to grab her hand as she swung it back.

'Get *off*, Ron!'

Hermione pulled out her wand. Malfoy stepped backwards. Crabbe and Goyle looked at him for instructions, thoroughly bewildered.

'C'mon,' Malfoy muttered, and next moment, all three of them had disappeared into the passageway to the dungeons.

'*Hermione!*' Ron said again, sounding both stunned and impressed.

'Harry, you'd better beat him in the Quidditch final!' Hermione said shrilly. 'You just better had, because I can't stand it if Slytherin win!'

'We're due in Charms,' said Ron, still goggling at Hermione. 'We'd better go.'

They hurried up the marble staircase towards Professor Flitwick's classroom.

'You're late, boys!' said Professor Flitwick reprovingly, as Harry opened the classroom door. 'Come along, quickly, wands out, we're experimenting with Cheering Charms today. We've already divided into pairs –'

Harry and Ron hurried to a desk at the back and opened their bags. Ron looked behind him.

'Where's Hermione gone?'

Harry looked around, too. Hermione hadn't entered the classroom, yet Harry knew she had been right next to him when he had opened the door.

'That's weird,' said Harry, staring at Ron. 'Maybe – maybe she went to the bathroom or something?'

But Hermione didn't turn up all lesson.

'She could've done with a Cheering Charm on her, too,' said Ron, as the class left for lunch, all grinning broadly – the Cheering Charms had left them with a feeling of great contentment.

Hermione wasn't at lunch either. By the time they had finished their apple pie, the after-effects of the Cheering Charms were wearing off, and Harry and Ron had started to get slightly worried.

'You don't think Malfoy did something to her?' Ron said anxiously, as they hurried upstairs towards Gryffindor Tower.

They passed the security trolls, gave the Fat Lady the password ('Flibbertigibbet') and scrambled through the portrait hole into the common room.

Hermione was sitting at a table, fast asleep, her head resting on an open Arithmancy book. They went to sit down either side of her. Harry prodded her awake.

'Wh-what?' said Hermione, waking with a start, and staring wildly around. 'Is it time to go? W-which lesson have we got now?'

'Divination, but it's not for another twenty minutes,' said Harry. 'Hermione, why didn't you come to Charms?'

'What? Oh no!' Hermione squeaked. 'I forgot to go to Charms!'

'But how could you forget?' said Harry. 'You were with us till we were right outside the classroom!'

'I don't believe it!' Hermione wailed. 'Was Professor Flitwick angry? Oh, it was Malfoy, I was thinking about him and I lost track of things!'

'You know what, Hermione?' said Ron, looking down at the enormous Arithmancy book Hermione had been using as a pillow. 'I reckon you're cracking up. You're trying to do too much.'

'No, I'm not!' said Hermione, brushing her hair out of her eyes and staring hopelessly around for her bag. 'I just made a mistake, that's all! I'd better go and see Professor Flitwick and say sorry ... I'll see you in Divination!'

Hermione joined them at the foot of the ladder to Professor Trelawney's classroom twenty minutes later, looking extremely harassed.

'I can't believe I missed Cheering Charms! And I bet they come up in our exams. Professor Flitwick hinted they might!'

Together they climbed the ladder into the dim, stifling tower room. Glowing on every little table was a crystal ball full of pearly white mist. Harry, Ron and Hermione sat down together at the same rickety table.

'I thought we weren't starting crystal balls until next term,' Ron muttered, casting a wary eye around for Professor Trelawney, in case she was lurking nearby.

'Don't complain, this means we've finished palmistry,' Harry muttered back. 'I was getting sick of her flinching every time she looked at my hands.'

'Good day to you!' said the familiar, misty voice, and Professor Trelawney made her usual dramatic entrance out of the shadows. Parvati and Lavender quivered with excitement, their faces lit by the milky glow of their crystal ball.

'I have decided to introduce the crystal ball a little earlier than I had planned,' said Professor Trelawney, seating herself with her back to the fire and gazing around. 'The fates have informed me that your examination in June will concern the Orb, and I am anxious to give you sufficient practice.'

Hermione snorted.

'Well, honestly ... "the fates have informed her" ... who sets the exam? She does! What an amazing prediction!' she said, not troubling to keep her voice low.

It was hard to tell whether Professor Trelawney had heard them, as her face was hidden in shadow. She continued, however, as though she had not.

'Crystal-gazing is a particularly refined art,' she said dreamily. 'I do not expect any of you to See when first you peer into the Orb's infinite depths. We shall start by practising relaxing the conscious mind and external eyes' – Ron began to snigger uncontrollably, and had to stuff his fist in his mouth to stifle the noise – 'so as to clear the Inner Eye and the superconscious. Perhaps, if we are lucky, some of you will See before the end of the class.'

And so they began. Harry, at least, felt extremely foolish, staring blankly at the crystal ball, trying to keep his mind empty when thoughts such as 'this is stupid' kept drifting across it. It didn't help that Ron kept breaking into silent giggles and Hermione kept tutting.

'Seen anything yet?' Harry asked them, after a quarter of an hour's quiet crystal-gazing.

'Yeah, there's a burn on this table,' said Ron, pointing. 'Someone's spilled their candle.'

'This is such a waste of time,' Hermione hissed. 'I could be practising something useful. I could be catching up on Cheering Charms –'

Professor Trelawney rustled past.

'Would anyone like me to help them interpret the shadowy portents within their Orb?' she murmured over the clinking of her bangles.

'I don't need help,' Ron whispered. 'It's obvious what this means. There's going to be loads of fog tonight.'

Both Harry and Hermione burst out laughing.

'Now, really!' said Professor Trelawney, as everyone's heads turned in their direction. Parvati and Lavender were looking scandalised. 'You are disturbing the clairvoyant vibrations!' She approached their table and peered into their crystal ball. Harry felt his heart sinking. He was sure he knew what was coming ...

'There is something here!' Professor Trelawney whispered, lowering her face to the ball, so that it was reflected twice in her huge glasses. 'Something moving ... but what is it?'

Harry was prepared to bet everything he owned, including his Firebolt, that it wasn't good news, whatever it was. And sure enough ...

'My dear ...' Professor Trelawney breathed, gazing up at Harry. 'It is here, plainer than ever before ... my dear, stalking towards you, growing ever closer ... the Gr–'

'Oh, for *goodness*' sake!' said Hermione, loudly. 'Not that ridiculous Grim *again*!'

Professor Trelawney raised her enormous eyes to Hermione's face. Parvati whispered something to Lavender, and they both glared at Hermione, too. Professor Trelawney stood up, surveying Hermione with unmistakeable anger.

'I am sorry to say that from the moment you have arrived in this class, my *dear*, it has been apparent that you do not have what the noble art of Divination requires. Indeed, I don't remember ever meeting a student whose mind was so hopelessly Mundane.'

There was a moment's silence. Then –

'Fine!' said Hermione suddenly, getting up and cramming *Unfogging the Future* back into her bag. 'Fine!' she repeated, swinging the bag over her shoulder and almost knocking Ron off his chair. 'I give up! I'm leaving!'

And to the whole class's amazement, Hermione strode over to the trapdoor, kicked it open, and climbed down the ladder out of sight.

It took a few minutes for the class to settle down again. Professor Trelawney seemed to have forgotten all about the Grim. She turned abruptly from Harry and Ron's table, breathing rather heavily as she tugged her gauzy shawl more closely to her.

'Ooooo!' said Lavender suddenly, making everyone start. 'Oooooo, Professor Trelawney, I've just remembered! You saw her leaving, didn't you? Didn't you, Professor? *"Around Easter, one of our number will leave us for ever!"* You said it *ages* ago, Professor!'

Professor Trelawney gave her a dewy smile.

'Yes, my dear, I did indeed know that Miss Granger would be leaving us. One hopes, however, that one might have mistaken the Signs ... the Inner Eye can be a burden, you know ...'

Lavender and Parvati looked deeply impressed, and moved over so that Professor Trelawney could join their table instead.

'Some day Hermione's having, eh?' Ron muttered to Harry, looking awed.

'Yeah ...'

Harry glanced into the crystal ball, but saw nothing but swirling white mist. Had Professor Trelawney really seen the Grim again? Would he? The last thing he needed was another near-fatal accident, with the Quidditch final drawing ever nearer.

*

The Easter holidays were not exactly relaxing. The third-years had never had so much homework. Neville Longbottom seemed close to a nervous collapse, and he wasn't the only one.

'Call this a holiday!' Seamus Finnigan roared at the common room one afternoon. 'The exams are ages away, what're they playing at?'

But nobody had as much to do as Hermione. Even without Divination, she was taking more subjects than anybody else. She was usually last to leave the common room at night, first to arrive at the library next morning; she had shadows like Lupin's under her eyes, and seemed constantly close to tears.

Ron had taken over responsibility for Buckbeak's appeal. When he wasn't doing his own work, he was poring over enormously thick volumes with names like *The Handbook of Hippogriff Psychology* and *Fowl or Foul? A Study of Hippogriff Brutality*. He was so absorbed, he even forgot to be horrible to Crookshanks.

Harry, meanwhile, had to fit in his homework around Quidditch practice every day, not to mention endless discussions of tactics with Wood. The Gryffindor–Slytherin match would take place on the first Saturday after the Easter holidays. Slytherin were leading the tournament by exactly two hundred points. This meant (as Wood constantly reminded his team) that they needed to win the match by more than that amount to win the Cup. It also meant that the burden of winning fell largely on Harry, because capturing the Snitch was worth one hundred and fifty points.

'So you must *only* catch it if we're *more* than fifty points up,' Wood told Harry constantly. 'Only if we're more than fifty points up, Harry, or we win the match but lose the Cup. You've got that, haven't you? You must only catch the Snitch if we're –'

'I KNOW, OLIVER!' Harry yelled.

The whole of Gryffindor house was obsessed with the coming match. Gryffindor hadn't won the Quidditch Cup since the legendary Charlie Weasley (Ron's second-oldest brother) had been

Seeker. But Harry doubted whether any of them, even Wood, wanted to win as much as he did. The enmity between Harry and Malfoy was at its highest point ever. Malfoy was still smarting about the mud-throwing incident in Hogsmeade, and even more furious that Harry had somehow wormed his way out of punishment. Harry hadn't forgotten Malfoy's attempt to sabotage him in the match against Ravenclaw, but it was the matter of Buckbeak that made him most determined to beat Malfoy in front of the entire school.

Never, in anyone's memory, had a match approached in such a highly charged atmosphere. By the time the holidays were over, tension between the two teams and their houses was at breaking-point. A number of small scuffles broke out in the corridors, culminating in a nasty incident in which a Gryffindor fourth-year and a Slytherin sixth-year ended up in the hospital wing with leeks sprouting out of their ears.

Harry was having a particularly bad time of it. He couldn't walk to class without Slytherins sticking out their legs and trying to trip him up; Crabbe and Goyle kept popping up wherever he went, and slouching away looking disappointed when they saw him surrounded by people. Wood had given instructions that Harry should be accompanied everywhere, in case the Slytherins tried to put him out of action. The whole of Gryffindor house took up the challenge enthusiastically, so that it was impossible for Harry to get to classes on time because he was surrounded by a vast, chattering crowd. Harry was more concerned for his Firebolt's safety than his own. When he wasn't flying it, he locked it securely in his trunk, and frequently dashed back up to Gryffindor Tower at break-times to check that it was still there.

*

All usual pursuits were abandoned in the Gryffindor common room the night before the match. Even Hermione had put down her books.

'I can't work, I can't concentrate,' she said nervously.

There was a great deal of noise. Fred and George Weasley were dealing with the pressure by being louder and more exuberant than ever. Oliver Wood was crouched over a model of a Quidditch pitch in the corner, prodding little figures across it with his wand and muttering to himself. Angelina, Alicia and Katie were laughing at Fred and George's jokes. Harry was sitting with Ron and

Hermione, removed from the centre of things, trying not to think about the next day, because every time he did, he had the horrible sensation that something very large was fighting to get out of his stomach.

'You're going to be fine,' Hermione told him, though she looked positively terrified.

'You've got a *Firebolt*!' said Ron.

'Yeah ...' said Harry, his stomach writhing.

It came as a relief when Wood suddenly stood up and yelled, 'Team! Bed!'

*

Harry slept badly. First he dreamed that he had overslept, and that Wood was yelling, 'Where were you? We had to use Neville instead!' Then he dreamed that Malfoy and the rest of the Slytherin team arrived for the match riding dragons. He was flying at breakneck speed, trying to avoid a spurt of flames from Malfoy's steed's mouth, when he realised he had forgotten his Firebolt. He fell through the air and woke with a start.

It was a few seconds before Harry remembered that the match hadn't taken place yet, that he was safe in bed and that the Slytherin team definitely wouldn't be allowed to play on dragons. He was feeling very thirsty. As quietly as he could, he got out of his four-poster and went to pour himself some water from the silver jug beneath the window.

The grounds were still and quiet. No breath of wind disturbed the treetops in the Forbidden Forest; the Whomping Willow was motionless and innocent-looking. It looked as though conditions for the match would be perfect.

Harry set down his goblet and was about to turn back to his bed when something caught his eye. An animal of some kind was prowling across the silvery lawn.

Harry dashed to his bedside table, snatched up his glasses and put them on, then hurried back to the window. It couldn't be the Grim – not now – not right before the match –

He peered out at the grounds again and, after a minute's frantic searching, spotted it. It was skirting the edge of the Forest now ... it wasn't the Grim at all ... it was a cat ... Harry clutched the window-ledge in relief as he recognised the bottle-brush tail. It was only Crookshanks ...

Or *was* it only Crookshanks? Harry squinted, pressing his nose flat against the glass. Crookshanks seemed to have come to a halt. Harry was sure he could see something else moving in the shadow of the trees, too.

And next moment, it had emerged: a gigantic, shaggy black dog, moving stealthily across the lawn, Crookshanks trotting at its side. Harry stared. What did this mean? If Crookshanks could see the dog as well, how could it be an omen of Harry's death?

'Ron!' Harry hissed. 'Ron! Wake up!'

'Huh?'

'I need you to tell me if you can see something!'

''S all dark, Harry,' Ron muttered thickly. 'What're you on about?'

'Down here –'

Harry looked quickly back out of the window.

Crookshanks and the dog had vanished. Harry climbed onto the window-sill to look right down into the shadows of the castle, but they weren't there. Where had they gone?

A loud snore told him Ron had fallen asleep again.

*

Harry and the rest of the Gryffindor team entered the Great Hall next day to enormous applause. Harry couldn't help grinning broadly as he saw that both the Ravenclaw and Hufflepuff tables were clapping them, too. The Slytherin table hissed loudly as they passed. Harry noticed that Malfoy looked even paler than usual.

Wood spent the whole of breakfast urging his team to eat, while touching nothing himself. Then he hurried them off to the pitch before anyone else had finished, so they could get an idea of the conditions. As they left the Great Hall, everyone applauded again.

'Good luck, Harry!' called Cho Chang. Harry felt himself blushing.

'OK ... no wind to speak of ... sun's a bit bright, that could impair your vision, watch out for it ... ground's fairly hard, good, that'll give us a fast kick-off ...'

Wood paced the pitch, staring around with the team behind him. Finally they saw the front doors of the castle open in the distance, and the rest of the school spill onto the lawn.

'Changing rooms,' said Wood tersely.

None of them spoke as they changed into their scarlet robes. Harry wondered if they were feeling like he was: as though he'd eaten something extremely wriggly for breakfast. In what seemed like no time at all, Wood was saying, 'OK, it's time, let's go ...'

They walked out onto the pitch to a tidal wave of noise. Three-quarters of the crowd were wearing scarlet rosettes, waving scarlet flags with the Gryffindor lion upon them or brandishing banners with slogans such as 'GO GRYFFINDOR!' and 'LIONS FOR THE CUP!' Behind the Slytherin goalposts, however, two hundred people were wearing green; the silver serpent of Slytherin glittered on their flags, and Professor Snape sat in the very front row, wearing green like everyone else, and a very grim smile.

'And here are the Gryffindors!' yelled Lee Jordan, who was acting as commentator as usual. 'Potter, Bell, Johnson, Spinnet, Weasley, Weasley and Wood. Widely acknowledged as the best side Hogwarts has seen in a good few years –'

Lee's comments were drowned by a tide of 'boos' from the Slytherin end.

'And here come the Slytherin team, led by captain Flint. He's made some changes in the line-up and seems to be going for size rather than skill –'

More boos from the Slytherin crowd. Harry, however, thought Lee had a point. Malfoy was easily the smallest person on the Slytherin team; the rest of them were enormous.

'Captains, shake hands!' said Madam Hooch.

Flint and Wood approached each other and grasped each other's hands very tightly; it looked as though each was trying to break the other's fingers.

'Mount your brooms!' said Madam Hooch. 'Three ... two ... one ...'

The sound of her whistle was lost in the roar from the crowd as fourteen brooms rose into the air. Harry felt his hair fly back off his forehead; his nerves left him in the thrill of the flight; he glanced around, saw Malfoy on his tail, and sped off in search of the Snitch.

'And it's Gryffindor in possession, Alicia Spinnet of Gryffindor with the Quaffle, heading straight for the Slytherin goalposts, looking good, Alicia! Argh, no – Quaffle intercepted by Warrington, Warrington of Slytherin tearing up the pitch – WHAM! – nice Bludger work there by George Weasley, Warrington drops the Quaffle, it's caught by – Johnson, Gryffindor back in possession, come on, Angelina – nice swerve round Montague – *duck, Angelina, that's a Bludger!* – SHE SCORES! TEN–ZERO TO GRYFFINDOR!'

Angelina punched the air as she soared round the end of the

pitch; the sea of scarlet below was screaming its delight –

'OUCH!'

Angelina was nearly thrown from her broom as Marcus Flint went smashing into her.

'Sorry!' said Flint, as the crowd below booed. 'Sorry, didn't see her!'

Next moment, Fred Weasley had chucked his Beater's club at the back of Flint's head. Flint's nose smashed into the handle of his broom and began to bleed.

'That will do!' shrieked Madam Hooch, zooming between them. 'Penalty to Gryffindor for an unprovoked attack on their Chaser! Penalty to Slytherin for deliberate damage to *their* Chaser!'

'Come off it, Miss!' howled Fred, but Madam Hooch blew her whistle and Alicia flew forward to take the penalty.

'Come on, Alicia!' yelled Lee into the silence that had descended on the crowd. 'YES! SHE'S BEATEN THE KEEPER! TWENTY–ZERO TO GRYFFINDOR!'

Harry turned the Firebolt sharply to watch Flint, still bleeding freely, fly forwards to take the Slytherin penalty. Wood was hovering in front of the Gryffindor goalposts, his jaw clenched.

''Course, Wood's a superb Keeper!' Lee Jordan told the crowd, as Flint waited for Madam Hooch's whistle. 'Superb! Very difficult to pass – very difficult indeed – YES! I DON'T BELIEVE IT! HE'S SAVED IT!'

Relieved, Harry zoomed away, gazing around for the Snitch, but still making sure he caught every word of Lee's commentary. It was essential that he hold Malfoy off the Snitch until Gryffindor was more than fifty points up ...

'Gryffindor in possession, no, Slytherin in possession – no! – Gryffindor back in possession and it's Katie Bell, Katie Bell for Gryffindor with the Quaffle, she's streaking up the pitch – THAT WAS DELIBERATE!'

Montague, a Slytherin Chaser, had swerved in front of Katie, and instead of seizing the Quaffle, had grabbed her head. Katie cartwheeled in the air, managed to stay on her broom but dropped the Quaffle.

Madam Hooch's whistle rang out again as she soared over to Montague and began shouting at him. A minute later, Katie had put another penalty past the Slytherin Keeper.

'THIRTY–ZERO! TAKE THAT, YOU DIRTY, CHEATING –'

'Jordan, if you can't commentate in an unbiased way –!'

'I'm telling it like it is, Professor!'

Harry felt a huge jolt of excitement. He had seen the Snitch – it was shimmering at the foot of one of the Gryffindor goalposts – but he mustn't catch it yet. And if Malfoy saw it ...

Faking a look of sudden concentration, Harry pulled his Firebolt round and sped off towards the Slytherin end. It worked. Malfoy went haring after him, clearly thinking Harry had seen the Snitch there ...

WHOOSH.

One of the Bludgers came streaking past Harry's right ear, hit by the gigantic Slytherin Beater, Derrick. Next moment –

WHOOSH.

The second Bludger had grazed Harry's elbow. The other Beater, Bole, was closing in.

Harry had a fleeting glimpse of Bole and Derrick zooming towards him, clubs raised –

He turned the Firebolt upwards at the last second, and Bole and Derrick collided with a sickening crunch.

'Ha haaa!' yelled Lee Jordan, as the Slytherin Beaters lurched away from each other, clutching their heads. 'Too bad, boys! You'll need to get up earlier than that to beat a Firebolt! And it's Gryffindor in possession again, as Johnson takes the Quaffle – Flint alongside her – poke him in the eye, Angelina! – it was a joke, Professor, it was a joke – oh, no – Flint in possession, Flint flying towards the Gryffindor goalposts, come on, now, Wood, save –!'

But Flint had scored; there was an eruption of cheers from the Slytherin end and Lee swore so badly that Professor McGonagall tried to tug the magical megaphone away from him.

'Sorry, Professor, sorry! Won't happen again! So, Gryffindor in the lead, thirty points to ten, and Gryffindor in possession –'

It was turning into the dirtiest match Harry had ever played in. Enraged that Gryffindor had taken such an early lead, the Slytherins were rapidly resorting to any means to take the Quaffle. Bole hit Alicia with his club and tried to say he'd thought she was a Bludger. George Weasley elbowed Bole in the face in retaliation. Madam Hooch awarded both teams penalties, and Wood pulled off another spectacular save, making the score forty–ten to Gryffindor.

The Snitch had disappeared again. Malfoy was still keeping

close to Harry as he soared over the match, looking around for it – once Gryffindor were fifty points ahead ...

Katie scored. Fifty–ten. Fred and George Weasley were swooping around her, clubs raised, in case any of the Slytherins were thinking of revenge. Bole and Derrick took advantage of Fred and George's absence to aim both Bludgers at Wood; they caught him in the stomach, one after the other, and he rolled over in the air, clutching his broom, completely winded.

Madam Hooch was beside herself.

'*You do not attack the Keeper unless the Quaffle is within the scoring area!*' she shrieked at Bole and Derrick. 'Gryffindor penalty!'

And Angelina scored. Sixty–ten. Moments later, Fred Weasley pelted a Bludger at Warrington, knocking the Quaffle out of his hands; Alicia seized it and put it through the Slytherin goal: seventy–ten.

The Gryffindor crowd below were screaming themselves hoarse – Gryffindor were sixty points in the lead, and if Harry caught the Snitch now, the Cup was theirs. Harry could almost feel hundreds of eyes following him as he soared around the pitch, high above the rest of the game, with Malfoy speeding along behind him.

And then he saw it. The Snitch was sparkling twenty feet above him.

Harry put on a huge burst of speed, the wind roaring in his ears; he stretched out his hand, but suddenly, the Firebolt was slowing down –

Horrified, he looked around. Malfoy had thrown himself forward, grabbed hold of the Firebolt's tail and was pulling it back.

'You –'

Harry was angry enough to hit Malfoy, but he couldn't reach. Malfoy was panting with the effort of holding onto the Firebolt, but his eyes were sparkling maliciously. He had achieved what he'd wanted – the Snitch had disappeared again.

'Penalty! Penalty to Gryffindor! I've never seen such tactics!' Madam Hooch screeched, shooting up to where Malfoy was sliding back onto his Nimbus Two Thousand and One.

'YOU CHEATING SCUM!' Lee Jordan was howling into the megaphone, dancing out of Professor McGonagall's reach. 'YOU FILTHY, CHEATING B–'

Professor McGonagall didn't even bother to tell him off. She was actually shaking her fist in Malfoy's direction; her hat had fallen off, and she, too, was shouting furiously.

Alicia took Gryffindor's penalty, but she was so angry she missed by several feet. The Gryffindor team was losing concentration and the Slytherins, delighted by Malfoy's foul on Harry, were being spurred on to greater heights.

'Slytherin in possession, Slytherin heading for goal – Montague scores –' Lee groaned. 'Seventy–twenty to Gryffindor ...'

Harry was now marking Malfoy so closely their knees kept hitting each other. Harry wasn't going to let Malfoy anywhere near the Snitch ...

'Get out of it, Potter!' Malfoy yelled in frustration, as he tried to turn and found Harry blocking him.

'Angelina Johnson gets the Quaffle for Gryffindor, come on, Angelina, COME ON!'

Harry looked round. Every single Slytherin player apart from Malfoy, even the Slytherin Keeper, was streaking up the pitch towards Angelina – they were all going to block her –

Harry wheeled the Firebolt about, bent so low he was lying flat along the handle and kicked it forwards. Like a bullet, he shot towards the Slytherins.

'AAAAAAARRRGH!'

They scattered as the Firebolt zoomed towards them; Angelina's way was clear.

'SHE SCORES! SHE SCORES! Gryffindor lead by eighty points to twenty!'

Harry, who had almost pelted headlong into the stands, skidded to a halt in mid-air, reversed and zoomed back into the middle of the pitch.

And then he saw something to make his heart stand still. Malfoy was diving, a look of triumph on his face – there, a few feet above the grass below, was a tiny, golden glimmer.

Harry urged the Firebolt downwards but Malfoy was miles ahead.

'Go! Go! Go!' Harry urged his broom. They were gaining on Malfoy ... Harry flattened himself to the broom handle as Bole sent a Bludger at him ... he was at Malfoy's ankles ... he was level –

Harry threw himself forwards, taking both hands off his broom. He knocked Malfoy's arm out of the way and –

'YES!'

He pulled out of his dive, his hand in the air, and the stadium exploded. Harry soared above the crowd, an odd ringing in his ears. The tiny golden ball was held tight in his fist, beating its wings hopelessly against his fingers.

Then Wood was speeding towards him, half-blinded by tears; he seized Harry around the neck and sobbed unrestrainedly into his shoulder. Harry felt two large thumps as Fred and George hit them; then Angelina, Alicia and Katie's voices, 'We've won the Cup! We've won the Cup!' Tangled together in a many-armed hug, the Gryffindor team sank, yelling hoarsely, back to earth.

Wave upon wave of crimson supporters was pouring over the barriers onto the pitch. Hands were raining down on their backs. Harry had a confused impression of noise and bodies pressing in on him. Then he, and the rest of the team, were hoisted onto the shoulders of the crowd. Thrust into the light, he saw Hagrid, plastered with crimson rosettes – 'Yeh beat 'em, Harry, yeh beat 'em! Wait till I tell Buckbeak!' There was Percy, jumping up and down like a maniac, all dignity forgotten. Professor McGonagall was sobbing harder even than Wood, wiping her eyes with an enormous Gryffindor flag; and there, fighting their way towards Harry, were Ron and Hermione. Words failed them. They simply beamed, as Harry was borne towards the stands, where Dumbledore stood waiting with the enormous Quidditch Cup.

If only there had been a Dementor around ... As a sobbing Wood passed Harry the Cup, as he lifted it into the air, Harry felt he could have produced the world's best Patronus.

— CHAPTER SIXTEEN —

Professor Trelawney's Prediction

Harry's euphoria at finally winning the Quidditch Cup lasted at least a week. Even the weather seemed to be celebrating; as June approached, the days became cloudless and sultry, and all anybody felt like doing was strolling into the grounds and flopping down on the grass with several pints of iced pumpkin juice, perhaps playing a casual game of Gobstones or watching the giant squid propel itself dreamily across the surface of the lake.

But they couldn't. The exams were nearly upon them, and instead of lazing around outside, the students were forced to remain inside the castle, trying to bully their brains into concentrating while enticing wafts of summer air drifted in through the windows. Even Fred and George Weasley had been spotted working; they were about to take their O.W.Ls (Ordinary Wizarding Levels). Percy was getting ready to sit his N.E.W.Ts (Nastily Exhausting Wizarding Tests), the highest qualification Hogwarts offered. As Percy hoped to enter the Ministry of Magic, he needed top grades. He was becoming increasingly edgy, and gave very severe punishments to anybody who disturbed the quiet of the common room in the evenings. In fact, the only person who seemed more anxious than Percy was Hermione.

Harry and Ron had given up asking her how she was managing to attend several classes at once, but they couldn't restrain themselves when they saw the exam timetable she had drawn up for herself. The first column read:

MONDAY
9 o'clock, Arithmancy
9 o'clock, Transfiguration

Lunch
1 o'clock, Charms
1 o'clock, Ancient Runes

'Hermione?' Ron said cautiously, because she was liable to explode when interrupted these days. 'Er – are you sure you've copied down these times right?'

'What?' snapped Hermione, picking up the exam timetable and examining it. 'Yes, of course I have.'

'Is there any point asking how you're going to sit two exams at once?' said Harry.

'No,' said Hermione shortly. 'Has either of you seen my copy of *Numerology and Grammatica*?'

'Oh, yeah, I borrowed it for a bit of bedtime reading,' said Ron, but very quietly. Hermione started shifting heaps of parchment around on her table, looking for the book. Just then, there was a rustle at the window and Hedwig fluttered through it, a note clutched tightly in her beak.

'It's from Hagrid,' said Harry, ripping the note open. 'Buckbeak's appeal – it's set for the sixth.'

'That's the day we finish our exams,' said Hermione, still looking everywhere for her Arithmancy book.

'And they're coming up here to do it,' said Harry, still reading from the letter. 'Someone from the Ministry of Magic and – and an executioner.'

Hermione looked up, startled.

'They're bringing the executioner to the appeal! But that sounds as though they've already decided!'

'Yeah, it does,' said Harry slowly.

'They can't!' Ron howled. 'I've spent *ages* reading up stuff for him, they can't just ignore it all!'

But Harry had a horrible feeling that the Committee for the Disposal of Dangerous Creatures had had its mind made up for it by Mr Malfoy. Draco, who had been noticeably subdued since Gryffindor's triumph in the Quidditch final, seemed to regain some of his old swagger over the next few days. From sneering comments Harry overheard, Malfoy was certain Buckbeak was going to be killed, and seemed thoroughly pleased with himself for bringing it about. It was all Harry could do to stop himself imitating Hermione and hitting Malfoy in the face on these occasions. And the worst thing of all was that they had no time or opportunity to go and see Hagrid, because the strict new security measures had not been lifted, and Harry didn't dare retrieve his Invisibility Cloak from below the one-eyed witch.

*

Exam week began and an unnatural hush fell over the castle. The third-years emerged from Transfiguration at lunch-time on Monday limp and ashen-faced, comparing results and bemoaning the difficulty of the tasks they had been set, which had included turning a teapot into a tortoise. Hermione irritated the rest by fussing about how her tortoise had looked more like a turtle, which was the least of everyone else's worries.

'Mine still had a spout for a tail, what a nightmare ...'

'Were the tortoises *supposed* to breathe steam?'

'It still had a willow-patterned shell, d'you think that'll count against me?'

Then, after a hasty lunch, it was straight back upstairs for the Charms exam. Hermione had been right; Professor Flitwick did indeed test them on Cheering Charms. Harry slightly overdid his out of nerves and Ron, who was partnering him, ended up in fits of hysterical laughter and had to be led away to a quiet room for an hour before he was ready to perform the Charm himself. After dinner, the students hurried back to their common rooms, not to relax, but to start revising for Care of Magical Creatures, Potions and Astronomy.

Hagrid presided over the Care of Magical Creatures exam the following morning with a very preoccupied air indeed; his heart didn't seem to be in it at all. He had provided a large tub of fresh Flobberworms for the class, and told them that, to pass the test, their Flobberworm had to still be alive at the end of one hour. As Flobberworms flourished best if left to their own devices, it was the easiest exam any of them had ever sat, and also gave Harry, Ron and Hermione plenty of opportunity to speak to Hagrid.

'Beaky's gettin' a bit depressed,' Hagrid told them, bending low on the pretence of checking that Harry's Flobberworm was still alive. 'Bin cooped up too long. But still ... we'll know day after tomorrow – one way or the other.'

They had Potions that afternoon, which was an unqualified disaster. Try as Harry might, he couldn't get his Confusing Concoction to thicken, and Snape, standing watching with an air of vindictive pleasure, scribbled something that looked suspiciously like a zero onto his notes before moving away.

Then came Astronomy at midnight, up on the tallest tower; History of Magic on Wednesday morning, in which Harry scribbled everything Florean Fortescue had ever told him about medieval witch hunts, while wishing he could have had one of Fortescue's choco-nut sundaes with him in the stifling classroom. Wednesday afternoon meant Herbology, in the greenhouses under a baking hot sun; then back to the common room once more, with the backs of their necks sunburnt, thinking longingly of this time next day, when it would all be over.

Their second from last exam, on Thursday morning, was Defence Against the Dark Arts. Professor Lupin had compiled the most unusual exam any of them had ever taken; a sort of obstacle course outside in the sun, where they had to wade across a deep paddling pool containing a Grindylow, cross a series of potholes full of Red Caps, squish their way across a patch of marsh, ignoring the misleading directions from a Hinkypunk, then climb into an old trunk and battle with a new Boggart.

'Excellent, Harry,' Lupin muttered, as Harry climbed out of the trunk, grinning. 'Full marks.'

Flushed with his success, Harry hung around to watch Ron and Hermione. Ron did very well until he reached the Hinkypunk, which successfully confused him into sinking waist-high into the quagmire. Hermione did everything perfectly until she reached the trunk with the Boggart in it. After about a minute inside it, she burst out again, screaming.

'Hermione!' said Lupin, startled. 'What's the matter?'

'P-P-Professor McGonagall!' Hermione gasped, pointing into the trunk. 'Sh-she said I'd failed everything!'

It took a little while to calm Hermione down. When at last she had regained a grip on herself, she, Harry and Ron went back to the castle. Ron was still slightly inclined to laugh at Hermione's Boggart, but an argument was averted by the sight that met them on the top of the steps.

Cornelius Fudge, sweating slightly in his pinstriped cloak, was standing there staring out at the grounds. He started at the sight of Harry.

'Hello there, Harry!' he said. 'Just had an exam, I expect? Nearly finished?'

'Yes,' said Harry. Hermione and Ron, not being on speaking terms with the Minister for Magic, hovered awkwardly in the background.

'Lovely day,' said Fudge, casting an eye over the lake. 'Pity ... pity ...'

He sighed deeply and looked down at Harry.

'I'm here on an unpleasant mission, Harry. The Committee for the Disposal of Dangerous Creatures required a witness to the execution of a mad Hippogriff. As I needed to visit Hogwarts to check on the Black situation, I was asked to step in.'

'Does that mean the appeal's already happened?' Ron interrupted, stepping forwards.

'No, no, it's scheduled for this afternoon,' said Fudge, looking curiously at Ron.

'Then you might not have to witness an execution at all!' said Ron stoutly. 'The Hippogriff might get off!'

Before Fudge could answer, two wizards came through the castle doors behind him. One was so ancient he appeared to be withering before their very eyes; the other was tall and strapping, with a thin black moustache. Harry gathered that they were representatives of the Committee for the Disposal of Dangerous Creatures, because the very old wizard squinted towards Hagrid's cabin and said in a feeble voice, 'Dear, dear, I'm getting too old for this ... two o'clock, isn't it, Fudge?'

The black-moustached man was fingering something in his belt; Harry looked and saw that he was running one broad thumb along the blade of a shining axe. Ron opened his mouth to say something, but Hermione nudged him hard in the ribs and jerked her head towards the Entrance Hall.

'Why'd you stop me?' said Ron angrily, as they entered the Great Hall for lunch. 'Did you see them? They've even got the axe ready! This isn't justice!'

'Ron, your dad works for the Ministry. You can't go saying things like that to his boss!' said Hermione, but she, too, looked very upset. 'As long as Hagrid keeps his head this time, and argues his case properly, they can't possibly execute Buckbeak ...'

But Harry could tell Hermione didn't really believe what she was saying. All around them, people were talking excitedly as they ate their lunch, happily anticipating the end of exams that afternoon, but Harry, Ron and Hermione, lost in worry about

Hagrid and Buckbeak, didn't join in.

Harry and Ron's last exam was Divination; Hermione's, Muggle Studies. They walked up the marble staircase together. Hermione left them on the first floor and Harry and Ron proceeded all the way up to the seventh, where many of their class were sitting on the spiral staircase to Professor Trelawney's classroom, trying to cram in a bit of last-minute revision.

'She's seeing us all separately,' Neville informed them, as they went to sit down next to him. He had his copy of *Unfogging the Future* open on his lap at the pages devoted to crystal-gazing. 'Have either of you ever seen *anything* in a crystal ball?' he asked them unhappily.

'Nope,' said Ron, in an offhand voice. He kept checking his watch; Harry knew that he was counting down the time until Buckbeak's appeal started.

The queue of people outside the classroom shortened very slowly. As each person climbed back down the silver ladder, the rest of the class hissed, 'What did she ask? Was it OK?'

But they all refused to say.

'She says the crystal ball's told her that, if I tell you, I'll have a horrible accident!' squeaked Neville, as he clambered back down the ladder towards Harry and Ron, who had now reached the landing.

'That's convenient,' snorted Ron. 'You know, I'm starting to think Hermione was right about her' (he jabbed his thumb towards the trapdoor overhead), 'she's a right old fraud.'

'Yeah,' said Harry, looking at his own watch. It was now two o'clock. 'Wish she'd hurry up ...'

Parvati came back down the ladder glowing with pride.

'She says I've got all the makings of a true Seer,' she informed Harry and Ron. 'I saw *loads* of stuff ... well, good luck!'

She hurried off down the spiral staircase towards Lavender.

'Ronald Weasley,' said the familiar, misty voice from over their heads. Ron grimaced at Harry, and climbed the silver ladder out of sight. Harry was now the only person left to be tested. He settled himself on the floor with his back against the wall, listening to a fly buzzing in the sunny window, his mind across the grounds with Hagrid.

Finally, after about twenty minutes, Ron's large feet reappeared on the ladder.

'How'd it go?' Harry asked him, standing up.

'Rubbish,' said Ron. 'Couldn't see a thing, so I made some stuff up. Don't think she was convinced, though ...'

'Meet you in the common room,' Harry muttered, as Professor Trelawney's voice called, 'Harry Potter!'

The tower room was hotter than ever before; the curtains were closed, the fire was alight, and the usual sickly scent made Harry cough as he stumbled through the clutter of chairs and tables to where Professor Trelawney sat waiting for him before a large crystal ball.

'Good day, my dear,' she said softly. 'If you would kindly gaze into the Orb ... take your time, now ... then tell me what you see within it ...'

Harry bent over the crystal ball and stared, stared as hard as he could, willing it to show him something other than swirling white fog, but nothing happened.

'Well?' Professor Trelawney prompted delicately. 'What do you see?'

The heat was overpowering and his nostrils were stinging with the perfumed smoke wafting from the fire beside them. He thought of what Ron had just said, and decided to pretend.

'Er –,' said Harry, 'a dark shape ... um ...'

'What does it resemble?' whispered Professor Trelawney. 'Think, now ...'

Harry cast his mind around and it landed on Buckbeak.

'A Hippogriff,' he said firmly.

'Indeed!' whispered Professor Trelawney, scribbling keenly on the parchment perched upon her knees. 'My boy, you may well be seeing the outcome of poor Hagrid's trouble with the Ministry of Magic! Look closer ... does the Hippogriff appear to ... have its head?'

'Yes,' said Harry firmly.

'Are you sure?' Professor Trelawney urged him. 'Are you quite sure, dear? You don't see it writhing on the ground, perhaps, and a shadowy figure raising an axe behind it?'

'No!' said Harry, starting to feel slightly sick.

'No blood? No weeping Hagrid?'

'No!' said Harry again, wanting more than ever to leave the room and the heat. 'It looks fine, it's – flying away ...'

Professor Trelawney sighed.

'Well, dear, I think we'll leave it there ... a little disappointing ... but I'm sure you did your best.'

Relieved, Harry got up, picked up his bag and turned to go, but then a loud, harsh voice spoke behind him.

'*It will happen tonight.*'

Harry wheeled around. Professor Trelawney had gone rigid in her armchair; her eyes were unfocused and her mouth sagging.

'S-sorry?' said Harry.

But Professor Trelawney didn't seem to hear him. Her eyes started to roll. Harry stood there in a panic. She looked as though she was about to have some sort of seizure. He hesitated, thinking of running to the hospital wing – and then Professor Trelawney spoke again, in the same harsh voice, quite unlike her own:

'*The Dark Lord lies alone and friendless, abandoned by his followers. His servant has been chained these twelve years. Tonight, before midnight, the servant will break free and set out to rejoin his master. The Dark Lord will rise again with his servant's aid, greater and more terrible than ever before. Tonight ... before midnight ... the servant ... will set out ... to rejoin ... his master ...*'

Professor Trelawney's head fell forwards onto her chest. She made a grunting sort of noise. Then, quite suddenly, her head snapped up again.

'I'm so sorry, dear boy,' she said dreamily. 'The heat of the day, you know ... I drifted off for a moment ...'

Harry stood there, still staring.

'Is there anything wrong, my dear?'

'You – you just told me that the – the Dark Lord's going to rise again ... that his servant's going to go back to him ...'

Professor Trelawney looked thoroughly startled.

'The Dark Lord? He Who Must Not Be Named? My dear boy, that's hardly something to joke about ... rise again, indeed ...'

'But you just said it! You said the Dark Lord –'

'I think you must have dozed off too, dear!' said Professor Trelawney. 'I would certainly not presume to predict anything quite as far-fetched as *that*!'

Harry climbed back down the ladder and the spiral staircase, wondering ... had he just heard Professor Trelawney make a real prediction? Or had that been her idea of an impressive end to the test?

Five minutes later he was dashing past the security trolls

outside the entrance to Gryffindor Tower, Professor Trelawney's words still resounding in his head. People were striding past him in the opposite direction, laughing and joking, heading for the grounds and a bit of long-awaited freedom; by the time he had reached the portrait hole and entered the common room, it was almost deserted. Over in a corner, however, sat Ron and Hermione.

'Professor Trelawney,' Harry panted, 'just told me –'

But he stopped abruptly at the sight of their faces.

'Buckbeak lost,' said Ron weakly. 'Hagrid's just sent this.'

Hagrid's note was dry this time, no tears had splattered it, yet his hand seemed to have shaken so much as he wrote that it was hardly legible.

> *Lost appeal. They're going to execute at sunset. Nothing you can do. Don't come down. I don't want you to see it.*
> *Hagrid*

'We've got to go,' said Harry at once. 'He can't just sit there on his own, waiting for the executioner!'

'Sunset, though,' said Ron, who was staring out of the window in a glazed sort of way. 'We'd never be allowed ... specially you, Harry ...'

Harry sank his head into his hands, thinking.

'If we only had the Invisibility Cloak ...'

'Where is it?' said Hermione.

Harry told her about leaving it in the passageway under the one-eyed witch.

'... if Snape sees me anywhere near there again, I'm in serious trouble,' he finished.

'That's true,' said Hermione, getting to her feet. 'If he sees *you* ... how do you open the witch's hump again?'

'You – you tap it and say, "Dissendium",' said Harry. 'But –'

Hermione didn't wait for the rest of his sentence; she strode across the room, pushed the Fat Lady's portrait open and vanished from sight.

'She hasn't gone to get it?' Ron said, staring after her.

She had. Hermione returned a quarter of an hour later with the silvery Cloak folded carefully under her robes.

'Hermione, I don't know what's got into you lately!' said Ron, astounded. 'First you hit Malfoy, then you walk out on Professor Trelawney –'

Hermione looked rather flattered.

*

They went down to dinner with everybody else, but did not return to Gryffindor Tower afterwards. Harry had the Cloak hidden down the front of his robes; he had to keep his arms folded to hide the lump. They skulked in an empty chamber off the Entrance Hall, listening, until they were sure it was deserted. They heard a last pair of people hurrying across the Hall, and a door slamming. Hermione poked her head around the door.

'OK,' she whispered, 'no one there – Cloak on –'

Walking very close together so that nobody would see them, they crossed the Hall on tiptoe beneath the Cloak, then walked down the stone front steps into the grounds. The sun was already sinking behind the Forbidden Forest, gilding the top branches of the trees.

They reached Hagrid's cabin and knocked. He was a minute in answering, and when he did, he looked all around for his visitor, pale-faced and trembling.

'It's us,' Harry hissed. 'We're wearing the Invisibility Cloak. Let us in and we can take it off.'

'Yeh shouldn've come!' Hagrid whispered, but he stood back, and they stepped inside. Hagrid shut the door quickly and Harry pulled off the Cloak.

Hagrid was not crying, nor did he throw himself upon their necks. He looked like a man who did not know where he was or what to do. This helplessness was worse to watch than tears.

'Wan' some tea?' he said. His great hands were shaking as he reached for the kettle.

'Where's Buckbeak, Hagrid?' said Hermione hesitantly.

'I – I took him outside,' said Hagrid, spilling milk all over the table as he filled up the jug. 'He's tethered in me pumpkin patch. Thought he oughta see the trees an' – an' smell fresh air – before –'

Hagrid's hand trembled so violently that the milk jug slipped from his grasp and shattered all over the floor.

'I'll do it, Hagrid,' said Hermione quickly, hurrying over and starting to clean up the mess.

'There's another one in the cupboard,' Hagrid said, sitting down and wiping his forehead on his sleeve. Harry glanced at Ron, who looked back hopelessly.

'Isn't there anything anyone can do, Hagrid?' Harry asked fiercely, sitting down next to him. 'Dumbledore –'

'He's tried,' said Hagrid. 'He's got no power ter overrule the Committee. He told 'em Buckbeak's all right, but they're scared ... yeh know what Lucius Malfoy's like ... threatened 'em, I expect ... an' the executioner, Macnair, he's an old pal o' Malfoy's ... but it'll be quick an' clean ... an' I'll be beside him ...'

Hagrid swallowed. His eyes were darting all over the cabin, as though looking for some shred of hope or comfort.

'Dumbledore's gonna come down while it – while it happens. Wrote me this mornin'. Said he wants ter – ter be with me. Great man, Dumbledore ...'

Hermione, who had been rummaging in Hagrid's cupboard for another milk jug, let out a small, quickly stifled sob. She straightened up with the new jug in her hands, fighting back tears.

'We'll stay with you, too, Hagrid,' she began, but Hagrid shook his shaggy head.

'Yeh're ter go back up ter the castle. I told yeh, I don' wan' yeh watchin'. An' yeh shouldn' be down here anyway ... if Fudge an' Dumbledore catch yeh out without permission, Harry, yeh'll be in big trouble.'

Silent tears were now streaming down Hermione's face, but she hid them from Hagrid, bustling around making tea. Then, as she picked up the milk bottle to pour some into the jug, she let out a shriek.

'Ron! I – I don't believe it – it's *Scabbers*!'

Ron gaped at her.

'What are you talking about?'

Hermione carried the milk jug over to the table and turned it upside-down. With a frantic squeak, and much scrambling to get back inside, Scabbers the rat came sliding out onto the table.

'Scabbers!' said Ron blankly. 'Scabbers, what are you doing here?'

He grabbed the struggling rat and held him up to the light. Scabbers looked dreadful. He was thinner than ever, large tufts of hair had fallen out leaving wide bald patches, and he writhed in Ron's hands as though desperate to free himself.

'It's OK, Scabbers!' said Ron. 'No cats! There's nothing here to hurt you!'

Hagrid suddenly stood up, his eyes fixed on the window. His normally ruddy face had gone the colour of parchment.

'They're comin' ...'

Harry, Ron and Hermione whipped around. A group of men was walking down the distant castle steps. In front was Albus Dumbledore, his silver beard gleaming in the dying sun. Next to him trotted Cornelius Fudge. Behind them came the feeble old Committee member and the executioner, Macnair.

'Yeh gotta go,' said Hagrid. Every inch of him was trembling. 'They mustn' find yeh here ... go on, now ...'

Ron stuffed Scabbers into his pocket and Hermione picked up the Cloak.

'I'll let yeh out the back way,' said Hagrid.

They followed him to the door into his back garden. Harry felt strangely unreal, and even more so when he saw Buckbeak a few yards away, tethered to a tree behind Hagrid's pumpkin patch. Buckbeak seemed to know something was happening. He turned his sharp head from side to side, and pawed the ground nervously.

'It's OK, Beaky,' said Hagrid softly. 'It's OK ...' He turned to Harry, Ron and Hermione. 'Go on,' he said. 'Get goin'.'

But they didn't move.

'Hagrid, we can't –'

'We'll tell them what really happened –'

'They can't kill him –'

'Go!' said Hagrid fiercely. 'It's bad enough without you lot in trouble an' all!'

They had no choice. As Hermione threw the Cloak over Harry and Ron, they heard voices at the front of the cabin. Hagrid looked at the place where they had just vanished from sight.

'Go quick,' he said hoarsely. 'Don' listen ...'

And he strode back into his cabin as someone knocked at the front door.

Slowly, in a kind of horrified trance, Harry, Ron and Hermione set off silently around Hagrid's house. As they reached the other side, the front door closed with a sharp snap.

'Please, let's hurry,' Hermione whispered. 'I can't stand it, I can't bear it ...'

They started up the sloping lawn towards the castle. The sun was sinking fast now; the sky had turned to a clear, purple-tinged grey, but to the west there was a ruby-red glow.

Ron stopped dead.

'Oh, please, Ron,' Hermione began.

'It's Scabbers – he won't – stay put –'

Ron was bent over, trying to keep Scabbers in his pocket, but the rat was going berserk; squeaking madly, twisting and flailing, trying to sink his teeth into Ron's hand.

'Scabbers, it's me, you idiot, it's Ron,' Ron hissed.

They heard a door open behind them and men's voices.

'Oh Ron, please let's move, they're going to do it!' Hermione breathed.

'OK – Scabbers, stay *put* –'

They walked forwards; Harry, like Hermione, was trying not to listen to the rumble of voices behind them. Ron stopped again.

'I can't hold him – Scabbers, shut up, everyone'll hear us –'

The rat was squealing wildly, but not loudly enough to cover up the sounds drifting from Hagrid's garden. There was a jumble of indistinct male voices, a silence and then, without warning, the unmistakeable swish and thud of an axe.

Hermione swayed on the spot.

'They did it!' she whispered to Harry. 'I d-don't believe it – they did it!'

CHAPTER SEVENTEEN

Cat, Rat and Dog

Harry's mind had gone blank with shock. The three of them stood transfixed with horror under the Invisibility Cloak. The very last rays of the setting sun were casting a bloody light over the long-shadowed grounds. Then, behind them, they heard a wild howling.

'Hagrid,' Harry muttered. Without thinking about what he was doing, he made to turn back, but both Ron and Hermione seized his arms.

'We can't,' said Ron, who was paper white. 'He'll be in worse trouble if they know we've been to see him ...'

Hermione's breathing was shallow and uneven.

'How – could – they?' she choked. 'How *could* they?'

'Come on,' said Ron, whose teeth seemed to be chattering.

They set off back towards the castle, walking slowly to keep themselves hidden under the Cloak. Light was fading fast now. By the time they reached open ground, darkness was settling like a spell around them.

'Scabbers, keep still,' Ron hissed, clamping his hand over his chest. The rat was wriggling madly. Ron came to a sudden halt, trying to force Scabbers deeper into his pocket. 'What's the matter with you, you stupid rat? Stay still – OUCH! He bit me!'

'Ron, be quiet!' Hermione whispered urgently. 'Fudge'll be out here in a minute –'

'He won't – stay – put –'

Scabbers was plainly terrified. He was writhing with all his might, trying to break free of Ron's grip.

'What's the *matter* with him?'

But Harry had just seen – slinking towards them, his body low to the ground, wide yellow eyes glinting eerily in the darkness – Crookshanks. Whether he could see them, or was following the sound of Scabbers's squeaks, Harry couldn't tell.

'Crookshanks!' Hermione moaned. 'No, go away, Crookshanks! Go away!'

But the cat was getting nearer –

'Scabbers – NO!'

Too late – the rat had slipped between Ron's clutching fingers, hit the ground and scampered away. In one bound, Crookshanks sprang after him, and before Harry or Hermione could stop him, Ron had thrown the Invisibility Cloak off himself and pelted away into the darkness.

'*Ron!*' Hermione moaned.

She and Harry looked at each other, then followed at a sprint; it was impossible to run full out under the Cloak; they pulled it off and it streamed behind them like a banner as they hurtled after Ron; they could hear his feet thundering along ahead, and his shouts at Crookshanks.

'Get away from him – get away – Scabbers, come *here* –'

There was a loud thud.

'*Gotcha!* Get off, you stinking cat –'

Harry and Hermione almost fell over Ron; they skidded to a stop right in front of him. He was sprawled on the ground, but Scabbers was back in his pocket; he had both hands held tight over the quivering lump.

'Ron – come on – back under the Cloak –' Hermione panted. 'Dumbledore – the Minister – they'll be coming back out in a minute –'

But before they could cover themselves again, before they could even catch their breath, they heard the soft pounding of gigantic paws. Something was bounding towards them out of the dark – an enormous, pale-eyed, jet-black dog.

Harry reached for his wand, but too late – the dog had made an enormous leap and its front paws hit him on the chest. He keeled over backwards in a whirl of hair; he felt its hot breath, saw inch-long teeth –

But the force of its leap had carried it too far; it rolled off him; dazed, feeling as though his ribs were broken, Harry tried to stand up; he could hear it growling as it skidded around for a new attack.

Ron was on his feet. As the dog sprang back towards them, he pushed Harry aside; the dog's jaws fastened instead around Ron's outstretched arm. Harry lunged at it and seized a handful of the brute's hair, but it was dragging Ron away as easily as if he were a rag-doll –

Then, out of nowhere, something hit Harry so hard across the face he was knocked off his feet again. He heard Hermione shriek with pain and fall, too. Harry groped for his wand, blinking blood out of his eyes –

'*Lumos!*' he whispered.

The wand-light showed him the trunk of a thick tree; they had chased Scabbers into the shadow of the Whomping Willow and its branches were creaking as though in a high wind, whipping backwards and forwards to stop them going nearer.

And there, at the base of the trunk, was the dog, dragging Ron backwards into a large gap in the roots – Ron was fighting furiously, but his head and torso were slipping out of sight –

'Ron!' Harry shouted, trying to follow, but a heavy branch whipped lethally through the air and he was forced backwards again.

All they could see now was one of Ron's legs, which he had hooked around a root in an effort to stop the dog pulling him further underground. Then a horrible crack cut the air like a gunshot; Ron's leg had broken, and next second, his foot had vanished from sight.

'Harry – we've got to go for help –' Hermione cried; she was bleeding, too; the Willow had cut her across the shoulder.

'No! That thing's big enough to eat him, we haven't got time –'

'We're never going to get through without help –'

Another branch whipped down at them, twigs clenched like knuckles.

'If that dog can get in, we can,' Harry panted, darting here and there, trying to find a way through the vicious, swishing branches, but he couldn't get an inch nearer to the tree-roots without being in range of the tree's blows.

'Oh, help, help,' Hermione whispered frantically, dancing uncertainly on the spot, 'please ...'

Crookshanks darted forwards. He slithered between the battering branches like a snake and placed his front paws upon a knot on the trunk.

Abruptly, as though the tree had been turned to marble, it stopped moving. Not a leaf twitched or shook.

'Crookshanks!' Hermione whispered uncertainly. She now

grasped Harry's arm painfully hard. 'How did he know –?'

'He's friends with that dog,' said Harry grimly. 'I've seen them together. Come on – and keep your wand out –'

They covered the distance to the trunk in seconds, but before they had reached the gap in the roots, Crookshanks had slid into it with a flick of his bottle-brush tail. Harry went next; he crawled forwards, headfirst, and slid down an earthy slope to the bottom of a very low tunnel. Crookshanks was a little way along, his eyes flashing in the light from Harry's wand. Seconds later, Hermione slithered down beside him.

'Where's Ron?' she whispered in a terrified voice.

'This way,' said Harry, setting off, bent-backed, after Crookshanks.

'Where does this tunnel come out?' Hermione asked breathlessly from behind him.

'I don't know ... it's marked on the Marauder's Map but Fred and George said no one's ever got into it. It goes off the edge of the map, but it looked like it ends up in Hogsmeade ...'

They moved as fast as they could, bent almost double; ahead of them, Crookshanks's tail bobbed in and out of view. On and on went the passage; it felt at least as long as the one to Honeydukes. All Harry could think of was Ron, and what the enormous dog might be doing to him ... he was drawing breath in sharp, painful gasps, running at a crouch ...

And then the tunnel began to rise; moments later it twisted, and Crookshanks had gone. Instead, Harry could see a patch of dim light through a small opening.

He and Hermione paused, gasping for breath, edging forwards. Both raised their wands to see what lay beyond.

It was a room, a very disordered, dusty room. Paper was peeling from the walls; there were stains all over the floor; every piece of furniture was broken as though somebody had smashed it. The windows were all boarded-up.

Harry glanced at Hermione, who looked very frightened, but nodded.

Harry pulled himself out of the hole, staring around. The room was deserted, but a door to their right stood open, leading to a shadowy hallway. Hermione suddenly grabbed Harry's arm again. Her wide eyes were travelling around the boarded windows.

'Harry,' she whispered. 'I think we're in the Shrieking Shack.'

Harry looked around. His eyes fell on a wooden chair near them. Large chunks had been torn out of it; one of the legs had been ripped off entirely.

'Ghosts didn't do that,' he said slowly.

At that moment, there was a creak overhead. Something had moved upstairs. Both of them looked up at the ceiling. Hermione's grip on Harry's arm was so tight he was losing feeling in his fingers. He raised his eyebrows at her; she nodded again and let go.

Quietly as they could, they crept out into the hall and up the crumbling staircase. Everything was covered in a thick layer of dust except the floor, where a wide, shiny stripe had been made by something being dragged upstairs.

They reached the dark landing.

'*Nox*,' they whispered together, and the lights at the end of their wands went out. Only one door was open. As they crept towards it, they heard movement from behind it; a low moan, and then a deep, loud purring. They exchanged a last look, a last nod.

Wand held tightly before him, Harry kicked the door wide open.

On a magnificent four-poster bed with dusty hangings, lay Crookshanks, purring loudly at the sight of them. On the floor beside him, clutching his leg, which stuck out at a strange angle, was Ron.

Harry and Hermione dashed across to him.

'Ron – are you OK?'

'Where's the dog?'

'Not a dog,' Ron moaned. His teeth were gritted with pain. 'Harry, it's a trap –'

'What –'

'*He's the dog ... he's an Animagus ...*'

Ron was staring over Harry's shoulder. Harry wheeled around. With a snap, the man in the shadows closed the door behind them.

A mass of filthy, matted hair hung to his elbows. If eyes hadn't been shining out of the deep, dark sockets, he might have been a corpse. The waxy skin was stretched so tightly over the bones of his face, it looked like a skull. His yellow teeth were bared in a grin. It was Sirius Black.

'*Expelliarmus!*' he croaked, pointing Ron's wand at them.

Harry's and Hermione's wands shot out of their hands, high in the air, and Black caught them. Then he took a step closer. His eyes were fixed on Harry.

'I thought you'd come and help your friend,' he said hoarsely. His voice sounded as though he had long ago lost the habit of using it. 'Your father would have done the same for me. Brave of you, not to run for a teacher. I'm grateful ... it will make everything much easier ...'

The taunt about his father rang in Harry's ears as though Black had bellowed it. A boiling hate erupted in Harry's chest, leaving no place for fear. For the first time in his life, he wanted his wand back in his hand, not to defend himself, but to attack ... to kill. Without knowing what he was doing, he started forwards, but there was a sudden movement on either side of him and two pairs of hands grabbed him and held him back. 'No, Harry!' Hermione gasped in a petrified whisper; Ron, however, spoke to Black.

'If you want to kill Harry, you'll have to kill us, too!' he said fiercely, though the effort of standing up had drained him of still more colour, and he swayed slightly as he spoke.

Something flickered in Black's shadowed eyes.

'Lie down,' he said quietly to Ron. 'You will damage that leg even more.'

'Did you hear me?' Ron said weakly, though he was clinging painfully to Harry to stay upright. 'You'll have to kill all three of us!'

'There'll only be one murder here tonight,' said Black, and his grin widened.

'Why's that?' Harry spat, trying to wrench himself free of Ron and Hermione. 'Didn't care last time, did you? Didn't mind slaughtering all those Muggles to get at Pettigrew ... What's the matter, gone soft in Azkaban?'

'Harry!' Hermione whimpered. 'Be quiet!'

'HE KILLED MY MUM AND DAD!' Harry roared, and with a huge effort he broke free of Hermione and Ron's restraint and lunged forwards –

He had forgotten about magic – he had forgotten that he was short and skinny and thirteen, whereas Black was a tall, full-grown man. All Harry knew was that he wanted to hurt Black as badly as he could and that he didn't care how much he got hurt in return ...

Perhaps it was the shock of Harry doing something so stupid, but Black didn't raise the wands in time. One of Harry's hands fastened over Black's wasted wrist, forcing the wandtips away; the knuckles of Harry's other hand collided with the side of Black's head and they fell, backwards, into the wall –

Hermione was screaming; Ron was yelling; there was a blinding flash as the wands in Black's hand sent into the air a jet of sparks which missed Harry's face by inches; Harry felt the shrunken arm under his fingers twisting madly, but he clung on, his other hand punching every part of Black it could find.

But Black's free hand had found Harry's throat –

'No,' he hissed. 'I've waited too long –'

The fingers tightened, Harry choked, his glasses askew.

Then he saw Hermione's foot swing out of nowhere. Black let go of Harry with a grunt of pain. Ron had thrown himself on Black's wand hand and Harry heard a faint clatter –

He fought free of the tangle of bodies and saw his own wand rolling across the floor; he threw himself towards it but –

'Argh!'

Crookshanks had joined the fray; both sets of front claws had sunk themselves deep into Harry's arm; Harry threw him off, but Crookshanks now darted towards Harry's wand –

'NO YOU DON'T!' roared Harry, and he aimed a kick at Crookshanks that made the cat leap aside, spitting; Harry snatched up his wand and turned –

'Get out of the way!' he shouted at Ron and Hermione.

They didn't need telling twice. Hermione, gasping for breath, her lip bleeding, scrambled aside, snatching up her and Ron's wands. Ron crawled to the four-poster and collapsed onto it, panting, his white face now tinged with green, both hands clutching his broken leg.

Black was sprawled at the bottom of the wall. His thin chest rose and fell rapidly as he watched Harry walking slowly nearer, his wand pointing straight at Black's heart.

'Going to kill me, Harry?' he whispered.

Harry stopped right above him, his wand still pointing at Black's chest, looking down at him. A livid bruise was rising around Black's left eye and his nose was bleeding.

'You killed my parents,' said Harry, his voice shaking slightly, but his wand hand quite steady.

Black stared up at him out of those sunken eyes.

'I don't deny it,' he said, very quietly. 'But if you knew the whole story –'

'The whole story?' Harry repeated, a furious pounding in his ears. 'You sold them to Voldemort, that's all I need to know!'

'You've got to listen to me,' Black said, and there was a note of urgency in his voice now. 'You'll regret it if you don't ... you don't understand ...'

'I understand a lot better than you think,' said Harry, and his voice shook more than ever. 'You never heard her, did you? My mum ... trying to stop Voldemort killing me ... and you did that ... you did it ...'

Before either of them could say another word, something ginger streaked past Harry; Crookshanks leapt onto Black's chest, and settled himself there, right over Black's heart. Black blinked and looked down at the cat.

'Get off,' he murmured, trying to push Crookshanks off him.

But Crookshanks sank his claws into Black's robes and wouldn't shift. He turned his ugly, squashed face to Harry, and looked up at him with those great yellow eyes. To his right, Hermione gave a dry sob.

Harry stared down at Black and Crookshanks, his grip tightening on the wand. So what if he had to kill the cat, too? It was in league with Black ... if it was prepared to die, trying to protect Black, that wasn't Harry's business ... if Black wanted to save it, that only proved he cared more for Crookshanks than Harry's parents ...

Harry raised the wand. Now was the moment to do it. Now was the moment to avenge his mother and father. He was going to kill Black. He had to kill Black. This was his chance ...

The seconds lengthened, and still Harry stood frozen there, wand poised, Black staring up at him, Crookshanks on his chest. Ron's ragged breathing came from the bed; Hermione was quite silent.

And then came a new sound –

Muffled footsteps were echoing up through the floor – someone was moving downstairs.

'WE'RE UP HERE!' Hermione screamed suddenly. 'WE'RE UP HERE – SIRIUS BLACK – *QUICK*!'

Black made a startled movement that almost dislodged Crookshanks; Harry gripped his wand convulsively – *Do it now!* said a voice in his head – but the footsteps were thundering up the stairs and Harry still hadn't done it.

The door of the room burst open in a shower of red sparks and Harry wheeled around as Professor Lupin came hurtling into the room, his face bloodless, his wand raised and ready. His eyes flickered over Ron, lying on the floor, over Hermione, cowering next to the door, to Harry, standing there with his wand covering Black, and then to Black himself, crumpled and bleeding at Harry's feet.

'*Expelliarmus!*' Lupin shouted.

Harry's wand flew once more out of his hand; so did the two Hermione was holding. Lupin caught them all deftly, then moved into the room, staring at Black, who still had Crookshanks lying protectively across his chest.

Harry stood there, feeling suddenly empty. He hadn't done it. His nerve had failed him. Black was going to be handed back to the Dementors.

Then Lupin spoke, in an odd voice, a voice that shook with some suppressed emotion. 'Where is he, Sirius?'

Harry looked quickly at Lupin. He didn't understand what Lupin meant. Who was Lupin talking about? He turned to look at Black again.

Black's face was quite expressionless. For a few seconds, he didn't move at all. Then, very slowly, he raised his empty hand, and pointed straight at Ron. Mystified, Harry glanced around at Ron, who looked bewildered.

'But then ...' Lupin muttered, staring at Black so intently it seemed he was trying to read his mind, '... why hasn't he shown himself before now? Unless –' Lupin's eyes suddenly widened, as though he was seeing something beyond Black, something none of the rest could see, '– unless *he* was the one ... unless you switched ... without telling me?'

Very slowly, his sunken gaze never leaving Lupin's face, Black nodded.

'Professor Lupin,' Harry interrupted loudly, 'what's going –?'

But he never finished the question, because what he saw made his voice die in his throat. Lupin was lowering his wand. Next moment, he had walked to Black's side, seized his hand, pulled him to his feet so that Crookshanks fell to the floor, and embraced Black like a brother.

Harry felt as though the bottom had dropped out of his stomach.

'I DON'T BELIEVE IT!' Hermione screamed.

Lupin let go of Black and turned to her. She had raised herself off the floor, and was pointing at Lupin, wild-eyed. 'You – you –'

'Hermione –'

'– you and him!'

'Hermione, calm down –'

'I didn't tell anyone!' Hermione shrieked. 'I've been covering up for you –'

'Hermione, listen to me, please!' Lupin shouted. 'I can explain –'

Harry could feel himself shaking, not with fear, but with a fresh wave of fury.

'I trusted you,' he shouted at Lupin, his voice wavering out of control, 'and all the time you've been his friend!'

'You're wrong,' said Lupin. 'I haven't been Sirius' friend for twelve years, but I am now ... let me explain ...'

'NO!' Hermione screamed, 'Harry, don't trust him, he's been helping Black get into the castle, he wants you dead too – *he's a werewolf*!'

There was a ringing silence. Everyone's eyes were now on Lupin, who looked remarkably calm, though rather pale.

'Not at all up to your usual standard, Hermione,' he said. 'Only one out of three, I'm afraid. I have not been helping Sirius get into the castle and I certainly don't want Harry dead ...' An odd shiver passed over his face. 'But I won't deny that I am a werewolf.'

Ron made a valiant effort to get up again, but fell back with a whimper of pain. Lupin made towards him, looking concerned, but Ron gasped, *'Get away from me, werewolf!'*

Lupin stopped dead. Then, with an obvious effort, he turned to Hermione and said, 'How long have you known?'

'Ages,' Hermione whispered. 'Since I did Professor Snape's essay ...'

'He'll be delighted,' said Lupin coolly. 'He set that essay hoping someone would realise what my symptoms meant. Did you check the lunar chart and realise that I was always ill at the full moon? Or did you realise that the Boggart changed into the moon when it saw me?'

'Both,' Hermione said quietly.

Lupin forced a laugh.

'You're the cleverest witch of your age I've ever met, Hermione.'

'I'm not,' Hermione whispered. 'If I'd been a bit cleverer, I'd have told everyone what you are!'

'But they already know,' said Lupin. 'At least, the staff do.'

'Dumbledore hired you when he knew you were a werewolf?' Ron gasped. 'Is he mad?'

'Some of the staff thought so,' said Lupin. 'He had to work very hard to convince certain teachers that I'm trustworthy –'

'AND HE WAS WRONG!' Harry yelled. 'YOU'VE BEEN HELP-ING HIM ALL THE TIME!' He was pointing at Black, who had crossed to the four-poster bed and sunk onto it, his face hidden in one shaking hand. Crookshanks leapt up beside him and stepped onto his lap, purring. Ron edged away from both of them, drag-ging his leg.

'I have *not* been helping Sirius,' said Lupin. 'If you'll give me a chance, I'll explain. Look –'

He separated Harry, Ron and Hermione's wands and threw each back to its owner; Harry caught his, stunned.

'There,' said Lupin, sticking his own wand back into his belt. 'You're armed, we're not. Now will you listen?'

Harry didn't know what to think. Was it a trick?

'If you haven't been helping him,' he said, with a furious glance at Black, 'how did you know he was here?'

'The map,' said Lupin. 'The Marauder's Map. I was in my office examining it –'

'You know how to work it?' Harry said suspiciously.

'Of course I know how to work it,' said Lupin, waving his hand impatiently. 'I helped write it. I'm Moony – that was my friends' nickname for me at school.'

'You *wrote* –?'

'The important thing is, I was watching it carefully this evening, because I had an idea that you, Ron and Hermione might try and sneak out of the castle to visit Hagrid before his Hippogriff was executed. And I was right, wasn't I?'

He had started to pace up and down, looking at them. Little patches of dust rose at his feet.

'You might have been wearing your father's old Cloak, Harry –'

'How d'you know about the Cloak?'

'The number of times I saw James disappearing under it ...' said Lupin, waving an impatient hand again. 'The point is, even if you're wearing an Invisibility Cloak you show up on the Marauder's Map. I watched you cross the grounds and enter

Hagrid's hut. Twenty minutes later, you left Hagrid, and set off back towards the castle. But you were now accompanied by somebody else.'

'What?' said Harry. 'No, we weren't!'

'I couldn't believe my eyes,' said Lupin, still pacing, and ignoring Harry's interruption. 'I thought the map must be malfunctioning. How could he be with you?'

'No one was with us!' said Harry.

'And then I saw another dot, moving fast towards you, labelled Sirius Black ... I saw him collide with you, I watched as he pulled two of you into the Whomping Willow –'

'One of us!' Ron said angrily.

'No, Ron,' said Lupin. 'Two of you.'

He had stopped his pacing, his eyes moving over Ron.

'Do you think I could have a look at the rat?' he said evenly.

'What?' said Ron. 'What's Scabbers got to do with it?'

'Everything,' said Lupin. 'Could I see him, please?'

Ron hesitated, then put a hand inside his robes. Scabbers emerged, thrashing desperately; Ron had to seize his long bald tail to stop him escaping. Crookshanks stood up on Black's lap and made a soft hissing noise.

Lupin moved closer to Ron. He seemed to be holding his breath as he gazed intently at Scabbers.

'What?' Ron said again, holding Scabbers close to him, looking scared. 'What's my rat got to do with anything?'

'That's not a rat,' croaked Sirius Black suddenly.

'What d'you mean – of course he's a rat –'

'No, he's not,' said Lupin quietly. 'He's a wizard.'

'An Animagus,' said Black, 'by the name of Peter Pettigrew.'

— CHAPTER EIGHTEEN —

Moony, Wormtail, Padfoot and Prongs

It took a few seconds for the absurdity of this statement to sink in. Then Ron voiced what Harry was thinking.

'You're both mental.'

'Ridiculous!' said Hermione faintly.

'Peter Pettigrew's dead!' said Harry. 'He killed him twelve years ago!'

He pointed at Black, whose face twitched convulsively.

'I meant to,' he growled, his yellow teeth bared, 'but little Peter got the better of me ... not this time, though!'

And Crookshanks was thrown to the floor as Black lunged at Scabbers; Ron yelled with pain as Black's weight fell on his broken leg.

'Sirius, NO!' Lupin yelled, launching himself forwards and dragging Black away from Ron again, 'WAIT! You can't do it just like that – they need to understand – we've got to explain –'

'We can explain afterwards!' snarled Black, trying to throw Lupin off, one hand still clawing the air as it tried to reach Scabbers, who was squealing like a piglet, scratching Ron's face and neck as he tried to escape.

'They've – got – a – right – to – know – everything!' Lupin panted, still trying to restrain Black. 'Ron's kept him as a pet! There are parts of it even I don't understand! And Harry – you owe Harry the truth, Sirius!'

Black stopped struggling, though his hollowed eyes were still fixed on Scabbers, who was clamped tightly under Ron's bitten, scratched and bleeding hands.

'All right, then,' Black said, without taking his eyes off the rat. 'Tell them whatever you like. But make it quick, Remus. I want to commit the murder I was imprisoned for ...'

'You're nutters, both of you,' said Ron shakily, looking round at Harry and Hermione for support. 'I've had enough of this. I'm off.'

He tried to heave himself up on his good leg, but Lupin raised his wand again, pointing it at Scabbers.

'You're going to hear me out, Ron,' he said quietly. 'Just keep a tight hold on Peter while you listen.'

'HE'S NOT PETER, HE'S SCABBERS!' Ron yelled, trying to force the rat back into his front pocket, but Scabbers was fighting too hard; Ron swayed and overbalanced, and Harry caught him and pushed him back down to the bed. Then, ignoring Black, Harry turned to Lupin.

'There were witnesses who saw Pettigrew die,' he said. 'A whole street full of them ...'

'They didn't see what they thought they saw!' said Black savagely, still watching Scabbers struggling in Ron's hands.

'Everyone thought Sirius killed Peter,' said Lupin, nodding. 'I believed it myself – until I saw the map tonight. Because the Marauder's Map never lies ... Peter's alive. Ron's holding him, Harry.'

Harry looked down at Ron, and as their eyes met they agreed, silently: Black and Lupin were both out of their minds. Their story made no sense whatsoever. How could Scabbers be Peter Pettigrew? Azkaban must have unhinged Black after all – but why was Lupin playing along with him?

Then Hermione spoke, in a trembling, would-be calm sort of voice, as though trying to will Professor Lupin to talk sensibly.

'But Professor Lupin ... Scabbers can't be Pettigrew ... it just can't be true, you know it can't ...'

'Why can't it be true?' Lupin said calmly, as though they were in class, and Hermione had simply spotted a problem in an experiment with Grindylows.

'Because ... because people would know if Peter Pettigrew had been an Animagus. We did Animagi in class with Professor McGonagall. And I looked them up when I did my homework – the Ministry keeps tabs on witches and wizards who can become animals; there's a register showing what animal they become, and their markings and things ... and I went and looked Professor McGonagall up on the register, and there have only been seven Animagi this century, and Pettigrew's name wasn't on the list –'

Harry barely had time to marvel inwardly at the effort Hermione put into her homework, when Lupin started to laugh.

'Right again, Hermione!' he said. 'But the Ministry never knew that there used to be three unregistered Animagi running around Hogwarts.'

'If you're going to tell them the story, get a move on, Remus,' snarled Black, who was still watching Scabbers's every desperate move. 'I've waited twelve years, I'm not going to wait much longer.'

'All right ... but you'll need to help me, Sirius,' said Lupin, 'I only know how it began ...'

Lupin broke off. There had been a loud creak behind him. The bedroom door had opened of its own accord. All five of them stared at it. Then Lupin strode towards it and looked out into the landing.

'No one there ...'

'This place is haunted!' said Ron.

'It's not,' said Lupin, still looking at the door in a puzzled way. 'The Shrieking Shack was never haunted ... the screams and howls the villagers used to hear were made by me.'

He pushed his greying hair out of his eyes, thought for a moment, then said, 'That's where all of this starts – with my becoming a werewolf. None of this could have happened if I hadn't been bitten ... and if I hadn't been so foolhardy ...'

He looked sober and tired. Ron started to interrupt, but Hermione said, 'Shh!' She was watching Lupin very intently.

'I was a very small boy when I received the bite. My parents tried everything, but in those days there was no cure. The Potion that Professor Snape has been making for me is a very recent discovery. It makes me safe, you see. As long as I take it in the week preceding the full moon, I keep my mind when I transform ... I am able to curl up in my office, a harmless wolf, and wait for the moon to wane again.

'Before the Wolfsbane Potion was discovered, however, I became a fully fledged monster once a month. It seemed impossible that I would be able to come to Hogwarts. Other parents weren't likely to want their children exposed to me.

'But then Dumbledore became Headmaster, and he was sympathetic. He said that, as long as we took certain precautions, there was no reason I shouldn't come to school ...' Lupin sighed, and looked directly at Harry. 'I told you, months ago, that the

Whomping Willow was planted the year I came to Hogwarts. The truth is that it was planted *because* I had come to Hogwarts. This house –' Lupin looked miserably around the room, '– the tunnel that leads to it – they were built for my use. Once a month, I was smuggled out of the castle, into this place, to transform. The tree was placed at the tunnel mouth to stop anyone coming across me while I was dangerous.'

Harry couldn't see where this story was going, but he was listening raptly all the same. The only sound apart from Lupin's voice was Scabbers's frightened squeaking.

'My transformations in those days were – were terrible. It is very painful to turn into a werewolf. I was separated from humans to bite, so I bit and scratched myself instead. The villagers heard the noise and the screaming and thought they were hearing particularly violent spirits. Dumbledore encouraged the rumour ... even now, when the house has been silent for years, the villagers don't dare approach it ...

'But apart from my transformations, I was happier than I had ever been in my life. For the first time ever, I had friends, three great friends. Sirius Black ... Peter Pettigrew ... and, of course, your father, Harry – James Potter.

'Now, my three friends could hardly fail to notice that I disappeared once a month. I made up all sorts of stories. I told them my mother was ill, and that I had to go home to see her ... I was terrified they would desert me the moment they found out what I was. But of course, they, like you, Hermione, worked out the truth ...

'And they didn't desert me at all. Instead they did something for me that would make my transformations not only bearable, but the best times of my life. They became Animagi.'

'My dad, too?' said Harry, astounded.

'Yes, indeed,' said Lupin. 'It took them the best part of three years to work out how to do it. Your father and Sirius here were the cleverest students in the school, and lucky they were, because the Animagus transformation can go horribly wrong – one reason the Ministry keeps a close watch on those attempting to do it. Peter needed all the help he could get from James and Sirius. Finally, in our fifth year, they managed it. They could each turn into a different animal at will.'

'But how did that help you?' said Hermione, sounding puzzled.

'They couldn't keep me company as humans, so they kept me company as animals,' said Lupin. 'A werewolf is only a danger to people. They sneaked out of the castle every month under James's Invisibility Cloak. They transformed ... Peter, as the smallest, could slip beneath the Willow's attacking branches and touch the knot that freezes it. They would then slip down the tunnel and join me. Under their influence, I became less dangerous. My body was still wolfish, but my mind seemed to become less so while I was with them.'

'Hurry up, Remus,' snarled Black, who was still watching Scabbers with a horrible sort of hunger in his face.

'I'm getting there, Sirius, I'm getting there ... well, highly exciting possibilities were open to us now we could all transform. Soon we were leaving the Shrieking Shack and roaming the school grounds and the village by night. Sirius and James transformed into such large animals, they were able to keep a werewolf in check. I doubt whether any Hogwarts students ever found out more about the Hogwarts grounds and Hogsmeade than we did ... And that's how we came to write the Marauder's Map, and sign it with our nicknames. Sirius is Padfoot. Peter is Wormtail. James was Prongs.'

'What sort of animal −?' Harry began, but Hermione cut across him.

'That was still really dangerous! Running around in the dark with a werewolf! What if you'd given the others the slip, and bitten somebody?'

'A thought that still haunts me,' said Lupin heavily. 'And there were near misses, many of them. We laughed about them afterwards. We were young, thoughtless − carried away with our own cleverness.'

'I sometimes felt guilty about betraying Dumbledore's trust, of course ... he had admitted me to Hogwarts when no other Headmaster would have done so, and he had no idea I was breaking the rules he had set down for my own and others' safety. He never knew I had led three fellow students into becoming Animagi illegally. But I always managed to forget my guilty feelings every time we sat down to plan our next month's adventure. And I haven't changed ...'

Lupin's face had hardened, and there was self-disgust in his voice. 'All this year, I have been battling with myself, wondering whether I should tell Dumbledore that Sirius was an Animagus. But I didn't do it. Why? Because I was too cowardly. It would have meant admitting that I'd betrayed his trust while I was at school, admitting that I'd led others along with me ... and Dumbledore's trust has meant everything to me. He let me into Hogwarts as a boy, and he gave me a job, when I have been shunned all my adult life, unable to find paid work because of what I am. And so I convinced myself that Sirius was getting into the school using Dark Arts he learnt from Voldemort, that being an Animagus had nothing to do with it ... so, in a way, Snape's been right about me all along.'

'Snape?' said Black harshly, taking his eyes off Scabbers for the first time in minutes and looking up at Lupin. 'What's Snape got to do with it?'

'He's here, Sirius,' said Lupin heavily. 'He's teaching here as well.' He looked up at Harry, Ron and Hermione.

'Professor Snape was at school with us. He fought very hard against my appointment to the Defence Against the Dark Arts job. He has been telling Dumbledore all year that I am not to be trusted. He has his reasons ... you see, Sirius here played a trick on him which nearly killed him, a trick which involved me –'

Black made a derisive noise.

'It served him right,' he sneered. 'Sneaking around, trying to find out what we were up to ... hoping he could get us expelled ...'

'Severus was very interested in where I went every month,' Lupin told Harry, Ron and Hermione. 'We were in the same year, you know, and we – er – didn't like each other very much. He especially disliked James. Jealous, I think, of James's talent on the Quidditch pitch ... anyway, Snape had seen me crossing the grounds with Madam Pomfrey one evening as she led me towards the Whomping Willow to transform. Sirius thought it would be – er – amusing, to tell Snape all he had to do was prod the knot on the tree-trunk with a long stick, and he'd be able to get in after me. Well, of course, Snape tried it – if he'd got as far as this house, he'd have met a fully grown werewolf – but your father, who'd heard what Sirius had done, went after Snape and pulled him back, at great risk to his life ... Snape glimpsed me, though, at the end of the tunnel. He was forbidden to tell anybody by Dumbledore, but from that time on he knew what I was ...'

'So that's why Snape doesn't like you,' said Harry slowly, 'because he thought you were in on the joke?'

'That's right,' sneered a cold voice from the wall behind Lupin.

Severus Snape was pulling off the Invisibility Cloak, his wand pointing directly at Lupin.

CHAPTER NINETEEN

The Servant of Lord Voldemort

Hermione screamed. Black leapt to his feet. Harry jumped as though he'd received a huge electric shock.

'I found this at the base of the Whomping Willow,' said Snape, throwing the Cloak aside, careful to keep his wand pointing directly at Lupin's chest. 'Very useful, Potter, I thank you ...'

Snape was slightly breathless, but his face was full of suppressed triumph. 'You're wondering, perhaps, how I knew you were here?' he said, his eyes glittering. 'I've just been to your office, Lupin. You forgot to take your Potion tonight, so I took a gobletful along. And very lucky I did ... lucky for me, I mean. Lying on your desk was a certain map. One glance at it told me all I needed to know. I saw you running along this passageway and out of sight.'

'Severus –' Lupin began, but Snape overrode him.

'I've told the Headmaster again and again that you've been helping your old friend Black into the castle, Lupin, and here's the proof. Not even I dreamed you would have the nerve to use this old place as your hideout –'

'Severus, you're making a mistake,' said Lupin urgently. 'You haven't heard everything – I can explain – Sirius is not here to kill Harry –'

'Two more for Azkaban tonight,' said Snape, his eyes now gleaming fanatically. 'I shall be interested to see how Dumbledore takes this ... he was quite convinced you were harmless, you know, Lupin ... a *tame* werewolf ...'

'You fool,' said Lupin softly. 'Is a schoolboy grudge worth putting an innocent man back inside Azkaban?'

BANG! Thin, snake-like cords burst from the end of Snape's

wand and twisted themselves around Lupin's mouth, wrists and ankles; he overbalanced and fell to the floor, unable to move. With a roar of rage, Black started towards Snape, but Snape pointed his wand straight between Black's eyes.

'Give me a reason,' he whispered. 'Give me a reason to do it, and I swear I will.'

Black stopped dead. It would have been impossible to say which face showed more hatred.

Harry stood there, paralysed, not knowing what to do or who to believe. He glanced around at Ron and Hermione. Ron looked just as confused as he did, still fighting to keep hold of the struggling Scabbers. Hermione, however, took an uncertain step towards Snape and said, in a very breathless voice, 'Professor Snape – it – it wouldn't hurt to hear what they've got to say, w-would it?'

'Miss Granger, you are already facing suspension from this school,' Snape spat. 'You, Potter and Weasley are out of bounds, in the company of a convicted murderer and a werewolf. For once in your life, *hold your tongue.*'

'But if – if there *was* a mistake –'

'KEEP QUIET, YOU STUPID GIRL!' Snape shouted, looking suddenly quite deranged. 'DON'T TALK ABOUT WHAT YOU DON'T UNDERSTAND!' A few sparks shot out of the end of his wand, which was still pointing at Black's face. Hermione fell silent.

'Vengeance is very sweet,' Snape breathed at Black. 'How I hoped I would be the one to catch you ...'

'The joke's on you again, Severus,' snarled Black. 'As long as this boy brings his rat up to the castle –' he jerked his head at Ron, '– I'll come quietly ...'

'Up to the castle?' said Snape silkily. 'I don't think we need to go that far. All I have to do is call the Dementors once we get out of the Willow. They'll be very pleased to see you, Black ... pleased enough to give you a little kiss, I daresay ...'

What little colour there was in Black's face left it.

'You – you've got to hear me out,' he croaked. 'The rat – look at the rat –'

But there was a mad glint in Snape's eye that Harry had never seen before. He seemed beyond reason.

'Come on, all of you,' he said. He clicked his fingers, and the ends of the cords that bound Lupin flew to his hands. 'I'll drag the werewolf. Perhaps the Dementors will have a kiss for him, too –'

Before he knew what he was doing, Harry had crossed the room in three strides, and blocked the door.

'Get out of the way, Potter, you're in enough trouble already,' snarled Snape. 'If I hadn't been here to save your skin –'

'Professor Lupin could have killed me about a hundred times this year,' Harry said. 'I've been alone with him loads of times, having defence lessons against the Dementors. If he was helping Black, why didn't he just finish me off then?'

'Don't ask me to fathom the way a werewolf's mind works,' hissed Snape. 'Get out of the way, Potter.'

'YOU'RE PATHETIC!' Harry yelled. 'JUST BECAUSE THEY MADE A FOOL OF YOU AT SCHOOL YOU WON'T EVEN LISTEN –'

'SILENCE! I WILL NOT BE SPOKEN TO LIKE THAT!' Snape shrieked, looking madder than ever. 'Like father, like son, Potter! I have just saved your neck, you should be thanking me on bended knee! You would have been well served if he'd killed you! You'd have died like your father, too arrogant to believe you might be mistaken in Black – now get out of the way, or I will *make* you. GET OUT OF THE WAY, POTTER!'

Harry made up his mind in a split second. Before Snape could take even one step towards him, he had raised his wand.

'*Expelliarmus!*' he yelled – except that his wasn't the only voice that shouted. There was a blast that made the door rattle on its hinges; Snape was lifted off his feet and slammed into the wall, then slid down it to the floor, a trickle of blood oozing from under his hair. He had been knocked out.

Harry looked around. Both Ron and Hermione had tried to disarm Snape at exactly the same moment. Snape's wand soared in a high arc and landed on the bed next to Crookshanks.

'You shouldn't have done that,' said Black, looking at Harry. 'You should have left him to me ...'

Harry avoided Black's eyes. He wasn't sure, even now, that he'd done the right thing.

'We attacked a teacher ... we attacked a teacher ...' Hermione whimpered, staring at the lifeless Snape with frightened eyes. 'Oh, we're going to be in so much trouble –'

Lupin was struggling against his bonds. Black bent down

quickly and untied him. Lupin straightened up, rubbing his arms
where the ropes had cut into them.

'Thank you, Harry,' he said.

'I'm still not saying I believe you,' Harry retorted.

'Then it's time we offered you some proof,' said Black. 'You, boy
– give me Peter. Now.'

Ron clutched Scabbers closer to his chest.

'Come off it,' he said weakly. 'Are you trying to say you broke
out of Azkaban just to get your hands on *Scabbers*? I mean ...' he
looked up at Harry and Hermione for support. 'OK, say Pettigrew
could turn into a rat – there are millions of rats – how's he
supposed to know which one he's after if he was locked up in
Azkaban?'

'You know, Sirius, that's a fair question,' said Lupin, turning to
Black and frowning slightly. 'How *did* you find out where he was?'

Black put one of his claw-like hands inside his robes and took
out a crumpled piece of paper, which he smoothed flat, and held
out to show the others.

It was the photograph of Ron and his family that had appeared
in the *Daily Prophet* the previous summer, and there, on Ron's
shoulder, was Scabbers.

'How did you get this?' Lupin asked Black, thunderstruck.

'Fudge,' said Black. 'When he came to inspect Azkaban last
year, he gave me his paper. And there was Peter, on the front page
... on this boy's shoulder ... I knew him at once ... how many times
had I seen him transform? And the caption said the boy would be
going back to Hogwarts ... to where Harry was ...'

'My God,' said Lupin softly, staring from Scabbers to the picture
in the paper and back again. 'His front paw ...'

'What about it?' said Ron defiantly.

'He's got a toe missing,' said Black.

'Of course,' Lupin breathed, 'so simple ...so *brilliant* ... He cut it
off himself?'

'Just before he transformed,' said Black. 'When I cornered him,
he yelled for the whole street to hear that I'd betrayed Lily and
James. Then, before I could curse him, he blew apart the
street with the wand behind his back, killed everyone within
twenty feet of himself – and sped down into the sewer with the
other rats ...'

'Didn't you ever hear, Ron?' said Lupin. 'The biggest bit of Peter they found was his finger.'

'Look, Scabbers probably had a fight with another rat or something! He's been in my family for ages, right –'

'Twelve years, in fact,' said Lupin. 'Didn't you ever wonder why he was living so long?'

'We – we've been taking good care of him!' said Ron.

'Not looking too good at the moment, though, is he?' said Lupin. 'I'd guess he's been losing weight ever since he heard Sirius was on the loose again ...'

'He's been scared of that mad cat!' said Ron, nodding towards Crookshanks, who was still purring on the bed.

But that wasn't right, Harry thought suddenly ... Scabbers had been looking ill before he met Crookshanks ... ever since Ron's return from Egypt ... since the time when Black had escaped ...

'This cat isn't mad,' said Black hoarsely. He reached out a bony hand and stroked Crookshanks's fluffy head. 'He's the most intelligent of his kind I've ever met. He recognised Peter for what he was straight away. And when he met me, he knew I was no dog. It was a while before he trusted me. Finally, I managed to communicate to him what I was after, and he's been helping me ...'

'What do you mean?' breathed Hermione.

'He tried to bring Peter to me, but couldn't ... so he stole the passwords into Gryffindor Tower for me ... As I understand it, he took them from a boy's bedside table ...'

Harry's brain seemed to be sagging under the weight of what he was hearing. It was absurd ... and yet ...

'But Peter got wind of what was going on and ran for it ... this cat – Crookshanks, did you call him? – told me Peter had left blood on the sheets ... I suppose he bit himself ... well, faking his own death had worked once ...'

These words jolted Harry to his senses.

'And why did he fake his death?' he said furiously. 'Because he knew you were about to kill him like you killed my parents!'

'No,' said Lupin. 'Harry –'

'And now you've come to finish him off!'

'Yes, I have,' said Black, with an evil look at Scabbers.

'Then I should've let Snape take you!' Harry shouted.

'Harry,' said Lupin hurriedly, 'don't you see? All this time we've thought Sirius betrayed your parents, and Peter tracked him down

– but it was the other way around, don't you see? *Peter* betrayed your mother and father – Sirius tracked *Peter* down –'

'THAT'S NOT TRUE!' Harry yelled. 'HE WAS THEIR SECRET KEEPER! HE SAID SO BEFORE YOU TURNED UP, HE SAID HE KILLED THEM!'

He was pointing at Black, who shook his head slowly; the sunken eyes were suddenly over-bright.

'Harry ... I as good as killed them,' he croaked. 'I persuaded Lily and James to change to Peter at the last moment, persuaded them to use him as Secret Keeper instead of me ... I'm to blame, I know it ... the night they died, I'd arranged to check on Peter, make sure he was still safe, but when I arrived at his hiding place, he'd gone. Yet there was no sign of a struggle. It didn't feel right. I was scared. I set out for your parents' house straight away. And when I saw their house, destroyed, and their bodies – I realised what Peter must have done. What I'd done.'

His voice broke. He turned away.

'Enough of this,' said Lupin, and there was a steely note in his voice Harry had never heard before. 'There's one certain way to prove what really happened. Ron, *give me that rat.*'

'What are you going to do with him if I give him to you?' Ron asked Lupin tensely.

'Force him to show himself,' said Lupin. 'If he really is a rat, it won't hurt him.'

Ron hesitated, then at long last held out Scabbers and Lupin took him. Scabbers began to squeak without stopping, twisting and turning, his tiny black eyes bulging in his head.

'Ready, Sirius?' said Lupin.

Black had already retrieved Snape's wand from the bed. He approached Lupin and the struggling rat, and his wet eyes suddenly seemed to be burning in his face.

'Together?' he said quietly.

'I think so,' said Lupin, holding Scabbers tightly in one hand and his wand in the other. 'On the count of three. One – two – THREE!'

A flash of blue-white light erupted from both wands; for a moment, Scabbers was frozen in mid-air, his small black form twisting madly – Ron yelled – the rat fell and hit the floor. There was another blinding flash of light and then –

It was like watching a speeded-up film of a growing tree. A

head was shooting upwards from the ground; limbs were sprouting; next moment, a man was standing where Scabbers had been, cringing and wringing his hands. Crookshanks was spitting and snarling on the bed, the hair on his back standing up.

He was a very short man, hardly taller than Harry and Hermione. His thin, colourless hair was unkempt and there was a large bald patch on top. He had the shrunken appearance of a plump man who had lost a lot of weight in a short time. His skin looked grubby, almost like Scabbers's fur, and something of the rat lingered around his pointed nose, his very small, watery eyes. He looked around at them all, his breathing fast and shallow. Harry saw his eyes dart to the door and back again.

'Well, hello, Peter,' said Lupin pleasantly, as though rats frequently erupted into old schoolfriends around him. 'Long time, no see.'

'S-Sirius ... R-Remus ...' Even Pettigrew's voice was squeaky. Again, his eyes darted towards the door. 'My friends ... my old friends ...'

Black's wand arm rose, but Lupin seized him around the wrist, gave him a warning look, then turned again to Pettigrew, his voice light and casual.

'We've been having a little chat, Peter, about what happened the night Lily and James died. You might have missed the finer points while you were squeaking around down there on the bed –'

'Remus,' gasped Pettigrew, and Harry could see beads of sweat breaking out over his pasty face, 'you don't believe him, do you ... He tried to kill me, Remus ...'

'So we've heard,' said Lupin, more coldly. 'I'd like to clear up one or two little matters with you, Peter, if you'd be so –'

'He's come to try and kill me again!' Pettigrew shrieked suddenly, pointing at Black, and Harry saw that he used his middle finger, because his index was missing. 'He killed Lily and James and now he's going to kill me, too ... you've got to help me, Remus ...'

Black's face looked more skull-like than ever as he stared at Pettigrew with his fathomless eyes.

'No one's going to try and kill you until we've sorted a few things out,' said Lupin.

'Sorted things out?' squealed Pettigrew, looking wildly about him once more, eyes taking in the boarded windows and, again, the only door. 'I knew he'd come after me! I knew he'd be back for me! I've been waiting for this for twelve years!'

'You knew Sirius was going to break out of Azkaban?' said Lupin, his brow furrowed. 'When nobody has ever done it before?'

'He's got Dark powers the rest of us can only dream of!' Pettigrew shouted shrilly. 'How else did he get out of there? I suppose He Who Must Not Be Named taught him a few tricks!'

Black started to laugh, a horrible, mirthless laugh that filled the whole room.

'Voldemort, teach me tricks?' he said.

Pettigrew flinched as though Black had brandished a whip at him.

'What, scared to hear your old master's name?' said Black. 'I don't blame you, Peter. His lot aren't very happy with you, are they?'

'Don't know – what you mean, Sirius –' muttered Pettigrew, his breathing faster than ever. His whole face was shining with sweat now.

'You haven't been hiding from *me* for twelve years,' said Black. 'You've been hiding from Voldemort's old supporters. I heard things in Azkaban, Peter ... they all think you're dead, or you'd have to answer to them ... I've heard them screaming all sorts of things in their sleep. Sounds like they think the double-crosser double-crossed them. Voldemort went to the Potters' on your information ... and Voldemort met his downfall there. And not all Voldemort's supporters ended up in Azkaban, did they? There are still plenty out here, biding their time, pretending they've seen the error of their ways ... If they ever got wind that you were still alive, Peter –'

'Don't know ... what you're talking about ...' said Pettigrew again, more shrilly than ever. He wiped his face on his sleeve and looked up at Lupin. 'You don't believe this – this madness, Remus –'

'I must admit, Peter, I have difficulty in understanding why an innocent man would want to spend twelve years as a rat,' said Lupin evenly.

'Innocent, but scared!' squealed Pettigrew. 'If Voldemort's supporters were after me, it was because I put one of their best men in Azkaban – the spy, Sirius Black!'

Black's face contorted.

'How dare you,' he growled, sounding suddenly like the bear-sized dog he had been. 'I, a spy for Voldemort? When did I ever sneak around people who were stronger and more powerful than myself? But you, Peter – I'll never understand why I didn't see you were the spy from the start. You always liked big friends who'd look after you, didn't you? It used to be us ... me and Remus ... and James ...'

Pettigrew wiped his face again; he was almost panting for breath.

'Me, a spy ... must be out of your mind ... never ... don't know how you can say such a –'

'Lily and James only made you Secret Keeper because I suggested it,' Black hissed, so venomously that Pettigrew took a step backwards. 'I thought it was the perfect plan ... a bluff ... Voldemort would be sure to come after me, would never dream they'd use a weak, talentless thing like you ... it must have been the finest moment of your miserable life, telling Voldemort you could hand him the Potters.'

Pettigrew was muttering distractedly; Harry caught words like 'far-fetched' and 'lunacy', but he couldn't help paying more attention to the ashen colour of Pettigrew's face, and the way his eyes continued to dart towards the windows and door.

'Professor Lupin?' said Hermione timidly. 'Can – can I say something?'

'Certainly, Hermione,' said Lupin courteously.

'Well – Scabbers – I mean, this – this man – he's been sleeping in Harry's dormitory for three years. If he's working for You Know Who, how come he never tried to hurt Harry before now?'

'There!' said Pettigrew shrilly, pointing at Hermione with his maimed hand. 'Thank you! You see, Remus? I have never hurt a hair of Harry's head! Why should I?'

'I'll tell you why,' said Black. 'Because you never did anything for anyone unless you could see what was in it for you. Voldemort's been in hiding for twelve years, they say he's half-dead. You weren't about to commit murder right under Albus Dumbledore's nose, for a wreck of a wizard who'd lost all his power, were you? You'd want to be quite sure he was the biggest bully in the playground before you went back to him, wouldn't you? Why else did you find a wizard family to take you in? Keeping an ear out for news, weren't you, Peter? Just in case your old protector regained strength, and it was safe to rejoin him ...'

Pettigrew opened his mouth and closed it several times. He

seemed to have lost the ability to talk.

'Er – Mr Black – Sirius?' said Hermione timidly.

Black jumped at being addressed like this and stared at Hermione as though being spoken to politely was something he'd long forgotten.

'If you don't mind me asking, how – how did you get out of Azkaban, if you didn't use Dark Magic?'

'Thank you!' gasped Pettigrew, nodding frantically at her. 'Exactly! Precisely what I –'

But Lupin silenced him with a look. Black was frowning slightly at Hermione, but not as though he was annoyed with her. He seemed to be pondering his answer.

'I don't know how I did it,' he said slowly. 'I think the only reason I never lost my mind is that I knew I was innocent. That wasn't a happy thought, so the Dementors couldn't suck it out of me ... but it kept me sane and knowing who I am ... helped me keep my powers ... so when it all became ... too much ... I could transform in my cell ... become a dog. Dementors can't see, you know ...' He swallowed. 'They feel their way towards people by sensing their emotions ... they could tell that my feelings were less – less human, less complex when I was a dog ... but they thought, of course, that I was losing my mind like everyone else in there, so it didn't trouble them. But I was weak, very weak, and I had no hope of driving them away from me without a wand ...

'But then I saw Peter in that picture ... I realised he was at Hogwarts with Harry ... perfectly positioned to act, if one hint reached his ears that the Dark Side was gathering strength again ...'

Pettigrew was shaking his head, mouthing noiselessly, but staring all the while at Black as though hypnotised.

'... ready to strike the moment he could be sure of allies ... to deliver the last Potter to them. If he gave them Harry, who'd dare say he'd betrayed Lord Voldemort? He'd be welcomed back with honours ...

'So you see, I had to do something. I was the only one who knew Peter was still alive ...'

Harry remembered what Mr Weasley had told Mrs Weasley. 'The guards say he's been talking in his sleep ... always the same words ..."He's at Hogwarts".'

'It was as if someone had lit a fire in my head, and the Dementors couldn't destroy it ... it wasn't a happy feeling ... it was an obsession ... but it gave me strength, it cleared my mind. So, one night when they opened my door to bring food, I slipped past them as a dog ... it's so much harder for them to sense animal emotions that they were confused ... I was thin, very thin ... thin enough to slip through the bars ... I swam as a dog back to the mainland ... I journeyed north and slipped into the Hogwarts grounds as a dog ... I've been living in the Forest ever since ... except when I come to watch the Quidditch, of course ... you fly as well as your father did, Harry ...'

He looked at Harry, who did not look away.

'Believe me,' croaked Black. 'Believe me. I never betrayed James and Lily. I would have died before I betrayed them.'

And at long last, Harry believed him. Throat too tight to speak, he nodded.

'No!'

Pettigrew had fallen to his knees as though Harry's nod had been his own death sentence. He shuffled forward on his knees, grovelling, his hands clasped in front of him as though praying.

'Sirius – it's me ... it's Peter ... your friend ... you wouldn't ...'

Black kicked out and Pettigrew recoiled.

'There's enough filth on my robes without you touching them,' said Black.

'Remus!' Pettigrew squeaked, turning to Lupin instead, writhing imploringly in front of him. 'You don't believe this ... Wouldn't Sirius have told you they'd changed the plan?'

'Not if he thought I was the spy, Peter,' said Lupin. 'I assume that's why you didn't tell me, Sirius?' he said casually over Pettigrew's head.

'Forgive me, Remus,' said Black.

'Not at all, Padfoot, old friend,' said Lupin, who was now rolling up his sleeves. 'And will you, in turn, forgive me for believing *you* were the spy?'

'Of course,' said Black, and the ghost of a grin flitted across his gaunt face. He, too, began rolling up his sleeves. 'Shall we kill him together?'

'Yes, I think so,' said Lupin grimly.

'You wouldn't ... you won't ...' gasped Pettigrew. And he scrambled around to Ron.

'Ron ... haven't I been a good friend ... a good pet? You won't let them kill me, Ron, will you ... you're on my side, aren't you?'

But Ron was staring at Pettigrew with the utmost revulsion.

'I let you sleep in my *bed*!' he said.

'Kind boy ... kind master ...' Pettigrew crawled towards Ron, 'you won't let them do it ... I was your rat ... I was a good pet ...'

'If you made a better rat than human, it's not much to boast about, Peter,' said Black harshly. Ron, going still paler with pain, wrenched his broken leg out of Pettigrew's reach. Pettigrew turned on his knees, staggered forwards and seized the hem of Hermione's robes.

'Sweet girl ... clever girl ... you – you won't let them ... help me ...'

Hermione pulled her robes out of Pettigrew's clutching hands and backed away against the wall, looking horrified.

Pettigrew knelt, trembling uncontrollably, and turned his head slowly towards Harry.

'Harry ... Harry ... you look just like your father ... just like him ...'

'HOW DARE YOU SPEAK TO HARRY?' roared Black. 'HOW DARE YOU FACE HIM? HOW DARE YOU TALK ABOUT JAMES IN FRONT OF HIM?'

'Harry,' whispered Pettigrew, shuffling towards him, hands outstretched, 'Harry, James wouldn't have wanted me killed ... James would have understood, Harry ... he would have shown me mercy ...'

Both Black and Lupin strode forwards, seized Pettigrew's shoulders and threw him backwards onto the floor. He sat there, twitching with terror, staring up at them.

'You sold Lily and James to Voldemort,' said Black, who was shaking too. 'Do you deny it?'

Pettigrew burst into tears. It was horrible to watch: he looked like an oversized, balding baby, cowering on the floor.

'Sirius, Sirius, what could I have done? The Dark Lord ... you have no idea ... he has weapons you can't imagine ... I was scared, Sirius, I was never brave like you and Remus and James. I never meant it to happen ... He Who Must Not Be Named forced me –'

'DON'T LIE!' bellowed Black. 'YOU'D BEEN PASSING INFORMATION TO HIM FOR A YEAR BEFORE LILY AND JAMES DIED! YOU WERE HIS SPY!'

'He – he was taking over everywhere!' gasped Pettigrew. 'Wh-what was there to be gained by refusing him?'

'What was there to be gained by fighting the most evil wizard who has ever existed?' said Black, with a terrible fury in his face. 'Only innocent lives, Peter!'

'You don't understand!' whined Pettigrew. 'He would have killed me, Sirius!'

'THEN YOU SHOULD HAVE DIED!' roared Black. 'DIED RATHER THAN BETRAY YOUR FRIENDS, AS WE WOULD HAVE DONE FOR YOU!'

Black and Lupin stood shoulder to shoulder, wands raised.

'You should have realised,' said Lupin quietly. 'If Voldemort didn't kill you, we would. Goodbye, Peter.'

Hermione covered her face with her hands and turned to the wall.

'NO!' Harry yelled. He ran forwards, placing himself in front of Pettigrew, facing the wands. 'You can't kill him,' he said breathlessly. 'You can't.'

Black and Lupin both looked staggered.

'Harry, this piece of vermin is the reason you have no parents,' Black snarled. 'This cringing bit of filth would have seen you die, too, without turning a hair. You heard him. His own stinking skin meant more to him than your whole family.'

'I know,' Harry panted. 'We'll take him up to the castle. We'll hand him over to the Dementors. He can go to Azkaban ... just don't kill him.'

'Harry!' gasped Pettigrew, and he flung his arms around Harry's knees. 'You – thank you – it's more than I deserve – thank you –'

'Get off me,' Harry spat, throwing Pettigrew's hands off him in disgust. 'I'm not doing this for you. I'm doing it because I don't reckon my dad would've wanted his best friends to become killers – just for you.'

No one moved or made a sound except Pettigrew, whose breath was coming in wheezes as he clutched his chest. Black and Lupin were looking at each other. Then, with one movement, they lowered their wands.

'You're the only person who has the right to decide, Harry,' said Black. 'But think ... think what he did ...'

'He can go to Azkaban,' Harry repeated. 'If anyone deserves that place, he does ...'

Pettigrew was still wheezing behind him.

'Very well,' said Lupin. 'Stand aside, Harry.'

Harry hesitated.

'I'm going to tie him up,' said Lupin. 'That's all, I swear.'

Harry stepped out of the way. Thin cords shot from Lupin's wand this time, and next moment, Pettigrew was wriggling on the floor, bound and gagged.

'But if you transform, Peter,' growled Black, his own wand pointing at Pettigrew, too, 'we *will* kill you. You agree, Harry?'

Harry looked down at the pitiful figure on the floor, and nodded so that Pettigrew could see him.

'Right,' said Lupin, suddenly business-like. 'Ron, I can't mend bones nearly as well as Madam Pomfrey, so I think it's best if we just strap your leg up until we can get you to the hospital wing.'

He hurried over to Ron, bent down, tapped Ron's leg with his wand and muttered, *'Ferula.'* Bandages spun up Ron's leg, strapping it tightly to a splint. Lupin helped him to his feet; Ron put his weight gingerly on the leg and didn't wince.

'That's better,' he said. 'Thanks.'

'What about Professor Snape?' said Hermione in a small voice, looking down at Snape's prone figure.

'There's nothing seriously wrong with him,' said Lupin, bending over Snape and checking his pulse. 'You were just a little – over-enthusiastic. Still out cold. Er – perhaps it will be best if we don't revive him until we're safely back in the castle. We can take him like this ...'

He muttered, *'Mobilicorpus.'* As though invisible strings were tied to Snape's wrists, neck and knees, he was pulled into a standing position, head still lolling unpleasantly, like a grotesque puppet. He hung a few inches above the ground, his limp feet dangling. Lupin picked up the Invisibility Cloak and tucked it safely into his pocket.

'And two of us should be chained to this,' said Black, nudging Pettigrew with his toe. 'Just to make sure.'

'I'll do it,' said Lupin.

'And me,' said Ron savagely, limping forwards.

Black conjured heavy manacles from thin air; soon Pettigrew was upright again, left arm chained to Lupin's right, right arm to Ron's left. Ron's face was set. He seemed to have taken Scabbers's true identity as a personal insult. Crookshanks leapt lightly off the bed and led the way out of the room, his bottle-brush tail held jauntily high.

CHAPTER TWENTY

The Dementors' Kiss

Harry had never been part of a stranger group. Crookshanks led the way down the stairs; Lupin, Pettigrew and Ron went next, looking like contestants in a six-legged race. Next came Professor Snape, drifting creepily along, his toes hitting each stair as they descended, held up by his own wand, which was being pointed at him by Sirius. Harry and Hermione brought up the rear.

Getting back into the tunnel was difficult. Lupin, Pettigrew and Ron had to turn sideways to manage it; Lupin still had Pettigrew covered with his wand. Harry could see them edging awkwardly along the tunnel in single file. Crookshanks was still in the lead. Harry went right after Sirius, who was still making Snape drift along ahead of them; he kept bumping his lolling head on the low ceiling. Harry had the impression Sirius was making no effort to prevent this.

'You know what this means?' Sirius said abruptly to Harry, as they made their slow progress along the tunnel. 'Turning Pettigrew in?'

'You're free,' said Harry.

'Yes ...' said Sirius. 'But I'm also – I don't know if anyone ever told you – I'm your godfather.'

'Yeah, I knew that,' said Harry.

'Well ... your parents appointed me your guardian,' said Sirius stiffly. 'If anything happened to them ...'

Harry waited. Did Sirius mean what he thought he meant?

'I'll understand, of course, if you want to stay with your aunt and uncle,' said Sirius. 'But ... well ... think about it. Once my name's cleared ... if you wanted a ... a different home ...'

Some sort of explosion took place in the pit of Harry's stomach.

'What – live with you?' he said, accidentally cracking his head on a bit of rock protruding from the ceiling. 'Leave the Dursleys?'

'Of course, I thought you wouldn't want to,' said Sirius quickly. 'I understand. I just thought I'd –'

'Are you mad?' said Harry, his voice easily as croaky as Sirius'. 'Of course I want to leave the Dursleys! Have you got a house? When can I move in?'

Sirius turned right around to look at him; Snape's head was scraping the ceiling but Sirius didn't seem to care.

'You want to?' he said. 'You mean it?'

'Yeah, I mean it!' said Harry.

Sirius' gaunt face broke into the first true smile Harry had seen upon it. The difference it made was startling, as though a person ten years younger was shining through the starved mask; for a moment, he was recognisable as the man who had laughed at Harry's parents' wedding.

They did not speak again until they had reached the end of the tunnel. Crookshanks darted up first; he had evidently pressed his paw to the knot on the trunk, because Lupin, Pettigrew and Ron clambered upwards without any sound of savaging branches.

Sirius saw Snape up through the hole, then stood back for Harry and Hermione to pass. At last, all of them were out.

The grounds were very dark now, the only light came from the distant windows of the castle. Without a word, they set off. Pettigrew was still wheezing and occasionally whimpering. Harry's mind was buzzing. He was going to leave the Dursleys. He was going to live with Sirius Black, his parents' best friend ... he felt dazed ... What would happen when he told the Dursleys he was going to live with the convict they'd seen on television?

'One wrong move, Peter,' said Lupin threateningly, ahead. His wand was still pointed sideways at Pettigrew's chest.

Silently they tramped through the grounds, the castle lights growing slowly larger. Snape was still drifting weirdly ahead of Sirius, his chin bumping on his chest. And then –

A cloud shifted. There were suddenly dim shadows on the ground. Their party was bathed in moonlight.

Snape collided with Lupin, Pettigrew and Ron, who had stopped abruptly. Sirius froze. He flung out an arm to make Harry and Hermione stop.

Harry could see Lupin's silhouette. He had gone rigid. Then his limbs began to shake.

'Oh my –' Hermione gasped. 'He didn't take his Potion tonight! He's not safe!'

'Run,' Sirius whispered. 'Run! Now!'

But Harry couldn't run. Ron was chained to Pettigrew and Lupin. He leapt forwards but Sirius caught him around the chest and threw him back.

'Leave it to me – RUN!'

There was a terrible snarling noise. Lupin's head was lengthening. So was his body. His shoulders were hunching. Hair was sprouting visibly on his face and hands, which were curling into clawed paws. Crookshanks's fur was on end again, he was backing away –

As the werewolf reared, snapping its long jaws, Sirius disappeared from Harry's side. He had transformed. The enormous, bear-like dog bounded forwards. As the werewolf wrenched itself free of the manacle binding it, the dog seized it about the neck and pulled it backwards, away from Ron and Pettigrew. They were locked, jaw to jaw, claws ripping at each other –

Harry stood, transfixed by the sight; too intent upon the battle to notice anything else. It was Hermione's scream that alerted him –

Pettigrew had dived for Lupin's dropped wand. Ron, unsteady on his bandaged leg, fell. There was a bang, a burst of light – and Ron lay motionless on the ground. Another bang – Crookshanks flew into the air and back to the earth in a heap.

'*Expelliarmus!*' Harry yelled, pointing his own wand at Pettigrew; Lupin's wand flew high into the air and out of sight. 'Stay where you are!' Harry shouted, running forwards.

Too late. Pettigrew had transformed. Harry saw his bald tail whip through the manacle on Ron's outstretched arm, and heard a scurrying through the grass.

There was a howl and a rumbling growl; Harry turned to see the werewolf taking flight; it was galloping into the Forest –

'Sirius, he's gone, Pettigrew transformed!' Harry yelled.

Sirius was bleeding; there were gashes across his muzzle and back, but at Harry's words he scrambled up again, and in an instant, the sound of his paws was fading to silence as he pounded away across the grounds.

Harry and Hermione dashed over to Ron.

'What did he do to him?' Hermione whispered. Ron's eyes were only half-closed; his mouth hung open. He was definitely alive, they could hear him breathing, but he didn't seem to recognise them.

'I don't know.'

Harry looked desperately around. Black and Lupin both gone ... they had no one but Snape for company, still hanging, unconscious, in mid-air.

'We'd better get them up to the castle and tell someone,' said Harry, pushing his hair out of his eyes, trying to think straight. 'Come –'

But then, out of the darkness, they heard a yelping, a whining; a dog in pain ...

'Sirius,' Harry muttered, staring into the darkness.

He had a moment's indecision, but there was nothing they could do for Ron at the moment, and by the sound of it, Black was in trouble –

Harry set off at a run, Hermione right behind him. The yelping seemed to be coming from near the lake. They pelted towards it, and Harry, running flat out, felt the cold without realising what it must mean –

The yelping stopped abruptly. As they reached the lake's shore they saw why – Sirius had turned back into a man. He was crouched on all fours, his hands over his head.

'Nooo,' he moaned. 'Noooo .... please ...'

And then Harry saw them. Dementors, at least a hundred of them, gliding in a black mass around the lake towards them. He spun around, the familiar, icy cold penetrating his insides, fog starting to obscure his vision; more were appearing out of the darkness on every side; they were encircling them ...

'Hermione, think of something happy!' Harry yelled, raising his wand, blinking furiously to try and clear his vision, shaking his head to rid it of the faint screaming that had started inside it –

I'm going to live with my godfather. I'm leaving the Dursleys.

He forced himself to think of Sirius, and only Sirius, and began to chant: 'Expecto patronum! Expecto patronum!'

Black gave a shudder, rolled over and lay motionless on the ground, pale as death.

He'll be all right. I'm going to go and live with him.

'Expecto patronum! Hermione, help me! Expecto patronum!'

'Expecto –' Hermione whispered, 'expecto – expecto –'

But she couldn't do it. The Dementors were closing in, barely ten feet from them. They formed a solid wall around Harry and Hermione, and were getting closer ...

'EXPECTO PATRONUM!' Harry yelled, trying to blot the screaming from his ears. 'EXPECTO PATRONUM!'

A thin wisp of silver escaped his wand and hovered like mist before him. At the same moment, Harry felt Hermione collapse next to him. He was alone ... completely alone ...

'Expecto – expecto patronum –'

Harry felt his knees hit the cold grass. Fog was clouding his eyes. With a huge effort, he fought to remember – Sirius was innocent – innocent – *we'll be OK – I'm going to live with him –*

'Expecto patronum!' he gasped.

By the feeble light of his formless Patronus, he saw a Dementor halt, very close to him. It couldn't walk through the cloud of silver mist Harry had conjured. A dead, slimy hand slid out from under the cloak. It made a gesture as though to sweep the Patronus aside.

'No – *no* –' Harry gasped. 'He's innocent ... expecto – expecto patronum –'

He could feel them watching him, hear their rattling breath like an evil wind around him. The nearest Dementor seemed to be considering him. Then it raised both its rotting hands – and lowered its hood.

Where there should have been eyes, there was only thin, grey, scabbed skin, stretched blankly over empty sockets. But there was a mouth ... a gaping, shapeless hole, sucking the air with the sound of a death-rattle.

A paralysing terror filled Harry so that he couldn't move or speak. His Patronus flickered and died.

White fog was blinding him. He had to fight ... *expecto patronum* ... he couldn't see ... and in the distance, he heard the familiar screaming ... *expecto patronum* ... he groped in the mist for Sirius, and found his arm ... they weren't going to take him ...

But a pair of strong, clammy hands suddenly wrapped themselves around Harry's neck. They were forcing his face upwards ... he could feel its breath ... it was going to get rid of him first ... he could feel its putrid breath ... his mother was screaming in his ears ... she was going to be the last thing he ever heard –

And then, through the fog that was drowning him, he thought

he saw a silvery light, growing brighter and brighter ... he felt himself fall forwards onto the grass –

Face down, too weak to move, sick and shaking, Harry opened his eyes. The blinding light was illuminating the grass around him ... The screaming had stopped, the cold was ebbing away ...

Something was driving the Dementors back ... it was circling around him and Sirius and Hermione ... the rattling, sucking sounds of the Dementors were fading. They were leaving ... the air was warm again ...

With every ounce of strength he could muster, Harry raised his head a few inches and saw an animal amidst the light, galloping away across the lake. Eyes blurred with sweat, Harry tried to make out what it was ... it was bright as a unicorn. Fighting to stay conscious, Harry watched it canter to a halt as it reached the opposite shore. For a moment, Harry saw, by its brightness, somebody welcoming it back ... raising his hand to pat it ... someone who looked strangely familiar ... but it couldn't be ...

Harry didn't understand. He couldn't think any more. He felt the last of his strength leave him, and his head hit the ground as he fainted.

Hermione's Secret

'Shocking business ... shocking ... miracle none of them died ... never heard the like ... by thunder, it was lucky you were there, Snape ...'

'Thank you, Minister.'

'Order of Merlin, Second Class, I'd say. First Class, if I can wangle it!'

'Thank you very much indeed, Minister.'

'Nasty cut you've got there ... Black's work, I suppose?'

'As a matter of fact, it was Potter, Weasley and Granger, Minister ...'

'*No!*'

'Black had bewitched them, I saw it immediately. A Confundus Charm, to judge by their behaviour. They seemed to think there was a possibility he was innocent. They weren't responsible for their actions. On the other hand, their interference might have permitted Black to escape ... they obviously thought they were going to catch Black single-handed. They've got away with a great deal before now ... I'm afraid it's given them a rather high opinion of themselves ... and of course Potter has always been allowed an extraordinary amount of licence by the Headmaster –'

'Ah, well, Snape ... Harry Potter, you know ... we've all got a bit of a blind spot where he's concerned.'

'And yet – is it good for him to be given so much special treatment? Personally I try to treat him like any other student. And any other student would be suspended – at the very least – for leading his friends into such danger. Consider, Minister: against all school rules – after all the precautions put in place for his protection – out of bounds, at night, consorting with a werewolf and a murderer – and I have reason to believe he has been visiting Hogsmeade illegally, too –'

'Well, well ... we shall see, Snape, we shall see ... the boy has undoubtedly been foolish ...'

Harry lay listening with his eyes tight shut. He felt very groggy. The words he was hearing seemed to be travelling very slowly from his ears to his brain, so that it was difficult to understand. His limbs felt like lead; his eyelids too heavy to lift ... he wanted to lie here, on this comfortable bed, for ever ...

'What amazes me most is the behaviour of the Dementors ... you've really no idea what made them retreat, Snape?'

'No, Minister. By the time I had come round they were heading back to their positions at the entrances ...'

'Extraordinary. And yet Black, and Harry, and the girl –'

'All unconscious by the time I reached them. I bound and gagged Black, naturally, conjured stretchers and brought them all straight back to the castle.'

There was a pause. Harry's brain seemed to be moving a little faster, and as it did, a gnawing sensation grew in the pit of his stomach ...

He opened his eyes.

Everything was slightly blurred. Somebody had removed his glasses. He was lying in the dark hospital wing. At the very end of the ward, he could make out Madam Pomfrey with her back to him, bending over a bed. Harry squinted. Ron's red hair was visible beneath Madam Pomfrey's arm.

Harry moved his head over on the pillow. In the bed to his right lay Hermione. Moonlight was falling across her bed. Her eyes were open, too. She looked petrified, and when she saw that Harry was awake, pressed a finger to her lips, then pointed to the hospital-wing door. It was ajar, and the voices of Cornelius Fudge and Snape were coming through it from the corridor outside.

Madam Pomfrey now came walking briskly up the dark ward to Harry's bed. He turned to look at her. She was carrying the largest block of chocolate he had ever seen in his life. It looked like a small boulder.

'Ah, you're awake!' she said briskly. She placed the chocolate on Harry's bedside table and began breaking it apart with a small hammer.

'How's Ron?' said Harry and Hermione together.

'He'll live,' said Madam Pomfrey grimly. 'As for you two ... you'll be staying here until I'm satisfied you're – Potter, what do you think you're doing?'

Harry was sitting up, putting his glasses back on and picking up his wand.

'I need to see the Headmaster,' he said.

'Potter,' said Madam Pomfrey soothingly, 'it's all right. They've got Black. He's locked away upstairs. The Dementors will be performing the Kiss any moment now –'

'WHAT?'

Harry jumped up out of bed; Hermione had done the same. But his shout had been heard in the corridor outside; next second, Cornelius Fudge and Snape had entered the ward.

'Harry, Harry, what's this?' said Fudge, looking agitated. 'You should be in bed – has he had any chocolate?' he asked Madam Pomfrey anxiously.

'Minister, listen!' Harry said. 'Sirius Black's innocent! Peter Pettigrew faked his own death! We saw him tonight! You can't let the Dementors do that thing to Sirius, he's –'

But Fudge was shaking his head with a small smile on his face.

'Harry, Harry, you're very confused, you've been through a dreadful ordeal, lie back down, now, we've got everything under control ...'

'YOU HAVEN'T!' Harry yelled. 'YOU'VE GOT THE WRONG MAN!'

'Minister, listen, please,' Hermione said; she had hurried to Harry's side and was gazing imploringly into Fudge's face. 'I saw him, too. It was Ron's rat, he's an Animagus, Pettigrew, I mean, and –'

'You see, Minister?' said Snape. 'Confunded, both of them ... Black's done a very good job on them ...'

'WE'RE NOT CONFUNDED!' Harry roared.

'Minister! Professor!' said Madam Pomfrey angrily. 'I must insist that you leave. Potter is my patient, and he should not be distressed!'

'I'm not distressed, I'm trying to tell them what happened!' Harry said furiously. 'If they'd just listen –'

But Madam Pomfrey suddenly stuffed a large chunk of chocolate into Harry's mouth. He choked, and she seized the opportunity to force him back onto the bed.

'Now, *please*, Minister, these children need care. Please leave –'

The door opened again. It was Dumbledore. Harry swallowed his mouthful of chocolate with great difficulty, and got up again.

'Professor Dumbledore, Sirius Black –'

'For heaven's sake!' said Madam Pomfrey hysterically. 'Is this a hospital wing or not? Headmaster, I must insist –'

'My apologies, Poppy, but I need a word with Mr Potter and Miss Granger,' said Dumbledore calmly. 'I have just been talking to Sirius Black –'

'I suppose he's told you the same fairy tale he's planted in Potter's mind?' spat Snape. 'Something about a rat, and Pettigrew being alive –'

'That, indeed, is Black's story,' said Dumbledore, surveying Snape closely through his half-moon spectacles.

'And does my evidence count for nothing?' snarled Snape. 'Peter Pettigrew was not in the Shrieking Shack, nor did I see any sign of him in the grounds.'

'That was because you were knocked out, Professor!' said Hermione earnestly. 'You didn't arrive in time to hear –'

'Miss Granger, HOLD YOUR TONGUE!'

'Now, Snape,' said Fudge, startled, 'the young lady is disturbed in her mind, we must make allowances –'

'I would like to speak to Harry and Hermione alone,' said Dumbledore abruptly. 'Cornelius, Severus, Poppy – please leave us.'

'Headmaster!' spluttered Madam Pomfrey. 'They need treatment, they need rest –'

'This cannot wait,' said Dumbledore. 'I must insist.'

Madam Pomfrey pursed her lips and strode away into her office at the end of the ward, slamming the door behind her. Fudge consulted the large gold pocket watch dangling from his waistcoat.

'The Dementors should have arrived by now,' he said. 'I'll go and meet them. Dumbledore, I'll see you upstairs.'

He crossed to the door and held it open for Snape, but Snape hadn't moved.

'You surely don't believe a word of Black's story?' Snape whispered, his eyes fixed on Dumbledore's face.

'I wish to speak to Harry and Hermione alone,' Dumbledore repeated.

Snape took a step towards Dumbledore.

'Sirius Black showed he was capable of murder at the age of sixteen,' he breathed. 'You haven't forgotten that, Headmaster? You haven't forgotten that he once tried to kill *me*?'

'My memory is as good as it ever was, Severus,' said

Dumbledore quietly.

Snape turned on his heel and marched through the door Fudge was still holding. It closed behind them and Dumbledore turned to Harry and Hermione. They both burst into speech at the same time.

'Professor, Black's telling the truth – we *saw* Pettigrew –'

'– he escaped when Professor Lupin turned into a werewolf –'

'– he's a rat –'

'– Pettigrew's front paw, I mean, finger, he cut it off –'

'– Pettigrew attacked Ron, it wasn't Sirius –'

But Dumbledore held up his hand to stem the flood of explanations.

'It is your turn to listen, and I beg you will not interrupt me, because there is very little time,' he said quietly. 'There is not a shred of proof to support Black's story, except your word – and the word of two thirteen-year-old wizards will not convince anybody. A street full of eye-witnesses swore they saw Sirius murder Pettigrew. I myself gave evidence to the Ministry that Sirius had been the Potters' Secret Keeper.'

'Professor Lupin can tell you –' Harry said, unable to stop himself.

'Professor Lupin is currently deep in the Forest, unable to tell anyone anything. By the time he is human again, it will be too late, Sirius will be worse than dead. I might add that werewolves are so mistrusted by most of our kind that his support will count for very little – and the fact that he and Sirius are old friends –'

'But –'

'*Listen to me, Harry.* It is too late, you understand me? You must see that Professor Snape's version of events is far more convincing than yours.'

'He hates Sirius,' Hermione said desperately. 'All because of some stupid trick Sirius played on him –'

'Sirius has not acted like an innocent man. The attack on the Fat Lady – entering Gryffindor Tower with a knife – without Pettigrew, alive or dead, we have no chance of overturning Sirius' sentence.'

'*But you believe us.*'

'Yes, I do,' said Dumbledore quietly. 'But I have no power to make other men see the truth, or to overrule the Minister for Magic ...'

Harry stared up into the grave face and felt as though the ground beneath him was falling sharply away. He had grown used to the idea that Dumbledore could solve anything. He had expected Dumbledore to pull some amazing solution out of the air. But no ... their last hope was gone.

'What we need,' said Dumbledore slowly, and his light-blue eyes moved from Harry to Hermione, 'is more *time*.'

'But –' Hermione began. And then her eyes became very round. 'OH!'

'Now, pay attention,' said Dumbledore, speaking very low, and very clearly. 'Sirius is locked in Professor Flitwick's office on the seventh floor. Thirteenth window from the right of the West Tower. If all goes well, you will be able to save more than one innocent life tonight. But remember this, both of you. *You must not be seen*. Miss Granger, you know the law – you know what is at stake ... *you – must – not – be – seen*.'

Harry didn't have a clue what was going on. Dumbledore had turned on his heel and looked back as he reached the door.

'I am going to lock you in. It is –' he consulted his watch, 'five minutes to midnight. Miss Granger, three turns should do it. Good luck.'

'Good luck?' Harry repeated, as the door closed behind Dumbledore. 'Three turns? What's he talking about? What are we supposed to do?'

But Hermione was fumbling with the neck of her robes, pulling from beneath them a very long, very fine gold chain.

'Harry, come here,' she said urgently. '*Quick!*'

Harry moved towards her, completely bewildered. She was holding the chain out. He saw a tiny, sparkling hour-glass hanging from it.

'Here –'

She had thrown the chain around his neck, too.

'Ready?' she said breathlessly.

'What are we doing?' Harry said, completely lost.

Hermione turned the hour-glass over three times.

The dark ward dissolved. Harry had the sensation that he was flying, very fast, backwards. A blur of colours and shapes rushed past him; his ears were pounding. He tried to yell but couldn't hear his own voice –

And then he felt solid ground beneath his feet, and everything came into focus again –

He was standing next to Hermione in the deserted Entrance Hall and a stream of golden sunlight was falling across the paved floor from the open front doors. He looked wildly around at Hermione, the chain of the hour-glass cutting into his neck.

'Hermione, what –?'

'In here!' Hermione seized Harry's arm and dragged him across the hall to the door of a broom cupboard; she opened it, pushed him inside amongst the buckets and mops, followed him in, then slammed the door behind them.

'What – how – Hermione, what happened?'

'We've gone back in time,' Hermione whispered, lifting the chain off Harry's neck in the darkness. 'Three hours back ...'

Harry found his own leg and gave it a very hard pinch. It hurt a lot, which seemed to rule out the possibility that he was having a very bizarre dream.

'But –'

'Shh! Listen! Someone's coming! I think – I think it might be us!'

Hermione had her ear pressed against the cupboard door.

'Footsteps across the hall ... yes, I think it's us going down to Hagrid's!'

'Are you telling me,' Harry whispered, 'that we're here in this cupboard and we're out there, too?'

'Yes,' said Hermione, her ear still glued to the cupboard door. 'I'm sure it's us ... it doesn't sound like more than three people ... and we're walking slowly because we're under the Invisibility Cloak –'

She broke off, still listening intently.

'We've gone down the front steps ...'

Hermione sat down on an upturned bucket; looking desperately anxious, Harry wanted a few questions answered.

'Where did you *get* that hourglass thing?'

'It's called a Time-Turner,' Hermione whispered, 'and I got it from Professor McGonagall on our first day back. I've been using it all year to get to all my lessons. Professor McGonagall made me swear I wouldn't tell anyone. She had to write all sorts of letters to the Ministry of Magic so I could have one. She had to tell them that I was a model student, and that I'd never, ever use it for anything except my studies ... I've been turning it back so I could do hours over again, that's how I've been doing several lessons at once, see? But ...

'Harry, *I don't understand what Dumbledore wants us to do*. Why did he tell us to go back three hours? How's that going to help Sirius?'

Harry stared at her shadowy face.

'There must be something that happened around now he wants us to change,' he said slowly. 'What happened? We were walking down to Hagrid's three hours ago ...'

'This *is* three hours ago, and we *are* walking down to Hagrid's,' said Hermione. 'We just heard ourselves leaving ...'

Harry frowned; he felt as though he was screwing up his whole brain in concentration.

'Dumbledore just said – just said we could save more than one innocent life ...' And then it hit him. 'Hermione, we're going to save Buckbeak!'

'But – how will that help Sirius?'

'Dumbledore said – he just told us where the window is – the window of Flitwick's office! Where they've got Sirius locked up! We've got to fly Buckbeak up to the window and rescue Sirius! Sirius can escape on Buckbeak – they can escape together!'

From what Harry could see of Hermione's face, she looked terrified.

'If we manage that without being seen, it'll be a miracle!'

'Well, we've got to try, haven't we?' said Harry. He stood up and pressed his own ear against the door.

'Doesn't sound like anyone's there ... come on, let's go ...'

Harry pushed the cupboard door open. The Entrance Hall was deserted. As quietly and quickly as they could, they darted out of the cupboard and down the stone steps. The shadows were already lengthening, the tops of the trees in the Forbidden Forest gilded once more with gold.

'If anyone's looking out of the window –' Hermione squeaked, looking up at the castle behind them.

'We'll run for it,' said Harry determinedly. 'Straight into the Forest, all right? We'll have to hide behind a tree or something and keep a lookout –'

'OK, but we'll go round by the greenhouses!' said Hermione breathlessly. 'We need to keep out of sight of Hagrid's front door, or we'll see us! We must be nearly at Hagrid's by now!'

Still working out what she meant, Harry set off at a sprint, Hermione behind him. They tore across the vegetable gardens to the greenhouses, paused for a moment behind them, then set off again, fast as they could, skirting around the Whomping Willow, tearing towards the shelter of the Forest ...

Safe in the shadows of the trees, Harry turned around; seconds later, Hermione arrived beside him, panting.

'Right,' she gasped, 'we need to sneak over to Hagrid's. Keep out of sight, Harry ...'

They made their way silently through the trees, keeping to the very edge of the Forest. Then, as they glimpsed the front of Hagrid's house, they heard a knock upon his door. They moved quickly behind a wide oak trunk and peered out from either side. Hagrid had appeared in his doorway, shaking and white, looking around to see who had knocked. And Harry heard his own voice.

'It's us. We're wearing the Invisibility Cloak. Let us in and we can take it off.'

'Yeh shouldn've come!' Hagrid whispered. He stood back, then shut the door quickly.

'This is the weirdest thing we've ever done,' Harry said fervently.

'Let's move along a bit,' Hermione whispered. 'We need to get nearer to Buckbeak!'

They crept through the trees until they saw the nervous Hippogriff, tethered to the fence around Hagrid's pumpkin patch.

'Now?' Harry whispered.

'No!' said Hermione. 'If we steal him now, those Committee people will think Hagrid set him free! We've got to wait until they've seen he's tied outside!'

'That's going to give us about sixty seconds,' said Harry. This was starting to seem impossible.

At that moment, there was a crash of breaking china from inside Hagrid's cabin.

'That's Hagrid breaking the milk jug,' Hermione whispered. 'I'm going to find Scabbers in a moment –'

Sure enough, a few minutes later, they heard Hermione's shriek of surprise.

'Hermione,' said Harry suddenly, 'what if we – we just run in there, and grab Pettigrew –'

'No!' said Hermione in a terrified whisper. 'Don't you under- stand? We're breaking one of the most important wizarding laws!

Nobody's supposed to change time, nobody! You heard Dumbledore, if we're seen –'

'We'd only be seen by ourselves and Hagrid!'

'Harry, what do you think you'd do if you saw yourself bursting into Hagrid's house?' said Hermione.

'I'd – I'd think I'd gone mad,' said Harry, 'or I'd think there was some Dark Magic going on –'

'*Exactly!* You wouldn't understand, you might even attack your-self! Don't you see? Professor McGonagall told me what awful things have happened when wizards have meddled with time ... loads of them ended up killing their past or future selves by mistake!'

'OK!' said Harry. 'It was just an idea, I just thought –'

But Hermione nudged him, and pointed towards the castle. Harry moved his head a few inches to get a clear view of the dis-tant front doors. Dumbledore, Fudge, the old Committee member and Macnair the executioner were coming down the steps.

'We're about to come out!' Hermione breathed.

And sure enough, moments later, Hagrid's back door opened, and Harry saw himself, Ron and Hermione walking out of it with Hagrid. It was, without a doubt, the strangest sensation of his life, standing behind the tree, and watching himself in the pumpkin patch.

'It's OK, Beaky, it's OK ...' Hagrid said to Buckbeak. Then he turned to Harry, Ron and Hermione. 'Go on. Get goin'.'

'Hagrid, we can't –'

'We'll tell them what really happened –'

'They can't kill him –'

'Go! It's bad enough without you lot in trouble an' all!'

Harry watched the Hermione in the pumpkin patch throw the Invisibility Cloak over himself and Ron.

'Go quick. Don' listen ...'

There was a knock on Hagrid's front door. The execution party had arrived. Hagrid turned around and headed back into his cabin, leaving the back door ajar. Harry watched the grass flatten in patches all around the cabin and heard three pairs of feet retreating. He, Ron and Hermione had gone ... but the Harry and Hermione hidden in the trees could now hear what was happen-ing inside the cabin through the back door.

'Where is the beast?' came the cold voice of Macnair.

'Out – outside,' Hagrid croaked.

Harry pulled his head out of sight as Macnair's face appeared at Hagrid's window, staring out at Buckbeak. Then they heard Fudge.

'We – er – have to read you the official notice of execution, Hagrid. I'll make it quick. And then you and Macnair need to sign it. Macnair, you're supposed to listen too, that's procedure –'

Macnair's face vanished from the window. It was now or never.

'Wait here,' Harry whispered to Hermione. 'I'll do it.'

As Fudge's voice started again, Harry darted out from behind his tree, vaulted the fence into the pumpkin patch and approached Buckbeak.

'*It is the decision of the Committee for the Disposal of Dangerous Creatures that the Hippogriff Buckbeak, hereafter called the condemned, shall be executed on the sixth of June at sundown –*'

Careful not to blink, Harry stared up into Buckbeak's fierce orange eye once more, and bowed. Buckbeak sank to his scaly knees and then stood up again. Harry began to fumble with the rope tying Buckbeak to the fence.

'*... sentenced to execution by beheading, to be carried out by the Committee's appointed executioner, Walden Macnair ...*'

'Come on, Buckbeak,' Harry murmured, 'come on, we're going to help you. Quietly ... quietly ...'

'*... as witnessed below*. Hagrid, you sign here ...'

Harry threw all his weight onto the rope, but Buckbeak had dug in his front feet.

'Well, let's get this over with,' said the reedy voice of the Committee member from inside Hagrid's cabin. 'Hagrid, perhaps it would be better if you stayed inside –'

'No, I – I wan' ter be with him ... I don' wan' him ter be alone –'

Footsteps echoed from within the cabin.

'*Buckbeak, move!*' Harry hissed.

Harry tugged harder on the rope around Buckbeak's neck. The Hippogriff began to walk, rustling its wings irritably. They were still ten feet away from the Forest, in plain view of Hagrid's back door.

'One moment, please, Macnair,' came Dumbledore's voice. 'You need to sign, too.' The footsteps stopped. Harry heaved on the rope. Buckbeak snapped his beak and walked a little faster.

Hermione's white face was sticking out from behind a tree.

'Harry, hurry!' she mouthed.

Harry could still hear Dumbledore's voice talking from within the cabin. He gave the rope another wrench. Buckbeak broke into a grudging trot. They had reached the trees ...

'Quick! Quick!' Hermione moaned, darting out from behind her tree, seizing the rope too and adding her weight to make Buckbeak move faster. Harry looked over his shoulder; they were now blocked from sight; they couldn't see Hagrid's garden at all.

'Stop!' he whispered to Hermione. 'They might hear us –'

Hagrid's back door had opened with a bang. Harry, Hermione and Buckbeak stood quite still; even the Hippogriff seemed to be listening intently.

Silence ... then –

'Where is it?' said the reedy voice of the Committee member. 'Where is the beast?'

'It was tied here!' said the executioner furiously. 'I saw it! Just here!'

'How extraordinary,' said Dumbledore. There was a note of amusement in his voice.

'Beaky!' said Hagrid huskily.

There was a swishing noise, and the thud of an axe. The executioner seemed to have swung it into the fence in anger. And then came the howling, and this time they could hear Hagrid's words through his sobs.

'Gone! Gone! Bless his little beak, he's *gone*! Musta pulled himself free! Beaky, yeh clever boy!'

Buckbeak started to strain against the rope, trying to get back to Hagrid. Harry and Hermione tightened their grip and dug their heels into the Forest floor to stop him.

'Someone untied him!' the executioner was snarling. 'We should search the grounds, the Forest –'

'Macnair, if Buckbeak has indeed been stolen, do you really think the thief will have led him away on foot?' said Dumbledore, still sounding amused. 'Search the skies, if you will ... Hagrid, I could do with a cup of tea. Or a large brandy.'

'O' – o' course, Professor,' said Hagrid, who sounded weak with happiness. 'Come in, come in ...'

Harry and Hermione listened closely. They heard footsteps, the soft cursing of the executioner, the snap of the door, and then silence once more.

'Now what?' whispered Harry, looking around.

'We'll have to hide in here,' said Hermione, who looked very shaken. 'We need to wait until they've gone back to the castle. Then we wait until it's safe to fly Buckbeak up to Sirius' window. He won't be there for another couple of hours ...oh, this is going to be difficult ...'

She looked nervously over her shoulder into the depths of the Forest. The sun was setting now.

'We're going to have to move,' said Harry, thinking hard. 'We've got to be able to see the Whomping Willow, or we won't know what's going on.'

'OK,' said Hermione, getting a firmer grip on Buckbeak's rope. 'But we've got to keep out of sight, Harry, remember ...'

They moved around the edge of the Forest, darkness falling thickly around them, until they were hidden behind a clump of trees through which they could make out the Willow.

'There's Ron!' said Harry suddenly.

A dark figure was sprinting across the lawn and its shout echoed through the still night air.

'Get away from him – get away – Scabbers, come *here* –'

And then they saw two more figures materialise out of nowhere. Harry watched himself and Hermione chasing after Ron. Then he saw Ron dive.

'*Gotcha!* Get off, you stinking cat –'

'There's Sirius!' said Harry. The great shape of the dog had bounded out from the roots of the Willow. They saw him bowl Harry over, then seize Ron ...

'Looks even worse from here, doesn't it?' said Harry, watching the dog pulling Ron into the roots. 'Ouch – look, I just got walloped by the tree – and so did you – this is *weird* –'

The Whomping Willow was creaking and lashing out with its lower branches; they could see themselves darting here and there, trying to reach the trunk. And then the tree froze.

'That was Crookshanks pressing the knot,' said Hermione.

'And there we go ...' Harry muttered. 'We're in.'

The moment they disappeared, the tree began to move again. Seconds later, they heard footsteps quite close by. Dumbledore, Macnair, Fudge and the old Committee member were making their way up to the castle.

'Right after we'd gone down into the passage!' said Hermione. 'If *only* Dumbledore had come with us ...'

'Macnair and Fudge would've come, too,' said Harry bitterly. 'I bet you anything Fudge would've told Macnair to murder Sirius on the spot ...'

They watched the four men climb the castle steps and disappear from view. For a few minutes the scene was deserted. Then –

'Here comes Lupin!' said Harry, as they saw another figure sprinting down the stone steps and haring towards the Willow. Harry looked up at the sky. Clouds were obscuring the moon completely.

They watched Lupin seize a broken branch from the ground and prod the knot on the trunk. The tree stopped fighting, and Lupin, too, disappeared into the gap in its roots.

'If he'd only grabbed the Cloak,' said Harry. 'It's just lying there ...'

He turned to Hermione.

'If I just dashed out now and grabbed it, Snape'd never be able to get it and –'

'Harry, *we mustn't be seen*!'

'How can you stand this?' he asked Hermione fiercely. 'Just standing here and watching it happen?' He hesitated. 'I'm going to grab the Cloak!'

'Harry, *no*!'

Hermione seized the back of Harry's robes not a moment too soon. Just then, they heard a burst of song. It was Hagrid, making his way up to the castle, singing at the top of his voice, and weaving slightly as he walked. A large bottle was swinging from his hands.

'*See?*' Hermione whispered. '*See what would have happened? We've got to keep out of sight! No, Buckbeak!*'

The Hippogriff was making frantic attempts to get to Hagrid again; Harry seized his rope, too, straining to hold Buckbeak back. They watched Hagrid meander tipsily up to the castle. He was gone. Buckbeak stopped fighting to get away. His head drooped sadly.

Barely two minutes later, the castle doors flew open yet again, and Snape had come charging out of them, running towards the Willow.

Harry's fists clenched as they watched Snape skid to a halt next to the tree, looking around. He grabbed the Cloak and held it up.

'Get your filthy hands off it,' Harry snarled under his breath.

'Shh!'

Snape seized the branch Lupin had used to freeze the tree, prodded the knot, and vanished from view as he put on the Cloak.

'So that's it,' said Hermione quietly. 'We're all down there ... and now we've just got to wait until we come back up again ...'

She took the end of Buckbeak's rope and tied it securely around the nearest tree, then sat down on the dry ground, arms around her knees.

'Harry, there's something I don't understand ... why didn't the Dementors get Sirius? I remember them coming, and then I think I passed out ... there were so many of them ...'

Harry sat down, too. He explained what he'd seen; how, as the nearest Dementor had lowered its mouth to Harry's, a large silver something had come galloping across the lake and forced the Dementors to retreat.

Hermione's mouth was slightly open by the time Harry had finished.

'But what was it?'

'There's only one thing it could have been, to make the Dementors go,' said Harry. 'A real Patronus. A powerful one.'

'But who conjured it?'

Harry didn't say anything. He was thinking back to the person he'd seen on the other bank of the lake. He knew who he thought it had been ... but how *could* it have been?

'Didn't you see what they looked like?' said Hermione eagerly. 'Was it one of the teachers?'

'No,' said Harry. 'He wasn't a teacher.'

'But it must have been a really powerful wizard, to drive all those Dementors away ... If the Patronus was shining so brightly, didn't it light him up? Couldn't you see –?'

'Yeah, I saw him,' said Harry slowly. 'But ... maybe I imagined it ... I wasn't thinking straight ... I passed out right afterwards ...'

'*Who did you think it was?*'

'I think –' Harry swallowed, knowing how strange this was going to sound. 'I think it was my dad.'

Harry glanced up at Hermione and saw that her mouth was fully open now. She was gazing at him with a mixture of alarm and pity.

'Harry, your dad's – well – *dead*,' she said quietly.

'I know that,' said Harry quickly.

'You think you saw his ghost?'

'I don't know ... no ... he looked solid ...'

'But then – '

'Maybe I was seeing things,' said Harry. 'But ... from what I could see ... it looked like him ... I've got photos of him ...'

Hermione was still looking at him as though worried about his sanity.

'I know it sounds mad,' said Harry flatly. He turned to look at Buckbeak, who was digging his beak into the ground, apparently searching for worms. But he wasn't really watching Buckbeak.

He was thinking about his father, and about his three oldest friends ... Moony, Wormtail, Padfoot and Prongs ... Had all four of them been out in the grounds tonight? Wormtail had reappeared this evening when everyone had thought he was dead – was it so impossible his father had done the same? Had he been seeing things across the lake? The figure had been too far away to see distinctly ... yet he had felt sure, for a moment, before he'd lost consciousness ...

The leaves overhead rustled faintly in the breeze. The moon drifted in and out of sight behind the shifting clouds. Hermione sat with her face turned towards the Willow, waiting.

And then, at last, after over an hour ...

'Here we come!' Hermione whispered.

She and Harry got to their feet. Buckbeak raised his head. They saw Lupin, Ron and Pettigrew clambering awkwardly out of the hole in the roots, followed by the unconscious Snape, drifting weirdly upwards. Next came Harry, Hermione and Black. They all began to walk towards the castle.

Harry's heart was starting to beat very fast. He glanced up at the sky. Any moment now, that cloud was going to move aside and show the moon ...

'Harry,' Hermione muttered, as though she knew exactly what he was thinking, 'we've got to stay put. We mustn't be seen. There's nothing we can do ...'

'So we're just going to let Pettigrew escape all over again ...' said Harry quietly.

'How do you expect to find a rat in the dark?' snapped Hermione. 'There's nothing we can do! We came back to help Sirius. We're not supposed to be doing anything else!'

'*All right!*'

The moon slid out from behind its cloud. They saw the tiny

figures across the grounds stop. Then they saw movement –

'There goes Lupin,' Hermione whispered. 'He's transforming –'

'Hermione!' said Harry suddenly. 'We've got to move!'

'We mustn't, I keep telling you –'

'Not to interfere! But Lupin's going to run into the Forest, right at us!'

Hermione gasped.

'Quick!' she moaned, dashing to untie Buckbeak. 'Quick! Where are we going to go? Where are we going to hide? The Dementors will be coming any moment –'

'Back to Hagrid's!' Harry said. 'It's empty now – come on!'

They ran, fast as they could, Buckbeak cantering along behind them. They could hear the werewolf howling behind them ...

The cabin was in sight. Harry skidded to the door, wrenched it open and Hermione and Buckbeak flashed past him; Harry threw himself in after them and bolted the door. Fang the boarhound barked loudly.

'Shh, Fang, it's us!' said Hermione, hurrying over and scratching his ears to quieten him. 'That was really close!' she said to Harry.

'Yeah ...'

Harry was looking out of the window. It was much harder to see what was going on from here. Buckbeak seemed very happy to find himself back inside Hagrid's house. He lay down in front of the fire, folded his wings contentedly and seemed ready for a good nap.

'I think I'd better go outside again, you know,' said Harry slowly. 'I can't see what's going on – we won't know when it's time –'

Hermione looked up. Her expression was suspicious.

'I'm not going to try and interfere,' said Harry quickly. 'But if we don't see what's going on, how're we going to know when it's time to rescue Sirius?'

'Well ... OK, then ... I'll wait here with Buckbeak ... but Harry, be careful – there's a werewolf out there – and the Dementors –'

Harry stepped outside again and edged around the cabin. He could hear yelping in the distance. That meant the Dementors were closing in on Sirius ... he and Hermione would be running to him any moment ...

Harry stared out towards the lake, his heart doing a kind of drum-roll in his chest. Whoever had sent that Patronus would be appearing at any moment.

For a fraction of a second he stood, irresolute, in front of Hagrid's door. *You must not be seen.* But he didn't want to be seen. He wanted to do the seeing ... he had to know ...

And there were the Dementors. They were emerging out of the darkness from every direction, gliding around the edges of the lake ... they were moving away from where Harry stood, to the opposite bank ... he wouldn't have to get near them ...

Harry began to run. He had no thought in his head except his father ... If it was him ... if it really was him ... he had to know, had to find out ...

The lake was coming nearer and nearer, but there was no sign of anybody. On the opposite bank, he could see tiny glimmers of silver – his own attempts at a Patronus –

There was a bush at the very edge of the water. Harry threw himself behind it, peering desperately through the leaves. On the opposite bank, the glimmers of silver were suddenly extinguished. A terrified excitement shot through him – any moment now –

'Come on!' he muttered, staring about. 'Where are you? Dad, come on –'

But no one came. Harry raised his head to look at the circle of Dementors across the lake. One of them was lowering its hood. It was time for the rescuer to appear – but no one was coming to help this time –

And then it hit him – he understood. He hadn't seen his father – he had seen *himself* –

Harry flung himself out from behind the bush and pulled out his wand.

'EXPECTO PATRONUM!' he yelled.

And out of the end of his wand burst, not a shapeless cloud of mist, but a blinding, dazzling, silver animal. He screwed up his eyes, trying to see what it was. It looked like a horse. It was galloping silently away from him, across the black surface of the lake. He saw it lower its head and charge at the swarming Dementors ... now it was galloping around and around the black shapes on the ground, and the Dementors were falling back, scattering, retreating into the darkness ... they were gone.

The Patronus turned. It was cantering back towards Harry across the still surface of the water. It wasn't a horse. It wasn't a unicorn, either. It was a stag. It was shining brightly as the moon above ... it was coming back to him ...

It stopped on the bank. Its hooves made no mark on the soft ground as it stared at Harry with its large, silver eyes. Slowly, it bowed its antlered head. And Harry realised ...

'Prongs,' he whispered.

But as his trembling fingertips stretched towards the creature, it vanished.

Harry stood there, hand still outstretched. Then, with a great leap of his heart, he heard hooves behind him – he whirled around and saw Hermione dashing towards him, dragging Buckbeak behind her.

'What did you do?' she said fiercely. 'You said you were only going to keep a lookout!'

'I just saved all our lives ...' said Harry. 'Get behind here – behind this bush – I'll explain.'

Hermione listened to what had just happened with her mouth open yet again.

'Did anyone see you?'

'Yes, haven't you been listening? I saw me but I thought I was my dad! It's OK!'

'Harry, I can't believe it – you conjured up a Patronus that drove away all those Dementors! That's very, very advanced magic ...'

'I knew I could do it this time,' said Harry, 'because I'd already done it ... Does that make sense?'

'I don't know – Harry, look at Snape!'

Together they peered around the bush at the other bank. Snape had regained consciousness. He was conjuring stretchers and lifting the limp forms of Harry, Hermione and Black onto them. A fourth stretcher, no doubt bearing Ron, was already floating at his side. Then, wand held out in front of him, he moved them away towards the castle.

'Right, it's nearly time,' said Hermione tensely, looking at her watch. 'We've got about forty-five minutes until Dumbledore locks the door to the hospital wing. We've got to rescue Sirius and get back into the ward before anybody realises we're missing ...'

They waited, watching the moving clouds reflected in the lake, while the bush next to them whispered in the breeze. Buckbeak, bored, was ferreting for worms again.

'D'you reckon he's up there yet?' said Harry, checking his watch. He looked up at the castle, and began counting the windows to the right of the West Tower.

'Look!' Hermione whispered. 'Who's that? Someone's coming back out of the castle!'

Harry stared through the darkness. The man was hurrying across the grounds, towards one of the entrances. Something shiny glinted in his belt.

'Macnair!' said Harry. 'The executioner! He's gone to get the Dementors! This is it, Hermione –'

Hermione put her hands on Buckbeak's back and Harry gave her a leg up. Then he placed his foot on one of the lower branches of the bush and climbed up in front of her. He pulled Buckbeak's rope back over his neck and tied it to the other side of his collar like reins.

'Ready?' he whispered to Hermione. 'You'd better hold on to me –'

He nudged Buckbeak's sides with his heels.

Buckbeak soared straight into the dark air. Harry gripped his flanks with his knees, feeling the great wings rising powerfully beneath them. Hermione was holding Harry very tightly around the waist; he could hear her muttering, 'Oh, no – I don't like this – oh, I *really* don't like this –'

Harry urged Buckbeak forwards. They were gliding quietly towards the upper floors of the castle ... Harry pulled hard on the left-hand side of the rope, and Buckbeak turned. Harry was trying to count the windows flashing past –

'Whoa!' he said, pulling backwards as hard as he could.

Buckbeak slowed down and they found themselves at a stop, unless you counted the fact that they kept rising up and down several feet as he beat his wings to remain airborne.

'He's there!' Harry said, spotting Sirius as they rose up beside the window. He reached out, and as Buckbeak's wings fell, was able to tap sharply on the glass.

Black looked up. Harry saw his jaw drop. He leapt from his chair, hurried to the window and tried to open it, but it was locked.

'Stand back!' Hermione called to him, and she took out her wand, still gripping the back of Harry's robes with her left hand.

'*Alohomora!*'

The window sprang open.

'How – *how* –?' said Black weakly, staring at the Hippogriff.

'Get on – there's not much time,' said Harry, gripping Buckbeak firmly on either side of his sleek neck to hold him steady. 'You've got to get out of here – the Dementors are coming. Macnair's gone to get them.'

Black placed a hand on either side of the window-frame and heaved his head and shoulders out of it. It was very lucky he was so thin. In seconds, he had managed to fling one leg over Buckbeak's back, and pull himself onto the Hippogriff behind Hermione.

'OK, Buckbeak, up!' said Harry, shaking the rope. 'Up to the tower – come on!'

The Hippogriff gave one sweep of its mighty wings and they were soaring upwards again, high as the top of the West Tower. Buckbeak landed with a clatter on the battlements and Harry and Hermione slid off him at once.

'Sirius, you'd better go, quick,' Harry panted. 'They'll reach Flitwick's office any moment, they'll find out you've gone.'

Buckbeak pawed the ground, tossing his sharp head.

'What happened to the other boy? Ron?' said Sirius urgently.

'He's going to be OK – he's still out of it, but Madam Pomfrey says she'll be able to make him better. Quick – go!'

But Black was still staring down at Harry.

'How can I ever thank –'

'GO!' Harry and Hermione shouted together.

Black wheeled Buckbeak around, facing the open sky.

'We'll see each other again,' he said. 'You are – truly your father's son, Harry ...'

He squeezed Buckbeak's sides with his heels. Harry and Hermione jumped back as the enormous wings rose once more ... the Hippogriff took off into the air ... he and his rider became smaller and smaller as Harry gazed after them ... then a cloud drifted across the moon ... they were gone.

— CHAPTER TWENTY-TWO —

Owl Post Again

'Harry!'

Hermione was tugging at his sleeve, staring at her watch. 'We've got exactly ten minutes to get back down to the hospital wing without anybody seeing us – before Dumbledore locks the door –'

'OK,' said Harry, wrenching his gaze from the sky, 'let's go ...'

They slipped through the doorway behind them and down a tightly spiralling stone staircase. As they reached the bottom of it, they heard voices. They flattened themselves against the wall and listened. It sounded like Fudge and Snape. They were walking quickly along the corridor at the foot of the staircase.

'... only hope Dumbledore's not going to make difficulties,' Snape was saying. 'The Kiss will be performed immediately?'

'As soon as Macnair returns with the Dementors. This whole Black affair has been highly embarrassing. I can't tell you how much I'm looking forward to informing the *Daily Prophet* that we've got him at last ... I daresay they'll want to interview you, Snape ... and once young Harry's back in his right mind, I expect he'll want to tell the *Prophet* exactly how you saved him ...'

Harry clenched his teeth. He caught a glimpse of Snape's smirk as he and Fudge passed Harry and Hermione's hiding place. Their footsteps died away. Harry and Hermione waited a few moments to make sure they'd really gone, then started to run in the opposite direction. Down one staircase, then another, along a new corridor – then they heard a cackling ahead.

'*Peeves!*' Harry muttered, grabbing Hermione's wrist. 'In here!'

They tore into a deserted classroom to their left just in time. Peeves seemed to be bouncing along the corridor in tearing spirits, laughing his head off.

'Oh, he's horrible,' whispered Hermione, her ear to the door. 'I bet he's all excited because the Dementors are going to finish Sirius ...' She checked her watch. 'Three minutes, Harry!'

They waited until Peeves's gloating voice had faded into the distance, then slid back out of the room and broke into a run again.

'Hermione – what'll happen – if we don't get back inside – before Dumbledore locks the door?' Harry panted.

'I don't want to think about it!' Hermione moaned, checking her watch again. 'One minute!'

They had reached the end of the corridor with the hospital-wing entrance. 'OK – I can hear Dumbledore,' said Hermione tensely. 'Come on, Harry!'

They crept along the corridor. The door opened. Dumbledore's back appeared.

'I am going to lock you in,' they heard him saying. 'It is five minutes to midnight. Miss Granger, three turns should do it. Good luck.'

Dumbledore backed out of the room, closed the door and took out his wand to magically lock it. Panicking, Harry and Hermione ran forwards. Dumbledore looked up, and a wide smile appeared under the long silver moustache. 'Well?' he said quietly.

'We did it!' said Harry breathlessly. 'Sirius has gone, on Buckbeak ...'

Dumbledore beamed at them.

'Well done. I think –' he listened intently for any sound within the hospital wing. 'Yes, I think you've gone, too. Get inside – I'll lock you in –'

Harry and Hermione slipped back inside the dormitory. It was empty except for Ron, who was still lying motionless in the end bed. As the lock clicked behind them, Harry and Hermione crept back to their own beds, Hermione tucking the Time-Turner back under her robes. Next moment, Madam Pomfrey had come striding back out of her office.

'Did I hear the Headmaster leaving? Am I allowed to look after my patients now?'

She was in a very bad mood. Harry and Hermione thought it best to accept their chocolate quietly. Madam Pomfrey stood over them, making sure they ate it. But Harry could hardly swallow. He and Hermione were waiting, listening, their nerves jangling ... And then, as they both took a fourth piece of chocolate from Madam Pomfrey, they heard a distant roar of fury echoing from somewhere above them ...

'What was that?' said Madam Pomfrey in alarm.

Now they could hear angry voices, growing louder and louder. Madam Pomfrey was staring at the door.

'Really – they'll wake everybody up! What do they think they're doing?'

Harry was trying to hear what the voices were saying. They were drawing nearer –

'He must have Disapparated, Severus, we should have left somebody in the room with him. When this gets out –'

'HE DIDN'T DISAPPARATE!' Snape roared, now very close at hand. 'YOU CAN'T APPARATE OR DISAPPARATE INSIDE THIS CASTLE! THIS – HAS – SOMETHING – TO – DO – WITH – POTTER!'

'Severus – be reasonable – Harry has been locked up –'

BAM.

The door of the hospital wing burst open.

Fudge, Snape and Dumbledore came striding into the ward. Dumbledore alone looked calm. Indeed, he looked as though he was quite enjoying himself. Fudge appeared angry. But Snape was beside himself.

'OUT WITH IT, POTTER!' he bellowed. 'WHAT DID YOU DO?'

'Professor Snape!' shrieked Madam Pomfrey. 'Control yourself!'

'See here, Snape, be reasonable,' said Fudge. 'This door's been locked, we just saw –'

'THEY HELPED HIM ESCAPE, I KNOW IT!' Snape howled, pointing at Harry and Hermione. His face was twisted, spit was flying from his mouth.

'Calm down, man!' Fudge barked. 'You're talking nonsense!'

'YOU DON'T KNOW POTTER!' shrieked Snape. 'HE DID IT, I KNOW HE DID IT –'

'That will do, Severus,' said Dumbledore quietly. 'Think about what you are saying. This door has been locked since I left the ward ten minutes ago. Madam Pomfrey, have these students left their beds?'

'Of course not!' said Madam Pomfrey, bristling. 'I've been with them ever since you left!'

'Well, there you have it, Severus,' said Dumbledore calmly. 'Unless you are suggesting that Harry and Hermione are able to be in two places at once, I'm afraid I don't see any point in troubling them further.'

Snape stood there, seething, staring from Fudge, who looked thoroughly shocked at his behaviour, to Dumbledore, whose eyes were twinkling behind his glasses. Snape whirled about, robes swishing behind him, and stormed out of the ward.

'Fellow seems quite unbalanced,' said Fudge, staring after him. 'I'd watch out for him, if I were you, Dumbledore.'

'Oh, he's not unbalanced,' said Dumbledore quietly. 'He's just suffered a severe disappointment.'

'He's not the only one!' puffed Fudge. 'The *Daily Prophet*'s going to have a field day! We had Black cornered and he slipped through our fingers yet again! All it needs now is for the story of that Hippogriff's escape to get out, and I'll be a laughing stock! Well ... I'd better go and notify the Ministry ...'

'And the Dementors?' said Dumbledore. 'They'll be removed from the school, I trust?'

'Oh, yes, they'll have to go,' said Fudge, running his fingers distractedly through his hair. 'Never dreamed they'd attempt to administer the Kiss on an innocent boy ... completely out of control ... No, I'll have them packed off back to Azkaban tonight. Perhaps we should think about dragons at the school entrance ...'

'Hagrid would like that,' said Dumbledore, with a swift smile at Harry and Hermione. As he and Fudge left the dormitory, Madam Pomfrey hurried to the door and locked it again. Muttering angrily to herself, she headed back to her office.

There was a low moan from the other end of the ward. Ron had woken up. They could see him sitting up, rubbing his head, looking around.

'What – what happened?' he groaned. 'Harry? Why are we in here? Where's Sirius? Where's Lupin? What's going on?'

Harry and Hermione looked at each other.

'You explain,' said Harry, helping himself to some more chocolate.

*

When Harry, Ron and Hermione left the hospital wing at noon next day, it was to find an almost deserted castle. The sweltering heat and the end of the exams meant that everyone was taking full advantage of another Hogsmeade visit. Neither Ron nor Hermione felt like going, however, so they and Harry wandered into the grounds, still talking about the extraordinary events of the previous night and wondering where Sirius and Buckbeak were now. Sitting near the lake, watching the giant squid waving its tentacles lazily above the water, Harry lost the thread of the conversation as he looked across to the opposite bank. The stag had galloped towards him from there just last night ...

A shadow fell across them and they looked up to see a very bleary-eyed Hagrid, mopping his sweaty face with one of his tablecloth-sized handkerchiefs and beaming down at them.

'Know I shouldn' feel happy, after wha' happened las' night,' he said. 'I mean, Black escapin' again, an' everythin' – but guess what?'

'What?' they said, pretending to look curious.

'Beaky! He escaped! He's free! Bin celebratin' all night!'

'That's wonderful!' said Hermione, giving Ron a reproving look because he looked as though he was close to laughing.

'Yeah ... can't've tied him up properly,' said Hagrid, gazing happily out over the grounds. 'I was worried this mornin', mind ... thought he mighta met Professor Lupin in the grounds, but Lupin says he never ate anythin' las' night ...'

'What?' said Harry quickly.

'Blimey, haven' yeh heard?' said Hagrid, his smile fading a little. He lowered his voice, even though there was nobody in sight. 'Er – Snape told all the Slytherins this mornin' ... thought everyone'd know by now ... Professor Lupin's a werewolf, see. An' he was loose in the grounds las' night. He's packin' now, o' course.'

'He's *packing*?' said Harry, alarmed. 'Why?'

'Leavin', isn' he?' said Hagrid, looking surprised that Harry had to ask. 'Resigned firs' thing this mornin'. Says he can' risk it happenin' again.'

Harry scrambled to his feet.

'I'm going to see him,' he said to Ron and Hermione.

'But if he's resigned –'

'– doesn't sound like there's anything we can do –'

'I don't care. I still want to see him. I'll meet you back here.'

*

Lupin's office door was open. He had already packed most of his things. The Grindylow's empty tank stood next to his battered old suitcase, which was open and nearly full. Lupin was bending over something on his desk, and only looked up when Harry knocked on the door.

'I saw you coming,' said Lupin, smiling. He pointed to the parchment he had been poring over. It was the Marauder's Map.

'I just saw Hagrid,' said Harry. 'And he said you'd resigned. It's not true, is it?'

'I'm afraid it is,' said Lupin. He started opening his desk drawers and taking out the contents.

'*Why?*' said Harry. 'The Ministry of Magic don't think you were helping Sirius, do they?'

Lupin crossed to the door and closed it behind Harry.

'No. Professor Dumbledore managed to convince Fudge that I was trying to save your lives.' He sighed. 'That was the final straw for Severus. I think the loss of the Order of Merlin hit him hard. So he – er – *accidentally* let slip that I am a werewolf this morning at breakfast.'

'You're not leaving just because of that!' said Harry.

Lupin smiled wryly.

'This time tomorrow, the owls will start arriving from parents – they will not want a werewolf teaching their children, Harry. And after last night, I see their point. I could have bitten any of you ... that must never happen again.'

'You're the best Defence Against the Dark Arts teacher we've ever had!' said Harry. 'Don't go!'

Lupin shook his head and didn't speak. He carried on emptying his drawers. Then, while Harry was trying to think of a good argument to make him stay, Lupin said, 'From what the Headmaster told me this morning, you saved a lot of lives last night, Harry. If I'm proud of anything, it's how much you've learned. Tell me about your Patronus.'

'How d'you know about that?' said Harry, distracted.

'What else could have driven the Dementors back?'

Harry told Lupin what had happened. When he'd finished, Lupin was smiling again.

'Yes, your father was always a stag when he transformed,' he said. 'You guessed right ... that's why we called him Prongs.'

Lupin threw his last few books into his case, closed the desk drawers and turned to look at Harry.

'Here – I brought this from the Shrieking Shack last night,' he said, handing Harry back the Invisibility Cloak. 'And ...' he hesitated, then held out the Marauder's Map, too. 'I am no longer your teacher, so I don't feel guilty about giving you this back as well. It's no use to me, and I daresay you, Ron and Hermione will find uses for it.'

Harry took the map and grinned.

'You told me Moony, Wormtail, Padfoot and Prongs would've wanted to lure me out of school ... you said they'd have thought it was funny.'

'And so we would have done,' said Lupin, now reaching down to close his case. 'I have no hesitation in saying that James would have been highly disappointed if his son had never found any of the secret passages out of the castle.'

There was a knock on the door. Harry hastily stuffed the Marauder's Map and the Invisibility Cloak into his pocket.

It was Professor Dumbledore. He didn't look surprised to see Harry there.

'Your carriage is at the gates, Remus,' he said.

'Thank you, Headmaster.'

Lupin picked up his old suitcase and the empty Grindylow tank.

'Well – goodbye, Harry,' he said, smiling. 'It has been a real pleasure teaching you. I feel sure we'll meet again some time. Headmaster, there is no need to see me to the gates, I can manage ...'

Harry had the impression that Lupin wanted to leave as quickly as possible.

'Goodbye, then, Remus,' said Dumbledore soberly. Lupin shifted the Grindylow tank slightly so that he and Dumbledore could shake hands. Then, with a final nod to Harry, and a swift smile, Lupin left the office.

Harry sat down in his vacated chair, staring glumly at the floor. He heard the door close and looked up. Dumbledore was still there.

'Why so miserable, Harry?' he said quietly. 'You should be very proud of yourself after last night.'

'It didn't make any difference,' said Harry bitterly. 'Pettigrew got away.'

'Didn't make any difference?' said Dumbledore quietly. 'It made all the difference in the world, Harry. You helped uncover the truth. You saved an innocent man from a terrible fate.'

Terrible. Something stirred in Harry's memory. *Greater and more terrible than ever before* ... Professor Trelawney's prediction!

'Professor Dumbledore – yesterday, when I was having my Divination exam, Professor Trelawney went very – very strange.'

'Indeed?' said Dumbledore. 'Er – stranger than usual, you mean?'

'Yes ... her voice went all deep and her eyes rolled and she said ... she said Voldemort's servant was going to set out to return to him before midnight ... she said the servant would help him come back to power.' Harry stared up at Dumbledore. 'And then she sort of became normal again, and she couldn't remember anything she'd said. Was it – was she making a real prediction?'

Dumbledore looked mildly impressed.

'Do you know, Harry, I think she might have been,' he said thoughtfully. 'Who'd have thought it? That brings her total of real predictions up to two. I should offer her a pay rise ...'

'But –' Harry looked at him, aghast. How could Dumbledore take this so calmly?

'But – I stopped Sirius and Professor Lupin killing Pettigrew! That makes it my fault, if Voldemort comes back!'

'It does not,' said Dumbledore quietly. 'Hasn't your experience with the Time-Turner taught you anything, Harry? The consequences of our actions are always so complicated, so diverse, that predicting the future is a very difficult business indeed ... Professor Trelawney, bless her, is living proof of that. You did a very noble thing, in saving Pettigrew's life.'

'But if he helps Voldemort back to power –!'

'Pettigrew owes his life to you. You have sent Voldemort a deputy who is in your debt. When one wizard saves another wizard's life, it creates a certain bond between them ... and I'm much mistaken if Voldemort wants his servant in the debt of Harry Potter.'

'I don't want a bond with Pettigrew!' said Harry. 'He betrayed my parents!'

'This is magic at its deepest, its most impenetrable, Harry. But trust me ... the time may come when you will be very glad you saved Pettigrew's life.'

Harry couldn't imagine when that would be. Dumbledore looked as though he knew what Harry was thinking.

'I knew your father very well, both at Hogwarts and later, Harry,' he said gently. 'He would have saved Pettigrew too, I am sure of it.'

Harry looked up at him. Dumbledore wouldn't laugh – he could tell Dumbledore ...

'Last night ... I thought it was my dad who'd conjured my Patronus. I mean, when I saw myself across the lake ... I thought I was seeing him.'

'An easy mistake to make,' said Dumbledore softly. 'I expect you're tired of hearing it, but you do look *extraordinarily* like James. Except for your eyes ... you have your mother's eyes.'

Harry shook his head.

'It was stupid, thinking it was him,' he muttered. 'I mean, I knew he was dead.'

'You think the dead we have loved ever truly leave us? You think that we don't recall them more clearly than ever in times of great trouble? Your father is alive in you, Harry, and shows himself most plainly when you have need of him. How else could you produce that *particular* Patronus? Prongs rode again last night.'

It took a moment for Harry to realise what Dumbledore had said.

'Sirius told me all about how they became Animagi last night,' said Dumbledore, smiling. 'An extraordinary achievement – not least, keeping it quiet from me. And then I remembered the most unusual form your Patronus took, when it charged Mr Malfoy down at your Quidditch match against Ravenclaw. So you did see your father last night, Harry ... you found him inside yourself.'

And Dumbledore left the office, leaving Harry to his very confused thoughts.

*

Nobody at Hogwarts knew the truth of what had happened the night that Sirius, Buckbeak and Pettigrew had vanished except Harry, Ron, Hermione and Professor Dumbledore. As the end of term approached, Harry heard many different theories about what had really happened, but none of them came close to the truth.

Malfoy was furious about Buckbeak. He was convinced that Hagrid had found a way of smuggling the Hippogriff to safety, and seemed outraged that he and his father had been outwitted by a gamekeeper. Percy Weasley, meanwhile, had much to say on the subject of Sirius' escape.

'If I manage to get into the Ministry, I'll have a lot of proposals to make about Magical Law Enforcement!' he told the only person who would listen – his girlfriend, Penelope.

Though the weather was perfect, though the atmosphere was so cheerful, though he knew they had achieved the near impossible in helping Sirius to freedom, Harry had never approached the end of a school year in worse spirits.

He certainly wasn't the only one who was sorry to see Professor

Lupin go. The whole of Harry's Defence Against the Dark Arts class were miserable about his resignation.

'Wonder what they'll give us next year?' said Seamus Finnigan gloomily.

'Maybe a vampire,' suggested Dean Thomas hopefully.

It wasn't only Professor Lupin's departure that was weighing on Harry's mind. He couldn't help thinking a lot about Professor Trelawney's prediction. He kept wondering where Pettigrew was now, whether he had sought sanctuary with Voldemort yet. But the thing that was lowering Harry's spirits most of all was the prospect of returning to the Dursleys. For maybe half an hour, a glorious half hour, he had believed he would be living with Sirius from now on ... his parents' best friend ... it would have been the next best thing to having his own father back. And while no news of Sirius was definitely good news, because it meant he had successfully gone into hiding, Harry couldn't help feeling miserable when he thought of the home he might have had, and the fact that it was now impossible.

The exam results came out on the last day of term. Harry, Ron and Hermione had passed every subject. Harry was amazed that he had got through Potions. He had a shrewd suspicion that Dumbledore had stepped in to stop Snape failing him on purpose. Snape's behaviour towards Harry over the past week had been quite alarming. Harry wouldn't have thought it possible that Snape's dislike for him could increase, but it certainly had done. A muscle twitched unpleasantly at the corner of Snape's thin mouth every time he looked at Harry, and he was constantly flexing his fingers, as though itching to place them around Harry's throat.

Percy had got his top-grade N.E.W.Ts; Fred and George had scraped a handful of O.W.Ls each. Gryffindor house, meanwhile, largely thanks to their spectacular performance in the Quidditch Cup, had won the House Championship for the third year running. This meant that the end-of-term feast took place amid decorations of scarlet and gold, and that the Gryffindor table was the noisiest of the lot, as everybody celebrated. Even Harry managed to forget about the journey back to the Dursleys next day as he ate, drank, talked and laughed with the rest.

*

As the Hogwarts Express pulled out of the station next morning, Hermione gave Harry and Ron some surprising news.

'I went to see Professor McGonagall this morning, just before breakfast. I've decided to drop Muggle Studies.'

'But you passed your exam with three hundred and twenty per cent!' said Ron.

'I know,' sighed Hermione, 'but I can't stand another year like this one. That Time-Turner, it was driving me mad. I've handed it in. Without Muggle Studies and Divination, I'll be able to have a normal timetable again.'

'I still can't *believe* you didn't tell us about it,' said Ron grumpily. 'We're supposed to be your *friends*.'

'I promised I wouldn't tell *anyone*,' said Hermione severely. She looked around at Harry, who was watching Hogwarts disappear from view behind a mountain. Two whole months before he'd see it again ...

'Oh, cheer up, Harry!' said Hermione sadly.

'I'm OK,' said Harry quickly. 'Just thinking about the holidays.'

'Yeah, I've been thinking about them, too,' said Ron. 'Harry, you've got to come and stay with us. I'll fix it up with Mum and Dad, then I'll call you. I know how to use a fellytone now –'

'A *telephone*, Ron,' said Hermione. 'Honestly, *you* should take Muggle Studies next year ...'

Ron ignored her.

'It's the Quidditch World Cup this summer! How about it, Harry? Come and stay, and we'll go and see it! Dad can usually get tickets from work.'

This proposal had the effect of cheering Harry up a great deal.

'Yeah ... I bet the Dursleys'd be pleased to let me come ... especially after what I did to Aunt Marge ...'

Feeling considerably more cheerful, Harry joined Ron and Hermione in several games of Exploding Snap, and when the witch with the tea trolley arrived, he bought himself a very large lunch, though nothing with chocolate in it.

But it was late in the afternoon before the thing that made him truly happy turned up ...

'Harry,' said Hermione suddenly, peering over his shoulder. 'What's that thing outside your window?'

Harry turned to look outside. Something very small and grey was bobbing in and out of sight beyond the glass. He stood up for a better look and saw that it was a tiny owl, carrying a letter which was much too big for it. The owl was so small, in fact, that it kept tumbling over in the air, buffeted this way and that in the train's slipstream. Harry quickly pulled down the window, stretched out his arm and caught it. It felt like a very fluffy Snitch. He brought it carefully inside. The owl dropped its letter onto Harry's seat and began zooming around their compartment, apparently very pleased with itself for accomplishing its task. Hedwig clicked her beak with a sort of dignified disapproval. Crookshanks sat up in his seat, following the owl with his great yellow eyes. Ron, noticing this, snatched the owl safely out of harm's way.

Harry picked up the letter. It was addressed to him. He ripped open the letter and shouted, 'It's from Sirius!'

'What?' said Ron and Hermione excitedly. 'Read it aloud!'

Dear Harry,

I hope this finds you before you reach your aunt and uncle. I don't know whether they're used to owl post.

Buckbeak and I are in hiding. I won't tell you where, in case this falls into the wrong hands. I have some doubt about the owl's reliability, but he is the best I could find, and he did seem eager for the job.

I believe the Dementors are still searching for me, but they haven't a hope of finding me here. I am planning to allow some Muggles to glimpse me soon, a long way from Hogwarts, so that the security on the castle will be lifted.

There is something I never got round to telling you during our brief meeting. It was I who sent you the Firebolt –

'Ha!' said Hermione triumphantly. 'See! I *told* you it was from him!'

'Yes, but he hadn't jinxed it, had he?' said Ron. 'Ouch!'

The tiny owl, now hooting happily in his hand, had nibbled one of his fingers in what it seemed to think was an affectionate way.

Crookshanks took the order to the Owl Office for me. I used your name but told them to take the gold from Gringotts vault number seven hundred and eleven – my own. Please consider it as thirteen birthdays' worth of presents from your godfather.

I would also like to apologise for the fright I think I gave you, that night last year when you left your uncle's house. I had

only hoped to get a glimpse of you before starting my journey
north, but I think the sight of me alarmed you.
  I am enclosing something else for you, which I think will
make your next year at Hogwarts more enjoyable.
  If ever you need me, send word. Your owl will find me.
  I'll write again soon.
  Sirius

Harry looked eagerly inside the envelope. There was another
piece of parchment in there. He read it through quickly and felt
suddenly as warm and contented as though he'd swallowed a
bottle of hot Butterbeer in one go.

I, Sirius Black, Harry Potter's godfather, hereby give him per-
mission to visit Hogsmeade at weekends.

'That'll be good enough for Dumbledore!' said Harry happily. He
looked back at Sirius' letter.
  'Hang on, there's a PS ...

I thought your friend Ron might like to keep this owl, as it's my
fault he no longer has a rat.

Ron's eyes widened. The minute owl was still hooting excitedly.
  'Keep him?' he said uncertainly. He looked closely at the owl
for a moment, then, to Harry and Hermione's great surprise, he
held him out for Crookshanks to sniff.
  'What d'you reckon?' Ron asked the cat. 'Definitely an owl?'
  Crookshanks purred.
  'That's good enough for me,' said Ron happily. 'He's mine.'
  Harry read and re-read the letter from Sirius all the way back
into King's Cross station. It was still clutched tightly in his hand
as he, Ron and Hermione stepped back through the barrier of
platform nine and three-quarters. Harry spotted Uncle Vernon at
once. He was standing a good distance from Mr and Mrs Weasley,
eyeing them suspiciously, and when Mrs Weasley hugged Harry in
greeting, his worst suspicions about them seemed confirmed.
  'I'll call about the World Cup!' Ron yelled after Harry, as Harry
bid him and Hermione goodbye, then wheeled the trolley bearing
his trunk and Hedwig's cage towards Uncle Vernon, who greeted

him in usual fashion.

'What's that?' he snarled, staring at the envelope Harry was still clutching in his hand. 'If it's another form for me to sign, you've got another –'

'It's not,' said Harry cheerfully. 'It's a letter from my godfather.'

'Godfather?' spluttered Uncle Vernon. 'You haven't got a godfather!'

'Yes, I have,' said Harry brightly. 'He was my mum and dad's best friend. He's a convicted murderer, but he's broken out of wizard prison and he's on the run. He likes to keep in touch with me, though ... keep up with my news ... check I'm happy ...'

And grinning broadly at the look of horror on Uncle Vernon's face, Harry set off towards the station exit, Hedwig rattling along in front of him, for what looked like a much better summer than the last.